KISSING ANNE

"I don't want any husband but you," Anne whispered.

The words came out more strongly than she intended. Embarassed but defiant, she looked up at James. The laughter had left his face and he was looking down at her intently. "Truly?" he said. "Truly, Anne?"

"Yes, truly," she said, returning his look defiantly.

"Well, I am sure I want no other wife," he said. He began to draw her toward him. Anne went to him willingly, putting her arms around him and laying her head against his chest. It felt warm and secure within the circle of his arms.

"Anne, I want to kiss you."

"Then why don't you?" she asked.

"Because I am afraid I could not stop at just a kiss."

"Well, who said I wanted you to stop at a kiss?" she asked.

James lost no time in lowering his lips to Anne's. His first kiss was fleeting, almost tentative, but the second was more ardent, and before long his mouth was devouring Anne's with an urgency that left her breathless. . . .

Dear Romance Reader,

In July, we launched the Ballad line with four new series, and each month we'll present both new and continuing stories set everywhere from medieval England to the American West—the kind of passionate, romantic stories you love best, written by the most gifted authors. At the back of each book, we'll tell you when you can find subsequent books in the series that have captured your heart.

Debuting this month with a fabulous new series called *The Sword and the Ring,* Suzanne McMinn offers **My Lady Impostor.** The pageantry and adventure of medieval England come vividly to life in the rousing story of one incredible family in an age when men lived and died by the sword and a woman's life might be forever changed by a betrothal ring. Next, Alice Duncan continues *The Dream Maker* series with **Beauty and the Brain,** as an actress hiding her intelligence meets her match in a research assistant who knows everything . . . except about love.

Travel back to Regency England with Joy Reed's romantic *Wishing Well* trilogy. In **Anne's Wish,** a marriage of convenience promises unexpected love—unless a jealous rival comes between the newlyweds. Finally, the third book in Elizabeth Keys's charming *Irish Blessing* series reunites childhood companions, but will **Reilly's Pride** stand in the way of a love destined to unite two souls in matrimony?

Kate Duffy
Editorial Director

THE WISHING WELL

ANNE'S WISH

JOY REED

ZEBRA BOOKS
KENSINGTON PUBLISHING CORP.

http://www.zebrabooks.com

ZEBRA BOOKS are published by

Kensington Publishing Corp.
850 Third Avenue
New York, NY 10022

All Kensington titles, imprints and distributed lines are available at special quantity discounts for bulk purchases for sales promotion, premiums, fund-raising, educational or institutional use.

Special book excerpts or customized printings can also be created to fit specific needs. For details, write or phone the office of the Kensington Special Sales Manager: Kensington Publishing Corp., 850 Third Avenue, New York, NY 10022. Attn. Special Sales Department. Phone: 1-800-221-2647.

Zebra and the Z logo Reg. U.S. Pat. & TM Off.
Ballad is a trademark of Kensington Publishing Corp.

First Printing: May 2001
10 9 8 7 6 5 4 3 2 1

Printed in the United States of America

For Luc, amicalement

CHAPTER I

"The gentlemen are waiting for their tea, miss," said the servant.

Anne could not help jumping, though she had been expecting this summons for some time. "Thank you, Robert," she said, shutting her book with fingers that trembled. "You may tell the gentlemen I will be there directly."

"Very good, miss," said the servant. As he began to walk away, Anne nerved herself to ask a question.

"Are there many gentlemen tonight, Robert?"

The servant turned to regard her once more. It seemed to Anne that there was something uncomfortably knowing in his gaze. "No more than usual, miss. Only Mr. Young and Mr. Casey."

"Thank you, Robert," said Anne again. She tried to keep her voice even, but it trembled despite her best efforts. The servant gave her another knowing look, bowed, then turned and left the room.

After he had gone, Anne laid her book on the table beside the sofa and got to her feet. She did so with extreme care, for she felt ill, and her hands were shaking. "This won't do," she said aloud. "I mustn't let myself be so weak." The servant's news had been exactly what she had expected, yet it had been none the less painful on that account.

"But I mustn't let it affect me like this," she whispered. "I mustn't." Going to the chimney glass above the mantel, she surveyed her reflection. Her face looked even more colorless than usual, Anne observed gloomily, straightening the lace bertha about her shoulders and mechanically smoothing her hair. Her hair was very fair, almost as colorless as her face, a blond so pale it was more silver than gold. Indeed, as Anne regarded herself in the glass, it seemed to her that she looked wholly colorless apart from her eyes. These were very large, of a color between green and blue, and—it seemed to Anne—dangerously expressive. Even as she watched, they filled with tears.

"You mustn't be such a fool," she said aloud. "If anything could make your situation worse, it would be for Mr. Young and Mr. Casey to see you crying. They are both such dreadful gossips." No one knew better than she how fast rumors spread at Court. The news that Miss Anne Barrington had been crying at the tea table would be all over the Palace by tomorrow if she did not restrain herself. And there would be plenty of people able to guess what had made her cry. The servant's manner had been proof of that. Anne shut her eyes, drew a deep breath, and willed herself back into composure. But it was a tenuous composure, and as she went along the corridor to the parlor she hoped desperately it would hold until after Mr. Young and Mr. Casey were gone.

"Ah, here she is," cried Mr. Casey, rising to his feet as Anne came into the room. He was an elderly gentleman with a gallant manner and twinkling blue eyes, and Anne had always liked him in spite of his gossipy tendencies. "Good evening, Miss Barrington," he said, giving her the graceful bow that had been perfected by thirty-odd years at Court. "You look enchanting this evening."

As this was Mr. Casey's stock compliment to all females young and old, Anne was in no danger of overvaluing it. She merely gave Mr. Casey a brief smile before turning to greet Mr. Young. "Yes, enchanting," agreed Mr. Young, bowing and baring his teeth in a wolfish smile. "But if I may say so, perhaps a trifle pale? You are not feeling unwell, I trust, Miss Barrington?"

He spoke with exaggerated concern, yet even as he spoke his eyes were flickering over Anne's face and person. She felt sure he had noticed her red-rimmed eyes. "I trust not, indeed," she said shortly. "Won't you please sit down, Mr. Young, Mr. Casey? I will make you your tea."

As Anne set about making tea, she reflected for the thousandth time how unfair it was that she should have been burdened with such a task. It was no part of her duties as the Queen's Assistant Keeper of the Robes. Previous to her coming to Court, the Queen's Equerries and other visiting gentlemen had taken their tea where they could find it, but soon after Anne's arrival her superior, Mrs. Melkinthorpe, who was the Queen's First Keeper of the Robes, had suggested Anne might as well make their tea for them.

"You have nothing to do at that hour," Mrs. Melkinthorpe had told Anne in her thick, German-accented voice.

"You may as well make the gentlemen their tea as not. I will give you the use of my parlor to entertain them."

The parlor in question was really not Mrs. Melkinthorpe's parlor at all, but rather a joint parlor to be shared by both Keepers of the Robes. This was the theory at least, but in practice Mrs. Melkinthorpe had always behaved as though it were her property alone. Anne, at that time a shy, gauche seventeen-year-old newly arrived at Court, had not dared contest Mrs. Melkinthorpe's ownership. Likewise, she had not objected to making tea for the gentlemen, even though it encroached on one of the very few leisure hours she had in the day.

Looking at the matter from her present perspective, Anne could easily see how she had been imposed on. But it was less easy to recover the ground she had lost. Even now, when she had been seven years at Court, she was all too prone to give in to others' demands rather than dispute them. This was particularly true in the case of those demands made by Mrs. Melkinthorpe. The German woman had a ferocious temper and a hundred ways of making her assistant's life a misery when she was displeased, and after a trial or two, Anne had submitted to the fate of being imposed on as the lesser of the two evils.

But submission had brought her no reward in the long run. Rather, it had brought only a greater misery upon her. If she had refused at the start to make the gentlemen's tea, she never would have achieved more than a passing acquaintance with Timothy. If she had not become acquainted with Timothy, she would never have come to love him. And if she had not come to love him, she would not be enduring now the pain of having that love rejected and the mortification of knowing that others were aware of her misery.

There could be no doubt that Mr. Young knew of it.

Even as Anne handed him his tea, he fixed her with a bright, malicious eye. "It looks as though Timothy Linville's found himself a good thing," he said. "I have it on good authority that Miss Duval hasn't a penny less than thirty thousand pounds. What's more, she seems very *épris* of him—the Queen herself was remarking on it just the other day. It'd be a nice thing to have thirty thousand pounds, wouldn't it, Miss Barrington?"

Anne forced a smile. "It would indeed," she said. "Sugar, Mr. Young?"

Mr. Young declined sugar and went on, still fixing Anne with a malicious eye. "You and young Linville used to be pretty thick, didn't you, Miss Barrington? Why, there was a rumor running about not so long ago that he was going to marry *you.*"

With a terrible effort, Anne summoned another smile. "Do you still believe Court rumors, Mr. Young?" she said. "I learned never to do so years ago. If they are not fabrications from start to finish, they invariably prove to be much exaggerated."

"But you and Linville were friends, were you not? *Close* friends?"

"We were friends—or rather I should say we *are* friends," said Anne. Her voice was unsteady despite her best efforts, and she had to pause a minute before she could go on. "And like all Mr. Linville's friends, I must rejoice in his good fortune if he should be so lucky as to win the heart of Miss Duval. I am sure he will be as happy as he deserves to be."

Mr. Young raised an amused eyebrow at this speech, but to Anne's relief he did not pursue the subject of her and Timothy Linville. Instead he turned to Mr. Casey and began discussing the Regent's latest indiscretion. Anne was left to her own thoughts—and her own misery—once more.

She had met Timothy Linville a little more than a year ago. At the time, he had just taken a position at Court as one of the Queen's Equerries. He was a good-looking young man in his early twenties, and his appearance had caused a stir of interest among the ladies of the Court. The Queen had smiled upon him; several Ladies in Waiting had openly set their caps for him; and the Royal Princesses had indicated their approval by flirting with him in a restrained way. Even the redoubtable Mrs. Melkinthorpe was so far impressed with him as to curb the worst excesses of her temper in his company.

Anne, who was still as shy as she had been at seventeen if not quite so gauche, had never made any open bids for Timothy's attention. Yet she had always experienced a secret flutter of pleasure when he had appeared at the tea table with the other gentlemen. And when it happened one day that he was the only gentleman to show up in the Keeper's parlor for tea, she had been so flustered that it was a wonder she did not drop both pot and kettle in her excitement.

She had made an effort to overcome her shyness, however, and to treat this unlooked-for tête-à-tête as though it were merely commonplace. She had asked Timothy questions about himself: questions about his family and background and the nature of his present duties. Timothy had expanded under her interest. Soon he was telling Anne all about his hopes of one day attaining a position of eminence at Court.

"I thought when this business of Equerry came up that my fortune was made. It sounded like a good thing, you know—a position at Court, and everything made snug. But I soon learned my mistake. Why, the pay I get is

barely enough to keep me, what with all the expenses of
living in the Palace. What I need is a real position—
something with at least a thousand a year attached to it.
I've got my eye on one or two things, but since I'm
new at Court I can't look for advancement so soon. Her
Majesty as good as told me so when I ventured to drop
a hint in her ear last night.''

Anne could readily sympathize with Timothy's ambi-
tions. It seemed hard that such a brilliant and deserving
young man should be denied promotion simply because
there were others who had been longer at Court. Even
more could she sympathize with Timothy's laments about
money.

When she had first come to Court, her salary of two
hundred and fifty pounds a year had seemed unimaginable
riches. But she had soon learned how rapidly those riches
vanished when one was forced to buy a dozen or more
new dresses each year. The Queen expected her attendants
to be freshly and fashionably clothed for each of the
numerous Royal birthdays, as well as for such occasions
as Coronation Day, Christmas, and Easter. On really
important occasions two new toilettes were necessary,
one suitable for the Queen's Drawing Room and another
for the ball that took place later in the day. The cost of
plumes, lappets, hoopskirts, and other such trifles mounted
up in an alarming way, so much so that Anne had never
been able to save so much as a penny of her salary.
Indeed, she had a small but growing balance at the dressmaker's that showed no prospects of being paid off any-
time soon.

So she had been able to heartily sympathize with Timothy's plight. Timothy, for his part, had seemed pleased
by her sympathy. He had lingered long over his tea, and

when he had finally got up to go, he had told Anne he had enjoyed himself very much.

"You're a sweet girl, Miss Barrington," he told her. "I'm dashed if I don't feel better now I've told you all my troubles. I hope we'll have another chance to talk like this sometime soon."

Anne had hoped so, too, most fervently. And when, a few weeks later, it had once again chanced that Timothy was the only gentleman to come to tea, she had experienced something remarkably like a rush of elation.

On this occasion, as during their previous tête-à-tête, she and Timothy had talked long—or rather, Timothy had talked and Anne had listened. This was as it should be, according to Anne's way of thinking. What did she have to talk about, after all? The Court news was as well known to Timothy as herself, and she had no personal life to draw on for subjects of discussion. Every waking hour of her life was spent either serving her Royal Mistress or waiting for a summons to do so. As for her past, that was as dull as her present. Her birth had been genteel but undistinguished; she had passed her youth in rural surroundings far removed from celebrity or scandal, and her parents had been pleasant people of blameless life who had died as unobtrusively as they had lived. The only thing she had ever done worthy of notice was to be taken into Queen Charlotte's Court through the intercession of a distant cousin.

So Anne had listened to Timothy's talk with the keenest pleasure. Once more she had sympathized when he complained of the expenses of Court life and the injustice that kept him from promotion. When he had got up to leave, he had taken her hand in his and thanked her again for letting him air his grievances. "And if you *should* get a chance to drop a word in the Queen's ear about finding me a better place, I'd much appreciate it," he told her. "I daresay a clever girl like you would have as much influence with Her Majesty as anybody."

"I wouldn't," Anne told him honestly. "I don't have any influence at all."

But Timothy had refused to believe this. So flattering was his disbelief that Anne had broken down at last and given him a half promise to speak to the Queen, even though she knew how futile such an action must prove. Since there was no telling when they would have another tea table tête-à-tête, Timothy arranged to meet Anne in the Palace corridor in a few days' time to hear her report.

The report had been a negative one, as Anne had known it must be. She had felt badly as she described her failure to Timothy, fearing he would think she had let him down. But he had taken the news philosophically. "I don't doubt you tried, Miss Barrington," he had said, pressing her hand. "Of course I had hoped the Queen would be more understanding, but I certainly didn't count on it. After all, it's early days yet."

"Yes, it is," said Anne eagerly. "I'm sure you will be promoted very soon, Mr. Linville. The Queen likes you, I know, and Princess Sophia said just the other day that you were the most elegant man at Court."

"She did, did she?" said Timothy. "Well, that's something, at any rate." He paused a moment, thinking, then addressed Anne with his most appealing smile. "Look here, Miss Barrington," he said, "I wonder if you wouldn't mind doing another favor for me?"

In spite of the appeal of Timothy's smile, Anne had been forced to demur. "I really have no influence with the Queen, Mr. Linville," she told him. "It would do your cause no good at all if I were to try to talk to her again. Indeed, it might hurt it."

"Oh, but I'm not asking for you to talk to her again. All I want you to do is keep your eyes and ears open and let me know first thing if you hear of any nice, lucrative position opening up. Could you do that for me? And you might also put in a good word for me with the Queen and Princesses now and then if the opportunity presents itself. It'd mean a great deal to me to have someone in your position looking out for my interests."

This had sounded an easy enough task, and Anne had consented gladly to do what she could in Timothy's cause. "But how will I get word to you if I have anything to report?" she asked. "You know your duties do not always allow you to take tea with me, Mr. Linville. Even if they did, we couldn't count on having the privacy to discuss your personal affairs."

"Oh, that's easy. Nothing could be simpler. We'll meet here again, just like we did today," Timothy told her. "It's private and convenient, and we can hear anybody coming long before we see them. You usually have a few minutes free about this time of day, don't you, Miss Barrington?"

Anne admitted that she did, though she could not help thinking ruefully of this further intrusion on her all-too-scanty free time. But her ruefulness had vanished with Timothy's next words. "Bless you, you're an angel, Miss Barrington. I won't forget this, I promise you." And he had taken Anne's hand in his and kissed it.

That kiss on the hand had been a life-altering experience for Anne. For weeks afterward, it was the first thing she thought of when she awoke in the morning and the last thing she thought of before she dropped off to sleep at night. Timothy had probably not intended it as more than a friendly gesture, but it was the most nearly romantic thing that had ever happened in Anne's life, and it transformed her into Timothy's loyal partisan. All through the day she listened sharply for every word of him, good or bad, that anyone might utter in her presence, and each afternoon she would slip away to her and Timothy's rendezvous place to report to him her findings. Sometimes he was pleased by what she told him; other times he was displeased, but always, just before they parted, he would take her hand in his, kiss it again, and call her an angel.

Up till now, Anne's life at Court had been one of complete isolation. She had often longed for a friend, someone who would care about her and take an interest in her and allay the endless round of servitude that made up her whole existence. Timothy had performed this last function, and given the loneliness of Anne's position, it was perhaps not surprising that she soon began to imagine he might fulfill the others, too.

She began to read more into Timothy's thanks and kisses than simple gratitude. She began to imagine he looked at her with a certain tenderness, and that he took a pleasure in her company that had its root in more than just the information that he gained from her. She began to look forward to their daily meetings in the corridor as the most interesting part of her day, and the moment when Timothy kissed her hand as the most enjoyable.

From this point, of course, it was only a short step to fancying herself in love with Timothy. Anne imagined Timothy gaining the appointment he longed for, an appointment he had gotten with her help. She imagined how his thanks and gratitude would overflow into love and a proposal of marriage. And then she imagined herself the wife of Timothy, happy and busy in her own home and released forever from her life of servitude at Court.

Anne was too much a realist not to know that she was building these dream castles on a very unstable foundation. Yet she indulged in her imaginings, knowing full well that they were never likely to come to pass. It seemed to her merely a harmless amusement, a kind of continuing daydream that gave color and excitement to her dreary days and lonely nights. And then something happened that made her wonder if her dreams might someday become reality after all.

It happened the day she told Timothy that the Queen was looking for a new candidate to take over as Master of her Band. "Are you certain?" Timothy had demanded. "You are certain the position is available?" His eyes were aglow with excitement.

"Yes, quite certain," Anne had assured him. "Her Majesty spoke of it today while Mrs. Melkinthorpe and I were dressing her for dinner. And then, too, I heard a couple of gentlemen discussing it in the corridor as I came here to meet you."

"By Jove! Master of the Queen's Band! That would be a nice thing for me—a very nice thing indeed. I haven't heard what the position pays, but it stands to reason it must be more than I'm making now."

"You mean to apply for the position, then?" Anne had asked in surprise. "I did not know you were a musician, Mr. Linville. I only mentioned it because you asked to be kept informed about any positions that might be open."

Timothy clasped her hand. "Yes, and I'm dashed grateful to you. I'm no musician, of course, but I don't see that that makes any difference." He laughed. "Likely the Queen just wants somebody to keep an eye on the fellows who do the fiddling for her parties—make sure they show up on time, you know, and aren't in their cups when they get up to play. I can do that well enough, I hope. Indeed, I should think myself a poor sort of fellow if I couldn't!"

Anne was very conscious of the clasp of Timothy's

hand on hers "I am sure you could do anything to which you set your mind," she said warmly.

"Aye, trust me for that! I do believe my fortune is made, Miss Barrington. And I owe it all to you." With these words he had stooped and kissed Anne not on the hand, but full on the lips.

The next few weeks had been the happiest of Anne's life. Timothy had applied for the position of Master of the Queen's Band, and each day he and Anne would meet in the corridor to discuss the appointment and review all Anne had heard the Queen and others say concerning it. Timothy never doubted he would be chosen for the position. He was in the highest of high spirits, and as before, his spirits overflowed into lovemaking. He showered kisses, caresses, and extravagant compliments on Anne and begged for the privilege of calling her by her first name. "As I see it, we're partners, Anne. You've got a share in this, too, and if I succeed—well, time enough to think of that when I get the appointment. But I won't forget you, you may be sure of that. Has anyone ever told you what a sweet girl you are?"

Since nobody ever had, Anne came away from this meeting in a daze of happiness. She went through the rest of the day in the same happy daze, scarcely noticing even when the Queen rebuked her for bringing her the wrong jewels to wear with her evening toilette. But Anne's happiness was destined to come to an abrupt end. The very next morning, when she arrived in the Queen's dressing room to assist with Her Majesty's toilette, she was told that the position of Master of the Queen's Band had been given not to Timothy but to a German gentleman who, it appeared, was a respected musician in his own country.

Anne could think of nothing but what a blow this must

be for Timothy. Her heart bled for him when she remembered how much he had been counting on the promotion. All through that morning, as she went about her usual daily tasks, she was dreading the moment when she must meet Timothy in the corridor and tell him the sad news. But when she arrived in the corridor that afternoon, it was evident that Timothy had already heard it.

"Have you heard?" he demanded, as soon as Anne came in sight. "Have you heard about this infamous business?"

"About Dr. Lott? Yes, Timothy, I have heard. Indeed, it is very unfortunate."

"I could hardly believe it when I heard the news. Why, I can hardly believe it now. The insult of it all! For it *is* an insult, Anne—a damnable insult. For them to give the position to some old German fellow that nobody's ever heard of when it ought to have gone to me is as good as slapping me in the face."

Anne ventured to remark that Dr. Lott was said to be a very fine musician. "Apparently he is quite renowned on the Continent. And then, too, he is German, and you know the Queen has a partiality for Germans because she is German herself. I daresay that may have had something to do with it."

This thought seemed to cheer Timothy slightly, but he continued to dwell for some minutes longer on the insult that had been dealt him. "There must be more to it than I have heard," he insisted. "There must be some reason beyond the facts the Queen has let out. What exactly did she say about it, Anne? Did she mention me at all? Mention any reason why I was passed over?"

Anne opened her lips to reply, but at that moment both she and Timothy heard footsteps coming along the corridor. Timothy muttered an oath under his breath.

"Devil take it! Of all the times to be interrupted! I must hear what the Queen said about me, Anne—now, not tomorrow. I can't wait till tomorrow. Can you meet me tonight, after you are done undressing the Queen?"

Anne hesitated. "I suppose I could," she said. "But would it not look very peculiar if we are seen together so late? The Queen—"

"Damn the Queen! You speak as though the Queen is all you care about. I thought you cared about *me*." Grasping Anne's hand, Timothy spoke in a low, urgent voice. "Come to my room tonight, after everyone's gone to bed. You can tell me everything the Queen said without any risk of being interrupted. Then we can talk it over and decide what's best to do." Not giving Anne any chance to reply, he had released her hand and walked rapidly away.

Anne stood rooted to the spot, staring after him. Then as the footsteps drew nearer, she woke to her predicament and started down the corridor, trying to look as though she were merely returning to the Queen's rooms after performing some errand. Unfortunately, the footsteps proved to belong to Mr. Young, who had apparently recognized both Anne and Timothy's voices from the far end of the corridor and had come to find out what they were talking over in such a confidential manner.

"Oh, we were merely speaking of the rumor going about that Princess Charlotte is in an interesting condition," said Anne lightly. "I am sure that must be the foremost subject in everyone's minds right now. Indeed, I have heard nothing else discussed these last few weeks."

"To be sure," replied Mr. Young, but his smile was incredulous. Anne took leave of him, feeling that her efforts to throw him off the track had not been very successful.

At the moment, however, Mr. Young was the least of her worries. What was really occupying her was the question of whether or not she should go to Timothy's room that night.

It was not unheard of for ladies of the Court to visit gentlemen in their rooms. But the practice was certainly not encouraged. Queen Charlotte's Court was a straitlaced one, and the Queen herself rigidly disapproving of any moral lapse. Yet even in spite of the Queen's disapproval, romantic intrigues had been known to occur. Only the year before, a Lady-in-Waiting had been hastily married off to the Equerry who had gotten her with child.

In this case, of course, such moral objections did not apply, for it was business and not romance that would take Anne to Timothy's room. But the appearance would be the same to outsiders. Innocent or not, Anne knew she would be judged guilty if the incident ever came to the Queen's ears. Nor was the Queen the only one to be feared. The other members of the Court would be even quicker to judge her and talk about her, if she were seen entering or leaving Timothy's bedchamber in the middle of the night. She had heard enough Court gossip to know how unsparing their comments on her behavior would be.

But despite Anne's reluctance to become a subject of gossip, she could not stand the thought of disappointing Timothy. He had already suffered one disappointment that day, and for her to fail him at such a juncture would be another and perhaps greater disappointment. After all, he had told her many times how much he relied on her.

He needs me, Anne told herself. *It would be cruel to fail him now.*

Put like this, it seemed a noble thing to come to Timothy's aid. This was how Anne preferred to think of it, refusing to admit that she had another and less noble reason for going to him that night. The plain fact was that Timothy was a handsome, much admired young man and very popular among the Ladies of the Court. If she failed him now, he might well turn his attention to some other girl. And Anne could not bear that idea. He was the only thing resembling a real friend she had at Court. What was more, he had spoken of marriage—not in so many words, to be sure, but the inference was plain. Marriage would mean escape for her—a respectable escape from a life that was growing more unbearable by the day.

There was nothing Anne would not have done at this period to achieve such an escape. For seven long years she had been treated like the humblest of humble servants, summoned by a bell day and night in the midst of sleep and meals and too-brief hours of recreation. She was taken for granted by her Royal Mistress in all she did right and treated with icy contempt when she erred. She was continually barraged by the angry recriminations of Mrs. Melkinthorpe. She could not simply resign her position and look for other work. The Queen took it for granted that her Ladies were with her for life, and it was only in such cases as marriage or severe illness that she was reluctantly brought to release them from her service.

Even if Anne could have brought the Queen to release her, she knew how small were her chances of finding other work. She had little education and no accomplishments worth the mentioning. She was nearly fifty pounds in debt. And she had no family to whom she might turn for help. The distant cousin who had helped her to her present position had made it clear that such would be the extent of her assistance. She would not hesitate to wash her hands of her young relative if Anne were ungrateful enough to throw over such a desirable berth.

So driven by all these accumulated reflections, Anne made up her mind to go to Timothy's room that night.

It was some time after midnight when she stole cautiously along the corridor and up the stairs to Timothy's rooms. Her heart was beating fast, and every slightest noise made her start like a frightened deer. When she finally reached the wing where the Equerries lodged, she was trembling like a leaf. It was a relief to see a light shining from under Timothy's door. She had been half afraid he might have given her up and gone to bed. But he was clearly expecting her, for the door swung open almost as soon as she laid her hand upon it.

"You certainly took your time getting here," muttered Timothy. "I've been waiting for you this hour. Come in, quick, before somebody sees you."

Anne was a trifle taken aback by this ungracious greeting. But she dared not linger in the hall. So when Timothy swung the door wider and made an impatient gesture beckoning her in, she flitted across the doorstep.

It was a small room, dark and old-fashioned in its appointments and very similar in size and style to Anne's own bedchamber sitting room. Unlike Anne's room, however, it was very untidy. Clothes were strewn about the floor, a plate with some broken meat lay atop the writing table, and an empty brandy bottle stood on the chair beside it. Anne tried to keep her eyes from these things and fix them on Timothy, but when she looked at him she realized he was in no better condition than his room. His collar was undone, his hair in disorder, and there was a strong smell of brandy about him that suggested where the contents of the empty bottle had gone.

"Timothy!" she said in dismay. "Oh, Timothy, have you been drinking?"

Timothy made another impatient gesture. "Why the devil shouldn't I? I suppose I've as much right to a glass or two of brandy as anybody." With an uncertain gait, he walked over to the nearest chair and collapsed rather than sat on it. "Why shouldn't I have a drink or two?" he demanded again. "Seeing how my hopes have been cut up, I may as well go to the devil now and be done with it."

"That's not true." Seeing that he was not going to invite her to sit down, she went to the writing table, removed the brandy bottle from the chair beside it, and seated herself on the chair's extreme edge. "There will be other appointments, Timothy," she said, looking at him imploringly. "And some of them might even be better than this one. You must only be patient, and I'm sure the Queen will find you another position."

Timothy muttered that he was by no means sure of it himself. He then launched into a lengthy diatribe in which the Queen, Dr. Lott, and everyone else at Court came in freely for their share of blame in his disappointment. "Even you," he said, looking blearily at Anne. "Even you'd like to see me fail rather than succeed. You didn't want to come here tonight—you didn't want to talk to me—it's nothing to you whether I make good or not. You don't care about me at all."

"That's not true," said Anne. "That's not true in the least. I *do* care about you, Timothy."

"Do you?" said Timothy. His mood seemed to undergo an abrupt change. "Sweet Anne—darling Anne—best girl in the world. What would I do without you?" Rising from his chair, he stumbled toward her.

Anne also rose to her feet, half gratified and half alarmed. "Oh, Timothy," she said, "do you think—?"

Before she could finish, Timothy had caught her in his arms. "What I think is I'd like to kiss you," he said, and did so. But it was not a kiss like those he had given her before. Those had been, if not precisely chaste kisses, at least respectful ones. There was nothing respectful at all about the way Timothy was kissing her now. His mouth closed hard over hers while his tongue forced itself between her lips, and the fumes of brandy emanating from his mouth made Anne feel sick. She choked and sought to draw back.

"No!" she said. "No, Timothy!" But Timothy did not seem to hear her. Again he kissed her, holding her tight against him so she could not pull away. "No," whispered Anne again.

"Darling Anne," said Timothy fervently. "Darling, darling, Anne." His hands had begun to fumble with the hooks on the back of her dress.

"No!" said Anne again, but once more Timothy did not seem to hear her. She had a sense of being caught in a nightmare, of being held in the grip of a foe too strong to be resisted.

"Sweet, darling Anne," Timothy kept saying, "sweet darling Anne, you do like me, don't you? Don't you?"

"Yes," whispered Anne. "Yes, but—oh, don't, Timothy. I must go now, indeed I must. I must go to my own room."

"In a little while. In just a little while. Sweet, darling, Anne. You wouldn't leave me, would you?"

"No," said Anne helplessly. "But—oh, Timothy, not that. Please no—please not that."

But Timothy bore down on her relentlessly. All the while Anne protested and pleaded, right up till the last possible moment, yet she could not bring herself to really resist. It was as though some vital part of her was standing aside, watching her own violation but unable to do anything about it.

The violation, such as it was, was over quickly enough. One moment Timothy was atop her and grunting with animal passion; the next he had flung himself away with a muffled oath.

"Oh hell!" he said, burying his face in his hands. "Oh hell and the devil confound it!"

It did not appear to Anne that he had enjoyed himself any more than she had. Slowly and painfully, she got to her feet. Timothy continued to sit with his face buried in his hands. He did not look at Anne as she tried with shaking hands to straighten her disheveled hair and clothing. Nor did he look at her when, this task completed, she crossed to the door and prepared to let herself out. Anne paused with her hand on the doorknob, looking back at him. She felt she ought to say something, but when she considered it, she realized there was really nothing to say. So she went quickly out of the room and closed the door behind her.

She got back to her own room without being seen, a feat that had assumed a rather secondary importance in her mind. Once back in her room, she sank down in a chair and tried to realize the enormity of what had just happened to her.

She had just lost her virtue. She had lost it in the twinkling of an eye, and now she could never get it back again. Unbidden to her mind came the recollection of a pamphlet she had once seen in a maidservant's room— a pamphlet distributed by one of those well-meaning evangelical organizations that sought to stamp out vice among servants. *A Girl's Most Precious Treasure,* had been its rather sentimental title, and it had described in hair-raising terms the fate that awaited any young woman who lost her "treasure" outside the sanctity of marriage. Well, she had lost her treasure. She had sacrificed it to a drunken man and had gotten nothing in return. "Oh, Timothy, what have you done to me?" Anne whispered desolately. Yet desolate as she was, she did not quite despair.

It was, after all, no uncommon thing for a betrothed couple to indulge in marital intimacies before marriage. What had happened between her and Timothy was unfortunate, but so long as he was willing to do the honorable thing, it need not have any serious or lasting effects. *And of course he will do the honorable thing,* Anne told herself. *He spoke of marrying me before, or at least implied it. Of course he will marry me. He is a gentleman.* Yet her heart was full of unease. The plain fact was that Timothy had not behaved much like a gentleman tonight. On the contrary, he had behaved like the veriest blackguard.

And that was not the worst of it. The truth was that after what had happened, Anne was no longer sure she even wanted to marry Timothy. What he had done to her that evening had been so distasteful that she shrank from the thought of further such intimacies. To marry him would mean engaging in such intimacies frequently for the rest of her life.

"I can't," Anne whispered. "I simply can't. I would rather die than endure it."

It was almost a relief when, on the following afternoon, Timothy had failed to appear at their usual rendezvous. Nor had he appeared the day after that. It was not until several days later that Anne saw him again, and then it was not in a situation that admitted any privacy. He had just come back from attending the Queen during an airing in the Park, and several other Equerries and Court officials were with him, making private speech impossible. But even without private speech, Anne could see plainly enough that Timothy had no intention of behaving like a gentleman. The whole time they were together, he had avoided even looking at her, and when he presently took his leave, his farewells to the party had pointedly excluded her.

In spite of the fact that Anne had been expecting and almost hoping for this rejection, she found herself crushed by it. It was such a personal rejection, as though her very womanhood had been inspected and found wanting. She had always thought herself too small and thin and pale to be attractive. Now she saw herself as so small and thin and pale as to be completely insignificant. A part of her seemed to die that day, but it was not a quick or complete enough death to suit Anne. She was still horribly sensitive on the subject of Timothy. Every chance meeting was like salt in a raw wound, and the mere possibility of seeing him on any given day put her in such a nervous state that she could scarcely perform her duties.

Nor was this her worst cross. Somehow, either through the agency of Mr. Young or through her own transparent behavior or possibly through the actions of Timothy himself, his connection with Anne had become generally known at Court. She felt it in the eyes of those around her and in the pointed remarks that were made in her hearing. Naturally, this only added to Anne's misery. It was galling to know that people were whispering about her, and that she was held to have been jilted in favor of Miss Duval and her thirty thousand pounds. For Timothy had apparently abandoned the notion of making his fortune at Court in favor of the quicker and more expedient process of marrying an heiress. There could be no doubt that he was wooing Miss Duval most assiduously, and such gossips as Mr. Young seemed in no doubt that Miss Duval was inclined to favor his suit.

Anne hoped the heiress *would* accept him. If Timothy married Miss Duval, he would probably leave Court, and then the worst of her afflictions would be ended. But in the meantime they continued unabated. She was at the very apex of despair when she accompanied the Queen and her Court to St. James's for the annual celebration of the King's Birthday.

CHAPTER II

The celebration of the King's Birthday was one of the chief occasions in the Court calendar.

It mattered not a whit that a Regent was on the throne now and the old King confined to Kew Palace in what was whispered to be a state of irremediable madness. His Birthday was still celebrated annually by his Queen, and by a loyal populace that insisted on preferring him to his profligate son.

Anne could take no pleasure in the bustle surrounding the Court's removal to St. James. The transfer of such a large and unwieldy household was an onerous task for all concerned and one that always tried the Queen's uncertain temper. Since Her Majesty's Ladies usually bore the brunt of such temper, it was not surprising that Anne regarded the process with something less than enthusiasm. This year, beset by her own private worries, she was not merely unenthusiastic but miserable.

Anne had cause for misery even apart from her difficulties with Timothy. Every year on the King's Birthday, the Queen was accustomed to hold a Drawing Room, one of those formal occasions on which visitors were received into the Royal Presence. In the evening would follow the annual Birthday Ball. Anne would be expected to provide two toilettes for the occasion—two toilettes not merely new but very fashionable. This would put her yet deeper in debt and tighten the shackles that already bound her to life at Court.

Since it seemed to Anne that she was already bound there anyway, this ought not to have mattered greatly. Yet she had an innate dislike of debt that prevented her from spending as freely and thoughtlessly as her peers at Court. In the end, she decided to compromise by ordering one new dress for the Drawing Room and making over one of her existing dresses to wear that evening. She had no intention of attending the Ball anyway, and she reasoned that a made-over dress would serve just as well if she could make it over thoroughly enough to escape Royal censure.

By the time the day arrived, however, she was sorry that she had not simply ordered two new dresses in the beginning. The sewing and retrimming of her dress was weary work and had to be accomplished in those minutes she could snatch here and there amid constant interruptions. When the morning of the Birthday finally dawned, Anne was feeling more jaded and miserable than ever.

It did not help that she had to rise an hour earlier than usual to assist with the Royal Toilette, or that she had to dress, breakfast, and squeeze in an hour with the hairdresser as best she could while attending to Her Majesty's wishes. And when she went to put on the dress which the dressmaker had delivered only that morning, along with a pointed reminder about the balance Anne owed at her shop, Anne found in her new costume a fresh source of vexation.

Of course no Court dress could be really attractive, for the Queen still insisted on hoops being worn at her Drawing Rooms, and the effect of hoops beneath modern high-waisted dresses was ludicrous in the extreme. Likewise, the stipulation that ladies' coiffures be ornamented with large, upstanding ostrich plumes was one that accorded strangely with the present mode for classical chignons and demure ringlets. But Anne was used to these oddities and could view Drawing Room fashions without any thought of their essential discordance. Indeed, she had seen ladies who managed to make quite a handsome appearance in Court dress.

She, on the other hand, looked ridiculous in it. Such was Anne's unhappy conclusion as she regarded her reflection in the glass. Her slender figure was lost beneath the burden of a flounced and ruffled hoopskirt, and the height of her plumes only emphasized her own lack of inches. Her face looked as colorless as the lace lappets that dangled on either side of it, and the hairdresser had tortured the naturally smooth gloss of her hair into frizzy disorder. The lilac-pink watered silk of which her dress was fashioned was pretty enough in itself, but it might as well have been sackcloth, considering how little it did to make her attractive.

"I look ghastly," said Anne aloud. "Ghastly!"

The sound of her bell ringing forced her to abandon these unhappy reflections and hurry away to attend to the Queen. She found Her Majesty in a foul mood. Some of the ladies whispered that the Regent had been there, and that he and his mother had exchanged words. Whatever the cause, there could be no doubt that the Royal temper was sorely vexed.

The Queen's words were brusque and few as she ordered her attendants about. She rebuked Mrs. Melkin-thorpe sharply for being clumsy about lacing her stays, and she did not fail to remark that the white satin petticoat beneath Anne's open robe was the same one she had worn for the Princess Royal's birthday a few months previously. Anne had hoped this small economy would go unnoticed, but she saw now how vain that hope had been. With her Royal Mistress's words stinging in her ears and tears smarting in her eyes, Anne picked up the Queen's train and followed her into the Drawing Room.

Always before she had been struck by the pageantry of the Royal Drawing Room: the sea of waving plumes atop ladies' heads, the rich robes of every color in the rainbow, the gentlemen with their *chapeau bras* and satin breeches. Today, however, she stood silent and apathetic and took no notice of anything. Even when Timothy made his appearance in a velvet coat of rich plum and embroidered satin breeches of delicate oyster, she only raised her eyes for an instant and then lowered them again.

During the course of that long afternoon there was only one moment that made any real impression on Anne. The Queen, having received all the ladies being presented, had risen to leave the audience chamber. Anne had followed after her, once more bearing the Royal train. Their way led them back through a hall that contained several gentlemen who by their dress had evidently been attending the Prince Regent's Royal Levee, which was held concurrently with the Queen's Drawing Room to receive gentlemen to the Court. These gentlemen naturally stopped when they saw the Queen approaching and stood aside respectfully.

Among them was one gentleman, tall and rather sun-browned, who bowed deeply as the Queen's party approached. He did not bow with the polished grace of the courtiers, but still it was a very pleasing and masculine performance. Even Anne remarked it, sunk in apathy though she was. Looking at him with a closer attention, she discovered there was something very pleasing and masculine about his whole appearance. His black velvet coat was neatly fitted to his broad-shouldered figure, and the somberness of its hue made an attractive foil for his dark blond hair. His brown eyes looked out of his tanned face with an expression at once intelligent and good-humored.

It struck Anne that he did not seem to be taking the ceremony at all seriously. There was a suggestion of a smile about his lips as he watched the Queen pass with her Ladies and Equerries. This was very much an anomaly, for most first-time visitors to Court found the experience more awesome than amusing. Anne was moved to regard the gentleman with a still closer attention, and so evidently was Mr. Young, who inquired in a whisper of Mr. Casey beside him, "Who's the fellow in the black coat? His face looks familiar, but I'm damned if I can put a name to him."

"Oh, that's Lord Westland," Mr. Casey whispered back. "One of the Westlands of Devonshire, you know. This young man has just attained to the title upon his uncle's death. That's why he's wearing black, no doubt."

Again Anne looked at the young man. His eyes had been on the Queen all this while. Now they flickered to her Ladies behind her. His eye caught Anne's for an instant, and in that instant his expression changed. He stared at her, then bowed again hesitantly. There was no time for Anne to do more than bow her head in reply, even if it had been proper to do so, but she felt a betraying warmth in her cheeks. She was acutely conscious of Lord Westland's eyes lingering on her until she and the other Ladies had passed out of view.

Anne was curiously affected by this incident. For the rest of the afternoon, she found herself thinking about Lord Westland and wondering at his behavior. Later that afternoon she overheard two Maids of Honor discussing him as they stood waiting for their dismissal from the Queen. In an unobtrusive manner, Anne drew nearer to listen.

"Yes, Lord Westland is newly returned to England," one was saying. "He was an ambassador, or something of the sort to—to—Brazil, was it? Aye, I think it was Brazil, though it might have been one of those other outlandish countries in South America. I never can keep the half of them straight. He *is* handsome, isn't he? And enormously rich, too, they say. His old uncle left him a tremendous fortune in addition to the title."

"Rich and handsome and an earl besides," said the other with a sigh. "It's just my luck. Now all the match-making mamas in Town will be on the jump to catch him for their daughters, and I'll have no chance at all. I declare, it's the unfairest thing. *I've* no mama to invite him to parties and persuade him to dance with me and take me into supper, and yet I am sure I noticed Lord Westland first of anyone. I ought to get him if anybody does. It's a great handicap being all on one's own this way. I wonder if he will be at the ball tonight? I might find an excuse to walk by him and swoon into his arms."

"That's the oldest trick in the book," returned the other girl, laughing. "As well drop your handkerchief and be done with it!"

"Well, and I might try that, too! I am so glad I ordered

that delightful spotted silk for tonight. It was most dreadfully dear, but if Lord Westland is there, I am sure he cannot help being struck with it."

From here the two ladies' conversation devolved into a discussion of fashions, and Anne lost interest. She settled herself once more to silent endurance. But she could not quite lapse into her former apathy. The memory of Lord Westland's face kept recurring to her as she flew about that afternoon, attending to the Queen's wishes. She wondered why he had looked so strangely when he had seen her, as though—she groped for words—as though he had seen something strange and unexpected. She also found herself wondering, like the Maids of Honor, if he was to be at the ball that night. She almost wished she was going to be there, too, so she might see him again.

But that's nonsensical, she assured herself. *Why should I wish to see Lord Westland? He is nothing to me, nor I to him. Besides, I gave away my tickets, so there's no way I could go to the ball tonight even if I wanted to. And I don't want to. Timothy will be there, and probably Miss Duval, too. If anything could make me feel worse, it would be the sight of them dancing together.*

This being undeniably true, Anne tried to put Lord Westland out of her mind and concentrate on getting through the rest of the day's ordeal. She had to assist the Queen with her balldress, then hurry to change her own dress. While she was at it, she ordered warm water and washed her hair. It took so long to dry afterward that she was forced to go without dinner, but she felt ridding her hair of its unattractive hairdressing was the more urgent need. She had no real appetite in any case—had had none for weeks. So she brushed her hair until it was smooth and dry once more, arranged it in a simple chignon at the back of her neck, and surveyed her reflection in the glass.

What she saw pleased her far more than the reflection she had seen in the glass that afternoon. Shorn of her ridiculous plumes and hoopskirt, she still looked insignificant but not altogether undignified. Her figure might still be that of a schoolgirl, her complexion colorless, her face too thin, and her eyes too large, but at least these were faults of omission rather than commission. Her dress, laboriously made over and retrimmed in the minutes she had been able to snatch between duties, had turned out much better than she had dared hope. It was of white satin softened with clouds of netting, and it seemed to Anne that the floating draperies added something of shape and womanliness to her figure. At the very least, they helped distract from its inadequacies.

Her hair was still her hair, silver pale and devoid of the slightest trace of natural curl. But it looked better smooth than in the tortured mass of frizzy curls the hairdresser had left it in that morning, and on the whole, Anne was satisfied. She felt insensibly happier as she turned away from the glass. She could not imagine why this should be, for it made not one whit of difference whether she looked attractive or the greatest quiz imaginable. She was still a prisoner at Court, bereft of love and friendship and virtue and doomed to endure a monotonous round of servile duties all her life. But happier she was nonetheless, and she resolved to get what enjoyment she could from this brief respite from misery.

She had to wait on the Queen once more and attend to several other small duties attached to her position. But when these were done, she was free to do what she liked for the rest of the evening. The Queen had already told her she might be excused from attending the ball and that

her services would not be needed again until the ball
was over. Quickly Anne flitted through the labyrinthine
corridors of the Palace. Free evenings were all too rare
in her existence, and there were a number of things she
wanted to do with this one, but she had a fancy to look
in on the ball first. If possible, she wanted to see the
Queen make her entrance. This was a bit of pomp and
pageantry that Anne always enjoyed, in spite of being
familiar with the less glamorous behind-the-scenes reality
of Royalty.

She hurried along to a certain doorway, opening off
to a little-used corridor that commanded a view of the
ballroom. Few people passed this way, and the corridor
was dimly lit by a couple of branches of candles. Anne
cautiously opened the door a few inches and peeped out.
The Vice Chamberlain was just arriving with the Queen's
candle. Then came the Queen herself, magnificent in robes
of spangled velvet. She was followed by the Princesses,
who were likewise richly dressed and bejeweled. Then
came the Ladies of the Bedchamber and the Maids of
Honor.

Anne smiled a little to see the Maid she had overheard
talking that afternoon wearing the gown of spotted silk
with which she hoped to attract Lord Westland's notice.
The thought reminded Anne to wonder if Lord Westland
was there. She carefully examined the crowds of guests,
even opening the door a little wider to scrutinize them
more closely, but she saw no sign of him. Of course it
was difficult to be sure in such a crowd, but she thought
she should have seen him if he had been there.

Never mind, Anne told herself impatiently. *It's not as
though Lord Westland means anything to me. He's a
perfect stranger, and I will probably never see him again.*

*Only I should have liked to know why he looked at me
as he did this afternoon.*

Anne supposed she ought to go back to her room and
enjoy her evening alone as she had planned. There was
some mending she needed to do and a novel that she
had been trying to read for the last month amid many
interruptions, and she had looked forward to making fair
progress with both tonight. But still she lingered in the
corridor, watching the glittering company as they com-
ported themselves beneath the blaze of the great chande-
liers.

James, Earl of Westland, was feeling adrift in that company. He had arrived just in time for the Queen's entrance,
and he, like Anne, had watched the spectacle with a keen
appreciation for its theatrical qualities. But when it was
over, he found himself at loose ends.

It was not that he lacked for company. He knew a
few people among the guests, and those few had been
assiduous about introducing him to others. It was not
long, however, before James had begun to notice that a
large number of these new acquaintances were mothers
with daughters. And most of those mothers seemed intent,
even to the point of rude insistence, on his dancing with
their daughters.

James had never supposed he could have a surfeit of
feminine attention, but by the time an hour had gone by
he was beginning to feel not merely harassed but hunted.
After explaining for the twentieth time that he was not
dancing that evening, owing to his uncle's recent death,
he fled the ballroom and took refuge in the refreshment
room.

In a way, his excuse had been a false one, for the six

months of formal mourning due an uncle's death had already passed. James had been working in Brazil as an adjunct to the British ambassador when the news of his uncle's passing had reached him some months after the actual event. There had been further delays involved in resigning his position, packing his things, and returning to England, and yet another delay before he was ready to come to London to be presented in his new title to his sovereign. Under such circumstances, it seemed to James only right that he should extend the mourning period slightly beyond its formal requirement.

Yet he had been little acquainted with the elusive man who had been his uncle. Almost no one had been much acquainted with the old Lord Westland, unless it was the taciturn Scots servants who tended the modest farmhouse where he had spent the last thirty years of his life. It had been accounted odd of him to live in such a modest way when he possessed one of the largest private fortunes in England, and even odder of him to bury himself in Scottish obscurity while his family estate in Devonshire was leased to strangers. But such had been his choice, and James could only suppose he had been happy in it.

For himself, he had no wish to enjoy a similar obscurity. He had found it intoxicating to realize that after a lifetime of hard work and forced economy, he was now a wealthy earl. Of course he had known ever since he was a boy that he was his uncle's heir, but so eccentric and secretive had his uncle been that James was not inclined to presume upon that position. He would not have been surprised at any time during the past thirty years if old Lord Westland had suddenly produced a Scots wife and half-a-dozen strapping sons and effectively removed James from the succession. But no wife or sons had appeared, and James was encouraged to think now that his inheritance was secure. It was the question of what he was to do with that inheritance that was concerning him at the moment.

It had seemed at first as though, having achieved wealth and title, he could want for nothing more. But several meetings with his uncle's men of business had gradually brought James to the realization that his new position carried with it almost as many responsibilities as perquisites. He did not mind most of his new responsibilities, for he had worked ever since leaving Oxford and had no objection to working now in the manner his new station demanded of him. But there was one responsibility—the responsibility of providing himself with an heir—that had come as an unpleasant shock to him.

When his solicitor had first delicately pointed out this duty to him, James had laughed. "Oh, I daresay I will marry and produce an heir in due time," he had told the man. "I don't see that there's any hurry about it at this stage."

"No, hurry, no. But you do realize, my lord, that without a direct heir, the title and property will automatically pass at your death to your next of kin?" The solicitor looked down at his papers. "That would be your brother Thomas."

"Half brother," had said James with some emphasis. "Yes, the estate would go to Thomas, I suppose."

He had said nothing more at the time, but the idea had recurred to him frequently and unpleasantly in the days that followed. Life was such an uncertain thing. Only a few months before he had endured a bout of fever in Brazil that had nearly proved fatal. Some such thing might easily happen again, and then, if he should die, Thomas would get the title—Thomas, who had always gotten what he wanted even as a boy and had taken as an adult the thing James had desired most. It was unbearable to think of Thomas getting his title and fortune, too. Yet the only way James could prevent it from happening would be to marry and produce an heir. And given that Thomas had always been lucky, and he, by contrast, notably unlucky, James felt there was no time to be lost in setting about this venture.

So he had been looking about him for a bride, but he was handicapped in having little knowledge of English society. At the Palace that afternoon, he had looked with bemusement at the ladies in their hoopskirts and diamonds and waving plumes. They seemed magnificent creatures, but completely artificial—as though they had been turned out in round lots by some elite manufactory. Human hearts might beat beneath their robes of silk and satin and brocade, but how could he tell which one would suit him best? He would have to bear with his choice for a lifetime, and he had seen enough combative and loveless marriages to know they were to be avoided at all costs.

By the time the Queen had left her audience chamber, he was glad to abandon this puzzle and concentrate on the experience of seeing Charlotte of Mecklenburg-Strelitz for the first time. She had not impressed him particularly, but as he had stood watching her sweep past he had caught the eye of a young lady among the other Royal attendants. She was a very small young lady, hardly more than a child in appearance, and she was regarding him with a pair of grave eyes of a peculiarly beautiful aquamarine blue. Something in her calm, clear-eyed gaze made James feel as though she could read the thoughts passing in his head. He had kept looking at her as she followed after her Royal Mistress, until at last she was lost from view behind a sea of hoopskirts and nodding plumes.

It had been a trifling incident, yet it had made a strong

impression on James. He had wondered many times since then who the young lady was. He was sorry he had not made inquiries then and there as to her identity. Yet somehow he had been reluctant to ask any questions. That look had seemed such a private thing—merely a look, but a look that somehow carried significance. He felt he would like to see the young lady again and talk to her. Indeed, more than half his hopes in coming to the ball that evening were concerned with that very thing.

But circumstances had thwarted him. He had caught no glimpse of the young lady all that evening. Or was it merely that he did not recognize her? He had seen her only once, after all, and that in rather distracting circumstances. All he could say for certain was that she was small and fair-haired and that she had remarkably beautiful eyes.

After an hour spent enduring the assaults of marriage-minded maidens and their mothers, James was in no mood to look for ladies, even ladies with remarkably beautiful eyes. So he had retreated to a far corner of the crowded refreshment room and sought to solace his harassed state with a glass of champagne punch. But hardly had he lifted the glass to his lips when, to his horror, he saw a middle-aged lady enter the room—one of the matrons who had been most determined in her pursuit of him. Even after he had explained he was not dancing, she had not let him alone, but had urged him in strongest terms to take her "dear Amelia" in to supper.

The lady was looking around the room with a narrow attention. James felt certain that she was looking for him. She had not seen him yet, but she soon would if he did not take immediate action. James glanced around the room. There was a doorway just behind him that led into an adjoining saloon. James ducked quickly through this doorway, crossed the saloon, and made for the door on its further side.

This door opened onto a long corridor. A lackey in the Queen's livery was standing on guard there. He looked frowningly at James and opened his mouth to speak, but James forestalled him. "I'm in a hurry," he said rapidly. "Is there another way out of the Palace? It's most important that I not go back through the ballroom."

The lackey looked down at the golden coin James had thrust into his hand. His frown vanished. "Yes, *sir,*" he said fervently, and proceeded to give James a set of complex instructions on how to reach the nearest exit. "Just follow this corridor here—turn left—then right again—"

James, in a hurry to avoid pursuit, thanked him quickly and set off down the corridor. But though he followed the lackey's instructions as well as he could, it was soon obvious he had taken a wrong turning somewhere.

"I hope I haven't gone from the frying pan into the fire," he muttered to himself. "If the Queen's Guards find me wandering the corridors of the Palace, I'll be lucky not to be arrested as a suspicious character!" It was hardly likely that an earl would be subject to any very serious penalty, even for such an impertinent crime as trespassing in the Royal chambers, but still it would be embarrassing. In desperation James chose a turning to the right. He found himself in a dimly lit corridor that seemed to lead back to the ballroom. So at least he judged from the sound of music and laughter that came from the half-open door at the far end of the corridor. James made for it with relief, feeling that the ballroom was the lesser of the two evils at this stage of events. Then he stopped. A lady was standing in the doorway, looking out.

She was a very small lady, clothed in misty white and

with hair so pale it gleamed like silver in the dim light. Indeed, there was something ephemeral about her whole figure that made James wonder for a startled instant if she might be a phantom rather than a living woman. Then she turned to look at him, and he saw to his amazement that she was the same lady he had noticed that afternoon.

CHAPTER III

For a moment James stood regarding the lady with amazement. She had turned at his approach, and now she looked back at him, her expression as amazed at his own. "Lord Westland!" she exclaimed.

"Yes," said James, more amazed than ever. It seemed to him remarkable that she should know his name. But then the whole incident seemed to him remarkable. He had been searching for her all evening, and now here she was, standing right in front of him. Pulling himself together, he bowed. "James Westland, at your service, ma'am. I—er—I believe you have the advantage of me."

The lady immediately dropped him a graceful curtsy. "Barrington," she said softly. "My name is Anne Barrington."

"I am pleased to meet you, Miss Barrington," said James. He noticed that her eyes were as clear and beautiful as he remembered. He stood looking down at her with pleasure until the beautiful eyes dropped with a look of confusion. Once more James was recalled to a sense of his manners.

"Forgive me," he said. "I didn't mean to stare. But I believe I have seen you before, haven't I? At the Drawing Room this afternoon, attending the Queen?"

"Yes," admitted Anne. "I was at the Drawing Room."

"I thought so. I noticed you, you see."

"I noticed you, too," said Anne in a barely audible voice. "Please excuse me, my lord. It has been delightful meeting you, but I must be going now."

"But why?" asked James. The idea of her leaving filled him with an irrational dismay. "Must you go so soon? I had hoped—I had hoped you might consent to dance with me."

The words slipped out without any conscious thought, and James was aghast as soon as they were spoken. He had excused himself from dancing all evening on the grounds of his uncle's recent death. If he stood up now, he would undoubtedly give offense to a great many people as well as show disrespect for his uncle's memory. Yet he could not bring himself to renege on his impulsive invitation, even in spite of the possible consequences. *If my dancing offends them, then so be it,* he told himself recklessly. *I suppose I have a right to dance with whom I wish.*

Anne shook her head, however, her eyes wide and affrighted. "Oh, no! I am afraid I cannot dance with you, my lord. Though I am sure I am very much obliged that you should ask me," she added with punctilious politeness. "But you see I am not dancing tonight. Indeed, I am not really even attending the ball. I only came here to watch for a minute, and now I must be going."

"Must you?" said James wistfully. "But you looked

comfortable enough before I came. I would not like to think I drove you away.''

She threw him an indefinable look. "No, you didn't drive me away. And I was not—I was not comfortable. I was only interested.''

James surveyed her with new interest. "Were you? So was I. All evening I have been interested rather than comfortable. That's why I am here instead of being out there.'' He nodded toward the ballroom.

Anne looked at him with astonishment. "Indeed? I would not have thought it possible, my lord. Surely a man in your position must have many friends.''

James shook his head. "Nary a one. I haven't been in England long enough to make any. I just came here from Brazil a few weeks ago.''

"But surely,'' began Anne, then stopped. After a moment she went on, more slowly. "But surely, there are many people eager to make your acquaintance, my lord? I know there must be. I even heard two of them talking about it at the Drawing Room this afternoon, and I am sure there are many more besides who would count themselves honored to be your friend.''

"Yes, there are plenty of people eager to become my friends. But as far as I can tell, it's not I but my title that inspires them with such an urgent desire for friendship. You can't think how lowering that is.''

Anne gave him another look, this one mingled with sympathy. "I suppose it must be. I confess I never looked at it in that light, my lord. But never fear. I am sure that after you have been in England a little longer you will find friends.''

James shook his head despondently. "I doubt it. The truth is, I don't have much to say to most of the people I've met since returning to England. I've worked all my adult life, you see, and I just don't seem to have much in common with these society folk who make seeking pleasure the whole business of their life." He smiled at Anne. "Why, since coming to England, you're the person I've talked to most, setting aside such worthies as attorneys and bailiffs!"

Anne looked at her feet. "Perhaps that is because I have nothing in common with society people either," she said softly. "Like you, I, too, have been obliged to work for my living."

"Have you? What do you do? Are you attached to the Court in some way?"

"Yes, I am a Keeper of the Robes," she said. "*Second* Keeper of the Robes." It was obvious from the way she spoke that the words aroused some painful reflection.

James wondered why she looked and sounded so gloomy. "Your position sounds rather an interesting one," he ventured. Anne gave him a quick look, but did not answer. "Isn't it interesting?" he asked curiously.

Again Anne did not answer. Looking at her closely, James was aghast to see a tear trickling down her cheek. "I'm sorry!" he said. "Have I said something amiss? Do forgive me, Miss Barrington. Upon my word, I didn't mean to hurt you."

She shook her head. "It's nothing," she said, but her voice broke in midsentence. James looked at her with consternation.

"I'm sorry, Miss Barrington—upon my word, I truly am sorry. Is there something I can do?"

She shook her head. "No," she said. "There is nothing—nothing you can do. Nothing *anyone* can do." Burying her face in her hands, she began to weep in earnest.

James, looking at her in a panic, wondered what to do. He felt he ought to try to comfort her, but feared such an act would be presumption in a stranger. "Don't cry, Miss Barrington," he pleaded. "Please don't cry. Here, take my handkerchief." She accepted the handkerchief that he pressed into her hand, but as far as he could tell it did nothing toward stemming the flood of her tears. "Can I do anything?" he asked urgently. "Should I call your maid, Miss Barrington? Or fetch you some smelling salts?"

"No," she said. "No, I want nothing at all, my lord. If you would be so good as to leave me—"

"But I can't leave you when you are so distressed. If you will not let me fetch your maid or smelling salts, at least let me get you a glass of wine." After urging this request several times, he managed to gain a weak affirmative. "Excellent! I'll be back with your wine in two shakes, Miss Barrington. Mind you don't stir from this spot. If you run away, I'll have to ask the Palace servants to call you for me. You can't escape me, for now I know your name."

This weak witticism caused Anne to smile briefly through her tears. Feeling heartened by the circumstance, James hurried away to execute his commission.

He was back with the wine in less than five minutes and found Anne sitting slumped against the wall, dabbing dejectedly at her eyes. She seemed to have stopped crying, however, and accepted the glass of wine he offered her with another of her watery smiles. "Thank you, my lord," she said. "I think the worst of the storm is over. Please forgive me for putting you to so much trouble. I can't think how I came to be such a wet-goose."

James stood watching her as she took a few sips of the wine. After she had drunk about half of it, she glanced up at him. "Indeed, I think all is well now, my lord. I feel much better now, and you need not stay any longer on my account.''

James hesitated. "You don't mind if I do stay, though, do you? Just to make certain you are recovered?''

"To be quite honest, I would rather you did not," said Anne. She gave him another watery smile. "I am deeply ashamed of having behaved like such a fool. And not only that: I am sure I must look a fright after crying so much.''

"You do not look a fright to me," said James honestly. In the dim light of the corridor he could see the tears had left her eyelids stained with pink, but they had detracted nothing from the beauty of those aquamarine eyes.

Anne turned her face away. "You are very kind to say so, my lord, but I know I do look a fright. I cannot bear for you to see me like this. Please, I would rather you went away.''

"Well, if it's only the way you look that concerns you, we can soon attend to that." Walking over to the branches of candles on the wall, James snuffed them out one by one until only the furthermost branch at the far end of the hall remained to cast a dim glow along its length. "That's better! Now I cannot tell you have been crying at all.''

Anne looked at him doubtfully, then smiled. It was the first real smile she had given him, and it transfigured her pale, grave face with amazing effect. James felt a little dizzy. To disguise his confusion, he gestured to the floor beside her. "Do you mind if I sit down with you?''

"Certainly not, my lord. You are quite welcome to sit down. But are you sure you would not rather return to the ballroom?''

"Quite sure," said James fervently. He seated himself on the floor.

Once there, he found himself with nothing to say. Anne said nothing either, for a considerable time, but at last she roused herself to speak again. "I suppose you must be wondering at the way I have behaved, my lord?"

James shook his head. "No. Grieved, perhaps, but I see nothing to wonder at."

Anne gave him a startled look. "Don't you? But how can that be?"

"Well, it's plain to see you are unhappy. Unhappy with your position here at Court, I suppose. Is that it?"

She nodded. "Yes, that is it," she said in a low voice. "Or rather that is most of it."

"Tell me about it," said James.

As he spoke these words, he wondered at himself. It was not like him to interest himself in the affairs of a bare acquaintance—a lady whose existence he had not known of twenty-four hours before. Likewise, it seemed the height of presumption to ask that lady to confide her secret sorrows to him as though he were a bosom friend. But to his surprise, she began at once to speak in a low, clear voice.

"I have been a Keeper of the Queen's Robes for seven years now. I came to Court when I was seventeen. My parents had died, and they were not at all well-off people. There was almost nothing left after the expense of burying them and settling their debts. Without some kind of position, I wouldn't have had enough to keep me."

"I'm sorry," said James with sympathy. She flashed him a quick, shy smile.

"Thank you, my lord. As I said, I hadn't enough to keep me, so I was very relieved when a relative of my father's who had some influence at Court was able to get me this position. That is, I was relieved at first. But then after I had been here for a while—oh, I ought not to be speaking like this!'' She looked aghast. "Indeed, I did not mean to speak against the Queen, my lord. You must think me very wrong and ungrateful to be saying such things."

"Not at all," said James. "Why should it be wrong and ungrateful to say what you think?"

"Why, because so much has been done for me. I might easily be a pauper in a workhouse if I had not gotten this position. And the Queen and everyone else have been very kind to me according to their lights."

James shook his head. "I met the Queen for the first time this afternoon, so perhaps I am not competent to judge. But it did not strike me that kindness was her outstanding characteristic."

Anne looked almost frightened by these words. After a minute, however, she nodded. "No . . . no, she is not what you or I should call kind. But she is Queen, you know, and for someone in such a high position, she is really quite kind and thoughtful."

"It does not seem to me that high position should excuse one from the exercise of ordinary kindness and thoughtfulness," said James. "But go on."

Thus encouraged, Anne went on to describe an existence that sounded to James's ears like nothing so much as slavery. He heard of summonses early and late; of meals and recreation interrupted or cut short with Royal disregard; and of the petty tyranny of her superior, Mrs. Melkinthorpe, who raged for hours about something as trifling as a window opened without her permission. He heard of an isolation so complete that the outside world seemed not to exist; of a ceaseless round of duties completed in an atmosphere of criticism and watchful jealousy; of companions whose minds were wholly given up to intrigue and jockeying for personal gain.

"But what were your friends and relatives thinking about, to allow you to live in such surroundings?" James demanded. "Did they not see what it was doing to you?"

Anne shook her head. "You do not understand, my lord. It is a great honor to be one of the Queen's Ladies. I was considered very fortunate to be made her Assistant Keeper of the Robes, and there are dozens who would be glad to take my place if ever the position should come open."

"It doesn't sound much like an honor to *me*," said James with emphasis. "It sounds like slavery. And I still say your friends and relatives are wrong not to take you away from it."

"But you see I have no friends, my lord. And no relatives either, apart from the cousin who got me the post. And she told me at the outset that I had better make good, for she was in no position to do anything else for me."

James was silent. The idea of any Englishwoman finding herself in such a predicament was a new one to him. He glanced at Anne, who sat twisting his handkerchief between her hands, seeming almost to have forgotten his presence. "It sounds an awkward enough situation," he admitted. "But there must be *some* way out of it. Cannot you simply resign your position?"

Anne gave him an almost pitying look. "You don't understand, my lord," she said. "When the Queen appoints a woman to a position such as mine, she expects her to remain there for life. One cannot simply resign. I have never known anyone released from Her Majesty's service, unless it was because of illness or marriage."

James caught eagerly at these words. "But there you are! If illness is a legitimate excuse for leaving, then nothing could be simpler. You need only tell the Queen that your health is breaking down under such a demanding

schedule of duties. I don't think it would be a lie, either.''
He regarded his companion's pale face and slender figure
with compassion. "You look very frail."

But Anne brushed his words aside. "It would not
answer, my lord," she said. "What would I do even if
Her Majesty did release me? I have no home to return
to—no friends or relatives to take me in. I would have
to find a position, and since I have no education or accomplishments to speak of, what kind of position could I get?
Chances are it would be no better than this one, and very
possibly it would be worse.''

James was forced to admit that this seemed probable.
He sat frowning into space as Anne continued to twist
his handkerchief between her hands. "I see your point.
Yes, assuredly I see your point," he told her. "You don't
think—? No, I daresay that would not answer either.''

"Nothing will answer," said Anne hopelessly. "I will
serve the Queen until I die, or until I become too ill to
fulfill my duties. Those are my only choices, and I am
quite resigned to that fact.''

James, looking down at her, was filled with an infinite
pity, and also with something else. Before he had time
to reflect, the words were out of his mouth.

"Look here," he said. "How would you like to marry
me?''

CHAPTER IV

For a moment Anne did not think she had heard James correctly. She turned to look at him, and all the doubt and skepticism in her mind was visible in her eyes.

"What did you say?" she asked.

"I asked if you wouldn't like to marry me," James repeated. His voice sounded diffident, but Anne observed there was a determined set to his jaw.

"You must be joking," she said flatly.

"And why would I be joking? I assure you I am quite in earnest. Looking at the matter impartially, I can see no other solution to your difficulties."

"But that's ridiculous," said Anne, who was finding the whole conversation increasingly surreal. "Simply ridiculous. You cannot really wish to marry me!"

"Why shouldn't I?" James responded.

Anne found this question as difficult to answer as the other. "Because—because you have only just met me.

And you know nothing about me. And—oh, it's ridiculous, my lord. You cannot really wish to marry me!''

"But I do," said James.

Looking at him again, Anne was struck by something in his eyes—an expression that made her drop her own in haste. "I am sure you do not," she said. "Why should you? If you really wanted to marry, you might have almost any lady in the kingdom for your wife.''

"True," he agreed equably. "I have met quite a number of ladies just this evening who gave me to understand my addresses would be very acceptable to them. But I know full well that it is only my title that interests them— my title and my money. For me personally they do not care a button, and if my worldly goods and estate were transferred tomorrow to some other fellow, they would be off in full cry after him with never another thought for me.''

"That may be true of most of them," acknowledged Anne. "But I cannot believe there is not one lady in England who would not marry you simply for yourself.''

"Possibly there might be. But there are reasons—essential reasons—why I must marry soon. I cannot afford to take months or even years to search all England for the one disinterested lady who might wish to become my bride.''

Anne thought she was beginning to understand. "I see," she said. "It is a marriage of convenience you are proposing?''

There was a pause before James answered. "Yes, if you like to put it that way," he said. "Certainly we would both gain something by such a marriage. I would gain the wife I need, and you would gain an honorable excuse for leaving the service of the Queen.''

James spoke carefully, keeping his eyes averted from

Anne as he spoke. He had the sense that he was telling a falsehood, although that made no sense under the circumstances. After all, everything he had just told Anne was the truth. He did need a wife, and she did need an excuse to leave the Queen, and marriage would provide a convenient solution to both their difficulties.

But though Anne showed no signs of suspecting his veracity, neither did she seem eager to embrace the solution he proposed. She shook her head slowly. "It's very good of you to make me such an offer, my lord," she said. "But I couldn't think of accepting it. I should think myself iniquitous to make use of you in such a way."

"But I would be using you, too," pointed out James. "Besides, there is using and using. By marrying me, you might be using me in a sense, but you would not be using me to merely gain a title and fortune. That, of all things, is what I should find most distasteful. Of course my offer is an unconventional one, but you must see that I could never be sure of the motives of a lady to whom I proposed in a more conventional way. Your motives I both understand and approve. Indeed, I would be glad to think I might be of service to you."

Anne twisted the handkerchief between her hands once more. "Still, it does not seem right, my lord," she said. "You offer me so much, and I—I can give you so little in return."

James thought he understood. "Of course we are strangers," he said. "If we were to marry, I would not expect you to—I would not expect you to give me your affections as though we were marrying for love."

Anne threw him a fleeting glance, then looked quickly away. "It's not that," she said. But she did not expand on this statement, and after a moment James went on in a quiet voice.

"I can understand that my proposals have taken you by surprise. Naturally you would not wish to make such an important decision at a moment's notice. You will want time to think about it and decide what is best to do. Why don't I give you my direction here in London, and you can write to me as soon as you make up your mind?"

Producing a diminutive pencil and memorandum book from his pocket, he began to write. Anne opened her mouth to object, then shut it again. She knew perfectly well she ought to stop him. It would be wrong to let him think even for a moment that she could accept such staggering generosity from a stranger. Yet it seemed so much like an answer to a prayer—an answer to a prayer she would never have dared make, so extravagant and unlikely did it seem. To think she might marry Lord Westland! She looked at him, marveling that this man with so much to offer should think of offering it to someone as insignificant as Anne Barrington.

He caught her eye upon him and smiled. Anne smiled back and was aware of a small flutter within her heart. *If he wanted my affections, he might win them very easily,* she thought. *He is far too modest in thinking women find him attractive only because of his money and title.*

This train of thought embarrassed her, and she got to her feet, making a great show of smoothing and settling her skirts. James got to his feet, too, and handed her the slip of paper. "You will let me know?" he said. "You will write and tell me if you wish to accept my offer? Or if there is anything else I can do for you? You must know I will be glad to do anything I can."

Again he looked down at her, and again Anne was struck by the expression in his eyes. Averting her own eyes, she nodded, saying with difficulty, "But you have done so much for me already, my lord. Listening to my problems, and bringing me wine, and behaving so kindly to me. I couldn't think of asking you for anything more."

"Nevertheless, I hope you will ask," he said. In silence he stood a moment, looking down at her. Anne looked back at him. It was dark in the hallway, lit only by the single far-off branch of candles. Music came drifting in from the ballroom, the strains of a country dance mingled with voices and laughter. "We are friends now, you see—at least I hope we are. I should like to be your friend, Miss Barrington. Will you allow me that place?"

"Of course," said Anne in wonder. Her wonderment grew greater when he bent and kissed her on the lips.

"Forgive me," he said, looking down at her with a hint of apprehension in his eyes. "I ought not to have done that, but I meant no disrespect. It was only that—it was only that—"

"It's all right," said Anne. Curiously enough, it *was* all right. She could not have explained why it was all right that a man she had met only an hour ago should kiss her in such an intimate way, yet she felt instinctively that there had been nothing irreverent or impertinent in the intimacy. "I will gladly be your friend, gladly," she told him. "But in that case you must call me Anne and not Miss Barrington."

"And you must call me James and not 'my lord,' " he returned, smiling. "And you must also let me know if there is ever the slightest service I can perform for you. You will do that, Anne?"

"Yes, I will do that," she said. Rather shyly she gave him her hand. He took it, bowed low over it, then released it. "Good night, my lord—or James, as I should say. And thank you again."

"Good night to you, Anne. I hope it will all go better

with you after this. But if it doesn't, write and let me know.''

"I will," said Anne, though she had no intention of doing so. As she flitted away, she could not resist the urge to look back at him. He was standing looking after her, and when he saw her looking back he bowed again. Anne dropped a curtsy in return, then hastened on down the corridor.

Once out of sight, she took to her heels and ran as though her life depended on it. She could not decide if she was more gladdened or embarrassed by the interview just past. There was a strange exhilaration in the memory of it, yet also much that was mortifying. She had just spread out the whole shabby fabric of her life for a stranger to inspect—and such a stranger, too! A wealthy, handsome, and eligible earl, who might be expected to only sneer at it.

But he's not like that, Anne told herself. *That is dismissing him as nothing more than his title and fortune, and he is much more than that. He is a gentleman—a gentleman in the best sense of the word. I only wish I could have met him under other circumstances.*

She was still reflecting on this theme when she reached her room. There she halted, for Mrs. Melkinthorpe was standing just outside the door. The German woman's eyes were snapping, and her always ruddy face was suffused with choler, so that it was redder than ever.

"Where haf you been?" she demanded of Anne, her anger intensifying the slight German accent she retained despite twenty years of Court life and ten years of marriage to an Englishman. "We haf for you been looking this twenty minutes at least. Her Majesty has been for you waiting—for you, you lazy and ungrateful girl! Haf you no respect, no consideration for Her whom you serve?''

"I'm sorry," said Anne, stammering. "I didn't know. I had thought—Her Majesty said I might have the evening to myself—"

"An evening to yourself!" repeated Mrs. Melkinthorpe with scorn. "Me, I think it is honor enough to serve my Queen, without asking for evenings to myself. But then I am not you—you with your airs and graces and independence. And so you thought I should do all the work of undressing Her Majesty myself?"

Anne protested that such was not her thought at all, but Mrs. Melkinthorpe paid no attention. Still scolding, she conducted Anne along the corridor until they reached the Queen's Dressing Room.

It was clear to Anne that she was in disgrace here as well. She was received with frosty silence and not a word was spoken to her as she went about removing the Royal garments and readying the Queen for bed. "I will let you go now, Miss Barrington," said Her Majesty coldly at the conclusion of this task. "Hereafter, you will perhaps have the goodness to let us know where you can be found of an evening, so we need not be kept waiting for your assistance."

"Yes, of course," said Anne, blinking back the tears. "Good night, Your Majesty."

She knew she had not heard the last of this incident. Nor was she wrong, for Mrs. Melkinthorpe referred to it countless times in the weeks that followed, describing Anne's negligence in such terms that a listener might have been pardoned for supposing she had deliberately fled from the Royal summons. The other members of the Court, well familiar with Mrs. Melkinthorpe's personality, took none of her diatribe seriously, yet it was an incident in their stagnant and self-contained lives, and they deliberately exploited it for all it was worth. Anne spent her days in an almost constant state of humiliation.

And even this was not her worst cause of humiliation. In the days following the Birthday Ball, she began to notice among the Equerries and other men at Court a change in demeanor—a certain increased boldness allied with a decrease in respect. When Mr. Young waylaid her in the hall and tried to inveigle her into kissing him in a manner that was little short of bullying, Anne knew that the worst had happened. Timothy had clearly been talking. He must have described something of what had passed between them that night she had gone to his room, and the knowledge that she had enjoyed intimate relations with him (though of enjoyment there had been none) was now widely known, or at least suspected, by others at Court.

In this atmosphere, Anne quickly lost what little joy of living she had possessed. Her appetite, always small, began to fail her completely. Her throat seemed blocked, so that the act of swallowing food was nauseating. The daily walks and airings she had always striven to take as a safeguard to health seemed too much trouble to be bothered with. Even reading, which had been her one real escape, now lost its charms. When she was summoned to her Royal duties, she performed them like an automaton; when she was not, she merely sat in her room, listlessly awaiting the next summons.

It struck her now and then that if she continued the way she was going, she would probably fall into a decline. Sometimes she suspected she was already falling into one. There was a sense of inevitability, of being pulled down a long downhill slope, that gave the term a certain aptness. In a detached sort of way, Anne found the experience almost interesting. But then James's letter arrived, and her detachment was shaken by a new and different set of emotions.

She received the letter from Mrs. Melkinthorpe, who lingered to ask suspiciously whom it was from. "I don't know," said Anne, looking at the letter's superscription with puzzlement. She almost never received letters, and the handwriting of this one was unfamiliar to her.

Mrs. Melkinthorpe took this as mere evasion, however. After castigating Anne as "a sly creature, my Gott! Always the secrets, the mysteries," she went stomping off in a rage. Anne broke the letter's seal, unfolded the letter, and read the following:

Dear Miss Barrington,

I have thought of you many times since our conversation the night of the King's Birthday Ball. I hope things have been going better for you in the weeks since then.

As I have not heard from you, I presume this must be the case. But if you are still unhappy in your position, I beg to assure you that my offer still stands. Nothing that has happened in the past weeks has shaken my conviction that we might deal very well together as husband and wife. I stand ready to bestow on you all I possess at a moment's notice. Only send me a word, and I will come to you, and we can plan how best this may be accomplished.

Yours, etc.,

James Westland

Anne read through this letter once, then read it through again in bemusement. Bemusement was indeed her chief emotion. Yet at the same time she had a curious sense of something stirring to life within her.

She had thought of James often in the weeks that had passed since the Birthday Ball. Yet the events that had elapsed since that evening had served to blur its memory in her mind and make it seem little more than a brief, pleasant dream in the midst of nightmares. Now it sprang into sudden vividness again. She remembered James as he had stood before her that night: the concern he had shown for her distress, and the sympathy that he had expressed for her plight. She remembered how he had looked, how he had spoken—how he had kissed her. And she realized that here was a real way out of her difficulties, if only she dared to take it.

"I can't," whispered Anne, looking at the letter. "It would be taking dreadful advantage of him. I simply cannot!" But then the alternative loomed before her. If she went on in the way she was going, it would almost certainly be the death of her. Indeed, what was facing her now was really a choice between life and death. Did she truly wish to die?

"No, I do not," said Anne, and with those words, she found her choice was made. Drawing ink, paper, and pen toward her, she wrote swiftly:

Dear Lord Westland,
*   If your offer still stands, I am willing to accept it. You may call on me at your earliest convenience to discuss such arrangements as must be made.*
*   Yours, with gratitude,*

*   Anne Barrington*

Having sanded and sealed this epistle, she rang for her servant and told him to carry it to Lord Westland at the address James had given her.

The servant received these orders with a murmured, "Very good, miss," though if Anne had been paying attention she would have seen his eyes widen. But her thoughts were otherwise occupied. She wondered how long it would be before James received the note, and what he would do when he read it.

I hope he won't be too long in replying, she told herself. She felt all at once very nervous and apprehensive. But though these were not comfortable emotions, they were better by far than the cold, dead feeling of hopelessness that had haunted her so long. When dinnertime came, she was able to eat a real meal for the first time in days, and that made her feel better still.

By the time James's reply came, she felt ready to face whatever it might contain. In the event, its contents were brief enough:

Dear Anne,
 Your note has made me very happy. I will wait upon you tomorrow, so we may discuss the necessary arrangements.

Yours in expectation,

James

CHAPTER V

Although James had told Anne that her message had made him very happy, happiness was not his predominant state of mind in the days that followed. What he was feeling was such a contradictory jumble of emotions, good and bad, that he was exasperated by his own ambivalence.

I must have been mad, he told himself. *It's the only thing that can explain my doing such a foolish thing. Why, I hardly know this girl! And now I am engaged to marry her!*

In his memory he went over his two meetings with Anne. The first had hardly counted, seeing that it had consisted merely of an exchange of looks. It was only on their second meeting that they had come to know each other in some degree. He had described his difficulties in returning to London in his changed condition, and Anne had confided to him the story of her own difficulties. Moved by pity for her plight—and by some other emotion harder to define—he had offered marriage to her. Anne had demurred, whereupon he had given her his name and address and urged her to write to him if she should think better of her decision.

For a week after this incident, James had been in a fever lest Anne take him at his word. The thought that she might force him to carry through on his impulsive proposal filled him with nothing but horror. He could not imagine what had inspired him to offer marriage to a girl who was a virtual stranger to him. But as the weeks had slipped by and he had heard nothing from her, his feelings had insensibly shifted from relief to resentment. He felt injured that Anne should have rejected him and his offer. He kept thinking of her as he had seen her, with her beautiful clear eyes, silver blond hair, and slender figure in its floating draperies of white. There was something about her that caught his imagination and refused to let it go. In the end, moved by the same madness he could not explain, he had written to her, repeating his offer of marriage and urging her a second time to accept it.

And now she had accepted it, and he was filled with horror again. *I must have been mad,* he repeated to himself. *There is no need at all for me to be in such haste to marry. And if I did insist on marrying, I would have done better to choose a different kind of girl—a strong, healthy girl suited to childbearing. After all, the whole point of my marrying is to get an heir.* Given Anne's childlike stature, he doubted her suitability to this purpose. She was so small and fragile-looking, so almost ethereal in appearance. Yet when he thought of her, there was a part of him that responded as it had never responded to any other woman.

And so in a mixture of excitement, regret, and bewilderment, he prepared to go and interview his bride-to-be.

Since the Birthday Ball, the Court had removed again to Windsor, so it was a considerable drive that brought him at last to the doors of the Palace. He bribed a flunky to carry word to Anne that he was there, and presently he was shown into a small sitting room on the first floor. Anne was seated there, nervously plaiting her hands together.

Once again, James was struck by her air of fragility. The hand she gave him in greeting was so small and fine-boned that he hardly dared touch it for fear of crushing it. She was wearing a dress of green jaconet muslin, richly flounced and trimmed with rows of pleatings and braid. Even James's ignorant eyes recognized it as the height of fashion, but the effect was less one of intimidation than of a small girl dressed up in her mother's clothes. These details vanished from his mind, however, as soon as he looked into her eyes. They were shadowed and weary, and her whole face had a pinched look about it. It shocked him so much that he spoke out without thinking.

"What have they been doing to you?"

Anne was surprised by the indignation in his voice. She had expected this first meeting to be an awkward and formal business, and for the past twelve hours she had been trying to think what she might say, in between fits of wondering whether she had better not simply say it had all been a mistake and she could not marry him after all. Now, however, she found herself responding to James's question quite naturally.

"What have they been doing to me?" she repeated. "Why, nothing, James—nothing worth mentioning." She had no sense that she was speaking an untruth. So strong and warm and vital was his presence that all the slights and slurs of the previous weeks seemed to fade to nothing-ness in comparison. Even the thought of Timothy was nothing more than a dim shadow lurking on the fringes of her memory.

"But you look tired to death! It is as I said before—the work here is too much for you. You should have written me sooner and let me take you away from it."

"Perhaps," said Anne. Nervously she began to plait her hands together once more. "But I could not feel it right to take advantage of such a generous offer. Indeed, I cannot think it right even now, James." She looked up at him appealingly. "Are you quite, quite sure that you want to marry me?"

"Yes, I am," said James. To his surprise, he found that he meant it. When he looked in her eyes, he forgot all about her fragility and her immature figure and her probable unsuitability for childbearing. She was simply a woman—a woman to whom he felt connected on some strange, underlying level. "As far as I can see, the sooner I marry you and take you away from here, the better," he told her. "If I get a special license, we might be able to marry as early as the day after tomorrow. Have you told the Queen you are leaving her?"

"No, not yet," said Anne. She began to twist her hands together once more. "Indeed, I hardly know how I am to tell her. I am afraid she will think our engagement very strange and sudden. As will everyone else, of course."

"Let them think what they like," said James. On an impulse he reached out and gathered her into his arms. The movement was instinctive on his part, and for an instant he was afraid Anne would be frightened or offended by it. But she came to him willingly, wrapping her own arms around him and laying her head against his chest with a sigh.

"Oh, James," she whispered. James reached down to stroke her silver blond head with fingers that trembled slightly. He felt shaken, yet exhilarated, full of a strange, glowing delight. It was as though some timid wild animal had come to him of its own accord. He was afraid to move, almost afraid to breathe, lest he frighten Anne away. But when she had lain in his arms several minutes without making any move to break away, he ventured to stoop and kiss her on the brow. She looked up at him then, and something in her expression inspired him to kiss her again, this time full on the lips. It was at that moment that Mrs. Melkinthorpe walked into the room.

"Miss Barrington, I haf—" she began, then stopped with a gasp. "My Gott! What is this?" She looked from James to Anne with kindling eyes. "I knew you were for to be sly, but this—this goes beyond everything. To bring a man to your room and there conduct yourself like a woman of the streets—"

James opened his mouth to interrupt this diatribe, but Anne forestalled him. "You misunderstand the situation, Mrs. Melkinthorpe," she said, with a dignity that surprised even herself. "This is my fiancé, Lord Westland."

If Anne had been a vengeful or malicious woman, she might have felt any number of old scores were evened at that moment. Mrs. Melkinthorpe drew in her breath sharply, then let it out again, looking absurdly like a deflated balloon. "Your fiancé!" she exclaimed. "You do not mean to tell me you are betrothed, Miss Barrington?"

"Yes, I am," said Anne, with more dignity still.

"But how then have I never heard of this before? I knew not even that you and Lord Westland were acquainted."

Anne threw an imploring look at James, who answered quickly, "Miss Barrington and I have thought it best to keep the news of our engagement private until now. I have been in South America for some years and only recently achieved a position where I might support a wife.''

''My Gott, but it is as I have always said. You are the sly one,'' Mrs. Melkinthorpe told Anne. She said it more with the air of a compliment than an insult, however, and Anne merely smiled and said nothing. ''But this engagement of yours—it does not mean you are to leave the Queen's service, does it, Miss Barrington? Lord Westland will not mind your continuing here at the Palace, I suppose?''

''On the contrary, I mind very much,'' said James, once more answering before Anne could respond. ''In my opinion, Anne has been working far too hard, and her health is beginning to suffer. I was quite shocked to see how she looked when I came in today. I want to take her right away from here as soon as possible.''

''But it is not that you can leave Her Majesty in the lurch!'' said Mrs. Melkinthorpe, looking aghast. ''It is the Queen, you understand! If she does release Miss Barrington from her service, it will only be after she has had time to find another lady to take her place.''

''Let us hope she can do that within two days, then,'' said James with determination. ''Because I do not intend to wait any longer to claim my wife.''

Anne fully expected an explosion at these words. But after Mrs. Melkinthorpe had surveyed James for a moment or two in apoplectic silence, she threw up her hands. ''It is that you do not understand, my lord! All cannot be done in an instant. Why, Her Majesty does not even know that Miss Barrington means to marry.''

''Yes, and that is why I would like to inform her of the fact as soon as possible. Would it be possible for me to see Her Majesty for a moment or two?''

Mrs. Melkinthorpe threw up her hands once more, but

her voice was unexpectedly submissive as she replied, "I will make inquiry, if you like. Do you wait here, my lord, and I will see if Her Majesty finds it convenient to see you."

After she had gone, Anne looked up at James. "Oh, James," she said penitently. "What a scene for you to have to endure! And I am afraid there will be a worse scene when you tell the Queen about our plans. I almost think it would be better to write to her rather than tell her face-to-face."

"No, I'd sooner break the news to her in person and get it over with," said James. "What can she do, after all? She might cut up a bit rough at first, but she can't eat me." He smiled down at Anne. "All this is happening rather fast, isn't it? But as far as I am concerned, it can't be settled fast enough. I find myself quite eager to be married of a sudden."

There was a kindling light in his dark eyes as he looked down at Anne. It aroused an answering glow in Anne's heart. Yet at the same time, she was smitten by a feeling of guilt. He looked so happy and so confident—so confident that he was gaining a wife who would do him credit. And what he was gaining was plain, thin, awkward Anne Barrington, a girl who not only lacked the treasure of virtue but was so lacking in worldly treasure that she was some forty-odd pounds in debt.

Anne suddenly felt she could not go a moment longer without undeceiving him. "James," she said in a faltering voice. "Things are indeed going very fast, as you say. I wonder—I wonder if they are not going too fast. You know you are really very little acquainted with me. If you knew everything about me, I think—I am afraid you would not wish to marry me."

She felt like a monster of cruelty as the light died from

James's eyes. "You don't wish to marry me?" he asked. Although his voice was quiet, Anne could sense the hurt in it.

"I do wish to marry you!" she said desperately. "But you don't know me, James. Indeed, there are a great many things about me you don't know."

"Nor do you know everything about me," pointed out James. "This marriage will be quite as much an act of faith on your part as on mine."

"Yes, perhaps. But I have nothing to lose, whereas you have a great deal. And I would not bring shame on you for anything, James."

"If that is so, then you won't," said James. "I trust you, Anne. I am sure you would never do anything to hurt me."

"But I might hurt you without trying! I wish I could make you understand." Even as she spoke, Anne felt the impossibility of speaking a truth so sordid and ugly. James looked down at her with furrowed brow.

"I am willing to take the chance if you are," he said. "As I see it, it's another of those matters where we must take each other on faith."

Anne made one last desperate effort. "Yes, but you ought to know the difficulties that marrying me will involve you in. The fact is that I am—that I am in *debt*, James." Averting her face, she added, "And there are other things I have done in my life of which I am even more ashamed."

James reached out and gently turned her face toward him again. "Well, and so are there things in my life of which I am ashamed," he said. "So are there in any adult person's, I suppose. But that need not affect our future as far as I can see. Just how much is this debt of yours?"

"Almost fifty pounds," said Anne despairingly.

James gave a whoop of laughter. "My dear girl! And you call that being in debt? I assure you, I am quite capable of shouldering a much greater burden than that. Indeed, I would do so willingly even if your debt were a hundred times as much."

"It might as well be, for all the ability I have to pay it. Can't you see, James? It fills me with shame that I must ask my husband to pay my debts before even the marriage vows are pronounced."

"Yes, I see," said James, patting her hand. "But indeed, what you ask is only a trifle, Anne. Don't let it make you feel badly. And if there are other such considerations that are disturbing you, I would beg of you not to let them make you feel badly, either. Whatever they are, I am sure I should not regard them any more than this one."

Anne was not so sure. But so little did she wish to talk of her other concern, and so badly did she want to believe him, that she said nothing more. There would have been little time for discussion in any case, for Mrs. Melkinthorpe came bursting in a moment later with a self-important face.

"The Queen will see you, my lord," she said. "If you will follow me, please?"

Anne was prey to considerable nervousness while James's Royal interview was going on. It was quite possible that the Queen would object to the hasty marriage he was proposing and contrive somehow to put a stop to it. Anne wondered that she herself was not more diffident on the subject, but in fact she felt very willing and even eager to be married. "It will take me away from Court, at least," she rationalized. "And I have been wanting to escape so long that it stands to reason I should gladly embrace any means that is offered.''

It was almost an hour later that James reappeared. He had the appearance of a man who had passed through a major ordeal, but there was a triumphant smile on his face as he bowed over Anne's hand.

''It is all settled,'' he told her. ''After tomorrow you are no longer in the Queen's service.''

Anne shut her eyes. ''Thank God,'' she said. ''But was it not very difficult to convince her, James? She cannot have been happy to let me go on such short notice.''

''No, she wasn't happy about it,'' agreed James with a reminiscent grimace. ''But I made her see the necessity of it in the end. Indeed, I cannot think the worse of her for her reluctance to let you go. She had nothing but the highest praise for your character, conduct, and industry.''

''Had she?'' said Anne in disbelief. ''The *Queen* praised me? I would not have expected it.''

''Indeed she did. What is more, she means to make you some reward for it. She has agreed to give you a hundred pounds on your marriage and to continue your salary at half-pay afterwards in the form of an annuity.''

Anne's mouth opened, but no words came out. James smiled down at her flabbergasted face. ''So you see, your worries about debt were quite needless. Not only will you be able to pay your debt, you will have money enough to buy bride-clothes, too, if you like.''

Anne shuddered. ''If you do not mind, James, I think I shall not bother with bride-clothes. As we are to be married so hastily, there can be no necessity. And really I have clothes enough as it is.'' She gave him an apologetic smile. ''The truth is that I am sick to death of the whole subject of clothes. I have spent all the last seven years pinching and scraping and trying to contrive the maximum

show for the minimum outlay, and it will be a relief—
an unspeakable relief—not to have to do so anymore.''

"As you like," said James, pressing her hand. ''I'm
sure it's no concern of mine.''

He went on to talk of the other arrangements for their
marriage. ''We are to be married the day after tomorrow
in the King's Chapel. I have arranged for a clergyman to
officiate, but I must still obtain the necessary license. That
must be my task for tomorrow.''

"I suppose I will not see you tomorrow, then," said
Anne. She was surprised to find how disappointed the
idea made her feel.

"No, I expect not. But the next day you shall see me,
never fear!" Smiling, James took her hand in his and
kissed it. "Until then, my dear," he said.

"Until then," echoed Anne. She accompanied him to
the door and remained there watching as he strode off
down the corridor.

CHAPTER VI

In the beginning, Anne had wondered how she would ever get through the forty-odd hours that remained till her wedding. But as things turned out, those hours flew by in such a hectic rush that she had no time to be impatient at all.

The astounding news that Miss Anne Barrington was engaged to marry the Earl of Westland had spread through the Queen's household like an outbreak of some virulent disease. Like such a disease, it had the effect of drastically altering its victims' temperaments. Ladies who had formerly snubbed or patronized Anne became suddenly oppressively friendly, while gentlemen who had formerly declared her a mousy little thing not worth looking at stopped her in the corridor to give her their best wishes and assure her they had always had her welfare in mind. She no longer had to ring repeatedly (and sometimes in vain) to summon a servant. Her summonses were always answered promptly and her orders received with so many obsequious smiles and smirks that Anne found herself quite nauseated. Even the Queen addressed her with added respect now that she was a future countess. It was more than Anne would have imagined possible, and sometimes almost more than she could bear.

She also found, to her sorrow, that she could not entirely escape the matter of bride-clothes. The idea that she could be married without making some addition to her wardrobe was received with such an outcry that she had to give it up. "You must have a proper wedding dress," cried the other ladies of the Court. "And a dress to go away in— and new linen, of course. Does Lord Westland mean to take you on a wedding trip?"

Since Anne knew nothing of her future bridegroom's plans, she was forced to be evasive on this point. She said merely that she believed Lord Westland intended to take her into the country and that she would thus have no need for many new dresses. But she could not escape the wedding and going-away dresses, or the new linen that the other ladies prescribed for her. And much as she disliked the necessity of further outlay for clothing, it struck her as being only fit and proper that she should make at least this much preparation for her marriage. She had no wish to shame James before others by appearing shabby or second-rate in any way.

It might have been thought difficult to put together even such a reduced trousseau as this in the time Anne was allowed, but in practice it was not difficult at all. There were many willing hands to help her choose, cut, and sew her bridal garments. Of course Anne knew perfectly well that most of them would never have lifted a finger on her behalf if her bridegroom had been of humbler estate, but she still could not help feeling more kindly toward them for their assistance. Even Mrs. Melkinthorpe redeemed herself by donating a length of fine lace and a pair of beautifully embroidered garters, while the Queen so far overcame her displeasure at Anne's marriage as to present her with a length of magnificent silver brocade.

On the morning of her wedding day, all was in readiness. Anne had nothing to do but bathe and array herself in her bridal garments.

Her dress was of white taffeta trimmed with silver embroidery and worn open over a petticoat made from the Queen's silver brocade. She wore a wreath of silver flowers on her head over a veiling of white lace, and her hair beneath was twisted up in the elaborate arrangement of coils and braids that the Queen's own dressing woman had assured her was the latest fashion. Anne was not sure it was a fashion that became her, but it was better by far than the tortured curls she had worn at the last Drawing Room, and so she let it pass. She was likewise not sure that her white and silver garments became her as well as some brighter color would have done, but when she surveyed herself in the glass she decided that on the whole she looked rather well. Her garments fit her neatly, were elegant in cut, and represented the latest in bridal fashion. Nothing more could be asked under the circumstances.

Several Court ladies had insisted on helping her dress, and now they hung about her room, peeking into her packed belongings, chattering excitedly, and making general nuisances of themselves. Anne was undisturbed by their chatter, however. She was beginning to be very nervous. Up till now, the magnitude of what she was doing had hardly registered upon her.

She had known, in an intellectual sense, that she was about to be married. She had known that marriage was a serious and irrevocable act that must affect the whole future pattern of her life. But she had been so eager to escape the past pattern of her life that she had hardly spent any time wondering what the new one would be like.

Now she did find herself wondering, and some of her wonderings were very uncomfortable. It did not help that several of the other ladies kept making sly allusions to bridal nights and eager bridegrooms. Of course they did not know that her marriage was a marriage of convenience, but it suddenly occurred to Anne that this circumstance would probably make no difference where her bridal night was concerned. James had spoken of needing a wife, and what that meant, in all likelihood, was simply that he needed children—more specifically, a male heir. In that case, he could hardly fail to insist on his conjugal rights.

The thought made Anne's blood run cold. She had been trying very hard not to think of the night she had gone to Timothy's room, but now all the shame and horror of that experience came flooding back to her. Could she really face such an experience again? And even if she could, there was still James to be considered. He would undoubtedly expect his bride to be a virgin. She, Anne, was not a virgin. Her upcoming marriage might have redeemed her character in the eyes of her peers, but Anne knew the ways of Court gossip too well to doubt that there would always be whispers about her even if Timothy held his tongue from now on. And there was no guarantee whatever that he would.

More and more, she found herself wishing she knew Timothy's intentions. If he was engaged himself, there seemed no reason for him to put a spoke in the wheel of her own engagement. Yet she had heard no news of him or of his courtship of Miss Duval for some weeks. In fact, now that she considered it, she had hardly seen Timothy during the last few weeks. He, alone of the Equerries, had abstained from wishing her well on the event of her coming marriage, an abstinence for which she had been grateful. But now she would have been glad to know his intentions toward her. She had hideous visions of him showing up during the ceremony and denouncing her as unchaste before the altar.

"But it wasn't I who did anything shameful," she whispered to herself. "I was only a fool."

"Fool indeed!" One of the other ladies who had caught these last words laughed. "I wish I were half the fool you are, Miss Barrington. You have done very nicely for yourself, catching an earl as a bridegroom. Tell me, how did you come to be acquainted with Lord Westland in the first place? I never heard the way of it."

Fortunately for Anne, a servant appeared just then to inform her that James was waiting for her in the chapel. She sprang to her feet. "Yes, I am ready," she said breathlessly. "Tell Lord Westland that I will be there as soon as I may."

The other ladies insisted on accompanying her to the chapel. Anne made no protest as they trailed along behind her. She did not care enough to object. All her thoughts were of her waiting bridegroom. Even her worries about Timothy had vanished in the excitement that now possessed her. Her nerves were keyed to an unbearable pitch, and she felt as if she might be about to be sick.

Yet when she saw her bridegroom, she wondered why she had been so nervous. James was still James, whatever else might be changed. In his fawn-colored Inexpressibles and handsome blue coat adorned with a wedding favor, he looked incredibly handsome but also very real and solid and reassuring. Anne let out her breath in a sigh. Several of the other ladies sighed also, and one remarked audibly, "Isn't he *divine!* And an earl besides. It isn't fair, upon my word."

James caught Anne's eye, and his lip quivered. Her own lips trembled into an answering smile. James bent down to address her in a whisper. "Anne," he said. "I was half afraid you wouldn't come. But I am so very glad you did. You look beautiful."

"And you look beautiful, too," said Anne. "Or should I say divine?"

"You shouldn't," he said, and they both laughed. The ladies gave them curious looks, and the waiting clergyman a shocked one. Anne and James immediately sobered and with suitable gravity came forward to take their places at the altar.

The ceremony was a very brief one and over in a matter of minutes. It seemed strange to Anne that a few words could bind her so irrevocably to another human being. Yet she could not help being impressed by the beauty and power of those words. When she was called on to pronounce her vows, her "I will" came out clear and strong. The ladies all sighed again; the clergyman smiled, and Mrs. Melkinthorpe let out a lugubrious sob from the back pew into which she had slipped just as the ceremony was beginning.

When it was over, and the wedding ring was on Anne's finger, and she was receiving the congratulations of the other ladies (including Mrs. Melkinthrope, who kept saying "Gott bless you, my dear," and enveloping her in a series of painful hugs), Anne looked at James. She found it impossible to believe that this man was now her husband. He looked as though he were having similar doubts. He was regarding her with a fixed expression, but when Anne looked at him he looked quickly away. "Well," he said, "I suppose that's that. Are your things packed and ready to go?"

Anne said that they were, and one of the ladies volunteered to have a servant fetch them to the carriage. "But I must go to my room to change my dress anyway," said Anne. "I can see to it myself."

"Change your dress?" said James. "Must you change your dress?"

"Yes, I can hardly travel in this," said Anne. "Can I?" she added doubtfully, seeing the disappointment in his face.

"You can as far as I am concerned," said James. He spoke with such sincerity that Anne instantly resolved to leave on her bridal garments no matter how unconventional such an action might be. It certainly simplified her leave-taking. She had only to wait with James while her bags and boxes were brought down and loaded into his chaise, then take her own place inside it.

"Is your woman going with us?" questioned James, as he joined her on the banquette. "I forgot to ask if you had a servant."

"Yes, I have one—or rather, had one. Since he is a manservant rather than a woman, I thought it better to give him his notice when I announced my engagement," said Anne. "He will have no trouble finding new work. In fact, I think one of the other ladies at the Palace has already taken him into her employ."

"That's good," said James. "We will find a suitable

woman to wait on you when we get to the country. But for now I am just as glad it is only us.''

Anne threw him a look. All at once she felt nervous again. To distract herself from her thoughts, she asked, ''Where in the country are we going? It's very foolish of me, but I do not even know where your house is located.''

''I own several houses now, but it is to my principal seat that I am taking you. It is called Honeywell House, and it is located in Devon.''

''Devon,'' said Anne. ''Honeywell House.'' The words had a delicious taste on her lips and an almost magical sound to her ears. ''I have heard Devon is a very beautiful county.''

''Yes, it is. So beautiful you can hardly believe it's real at times. And more magic to the square foot than any other county in England, as my old nurse used to say. She was a native of Devonshire, and she used to tell me stories about the ghosts and hobgoblins and haunted houses back home until I fancied the entire county solidly carpeted with spirits.''

Anne laughed. ''I hope Honeywell House is not haunted,'' she said. ''I should think it would be nerve-wracking to share one's home with a ghost!''

''You needn't fear as to that. There's no ghost at Honeywell House that I ever heard of. But we do have a very celebrated wishing well. For my part, I consider that confers a deal more distinction on the property than anything as commonplace as a ghost!''

''A wishing well?'' said Anne, looking at James with disbelief. ''Have you really one, James?''

''Yes, we do. At least—well, perhaps not precisely a

wishing well. As I recall, it's really more on the order of a divination well. One sees one's future in it, or something of the sort.''

"Truly?" said Anne, more disbelievingly still.

James laughed and shrugged his shoulders. "Truly, I know only what I have been told. I never even visited the property until a few weeks ago, so I'm not really acquainted with the well and its powers. But it sounds impressive, doesn't it?"

Anne agreed that it did, and asked him other questions concerning Honeywell House. She was sincerely interested to learn more of her new home, but she was also conscious of having an ulterior motive in keeping him talking. He was her husband now, and she was alone in a chaise with him. All her nerves were aquiver with the thought that he might at any moment decide to make love to her.

Of course he had already kissed her a couple of times, and she had found the experience not at all unpleasant. But when she tried to go further and imagine him taking those liberties to which a husband was entitled, her mind would go only so far in its speculations before drawing back upon itself with a frightened jerk. The idea of making love to him simultaneously fascinated and repelled her. She stared at his strong, clear-cut profile—still so much the profile of a stranger—and wondered if it would ever seem familiar and natural to think of him in those terms.

Fortunately, James showed no signs of becoming amorous. Indeed, as the journey wore on, he began to show signs of weariness instead. He fell silent, yawned repeatedly, and finally told Anne that he was afraid he was not proving very good company.

"The fact is, I'm tired to death. I hardly slept last night,

I was so dashed nervous—'' He broke off with a guilty look at Anne.

Anne laughed. "I was nervous, too! I lay awake for hours and hours before I could fall asleep."

A sparkle appeared in James's eyes. "And did you, like me, wonder if you were making a terrible mistake?" he said. "Did you imagine you must have been mad to commit yourself to such a reckless enterprise?"

"Yes, I certainly did. Did you?"

"Yes. About three A.M., I was sure of it. But now I feel much easier in my mind. What about you?"

"Yes," said Anne slowly. "Yes, I do feel better, James. But that's not to say I don't still feel nervous."

"Well, I feel nervous, too," said James. "And I suppose it's not to be wondered at. It's a momentous thing to get married in any fashion, and the way we managed it didn't leave much time to get acquainted. We shall have to take our time getting acquainted after the ceremony instead of before."

Anne looked at him, wondering if he was talking about getting acquainted in a physical sense. He seemed to understand her thoughts, for he smiled. "No, I'm not going to try to make love to you here in the chaise," he said. "For one thing, I strongly suspect I should come to grief in such an enterprise. I am very tired, as I mentioned before, and hardly equal to a task that demands a certain amount of stamina as well as skill. For another, I am just plain afraid."

"Afraid?" said Anne in amazement. "*You* are afraid, James? Afraid of what?"

"Afraid of doing something wrong and putting you off me for life," said James. He looked into Anne's eyes. "I know we're still almost strangers, but I do care about

you, Anne. I want you to be happy. I think you deserve
to be, after all you have suffered.''

Anne felt tears springing to her eyes, accompanied by
a strange suffusing warmth. She suddenly felt she would
not have minded very much even if he had demanded his
full conjugal rights on the spot. "I *am* happy, James,"
she said. "Happier than I have been in years."

"Good. I mean to keep you that way." James drew
her hand into his. "But I do trust that your happiness
does not depend on my being an entertaining companion
for the next hour or two. In spite of all my best efforts,
I am afraid I am about to fall asleep."

"I don't mind if you fall asleep," said Anne. "But I
cannot think you will be very comfortable, trying to sleep
sitting up in a moving chaise." In a hesitant voice, she
added, "Would you—would you like to lie down and
put your head in my lap?"

James leaned over and kissed her on the brow. "I can
think of nothing I would like better," he said. "You are
the best and most understanding of wives, Anne, and I
am thoroughly glad I married you."

"I'm glad I married you, too," said Anne. She moved
over on the banquette so that James could stretch at full
length, or as nearly full length as the width of the chaise
would allow. He laid his head in Anne's lap and shut his
eyes. At first Anne could only think how strange it was
to be sitting with him like this when they were so little
acquainted, but there was nothing unpleasant about it. On
the contrary, she found herself feeling quite tender and
protective toward him. He seemed so vulnerable in sleep,
not like a wealthy and powerful earl at all, but merely
like a man who was unutterably weary.

Anne was weary, too, but she did not feel like sleeping.
She sat as still as she could, determined not to wake

James. Her limbs grew steadily more cramped as the afternoon wore on, but she endured the small pains stoically and was rewarded by seeing him awake spontaneously as the chaise slowed to negotiate a sharp turn in the road.

"What time is it? Good God, I did sleep, didn't I? Do forgive me, Anne. You must have grown very weary, bearing with me all afternoon."

"I didn't mind," said Anne, stretching her legs surreptitiously. "In fact, I was glad to see you resting so comfortably. I hope you feel better now."

"Better, yes, but I'm getting hungry. Though it's still rather early for dinner." Again James consulted his watch. "I'll just grab a standing bite at the next change and wait to dine until we stop for the evening. Unless you would rather dine now?"

Anne said she would rather wait to dine, so James assuaged his appetite with a few sandwiches at the next posting house, and they pushed on through the late afternoon till evening. When it started to grow dark, they began to look about them for a suitable place to stop. They finally settled on a pleasant inn advertising clean rooms and good dinners.

"We have made excellent time," said James, as he helped Anne out of the chaise. "I believe if we made an early enough start tomorrow, we might reach Honeywell House by evening. But that would be a long day's driving, and I see no need to make an ordeal of the journey. We'll drive another six hours or so tomorrow, find someplace to spend the night, and reach Honeywell House early the day after tomorrow."

Anne had nothing to say against this plan, and they went into the inn together. The style of their servants and carriage, James's title, and Anne's bridal attire combined to make a powerful impression on the landlady. She was extremely civil in greeting them, and when she learned Anne and James had only been married that day her civility erupted in an embarrassing tendency to fuss. The commercial gentleman occupying the best parlor was summarily ejected so they might occupy it instead; extra candles were brought in ("Wax candles, mind you, Jenny—none of your tallow ones!") and a meal that would not have disgraced Lucullus was presently set before them.

"Wedding cake!" said James, looking in a stunned way at the centerpiece of this feast. "How in the name of heaven did you manage a wedding cake on such short notice?"

The landlady beamed. "Ah, 'twas made for my niece, my lord. She's to be married this day fortnight and so I had it all ready save the icing of it. No, 'tis no matter, my lord," she said firmly, seeing James was about to protest this misappropriation of cake. "I've plenty of time to make Sarah another afore then. I'm only glad I happened to have such a thing to hand, for 'twould be a great shame to be married and have not a bit of bridal cake with your supper. Just you ring if you need anything else, my lord and my lady. I'll see to your rooms while you're eating. Clean sheets—aye, clean sheets, to be sure! I've some put by just for such occasions that are as fine and soft as silk. You'll do as well as kings on those, I'm thinking."

She bustled out amidst these all too audible reflections, leaving Anne much embarrassed. She glanced at James and thought he looked embarrassed, too. The subject of their wedding night had been hanging in the air above them all day and was beginning to take on a certain urgency in Anne's mind. James had refrained from mak-

ing love to her in the chaise, true, but that did not mean
he would refrain in this different setting. Anne found her
insides suddenly twisted by anxiety. Abruptly she put
down the bite of roast pullet she had been about to eat.
But as though James had caught her thought, he spoke
out suddenly.

"Don't be nervous, Anne," he said. "Being married
is excitement enough for one day. I shall not disturb you
tonight, not even for the lure of fine linen sheets!" He
smiled at her. "Anyway, a public inn isn't my idea of a
proper venue for such a ticklish venture as one's wedding
night."

Anne felt her cheeks turn pink. "Thank you, James,"
she said faintly. She took up her fork again, but as she
began once more to eat, she was surprised to find that
mingled with the relief in her heart was something almost
like disappointment.

I daresay he is not very eager to make love to me, she
thought. *It's not as though I am a beauty, or even pretty.*
The thought rankled, but she did her best to push it from
her thoughts and behave normally throughout the rest of
the meal.

After dinner, she was taken to her room. The landlady
insisted on helping her undress, and she made such a
point of showing Anne the communicating door into
James's room that Anne was reduced to blushes once
more. But at last the landlady took herself off, and Anne
climbed into bed.

She was very tired, but her mind still insisted on keeping
her awake long after the lights were extinguished. She
looked at the communicating door to James's room and
wondered what he was doing behind it. Strange as it
would have been to have him with her, it seemed even
stranger to sleep like strangers in separate rooms when

they were husband and wife. The idea made her feel rather sad. Her last thought, as she drifted off to sleep, was to wonder uneasily how long it would be before James would think it proper to consummate their relationship.

CHAPTER VII

James, meanwhile, was finding it very difficult to sleep. The hours he had slept in the carriage that afternoon had erased the greater part of his fatigue, and a cup of strong tea after dinner had served to waken him still further. He felt alert, restless, and anything but sleepy. He paced back and forth across his room, wondering what he ought to do. The idea of the taproom occurred to him, and for a moment he considered going down and seeking what entertainment he could find there. But then he realized how odd that would look. This was his wedding night, and to spend it drinking beer with a company of farmers, tradesmen, and commercial travelers rather than making love to his bride would cause remark at the very least.

Indeed, such a singular occurrence as the Earl of Westland's eschewing his bride's company on his wedding night might even make it into the London papers. For

Anne's sake, if not for his own, he must avoid any hint of such scandal. Somehow he must pass the hours without letting anyone know his occupation was not that which everyone supposed it to be. A search of his room turned up a pack of dog-eared cards, along with an ancient copy of *Humphrey Clinker*. With these meager amusements, James settled down to get himself through the evening.

His valet had already undressed him, so when at last he did grow tired he had only to extinguish the lights and go to bed. As he lay alone in the great four-poster with its frowzy curtains and worn sheets, he reflected with grim amusement that it was hardly his notion of an ideal way to spend one's wedding night. The door to Anne's room seemed to beckon to him temptingly from across the shadowy room, but he thrust the temptation aside.

She looked frightened to death earlier, when the landlady spoke about the sheets, he thought. *I would rather wait until she is no longer frightened of me before I try to do more than kiss her.*

He reflected with pleasure that she did not seem to mind his kisses, at any rate. And there was also a great comfort in knowing she was married to him and that he now possessed the right to protect her. *I will make her happy if I can,* he swore to himself. *No matter if it's a year before I make love to her.*

Although James was quite sincere in these resolutions, he could not help hoping it would be rather less than a year before he might make love to Anne. She had looked so lovely that day in her bridal attire—feminine and delicate and altogether appealing. But she had looked heartbreakingly fragile, too. His heart misgave him when he thought of visiting his own gross male passions upon that slender body.

I will wait for her to be ready, he told himself. *I will wait as long as it takes.* And with this resolution for a pillow, he composed himself for sleep.

He awoke the next morning with a nagging sense of having forgotten something. Then suddenly he remembered what the something was and leaped out of bed. He dressed himself quickly without the aid of his valet, picked up one of his razors, then tapped on the door of Anne's room. "Anne?" he called.

"Yes?" said Anne's voice, sounding startled.

"May I come in?"

There was a silence, and then Anne's voice came again, sounding very shy. "Yes, if you like, James. Only—only you will find me not quite dressed, I am afraid."

James did his best to shut out the picture these words conjured in his mind. Nevertheless, he felt a noticeable quickening of his heart and a rising in his blood. "I'll wait," he said.

"No—no, it's all right. Do come in. The fact is, I believe I could use your help, James."

Full of equal parts suspense and excitement, James opened the door.

Anne was standing before the glass. She was wearing a dress of pale blue cambric, and he felt simultaneously pleased to see how pretty she looked and disappointed to see that she was dressed after all. Then he saw that the top of the gown gaped open in back. Anne was holding it closed with one hand, her face blushing but determined. "This is a new dress, and I find I can't fasten all the buttons by myself," she explained. "Would you mind very much, James . . . ?"

"I wouldn't mind at all," said James. In silence he buttoned up the remaining buttons. "Is that all?" he asked when he was done. "Is there anything else I can assist you with?"

"No, nothing," said Anne. Turning quickly toward the bed, she picked up the velvet spencer that was lying there.

"Let me," said James, and took it from her. Anne allowed him to help her into it, but James could see she was embarrassed. As soon as the spencer was on, he was careful to step away so she would not feel threatened.

Even so, it was a moment or two before she spoke. "You're awake early, James," she said.

"And so are you," said James. Anne merely nodded in reply. She turned away, under pretext of smoothing an unruly strand of hair. But James could see something was on her mind, and after a moment she spoke out with a hint of desperation in her voice. "James," she said. "I have been thinking. *The bedsheets.* Will not everyone be able to see that we—that last night we did not—?"

"Two minds with but a single thought," said James, smiling grimly. "That is why I am here." He showed Anne the razor in his hand.

Anne shrank back. "Oh!" she said. "Is that necessary, James?"

"I'm afraid so. But I shouldn't think I will have to do myself any serious injury to get the effect I want. Would you like to go to my room while I attend to it?"

Anne nodded vehemently and exited the room at a near run. Taking the razor, James lightly nicked one finger, then squeezed a few drops of blood onto the sheets. He had no real idea if this were a sufficient quantity of blood or not, but thought it was probably enough to allay suspicion. Then he thoroughly rumpled the bedclothes and disarranged the pillows. He could not help feeling a faint distaste that such a stratagem was necessary, but he reminded himself it was all for Anne's sake. And for Anne's sake, he would have done much more than this.

He and Anne breakfasted in the parlor downstairs, then took leave of their beaming landlady (who had all too evidently seen and approved the evidence of the sheets). They were both glad to be back in the chaise. As they settled down on the banquette, Anne noticed that James was holding a wooden box in his hands. She recalled that he had carried it carefully into the inn the night before and that she had seen the same box lying before the hearth in his room that morning.

"What is that?" she asked, pointing to the box.

"This?" said James, looking down at the box. He gave Anne a mischievous smile. "I'd tell you, but it might make you uncomfortable to ride in the carriage with it if you knew! It's by way of being a Bluebeard's secret, you see—one of those things wives sleep better for not knowing about their husbands."

Anne eyed him and the box doubtfully. "It can't be a very large secret," she objected. "That box is only a few inches deep, and it can't be more than a foot square."

"It is large enough of its kind, I assure you! Indeed, it is a most interesting creature. But I know ladies don't usually care for such things."

"A creature?" asked Anne, regarding the box with renewed interest. "It is a live animal you have there?"

"Yes—at least, it's living for now. But I am afraid despite my best efforts to keep it alive, it will soon give up the ghost. A pity, for I have never seen a more impressive specimen."

Anne's curiosity was thoroughly aroused. "Show me," she begged. "I won't be frightened, James. I am not the least bit afraid of animals—at least, not of any animal that would be small enough to fit in that box."

"Ah, but this is not an English animal! I got it from a fellow on the ship over from Brazil. It had stowed away amid some boxes of foodstuffs."

"Show me," begged Anne again. "I am sure I should like to see it, no matter what kind of animal it is."

"Very well, but don't say I didn't warn you." Laying the box on the banquette between them, James unfastened the small brass catch with which the box was closed. As he swung up the lid, Anne observed that it was perforated with a few holes, presumably to give the creature air. Then she saw what was inside, and a little shriek escaped her lips. James grinned.

"I told you so! But indeed the poor thing is at death's door and not, I believe, at all dangerous."

"Is that a *spider?*" said Anne, staring at the creature. She could scarcely believe her eyes. Huddled in one corner of the box was a spider so large that when its legs were extended it must have spanned a good eight inches. Even huddled as it was, it was an impressive sight. "Good heavens! Why, it is as large as my hand!" exclaimed Anne, holding out a gloved hand for comparison.

"A good deal larger, I should say," said James, looking also at her hand. "You have such small hands, Anne. This fellow is much closer to the size of my own hand." Looking down at the spider again, he added, "The man on the boat said this is what is called a bird-eating spider. Certainly it looks large enough to take on a finch or sparrow! But I haven't had any luck getting it to eat since returning to England. A pity, for I had fancied trying to keep it alive as a kind of curiosity. But I'm afraid death is inevitable for the poor thing. Once it dies, I'll send it to a fellow I know who works at the British Museum. He is an avid naturalist and very interested in all this sort of thing."

Anne looked again at the spider. There was indeed something eloquent of unhappiness in its immobility and huddled attitude. "Perhaps it is only cold," she suggested. "The English climate must be much cooler than the Brazilian one, even now that it is almost midsummer."

"Perhaps. I have tried to keep it warm, but of course that wasn't the easiest thing to do on board ship. And it hasn't been much easier since I've returned to England. I've had to lug it about from place to place with me, because I don't dare trust it to a servant. A couple of the housemaids at Honeywell House caught a glimpse of it one day when I was there, and you wouldn't believe the scene that ensued. One of them promptly gave notice, and the other went into such a fit of hysterics that she had to be dosed with brandy and laudanum."

"Well, we will be settled at Honeywell House for a while, I presume. Perhaps we can find a nice warm place for it there and nurse it back to health," said Anne. Frightening and grotesque as the great spider was, she felt a sort of pity for it. It was so obviously out of place in its environment. She, better than most people, could appreciate what that must mean.

James looked at her in surprise. "Well, I must say, I did not look for such a plucky attitude on your part, Anne! I've had grown men blench at the sight of this thing and beg me to destroy it out of hand. But you don't seem afraid of it at all."

"I *am* afraid of it, a little," said Anne honestly. "But I don't like to think of its dying. You don't think—you don't think it is dead already?"

"No, I think there's still a little life in it." Taking the pencil from his memorandum book, James gingerly prodded the spider's body. For a long time nothing happened, then at last one of its eight legs moved very slightly.

"It *is* alive," said Anne.

"Yes, barely. But God knows for how long. It seems more sluggish every time I touch it."

"I am sure that is only because it is cold," said Anne. "It's rather chilly this morning, for all it is mid-June. We must try to keep it as warm and comfortable as possible."

"Then you must hold it in your lap," returned James, laughing. "I am sure that is as warm and comfortable a place as anyone could desire!"

"I will, then," said Anne, and held out her hands for the box. James looked at her in amazement.

"I believe you mean it! You *are* plucky, aren't you? Most women would have fainted away at the first sight of this thing. But you don't seem frightened at all."

"I would be frightened to touch it by itself, but I'm not frightened of holding it in its box," said Anne. "Only latch the box first, if you will, James. Then I will not be frightened at all."

James relatched the box and handed it to Anne, who placed it carefully in her lap. All that day she held it there and even insisted on carrying it into the inns where they stopped for meals. "We will need a fire in the parlor," she told each landlord or landlady as soon as they had entered the hostelry. There were protests and looks of surprise at such a request on a warm June day, but in each case Anne carried her point, and the wooden box was tenderly deposited in front of the hearth and checked with anxious care every few minutes to make sure it was not too warm.

James was both amazed and amused to see Anne take up the spider's cause in this way. Yet it struck him that having this new interest had done her good. She had hardly spoken a word at any of the inns they had stopped at yesterday, except to timidly assent to whatever suggestions he or the innkeepers had made. But today here she was ordering about innkeepers, chambermaids, and his own servants with calm authority. So he refrained from teasing her about her new obsession and devoted himself instead to seeing that the human needs of their party were as well attended to as the spider's.

They spent that night at a busy posting house on the main highway. Having eaten her own share of the dinner of mutton, suet dumplings, and gooseberry pudding that the landlord set before them, Anne went upstairs to her room to check on the spider, which she had left comfortably disposed near a low fire in her bedchamber. She returned downstairs in a state of great excitement.

"James!" she said. "The spider has moved! It isn't nearly so huddled up as it was before."

She seemed anxious that James should witness this miracle firsthand, so he got up and followed her upstairs with indulgent amusement. Anne knelt and proudly opened the lid of the box to show him the spider sitting in a somewhat less huddled posture in the corner of the box.

"Yes, it has certainly moved," agreed James. "But whether that is a good thing or not, I do not know. I can't say it looks much better overall."

"It does," said Anne firmly. "Much better." Closing the box, she added, "It will be better still when we can find it a proper place to live. Staying in this closed-up box cannot be very pleasant or healthy for it. You say we will reach Honeywell House tomorrow?"

"Yes, assuming all goes well," said James. "We should be there by early afternoon."

He was conscious all at once of a certain tension in the atmosphere. While he and Anne had been talking of the spider, he had hardly been aware of his surroundings, but he was aware of them now. He was in Anne's bed-chamber, surrounded by the feminine clutter of her brushes on the washstand, her hat on the table, and her nightdress laid out ready for bed. He glanced at it, then hastily away. "Well," he said uncomfortably, "I suppose I ought to wish you good night."

"Oh!" said Anne, rather blankly. "Yes, it is growing late."

It struck James there was dissatisfaction in her voice. He glanced at her, but she looked quickly away. "Good night," he said. Feeling a fool, he bent to kiss her on the cheek.

As he did so, Anne turned her head sharply. The kiss aimed for her cheek landed on her lips instead. James drew back in a hurry, and for a moment he and Anne looked at each other. The tension in the atmosphere was more noticeable than ever.

"Well," said James.

"Well?" said Anne.

There was another brief silence. "Well, good night," said James, and turned away. But as he left the room, he had the sensation that he had failed to pass some subtle test.

After he had gone, Anne rang for hot water. The maid who brought it helped her undress, and soon Anne was ready for bed. As she settled herself between the sheets, she was conscious of a sense of disappointment.

It was ridiculous, of course, that she should be disappointed because James did not wish to make love to her. She told herself that after her experience with Timothy, she should have been glad to escape any repetition of the pain and suffering she had experienced. Yet somehow, her disappointment remained.

But that is understandable enough, she rationalized to

herself. *The only reason he married me was to get an heir, so it's inevitable that we shall have to make love sometime. I would rather get it over with sooner rather than later. As things stand now, it's like a sword of Damocles hanging over my head, and I can think of nothing else.*

Whatever the truth of the matter, it was certain that Anne thought of little else until she finally dropped off to sleep.

CHAPTER VIII

Anne awoke the next morning with a feverish sense of eagerness. *Today I will see my new home for the first time,* she told herself as she washed and dressed. *Honeywell House! I wonder what it will be like. I wonder if I will be happy there. Whatever it is like, I can hardly help being happier there than I was at Court.*

Her eagerness was such that she was able to put aside the hurt she had felt at James's rejection the night before and greet him with equanimity when she went down to breakfast. As soon as they had eaten, they took to the carriage again to begin the final stage of their journey.

As before, Anne held the box with the spider on her lap. She said little during the drive, and James said little, too. In fact, it seemed to Anne that some of the tension she had felt in the atmosphere the night before had returned. But before it could become too pronounced, the carriage began to slow, and Anne saw they were approaching a handsome set of iron gates set in a low stone wall. James indicated both gates and wall with a sweeping gesture.

"Here we are," he said. "Prepare yourself for your first sight of Honeywell House, ancient home of the West-lands."

Clutching the box on her lap, Anne stared out the window. The carriage had turned down a broad drive lined with a handsome avenue of limes. At the end stood a large house of gray stone with curving wings thrown out to each side. "Oh!" she said with pleasure. "It's beautiful, James."

"Yes, and you are seeing it at its best. I have no doubt it would still be an attractive place in midwinter, but midsummer in Devon is something quite out of the common way. For it *is* midsummer, or nearly so. This very night is Midsummer's Eve."

"Midsummer's Eve," repeated Anne. There was something intoxicating in those words, she thought. They held such promise of mystery and magic; one felt anything might happen.

In the meantime, events proceeded in a perfectly ordinary and straightforward course. The carriage stopped at the end of the drive in front of the house, and one of the footmen opened the carriage door and let down the steps for Anne and James. Another footman hurried to ply the knocker on the front door of the house while James and Anne followed after him, leaving James's valet to superintend the unloading of the luggage. But there was one piece of luggage that Anne carried herself: the wooden box containing the spider. So intent was she on settling it as soon as possible in a suitable place that even when she became aware that there were several dozen servants assembled to greet her and James inside the front hall of the house, she did not think to be nervous.

"Welcome, my lord, my lady," said the foremost servant, an elderly man in a sober frock coat who appeared to be the butler. "On behalf of all the staff at Honeywell House, we bid you welcome and wish you very happy on the event of your marriage."

The other servants murmured words of greeting and congratulation, then bowed or bobbed curtsies toward Anne and James. "Er—thank you," said James, glancing sideways at Anne. "Thank you for your kindness. I'm sure Lady Westland and I appreciate your gesture very much."

Again he glanced at Anne. Clutching the box, she bestowed a shy smile on the assembled servants and then, feeling some further gesture was necessary, she dropped them a curtsy. By habit it was the formal sweeping curtsy she had used at Court, and its effect on the servants was instantaneous. There was admiration or awe on every face, and one housemaid whispered audibly, "Coo! You can tell she was one of the Queen's Ladies, can't you? Graceful as a feather, and she didn't make no more of the business than if she was tying her shoe."

With this formality discharged, the servants all dispersed, save for an elderly woman in black who advanced toward them, stating that she was the housekeeper and that she expected Anne would like to see her rooms. Anne allowed herself to be led upstairs to her rooms and shown their different amenities, but when the housekeeper had finished with her tour Anne begged her to know if the house contained a conservatory.

"To be sure it does, my lady," said the housekeeper, looking surprised. "I can take you there now, if you like."

"I *would* like, very much," said Anne. Pausing only

to remove her hat and gloves, she picked up the wooden
box and accompanied the housekeeper back downstairs.

As soon as Anne entered the conservatory, she drew a
deep, pleasurable breath. The air within the conservatory
was warm and humid and scented with the blossoms of
hundreds of flowers. "Wonderful!" she said with enthusiasm. "This should do wonderfully. Thank you so much,
Mrs. Rhodes."

"You're very welcome, I'm sure," said the housekeeper. She looked and sounded puzzled, but when Anne
smiled at her she returned the smile before setting back
off across the hall with her keys jingling at her waist.

As soon as she had gone, Anne set out to systematically
explore the conservatory. She had not gone far before
she came upon an elderly man deadheading roses. He
gaped with astonishment at the sight of her, but quickly
recovered himself and tugged his forelock respectfully.
"Your ladyship!" he said. "Can I 'elp you with anything,
m'lady?"

His voice held no accent of Devon but was rather the
purest distillation of London cockney. "You are a Lon-
doner!" said Anne, momentarily distracted from her pre-
occupation.

"Aye, that I am—or used to be, m'lady. But I've
worked at 'oneywell 'ouse for a good thirty years now."

"Then you should be able to help me," said Anne. "I
need a—I don't know exactly what I need. Something
like a glass box? A small cucumber frame, perhaps?"

"Frames there be, in plenty," said the man. "But
they're not what you'd call small. What d'you want it
for, m'lady, if I may make so bold?"

"For this," said Anne, and opened the box.

The man drew in his breath sharply. "Gawdstrewth!"

he said. He came a step nearer, staring down into the box. "That's never a spider?"

"Yes, it *is* a spider. It is a Brazilian spider that Lord Westland brought back with him from South America."

"Gawdstrewth," said the man again, letting out his breath. "Must be a charming place, Brazil, I don't think! And to think one of the 'ousemaids was going about a few weeks ago with a story of his lordship 'aving a spider big as a fist in his room, and me not believing a word of it. Called 'er a little liar, I did, may the good Lord forgive me."

"It is rather difficult to believe in, even when you have seen it for yourself," said Anne, looking down at the spider. "But you can see it's a real spider. And now I am looking for a proper place to put it. I thought the conservatory would be good, as it is so warm and humid here."

"The lads won't 'alf like having a thing like that running loose in here," said the man with great conviction. "Nor will I, to speak truth, m'lady. It'd be enough to drive me into giving up gardening altogether and hiring on as a stable boy or some such thing!"

Anne laughed. "I don't mean to turn the spider loose in the conservatory," she said. "Of course it must be confined. Only I cannot think this box is the best home for it. If there was something like a small cucumber frame—"

"Ah, I see what you're getting at now, m'lady. Let me think. Oh, aye, what you need's a conservatory, I expect." Seeing Anne's confusion, he sketched a boxlike shape in the air. "Not a great conservatory like what we're standing in, but a little one like what ladies use to keep pot-plants in the house. That'd be just the thing."

He bustled off and returned in a few minutes with what looked like a miniature glass house. It was set on its own stand about waist-high, and the peaked roof was hinged so plants might be placed inside. "There you are, m'lady. What do you think? Will it do for your beast by way of h'accomodations?"

"It's perfect!" said Anne. She inspected the leaded panes of the glasshouse, noting that the lid did not fit tightly enough to exclude air, yet fastened with a positive latch. "This should serve wonderfully. Where can I put it that it will be out of the way?"

The man regarded the miniature glasshouse with a meditative eye. "I don't just know, m'lady. Raising flowers is my job, not spiders. But I wouldn't suppose strong light'd be the ticket, for it'd get mortal hot in that glass box once the sun got to shining through. Over by the warm wall in that shady corner'd be my best bet. That way you've got your steady heat and yet you're out of the sun. Besides," he added with a sardonic smile, "that way the lads won't have to go near it if they don't like to. They're a precious lot of delicate flowers, are my lads, just like them orchids over there. I wouldn't want to h'offend their sensibilities."

Anne laughed and agreed that the corner seemed the best place. The man carried the glasshouse over for her and set it carefully in place. "Looks kind of bare and empty to be growing anything in it, even a spider," he said, standing back to regard it.

"It does," agreed Anne. "Perhaps we could put some earth in the bottom of it? Of course if the spider makes a web, it won't much matter—but I don't know if spiders of this sort make webs."

The man gave a slight, involuntary shudder. "That'd be something to see, that would," he said. "But I wouldn't think so, myself. Doesn't have the build for it, if you get my meaning." Again he regarded the glasshouse. " 'Ere, how about I put in soil one side and moss on t'other? That way it can choose its own ground, so to speak, and we've a better chance of 'itting on something that takes its fancy.''

Anne agreed that this seemed reasonable, and the man went to fetch soil and moss. He troweled these commodities carefully into the glasshouse, then stood back to regard the effect. "Still looks a bit bare," he said. "How about I put in a plant or two to dress it up?''

"Will plants grow in such a low light?" asked Anne doubtfully

"Not all will, but there's some as don't mind shade. I've got just the thing." The man returned with a couple of small plants, which he set quickly and professionally into one corner of the glasshouse. "Will that do you?''

"That should do wonderfully," said Anne. "Now I wonder . . . do you suppose I should put a water dish in its cage, as one would do for a pet bird? Do spiders drink?''

She looked at the man, who shrugged his shoulders. "You're asking the wrong fellow, m'lady," he said. "Spiders ain't my business, except as I might run across one every now and then in the gardening line. But I shouldn't think it could do any 'arm to put in a dish of water. What I mean to say is, if it's got water it can drink if it wants to, and if it don't want to drink, then no 'arm done.''

Having fetched a shallow clay saucer for Anne, he filled it with clear water and watched as she set it into the conservatory. "Now to move the spider in," said Anne. She looked down dubiously at the box in her hand. The spider was sitting there as immobile as before, but she still felt a distinct disinclination to meddle with it.

"If it was me," said the man, who seemed to divine

Anne's thoughts, "I'd just put it in there box and all, m'lady, and let it come out in its own time."

"That is an *excellent* plan," said Anne, and did just that. Having hinged the lid shut on the glasshouse, she and the man stood watching the spider for a while. It did nothing but remain huddled in a corner of the box, however, and after a while the man gave a sigh.

"Seems kind of dull for being such a fierce-looking h'animal," he observed. "Was there anything else I could do for you, m'lady?"

"No, nothing," said Anne. She smiled at him shyly. "I am sorry to have taken you away from your other work, but I do appreciate your assisting me in this way. I couldn't have managed it without you."

The man made an embarrassed noise. "Pshaw, 'tis nothing. I was glad to be of 'elp, m'lady. After all, it isn't every day you get to see a spider the size of a bloomin' rat! Let me know if there's aught else I can do. Gardiner's the name—Joe Gardiner." He grinned at her. "Gardiner by name and gardener by nature, as you might say."

Anne laughed. "Thank you, Mr. Gardiner," she said, and they parted on the best of terms.

Just outside the conservatory door, Anne encountered Mrs. Rhodes, the housekeeper, once more. Mrs. Rhodes informed her that dinner would be served in a couple of hours. "The housemaids are unpacking your clothes, my lady," she said. "Being that you don't have a maid of your own, I took the liberty of asking Susan to wait on you. Her tongue runs faster than her hands, there's no denying, but she's a willing worker and should serve until your ladyship has time to make other arrangements."

Anne thanked the housekeeper and went upstairs to her room. She found the housemaids just finishing with the unpacking of her clothes. Susan, a stout country girl with cheeks like apples, curtsied and shyly introduced herself. "I'm sure I hope I'll prove to your satisfaction, m'lady," she said. "My, but you've got a lovely lot of clothes!"

Anne shuddered slightly. "Yes," she said without enthusiasm. "But many of them are Court dresses, you know. I don't suppose I'll have much use for them anymore."

Susan clasped her hands and gave a little shudder of ecstasy. "It must be so exciting to live at Court and wear lovely dresses and see the Queen and Princesses every day! Beg pardon, m'lady, but none of us here at Honeywell House can see how you could bear to leave it all—no, even to marry his lordship!"

Anne felt herself inadequate to any sort of explanation and so merely smiled. "I'm sure you and I will get along very well, Susan," she said. "Is there time for me to have a bath before dinner? I feel horridly dusty after traveling these last few days."

"It'll be a pinch, but we'll manage it," said Susan confidently. "Just you wait here, my lady, and I'll see to it all."

Susan was as good as her word. By the time the bell rang for dinner, Anne was freshly scrubbed from head to toe and dressed in a gown of watered silk that just matched her eyes, according to the enthusiastic Susan. "I never saw eyes the color of yours, m'lady," she said. "Beautiful they are—not exactly blue, and not exactly green, but something in between."

"Thank you, Susan," said Anne, looking in the glass. It struck her that she *was* looking rather well that evening. The dress of aquamarine silk brought out the color of her eyes, just as Susan said, and was tolerably flattering to her hair, too, making its silver blond sheen more a positive hue than a colorless nullity. And though the dress could not disguise the childlike slenderness of her figure, it was cut well enough so that this circumstance seemed less a flaw than usual.

"You look beautiful, m'lady," said Susan fervently. "How I wish I was as slim as you, then."

"Do you?" said Anne in astonishment. "I would much rather look like you, Susan." She looked enviously at Susan's generously curved figure.

Susan gave an amazed laugh. "Me?" she exclaimed. "Why, your ladyship must be joking. I've been plump all my life, and a terrible cross it's been to me, I do assure you." She shook her head sadly. "If I looked like you, m'lady, I'd be certain of seeing a husband in the well tomorrow morning instead of just my own face. You look so fine and graceful and—and elegant-like. Genteel, I mean to say. Which of course you are, m'lady, and no disrespect intended."

Anne assured her that none was taken. "But what do you mean, you'd be sure of seeing a husband in the well tomorrow if you looked like me?" she asked "You aren't talking about the fortune-telling well Lord Westland was telling me about, by any chance? The one that's supposed to predict the future?"

"So I am, then," said Susan with a vigorous nod. " 'Tis the only magic well hereabouts that I know of, and a powerful strong one by all accounts. Only I've never seen anything in the water myself in all the years I've been trying the charm. 'Witching the well,' we girls call it when we go there on Midsummer Day."

"And how does one go about 'witching the well'?"

"Why, you just go there on Midsummer Day before the sun's up and wash your face in the water. Once you've done that, you're supposed to be able to see your future.

But I've never seen anything at all in the water, let alone a husband, which is all the future that concerns *me,*" finished Susan disconsolately.

Anne smiled at her aggrieved tone. "Perhaps you will be more fortunate this year," she said. "Gracious, it's Midsummer Day tomorrow, isn't it? Lord Westland and I were talking about it on the way down, but it had almost slipped my mind."

Susan nodded vigorously. "Aye, and tonight's Midsummer's Eve, my lady," she said. "Be careful not to let moonlight fall on you tonight, or you'll be bewitched for sure."

Anne laughed and promised to take appropriate precautions against bewitchment. "But will you not be in danger yourself, if you go to the well tomorrow morning?" she asked. "If you must go before the sun's up, I don't see how you're to avoid being exposed to moonlight."

"Ah, it's different when you're going to the well," said Susan firmly. "The one charm's proof against the other, as you might say."

Anne found this reasoning amusing and was still smiling to herself as she went downstairs to the drawing room. James was waiting for her there. He rose as she came in and stood looking at her with bemusement.

"Anne," he said. "You look *happy.*"

He spoke as though he could hardly believe his eyes. Anne laughed. "Well, do you know, I think I *am* happy, James," she said. "This is a wonderful house—a *magical* house."

She was smiling as she looked up at him. James took her hand in his and kissed it. "I'm so glad," he said. "But speaking of magic—Anne, you must be a witch. How did you know to wear that particular dress tonight?"

"This dress?" said Anne, looking down at it. "Why, what is wrong with it, James?"

"Nothing is wrong with it. On the contrary, it is so right as to be positively eerie." James handed her a small leather box. "It's a gift I got for you earlier—a wedding gift. What with one thing and another I neglected to give it to you before. So I thought tonight would be an appropriate time. Our first night in our new home."

Anne took the box, slanting him a mischievous look. "It's not another spider, is it?" she asked.

James laughed. "No, it's not a spider! Open the box, Anne. I think you will admit it is an amazing coincidence."

Anne opened the box and gave a little cry. "How perfectly lovely."

Inside the box lay a necklace of aquamarines surrounded by diamonds. Matching earrings lay beside it. The stones were good-sized ones, but such was the delicacy of their setting that the overall effect was light and elegant instead of ponderous.

"How beautiful," repeated Anne, gazing down at the jewels. "What a wonderful gift."

James looked both pleased and embarrassed. "Do you really like them? I'm so glad, Anne. I saw them in a jeweler's window a week or two back, and they reminded me of you. Of your eyes, I mean."

"A week or two back?" said Anne in wonderment. "But it has been less than a week since I agreed to marry you."

"Yes, I know. But I thought of you when I saw them, and when you said you'd marry me, I went back and bought them for you."

Anne gave him an astonished look. James looked away quickly, his color rather heightened. "Well, shall I help

you put on your new gift?'' he asked. ''Or would you
feel uncomfortable wearing it tonight, when we are merely
having a family dinner?''

''I would not feel uncomfortable at all,'' said Anne.
''I should love to wear your gift, James. I have never
owned any real jewelry before.''

James smiled more easily as he took the box from her
hand. ''You own quite a bit of it now. Besides these
stones, there are some family heirlooms tucked away
somewhere that now belong to you. I'll have to look them
out for you.''

''Gracious,'' said Anne faintly. Seeing that James had
taken the necklace from the box, she turned around so
he might clasp it around her neck. It struck her that he
was rather a long time doing this. When his hands brushed
the nape of her neck, she shivered, and then was immediately embarrassed.

Fool, she told herself. *Don't be so foolish.* But as though
that touch had been a signal, she was all at once tremen-
dously aware of him standing close behind her, his hands
at her throat and his breath warm on the back of her head.

''There,'' he said at last. ''There's the necklace on.''

Anne turned around to face him. It struck her he was
looking a little agitated. She looked at him a long moment
and he looked back at her. ''Does it look well?'' she
asked at last.

''What?'' he said blankly. ''Oh, the necklace? Yes,
very well indeed.''

Something in the way he was looking moved Anne to
a sudden daring. Taking the earrings from the box, she
held them out to him. ''Will you put on the earrings for
me, too?'' she asked.

James looked at her a moment, then took the earrings
from her hand. He had to stoop slightly to reach her ears.

Anne stood very still, looking up at him as he fitted the earrings in her ears. His hands were unsteady, and she could sense his quickened breathing. Nor was he the only one so affected. When he finally straightened and stepped back, she could feel herself trembling like a leaf in the wind.

"Well," she said, then paused.

"Well?" said James, giving her look for look.

At that moment, the dining room door opened, and the butler appeared. "The dinner is served, my lord, my lady," he said, bowing.

"Thank you, Haywood," said James. But Anne could have sworn she heard him sigh as he gave her his arm and led her toward the dining room.

CHAPTER IX

The dinner that Anne and James sat down to that night was a very formal and lavish one, considering it was eaten by only two people. Anne supposed its lavishness was to celebrate her and James's arrival at Honeywell House, but soon learned that the circumstance of its being Midsummer's Eve had something to do with it, too.

"And here is the giblet pie, my lord," said the butler, as he set a steaming dish before James. "Shall I serve it for you, or would you and Lady Westland prefer to serve it yourselves?"

James looked surprised, but said politely, "We will serve it ourselves, thank you, Haywood. Giblet pie, you say?"

The butler bowed gravely. "On account of its being Midsummer Eve, my lord."

James looked puzzled; then, catching Anne's eye, smiled. "Oh, it's a custom, is it?" he said. "I should have guessed. There seem to be a great many customs connected with Midsummer's Eve here at Honeywell House.''

"As you say, my lord," said the butler gravely. "Along with the pie, there is a special beverage which Mrs. Rhodes brews herself according to an old family receipt. A sort of a mead it is, I believe, and traditionally drunk hereabouts on Midsummer's Eve. Would you care to try it?"

"Certainly," said James with cheerful resignation. "By all means let us taste Mrs. Rhodes's mead."

The butler helped James to the golden beverage, then turned to Anne. "I will try a little," she said politely. "It is a mead, you say? And home-brewed? How very interesting."

"And how very powerful," said James, choking slightly on a mouthful of mead. "I advise you to go carefully, Anne. Whatever else may be said about it, Mrs. Rhodes's family receipt packs a considerable wallop."

Thus advised, Anne was careful to do no more than sip at the glass of mead the butler poured for her. Since he refilled the glass at every sip, however, she had no way of knowing exactly how much she had drunk of it, and by the time the dessert course was finished she found that the room was having an alarming tendency to go in circles. James seemed to be experiencing much the same symptoms, for when dessert had been removed from the table he stood up abruptly.

"Anne, forgive me, but I must either get some fresh air or remain sitting here the rest of the night," he said. "Mrs. Rhodes's mead offers me no third choice."

Anne tried not to giggle and failed. "Thank heaven," she said. "I thought I was the only one!"

James grinned at her. "What, are you a victim of its powers, too? Never mind, we've plenty of time to sober up before we go to—'' He stopped as though struck, then went on with a pathetic attempt at dignity. ''Before we retire for the night, I mean.''

''Of course,'' said Anne, also striving for dignity. ''I never thought you meant anything else.'' A sudden thought occurred to her, and she looked up at James. ''Could we go to the conservatory before going outside, James? I have put the spider there, and I would like to see how it is faring.''

''Certainly,'' said James, and offered her his arm with an extravagantly sweeping gesture. Anne took it, and together they proceeded rather unsteadily across the hall to the conservatory.

The warm, moist air of the conservatory struck them as James swung open the doors. *''This* won't help my head,'' he remarked acutely as he led Anne inside. ''What I need is good, bracing, cold English air with no nonsense about it. Not 'the orange flower perfuming the bower.' ''

''The spider is over here,'' said Anne, tugging him toward the corner near the warm wall. ''But it's so dark that I can't see a thing. Is there a lamp somewhere?''

After a rather noisy search in which several objects unaccountably crashed to the ground, James unearthed a lantern. Lighting it, he carried it over to the spider's corner. Anne drew in her breath in a gasp.

''Look, James!'' she said. ''It's not in the wooden box any longer! It must have decided to explore its new home.'' Her eyes searched the glasshouse eagerly. ''But where is it—? Oh, there it is. James! What is it *doing?*''

''Speaking for myself,'' said James, looking critically at the spider, ''I should say it's doing the same thing we have been doing this evening—which is to say, drinking.''

''Drinking!'' said Anne, staring at the spider. It stood poised on its eight legs with its front end immersed in the saucer of water. "Do you think so? You don't think—you don't think it's *drowning,* do you, James?"

"Evidently not," said James, as the spider heaved its front end out of the water and backed away from the dish. It then set out on a leisurely exploration of the glasshouse. The corner with the plants seemed to find favor with it, for it settled down near them and began to groom itself, much after the fashion of a cat.

"Well!" said Anne in amazement.

"Remarkable," pronounced James. "Most remarkable. Do you know, Anne, I shouldn't be surprised if your protégé here pulls through after all. You seem to have done it proud in the matter of lodgings."

Anne explained how Joe Gardiner had found the glasshouse and assisted her in setting it up. "I am glad we decided to give it a dish of water. Perhaps what has ailed it all along is that it was merely thirsty."

"Possibly," agreed James. "But if water could cure it, only think what would have happened if you had given it some of Mrs. Rhodes's mead instead of water! That stuff is strong enough to raise the dead."

Anne laughed. "Yes, too strong for humans—and certainly too strong for spiders. I wonder if this spider will eat now that it has drunk? I must confess, I shudder a little at the thought. You say it eats *birds?*"

"That's the story, anyway. But I shouldn't think you'd have to feed it birds, Anne. When this one was captured on board ship it was actually in the act of eating a beetle, and I imagine it would eat other kinds of insects, too."

"Is that so? Well, insects of some sort ought not to be hard to find. I'll look for some tomorrow."

James smiled and shook his head. "You've taken a real fancy to this thing, haven't you? I must say I am amazed by your interest. I never would have supposed such an unlikely looking creature would win your heart.''

"It hasn't won my heart," said Anne with dignity. "I just feel sorry for it, that's all. It is far away from its natural environment, and there's nobody but me who cares about it."

"Well, I care sufficiently to help you look for insects tomorrow, but for tonight I would rather we went outside in quest of fresh air. This room is starting to go round and round, just as the dining room was doing."

Anne agreed fresh air would be prudent at that point, and they left the conservatory together. "Where would you like to go?" asked James. "Shall we walk a turn or two upon the terrace?"

"That sounds delightful," said Anne. "I would love to walk upon the terrace." To the terrace they went accordingly and walked back and forth along its length, looking out at the shadowy gardens and woods that lay beyond.

"How beautiful it is out here," said Anne. "And how lovely the air feels!" She drew in a deep breath. "It's positively balmy."

"Yes, not as bracing as two people in our condition could desire, but certainly pleasanter."

"I feel . . ." Anne hesitated, glancing up at James. "I feel as though I would like to go down into the garden for a while. Would you mind, James?"

"I would not mind at all. But will you be warm enough in just that thin dress and shawl? We could always ring one of the servants to bring your cloak."

"No, I'm sure I will not need it. If anything takes harm, it is likely to be my shoes." Anne glanced down at her satin slippers. "But I don't believe the grass is wet enough to hurt them."

"If it is, I'll buy you new ones," said James with another sweeping gesture. "What is a pair of shoes against the glory of a Midsummer night?"

"Nothing, to be sure," said Anne, laughing. Together they went down the terrace steps and into the garden.

It was delightful in the garden, with the scent of flowers perfuming the balmy air. Anne and James walked along a flagstone path that led past a pond studded with water lilies. They passed another garden devoted to flowers for cutting, then skirted a hedge of evergreen oak to admire a rose garden laid out in formal plots like an old-fashioned parterre.

"There is nothing like a rose garden at night," said Anne, drawing in a deep breath of rose-scented air. "Nothing!"

"No, it's as intoxicating as Mrs. Rhodes's mead," agreed James. "And look! The moon is just rising. Now we have all the essential elements for—for—"

"For what?" said Anne, looking at him inquiringly.

"Well, I was going to say, for romance," said James. He regarded Anne out of the corner of his eye. She was embarrassed, but at that moment a thought occurred to her that distracted her from her embarrassment.

"Oh, James! And Susan particularly warned me against being out in the moonlight tonight. She said it was likely to cause madness."

James shook his head gravely. "Too late now! We have both been exposed beyond redemption. Ah, well, never mind. So as long as we're doomed to be mad, we may as well be mad together." He took Anne's hand in his and bowed over it. "What mad thing shall we do next, oh wife of mine?"

Anne laughed. She felt suddenly exhilarated. "Do you

know, James, I think I should like to see this well everyone has been telling me about. Is it a long way from here?''

"A good way, but not a long way. What a splendid idea, Anne. By all means let us have a look at the well by moonlight. Who knows what visions we shall see on such a night as this?''

The way to the well led along a winding path that skirted a grove of trees and crossed a small stream by way of a quaint footbridge. Beyond the bridge, the path descended a set of steps that led into a sunken garden arranged in the Italian style. Statues and urns gleamed white in the moonlight, and water played in the fountain that stood at the garden's center. "Beautiful," said Anne, looking up at the spray of water. "Beautiful, beautiful.''

"Everything is beautiful tonight," agreed James.

He looked long and earnestly into Anne's face. She looked back at him a moment, then gave him her arm again. He took it in rather closer a grasp than before.

There was some excuse for this, for beyond the Italian garden was a stretch of wilderness. It was heavily wooded and dense with underbrush, and the path plunged in and around groves of trees, making walking slightly difficult. At last they came to a clearing. On one side of the clearing, toward the east, Anne could see ruined walls rising black against the moonlit sky. "What is this?" she asked in surprise. "A building of some kind?''

"Yes, this is the site of the old Honeywell House," said James. "If I were the Lord Westland of a few hundred years ago, this is the home to which I would have brought you.''

"What an odd thought that is," said Anne. "That we are only one out of a great many Lord and Lady Westlands. It gives me a queer feeling, James. We are part of a tradition that has been going on for hundreds of years.''

"More than a thousand," said James. "The Westlands are one of the oldest families in England, or so we like to boast. Our line stretches back well beyond the Norman Conquest. But we are rather an obscure family for all that. No Westland has ever achieved prominence as a statesman or soldier or man of learning. Keeping custody of the well seems to be our sole claim to fame."

"Yes, the well," said Anne, and was recalled to a sense of purpose. "Where is it, James? Is it near the ruins of the old house?"

"No, it is over there," said James, pointing to the west. "See that little round building that looks like a summerhouse? That is the well pavilion. It was built only a few hundred years ago, around the time of the present Honeywell House. The well itself is, of course, much older—indeed, I have heard it said it goes back to pre-Christian times. I understand there was a fuss a few years ago about a clergyman who wished to have it closed up, because he thought it pernicious that people should still use it for what he considered heathen rites. But the heathen rites won out, as they so often do, and I believe he was sent away with a flea in his ear. Our present clergyman, Mr. Hamthorpe, wisely turns a blind eye to the goings-on at the well this time of year."

"Indeed, it sounds a harmless enough business," said Anne. "If I were not a married woman, I should be tempted to try it myself." She threw James a shy smile.

"But married you are, my lady," said James, smiling back at her. "So I beg you will have no truck with the well, or its heathen goings-on."

They had reached the little pavilion by this time. James stood aside so that Anne might enter the building first. A few dilapidated garden seats were scattered around its perimeter, but its most striking furnishing was undoubtedly the well itself. This stood at the very center of the pavilion, and it was evident at once, as James had said, that the well was of far more ancient date than the building that now enshrined it. The waist-high circle of stone was crumbling at the edges and inscribed with worn and curious carvings. A dipper was fastened to its lip by an iron staple.

Anne went up to the very edge of the well and looked down. She could see the dark gleam of water, and after she had looked awhile she could make out her own features reflected dimly in its depths.

"No, you don't!" said James, taking her arm and making as though to pull her away. "Don't even think it! I won't have you looking for any husband but me."

"I don't want any husband but you," said Anne.

The words came out more strongly than she intended. Embarrassed but defiant, she looked up at James. The laughter had left his face, and he was looking down at her intently. "Truly?" he said. "Truly, Anne?"

"Yes, truly," she said, returning his look defiantly.

"Well, I am sure I want no other wife," he said. He began to draw her toward him. Anne went to him willingly, putting her arms around him and laying her head against his chest. It felt warm and secure within the circle of his arms, yet Anne was surprised to feel that he was trembling. "Anne," he said, "Anne!"

"Yes, James?" she said, looking up at him.

"I want to kiss you so badly!" he said.

"Then why don't you?" she asked.

"Because I am afraid I could not stop at just a kiss, Anne."

With a sense of unreality, Anne heard her own voice speaking with calm deliberation. "Well, and who said I wanted you to stop at a kiss?" she asked.

James's eyes widened. For a moment he stood looking down at her. Anne lifted her face, a movement of distinct provocation, and James lost no time in lowering his lips to hers. His first kiss was fleeting, almost tentative, but the second was more ardent, and before long his mouth was devouring Anne's with an urgency that left her breathless.

"You're so sweet, Anne," he whispered between kisses. "So very sweet."

Anne, clinging to him, made a small inarticulate noise. He redoubled his assault on her mouth, while his hands strayed from the small of her back to explore her body in ever-widening circles. Anne shivered at their touch. They seemed to awaken something inside her, a kind of hunger that rapidly fed on itself and grew to an aching desire. Before long, the touch of his hands and lips was only torment, because it left her longing for more. It was a longing that seemed impossible to satisfy. She let out a soft moan and moved restlessly in James's arms. "Anne," he whispered, "Anne."

"James," she whispered back. "I cannot bear it!"

He stopped kissing her long enough to look at her. "You want me to stop?" he asked.

"No!" said Anne. "I don't want you to stop. I—I do want you so badly."

For a moment she was shocked at this frank avowal. But it seemed to do her no disservice as far as James was concerned. "You cannot want me one-tenth as much as I want you—as I have been wanting you these last three days," he said. "I thought I should go mad. I have wanted so badly to kiss you—to taste you—" His lips strayed hungrily over her face and neck. "If you aren't careful, Anne, I shall lose my head and make love to you here and now, as though we were a couple of rustics in a haystack.''

For answer, Anne pressed herself yet more closely against him and raised her lips to his again. "On your head be it, then," he said. Holding her tightly against him, he lifted her off her feet and carried her over to a wicker settee that was among the furnishings of the well pavilion.

Anne sighed as he laid her on the settee. She sighed again and reached out to draw him close as he lowered his body over hers. This was a sensation more intimate and overwhelming than any that had gone on before. She exulted in the strength and solidity of his body atop hers. She was hardly aware of her own body except as a vehicle for pleasure. Yet when she presently became aware of his hands working at the buttons of her bodice, she felt a momentary flicker of shame and self-doubt. What if he was disgusted by the inadequacies of her figure? What if he no longer desired her when he saw she was more a child than a woman in appearance?

"Anne, oh, Anne," he whispered as he laid bare her chest. "My beautiful Anne." Then his mouth closed over her breast, and she forgot all else in the intensity of that sensation.

"James," she said with a soft cry. She put out a hand to touch his forehead, pulled it back, then put it out again, stroking the hair back over his brow. He caught her hand and kissed it before returning his attention to her breast. Anne writhed at the feel of his mouth, making little cries and half-intelligible pleas. "Oh, James, I cannot—oh! James, dear James, for God's sake—oh!"

She was aware of James's hands working at her clothing. One by one, strings, hooks and buttons gave way under his determined assault. Little by little her body was laid bare. In some corner of her mind, Anne felt she ought to shrink from this exposure, but instead she found herself welcoming it as James kissed and caressed each newly bared inch of skin. When he went to draw down her last petticoat, however, she clutched at it, seeking to retain the last shreds of a forgotten modesty.

Instead of trying to argue, James bent to kiss the hand clutching the petticoat. His lips ran over it lightly, lavishing kisses into its palm, and so pleasurable did Anne find this sensation that her hand gradually loosened its grip and allowed the petticoat to be drawn away.

"You are so beautiful, Anne," he whispered. "So perfect, and so very beautiful." His hands caressed her waist and hips and thighs, and where his hands went his mouth followed, until Anne felt every part of her body was ablaze with a frenzied desire. Yet there was one part that was more ablaze than the rest, and when his lips brushed across the soft flesh between her legs, then settled to a more leisurely examination, Anne drew a shuddering gasp and threw out a hand as though in protest.

"Ah, no! Dear God, James! What are you doing to me?"

The question was purely rhetorical, for it was already clear to Anne that he was intent on driving her mad with pleasure. She began to breathe heavily, turning her face from side to side and making an occasional moan. She felt flooded with sensation—a mounting tide of sensation from which she could not escape. It was like a pressure building inside her, building with unbearable force, and Anne was certain she must die if it continued one moment longer.

Then suddenly the sensation changed. Like music reaching a long-awaited climax, the tide of feeling within her seemed to buoy her up in a wave of feeling more

powerful and exquisite than any that had come before.
She cried out, half rising from the settee, then sank down
again in bewilderment.

"Anne," he said, raising his face to look at her. Anne
looked back at him a moment, then shuddered.

"Oh, James," she said. "How—how can you? But it
felt divine, James. So wonderful and so entirely divine."

"It felt divine to me, too," he said gravely. "I am glad
to give you pleasure, Anne."

"But—" Anne was filled with puzzlement. "But will
you not take your pleasure, too? Are you not going to—
to—"

James finished the sentence for her. "I would make
love most readily to you, Anne, if I felt the time were
right. But I think it important that you should be ready,
too."

Anne reached down to stroke the hair back from his
brow once more. "I am," she said. "I am ready, James."

Indeed, she felt quite ready to endure the pains of
lovemaking. It seemed to her the least she could do to
repay him for having given her such pleasure. She watched
as he removed his clothing piece by piece. When he
reached his underlinen, Anne shut her eyes instinctively,
but then she opened them again. That, too, seemed the
least she could do, in view of what he had done for her.
And when she looked, she was surprised to find his body
unexpectedly beautiful. She did not shrink even from the
sight of his sex, so strange in its swollen and unabashed
masculinity.

Moving with self-conscious care, James climbed onto
the settee and settled his body over Anne's. Anne put her
arms around him. He looked down at her, and there was
a tenderness in his eyes that brought a rush of tears to
Anne's own. "Anne?" he said.

"Yes, James," said Anne. At the last moment she shut her eyes, unable to resist this petty cowardice. Neither could she keep from bracing herself for the pain that she expected. But there was no pain. He entered her in a single smooth motion, and so far from painful was that entry that Anne's eyes flew open in surprise.

"James!" she said, looking up at him.

"Am I hurting you?" he asked anxiously.

"No!" said Anne. James looked at her and was apparently satisfied she was speaking the truth, for he began to thrust himself into her, slowly at first and then faster. With each thrust, a little of the tension seemed to leave Anne's body. Soon she was enveloped in a state of delicious lassitude. She sighed and shifted her body in a little voluptuous movement beneath him.

"Anne," he whispered. Anne looked up at him. Something in his eyes caught and held her own. She could not look away, but could only stare into those dark eyes that seemed curiously to mirror her own feelings. It was a strange sensation, and before long she was aware of another sensation, too, or rather a whole array of them. Eventually she recognized it as the same rising tide of sensations she had felt only a short time before. She found her body responding of its own accord to his, rising to meet his thrusts. She found herself whispering his name over and over, as the flood of feeling rose within her. And when it came to the crisis and she was carried out of herself with a piercing cry, she felt his hands grasp hers, heard him call her name, looked into his eyes, and saw clearly that the same enormity had just possessed them both.

James sighed, shuddered, and let his body go limp atop hers. But he kept hold of her hands, and raised himself a little on his elbows so he might continue to look into her eyes.

She wrapped her arms around him tightly. For a long time they said nothing. They lay there for what seemed hours, and still neither of them spoke, but only looked at each other and held each other in each other's arms.

At last James sighed and stirred. "God knows I don't want this to end, but I don't think I should keep you here any longer. Enjoyable as it would be in the short-term, the long-term consequences might be rather severe. If you were to take cold—"

"I'm not cold," said Anne, and smiled at him. "I'm not cold at all."

He smiled back and bent to kiss her on the brow. "Nevertheless, I'm afraid we must be going. If we stay much longer, we'll be in danger of meeting the girls when they come to wash their faces Midsummer morning. It must be after midnight already."

"Yes, I suppose so," said Anne. James sat up and began to draw on his discarded clothing. Anne did the same, throwing sideways glances at him as she dressed. She was obliged to call on him for assistance once or twice, but he gave it willingly, and when she was fully clothed once more he took her in his arms.

"Anne," he said. "*My* Anne." And he smiled at her.

"James," said Anne shyly, and then in a whisper, "My James."

"Yes," said James, and kissed her. "Your James. I'll never forget this night, never. What it meant to me— well, to put it into words would only diminish it. But I feel as if we really do belong to each other now. Why, I'd even let you wash your face in the well now, with a perfect confidence that I am the only husband it would ever show you."

"Would you?" said Anne, smiling.

"I would," said James. Solemnly he led her to the well and pointed down at the water. "Wash away. It's already Midsummer morning, and if the charm's going to work at all, it should work as well now as at five or six A.M."

Anne reached down into the well, gathered a little water in her hands, and splashed it on her face. "Now what?" she asked.

"You have to wish," said James. "You have to wish that your future be shown to you."

Anne shut her eyes, then opened them again. "I've wished," she said. "Now let us see what the well will show me."

She bent down to look into the water. James did the same beside her. "Do you see anything?" he asked anxiously.

"Nothing but my own face," said Anne. "And yours." She smiled at him.

"It's official, then," said James. "The well has sanctioned our marriage." And he proceeded to celebrate the well's sanction by taking her in his arms and kissing her once more.

CHAPTER X

It was very late that night—or rather very early the next morning—when Anne and James finally arrived back at Honeywell House. As they were entering the house, James put a question to Anne rather nervously.

"Anne, will you let me spend the night in your room? What remains of the night, that is?"

Anne was surprised by this question. She did not answer immediately, and James added quickly, "I don't mean to make a nuisance of myself. On my honor, I don't want anything but to just be with you. You needn't fear I will—er—plague you with any more attentions. But I would like just to be with you a little longer, if it wouldn't disturb you too much."

"It wouldn't disturb me at all," said Anne. "Not even if you did plague me with attentions." She smiled at him, and he smiled back at her.

"Anne," he said, and raised her hand to his lips. "My own Anne. I am glad to hear you say so."

They had to go through the formality of undressing in their own rooms, but as soon as their attendants were dismissed, James came into Anne's room and got into bed with her. For the rest of the night they lay together, talking. Anne told James about her childhood in Suffolk and about her deceased parents. He responded with anecdotes about his own youth and upbringing, and his years with the Brazilian Embassy. They talked until dawn began to color the eastern sky, at which point James drew Anne's head onto his chest, and they both fell abruptly asleep.

When Anne awoke, the morning was far advanced. James was still lying asleep beside her. She studied him, admiring the masculine beauty of his face and body and marveling at the fact that he was her husband—her husband most truly now. The memory of the night before made her shiver, and this movement, small as it was, made James stir and open his eyes. Seeing Anne, he smiled, put out an arm, and drew her close to him. "Good morning, dear wife," he said.

"Good morning, dear husband," returned Anne, snuggling against him. He ran both hands up and down her figure, pressing her against him. Anne was forcibly aware that he was aroused again, and she was beginning to be aroused herself when the door of her room opened and Susan came in carrying a can of hot water.

"Good morning, my lady. Good morning, m'lord," said Susan, her eyes studiously averted from the bed. "Here's your washing-up water, my lady. D'you want your chocolate now, or would you rather wait?"

"I will wait, if you please," said Anne, with all the dignity she could muster. As soon as the door closed behind her, she looked at James. He was smiling at her ruefully.

"What a thing it is to be a wealthy man," he said. "If we dwelt in a cottage, or were Gypsies living on the heath, we might have a degree of privacy. But since I am an earl, living in my ancestral home with several dozens of servants, I can be sure of having none at all."

"At least—" began Anne, then stopped with a blush.

"At least we had last night," said James, finishing the sentence for her with a grin. "An unconventional interlude, but on the whole satisfactory, I thought."

"Very satisfactory," said Anne with fervor.

James studied her soberly. "I am so glad I was able to give you pleasure, Anne," he said. "You must know I was afraid of hurting you."

Looking back at him, Anne felt a sudden chill. She looked away quickly, but not before the truth had impressed itself on her mind with devastating clarity.

Of course James had expected to hurt her last night. He had believed her to be a virgin. Strangely enough, her lack of virginity had not occurred to her last night while she and James were making love. So new and unexpected had been the pleasure he had given her that there had been nothing about it to remind her of that painful experience in Timothy's room. But she was reminded of it now, and it rose up like a ghost before her, haunting her with equal sensations of guilt and misery.

How could she have taken advantage of James's generosity in such a way? For Anne could not delude herself that she had not taken advantage of him. He had married her, believing she was something she was not. If he had known the truth about what she really was, he would never have wanted to marry her at all.

So convinced was Anne of this fact that it never

occurred to her to question it. Men might have love affairs prior to marriage without anyone thinking the worse of them for it, but women were expected to come to their marriage pure. She, Anne, was not pure. What was worse, she had compounded her impurity with deceit.

The thought filled Anne with dismay. Last night had been such a beautiful thing, not only because of the physical pleasure involved, but because there had been an intimacy and honesty about the whole experience that elevated it beyond the merely physical. She had revealed not only her body but some part of her real self to James in the process of making love to him, and he had seemed to cherish all she had revealed. Now she would never feel she had that freedom again. She could never be wholly honest with him, never be wholly at ease. She would always feel she was living a lie. Abruptly Anne rose from the bed. "Where are you going?" asked James in surprise.

"I—I think we had better get up now," said Anne, still with her face averted. Grasping for an excuse, she added, "If I wait to ring for my chocolate, the servants will think—they will know that we are—"

"That we are making love," finished James with a wry face. "Yes, I suppose so. Damn being an earl anyway! Forgive my language, Anne, but I have never felt the restrictions of my position more than at this moment. Still, they say that a pleasure anticipated is twice enjoyed. So I will look forward to tonight—if you've no objection?"

He looked at Anne, and so hopeful was his expression that she could not bear to disappoint him. "Certainly I have no objection, James," she said. "Tonight, if you like."

"I do like," said James emphatically. Rising from the

bed, he kissed her, then went off to his own room to dress.

Anne attended to her own dressing with the help of Susan, then went down to breakfast. Before entering the dining room, she stopped to visit the spider in the conservatory. It was still sitting beside the plants where she had last seen it the night before. "I will try to find something you can eat today," she told it, then glanced around with some embarrassment to see if anyone had overheard her talking to a spider. No one had, however, and so she went to her breakfast with her dignity intact.

She reminded James at breakfast of his promise to help her find food for the spider. "Yes, to be sure," he agreed. "But wouldn't you rather have a tour of the house first, Anne? Then afterwards we can look for insects while I give you a tour of the grounds. A *formal* tour," he added, with a hint of mischief in his eyes. "Last night's tour was by way of being an *informal* one."

Anne, blushing slightly, agreed to this agenda.

After breakfast, James took her all over the house, hindered slightly by the housekeeper, who insisted on accompanying them on the tour and on describing to Anne at great length all the house's unique and distinctive features. Both Anne and James bore with this as well as they could, but they were glad when she did not insist on accompanying them outside. Equipped with a jam jar that James had obtained from the kitchen to hold any suitable insects that might turn up, they set off down the terrace steps.

"It's beautiful," said Anne softly as they strolled amid fountains and flower beds. "Just as beautiful as it was last night, only in a different way."

"So it is," said James, surveying the landscape with an appraising air. "And I am in a mood to appreciate it fully, being in the company of my most delightful and discerning wife. Look, there's a grasshopper! Do you suppose your pet would eat a grasshopper?''

"It might," said Anne. Rather gingerly, she reached for the grasshopper. It evaded her grasp, however, and went leaping off into a nearby clump of shrubs.

"It's gone to covert," said James, laughing. "Tally-ho! After him, lads!'' Blowing an imaginary hunting horn, he plunged into the shrubbery after the grasshopper.

Anne, laughing helplessly, followed with the jam jar. After an exciting chase, they succeeded in capturing the grasshopper, and another chase ensued when a butterfly was unwary enough to flutter past James's nose. But when he finally succeeded in capturing it, Anne avowed it was too pretty to harm, so they let it go its own way and concentrated on catching grasshoppers and like prey. "Look, I've been blooded," said James, showing Anne a thumb stained with grasshoppers' "tobacco juice." "Do you think we have enough now? The jar's getting pretty full.''

"Yes, I think we have enough," agreed Anne. Looking at James's smiling face, she was overcome by a sense of unreality. It was unreal that she, Anne Barrington, should have spent a morning chasing grasshoppers with a belted earl who also happened to be her husband. It was unreal that she should be here, laughing in the sunlit gardens of Honeywell House instead of shivering in a drafty Palace corridor. It was unreal that she had lain in James's arms last night, and would lie in them again tonight if his words were true auguries. It was all unreal, but it was wonderful. As Anne fastened the lid on the jam jar, she reflected that the last twenty-four hours had been the happiest of her adult life.

James's next words put her happiness to flight, however.

"Since we're done hunting insects, why don't we go have another look at the well?" he suggested. "I have an urge to see if it's as attractive by sunlight as by moonlight." His eyes twinkled as he looked at Anne. "Though I can hardly hope it should hold the same attractions it did last night."

Anne managed to smile at him, but it was a strained smile. The thought of what had passed between her and James at the well last night reminded her once more of how she had deceived him. She had not been the innocent and virginal creature he had supposed her to be. And what if he even yet discovered his error? With a sensation of horror, she recalled the bloodletting James had performed at the inn on their wedding night. There would have been no bloodletting last night. The cushions on which she had lain would testify to her deceit if James were to think to consult them. With a tightness in her chest and a nauseated feeling in her stomach, she accompanied him through the Italian garden and into the woods where the well pavilion lay.

As soon as she entered the well pavilion, she looked anxiously at the settee where she and James had lain last night. Her relief was great when she saw that its cushions were so dark and weather-stained that it would have been impossible to detect any other stains upon them. She stood gazing at them in such relief that James noticed her fixed stare and threw her an amused look.

"Don't worry, Anne. Much as I would enjoy it, I haven't the courage to recreate our deed of last night here in broad daylight."

"I wasn't worrying," said Anne and came quickly over to join him beside the well. James looked closely into her face.

"Is everything well with you, Anne?" he asked.

"Of course," said Anne. "Why should it not be?"

She tried to make her tone light and playful, but James shook his head. "I'm asking you," he said. "You seem—different somehow. Not so happy as you were a little while ago. Is something wrong? Did I say something amiss?"

"You have said nothing wrong, James—nothing at all."

So great was the distress in her voice that James was partially relieved. "Well, I hope not," he said. "But if I do say or do anything wrong, you'll let me know right away, won't you? You know I'm rather new to this marriage business, and it's possible I might blunder inadvertently. Please believe I would never do anything purposely to hurt you, Anne—not for the world."

"Nor would I you," said Anne. But the words caught in her throat, and James looked at her closely once more.

"Anne, are you certain nothing is wrong?" he said. "If something is disturbing you, I wish you would tell me. You know you can tell me anything—anything at all."

Anne, looking into his eyes, thought he was in earnest. Here was another opportunity to tell him the whole story about her and Timothy. But when she thought of revealing that sordid tale here, where she and James had shared such an intimate and beautiful experience the night before, she simply could not do it. Besides, she reasoned, it was likely that when James assured her she might tell him anything, he was speaking of small and relatively harmless confessions—like her dressmaker's debt, for instance. This was a confession of an altogether different magnitude: a confession no husband could be expected to hear with equanimity. So she only shook her head.

"It's nothing, James," she said. "I am only a little tired, I think."

James looked contrite. "And no wonder if you are! Neither of us got much sleep last night, and we've been running about in the sun for over two hours now. I'd better be getting you back to the house. You must promise me that you will lie down for a while this afternoon, or I will never dare to come to your room tonight."

Anne threw him a fleeting look. "Very well," she said. In spite of her terrible secret and the misery it brought her, she could not help responding to the idea of James coming to her room that night. Was it right to accept the pleasure he offered her, when it had been obtained under what might be called false pretenses? Anne argued this question back and forth with herself as she and James walked back to the house. If his object was to get an heir, then clearly she must let him make love to her. To do otherwise would be to invalidate their marriage while at the same time cheating James of the thing he desired most from it—an heir to his name.

But perhaps it would be as well if their marriage *were* invalidated. A divorce or annulment would leave her exposed to shame and scandal, but at least she would have the comfort of knowing she had behaved honestly. But could she bring herself to behave honestly? Anne doubted it. She had not even the courage to tell James the truth about herself in private; it stood to reason that she would not have the courage to see it blared forth amid the harsh publicity of a divorce or annulment.

They had reached the terrace steps by the time Anne reached this point in her reasoning. She glanced up at James's profile as they went up the steps together. If only she could feel she was doing no wrong in keeping her secret from him. She wanted very much to stay married to him. *More than anything in the world,* Anne told herself.

She was still clutching the jam jar in one hand. As they reached the stairs, James reached out to take it from her. "I'll put that in the conservatory for you," he said. "You'd better go right upstairs and lie down."

Anne would not surrender the jar to him, however. "First I want to feed the spider," she said. "It has gone so long without eating, I would not want it to wait a minute longer than necessary."

James laughed. "Always solicitous of your spider! But you know it has gone months without eating, Anne. I have tried to feed it several times since I've been in England, but it showed no interest whatever."

"I want to try, at least," insisted Anne. "It won't take but a moment to try."

"Very well. But don't say I didn't warn you. It's my opinion these things don't eat in captivity. Some wild creatures don't, you know. They simply pine away and die once deprived of their freedom."

"It drank last night," said Anne stubbornly. "If it drinks, it will eat." But she feared James was right. Indeed, as she entered the conservatory, she almost shrank from approaching the spider's corner for fear she might find it already dead.

It was not dead, however, but grooming itself as it had done last night. Keeping a wary eye on it, Anne unfastened the catch on the glasshouse lid. She then went to extract a grasshopper from the jar, but in her nervousness she got two rather than one. "Put 'em both in," said James, who was watching these proceedings with an air of cynical amusement. "I can't see that it makes the least bit of difference. It might as well not eat one as two."

Setting her lips in a thin line, Anne dropped the grasshoppers into the glasshouse. One landed only a few inches from the spider. What happened next was too quick for the eye to follow. In a twinkling the spider had ceased to groom itself, whirled around, and pounced. The next moment it was sitting placidly once more, and the only difference between its past and present attitude was that there was now a grasshopper protruding from its mouth.

"The devil!" said James, gaping at the spider with his cynicism forgotten. "I don't believe it. It caught it! It's eating it."

"It is!" said Anne, nearly dropping the grasshopper jar in her excitement. "It *is* eating it. Good heavens, James! Did you see that?"

Even as she and James had been speaking, the other grasshopper had strayed too close to the spider and had suffered a fate like its fellow's. Now two grasshoppers protruded from the spider's mouth. "Two at once!" said James, staring at it in bemusement. "Here, Anne, put in another grasshopper. I wonder if it will take three?"

It took six in all, catching each one neatly while retaining the ones it had already captured. "Amazing," pronounced James, gazing down at the spider with incredulous eyes. "I guess it's making up for lost time."

"I am so glad," said Anne, hugging herself with delight. "I am so glad it's eating, James. Look, I think the spider is glad, too! It's dancing!"

The spider was indeed dancing, or something that looked very much like it. It swayed and turned on its eight legs, moving in a slow circle and swinging its body from side to side. "Amazing," said James again, and shook his head. "I never would have believed it if I hadn't seen it. Your instincts were obviously sound, Anne." He smiled at her. "You seem to have a knack for taking care of things. That's a comfort to know, seeing that I, like the spider, am now in your care.''

"So you are." Anne gave the jar in her hand a look of pretended appraisal. "I wonder if you, too, would thrive on grasshoppers?''

James laughed and caught her in his arms. "I beg you won't make the experiment! I don't know, though." He looked into her eyes. "As long as I have you, I think I would even eat grasshoppers without complaining—yes, and dance for joy afterwards.''

Looking back at him, Anne felt a surge of the purest happiness. The doubts and fears that had troubled her earlier seemed now ridiculously trivial. Of course it would have been better if she could have been a virgin when she married James. She still wished it had been possible, but there was no use crying over spilt milk. She was married to him, she was happy with him, and he was evidently happy with her. To renounce him because of a thing that she could not help and which had no real bearing on their relationship seemed quixotic in the extreme.

What does it matter, after all? she told herself. *I made a dreadful mistake over that business with Timothy, but it's in the past now. It would be ridiculous to let it spoil the rest of my life. There is no reason why James need ever know about it. I will simply be the best wife to him I can from now on, and leave the past to bury itself. What he doesn't know cannot hurt him.*

James was looking down at Anne quizzically, as though he sensed the tenor of her thoughts. "Why so serious, oh wife of mine?" he asked. "Dare I offer you a penny for your thoughts?''

"I was merely thinking that I want to be the best wife to you that I can, because you make me so happy," said Anne firmly.

"Why, that is more than a pennyworth of thoughts! A pound at the very least." James leaned down to kiss her again. "But you don't need to worry about wanting to be the best wife, because you *are* the best wife, Anne. The best wife in the whole world. Now let's go get ourselves a bite of something to eat. Watching this fellow eat all those grasshoppers has given me a tremendous appetite!"

CHAPTER XI

In the days that followed, Anne tried hard to fulfill her resolution of being the best wife she possibly could be to James.

It was an endeavor she found not only easy but enjoyable. She was not in any sense a skilled housekeeper, but since Honeywell House already possessed a skilled housekeeper in the person of Mrs. Rhodes, this was not a serious lack. Indeed, it was a question whether two skilled housekeepers could have coexisted in such harmony as that enjoyed by Anne and Mrs. Rhodes. Mrs. Rhodes went around telling the other servants that Anne was "a proper lady, as can't be said of everyone who's got a title. Nice-mannered and nicely spoken and elegant as you please—just what you might expect of one as was a lady of the Queen's Court." Anne, for her part, found Mrs. Rhodes an invaluable assistant and an authority on such issues as settling domestic disturbances, planning menus, and attending to the needs of a large household.

Being relieved of the greater share of household cares, she had all the more time to devote to James. He was much busier than she, for the work of managing the Honeywell House estate and his various other properties took a large part of every day. Anne could not help but contrast his busy and productive life with the idleness and dissolution she had seen among the gentlemen at Court.

At first James kept apologizing to Anne because his work kept him from entertaining her during the morning and afternoon hours. But Anne assured him she was quite capable of entertaining herself and indeed found no difficulty in doing so. After the restrictions of Court life, she could not get used to the freedom of having a whole day ahead of her in which she might do as she chose. She slept late, read for hours on end, went for long walks, and luxuriated in the possession of that greatest of all luxuries, time. There was time to watch the bees among the flowers in the garden; time to observe the haymakers working in the fields; time to drive about the neighborhood and surrounding countryside, acquainting herself with its beauties and points of interest.

Among all these activities, she did not neglect the spider in the conservatory. She had come to feel a proprietary interest in its well-being and disliked the idea of turning its care over to others. This was just as well, since no one else in the household wanted anything to do with it. Joe Gardiner would come and watch her if he happened to be in the conservatory while she was tending it, but though he admitted the spider was an interesting creature he was also firm in his insistence that it was ''h'unnatural.'' So Anne took charge of its care and daily scoured the gardens for grasshoppers, crickets, and other prey for it to eat.

After a few days of trying to catch insects with her hands, she had sent away for a net such as was manufactured for use by collectors of butterflies and moths. This greatly simplified the business of catching food for the spider. It never ate so many as six insects at one sitting after the first day, but it could usually be counted on to dispatch two or three. Anne begged the cook for a pair of tongs from the kitchen to remove insects from the jam jar and, when necessary, to return to the jar what the spider would not eat. These, with the net and the jam jar and a small, long-spouted watering can contributed by Joe Gardiner, made her spider husbandry equipment complete.

By this time the whole household knew about the exotic resident of the conservatory. Nearly all the maidservants had found a moment to slip down and look at the spider, shuddering with pleasurable horror at the idea of living in the same house with such a monstrosity. It was considered eccentric of Anne to take an interest in it, but like most eccentricities it was also felt to confer a certain distinction on its owner. "There goes my lady with her net. She's off to catch more food for that god-awful spider of hers," they would tell one another and agree there was no accounting for the tastes of the aristocracy.

"Most ladies in your position content themselves with lapdogs," James told her one day, when she had been particularly eloquent in describing the spider's activities. "A nice pug or spaniel."

"I don't want a pug or spaniel," said Anne. "In truth, James, I am a little—not afraid, exactly, but *nervous* around dogs."

James gave a shout of laughter. "But you're not nervous about an eight-inch spider?"

Anne reflected gravely, then shook her head. "No, I don't think I am. Though of course I am very careful not to give her a chance to harm me. But Arachne has never yet made any move to bite me, or indeed to bite anything except the insects she eats."

Arachne was the name Anne had settled on for her pet, as an appellation at once classical, dignified, and appropriate. James continued to tease her now and then about her wholesale adoption of the spider, but it was a friendly kind of teasing—almost a loving kind of teasing. And Anne was very happy to be subjected to it.

Her feelings for James had grown deeper with every day that passed. It seemed to her that no woman could have had a better husband. He was unfailingly kind and considerate, good-humored even under stress, and a most entertaining companion in the hours he could devote to her. And at night he was a lover such as she could not have dreamed of, because she had never dreamed such a one could exist. He came to her room almost every night and on the rare night he absented himself, she found herself missing him intensely. Indeed, if there was one cloud in her existence at all, it was the fact that she was coming to care for him a great deal more than was appropriate, considering that theirs was a marriage of convenience.

This fact came to plague Anne more and more as time went on. Try as she might, she could not forget that James had married her for reasons other than love. It was possible to put the idea out of her head for days at a time, but sooner or later it would arise again to trouble her. It was not that James's behavior was in any way responsible for her troubled state of mind. Indeed, as Anne frequently told herself, he could not have treated her more lovingly if he really had loved her.

But not once had he come out and said that he loved her, unless you counted that moment during the marriage ceremony in which he had promised to love her until death did them part. That, to Anne's mind, did not count. It was merely a formality to be gotten through, though she did not do James the injustice of thinking he had lied in pronouncing those solemn vows. She thought he did love her—in a way. But Anne was sure it was more an affectionate than a passionate love, a commonplace sort of love such as a man might feel for a favorite horse or loyal dog or anything else that was familiar, useful, and comfortable. And that was not at all the way she wanted him to love her. Not to put too fine a point on it, what she wanted was for him to love her in the way she was beginning to love him.

That she did love him, Anne could not doubt. The thought of him was in her mind all day long. When something interesting or humorous happened, she immediately stored it up in her memory to recount to him later. When something embarrassing or unfortunate happened—and such things do happen even to newly wed brides of earls—she automatically flew to him as to a source of comfort that never failed. When he complimented her on a dress or on a way of doing her hair, she had to fight an urge to wear that same dress or hair style over and over for the next fortnight. But it was at night, when she lay in his arms, that she felt it most surely. On more than one occasion she had been forced to literally bite her lips to keep from telling him how much and how deeply she loved him.

I can't tell him, she told herself. *He must never know what I feel for him. It would be different if he had ever said he loved me—but he hasn't. And I don't suppose he ever will. We have been married several months now, and if he hasn't developed such feelings by this time, it's not likely he ever will develop them. For me to lay claim to a love he does not share would only embarrass him and make him feel guilty. He might even feel obliged to lie about it and say he loved me in return—and that would be worse than his never saying it at all. It's bad enough there should be the dishonesty of what happened with Timothy and me between us. I would rather there was nothing else dishonest about our relationship.*

Anne still cringed when she thought of the deception she had practiced on James in regard to Timothy. But she thought of it less and less as the weeks slipped by. The fact was that nothing she had ever felt in regard to Timothy could compare with her feelings for James. Against the reality of her love for him, what had happened that night in Timothy's room seemed not only a vast time ago but utterly insignificant. She still regretted the incident and would have blotted it from the past if she could have, but since she could not, she put it from her mind and concentrated her thoughts on other and more important things—like not betraying herself when James did something that brought an involuntary "I love you" to her lips.

Being forced to practice a constant self-restraint in this respect was definitely the largest fly in the ointment of Anne's happiness. There were other small trials as well. As the weeks went by, and news spread throughout the neighborhood that the Earl of Westland had brought home a bride to Honeywell House, what seemed the whole populace of the county came to call on the newly wed couple to offer their respects and best wishes. And this could not be other than a trial for anyone of as shy and retiring a disposition as Anne.

The first of these callers arrived at an unfortunate time. Anne was engaged in one of her expeditions in search of insects and nearly bowled right into the visitors as she came round the corner of the house in hot pursuit of an athletic grasshopper. There were three callers altogether, all of them female. Two of them were elderly ladies; the other was younger, or at least dressed in a more youthful fashion, though there was something prematurely pinched and elderly about her face.

For a moment the four women stood looking at each other. As Anne's eyes traveled over the callers in their elaborate visiting attire, she was acutely conscious that her blue muslin dress was an old one, that her wide-brimmed straw hat was more utilitarian than beautiful, and that her hair was tumbling about her shoulders from the vigor of the chase. In particular was her appearance a contrast to the youngest lady, whose frilled and festooned dress and bonnet might have been designed as a display for milliner's trimmings. There was a contemptuous look in the lady's cold blue eyes that showed she appreciated this contrast as much as Anne.

The contempt in the stranger's eyes made Anne flush, but it also put her on her mettle. She had not lived seven years at Court without learning something of the art of rising to the occasion. Nor had she served in daily attendance upon the Queen of England without learning a few lessons in personal dignity. Whatever else might be said of Her Majesty, she had possessed to perfection the art of looking dignified even under trying circumstances— when being laced into her corsets, for instance, or when being cupped and blooded. This situation, embarrassing as it was, could not compare to such indignities as that.

So Anne lifted her chin and swept the ladies a very respectable curtsy in spite of the encumbrances of a butterfly net and a jar of grasshoppers. "Good afternoon," she said.

"Good afternoon," said the elder of the ladies. She was a stout dame with gray hair and a consequential manner, but there was doubt in her eyes as she surveyed Anne. "Are you—have I the honor of addressing—?"

"Lady Westland," said Anne, and curtsied again.

The elderly dame curtsied gravely in return. "I thought it must be Lady Westland," she remarked. "Although you are very much younger than I was led to expect. I am Lady Mabberly."

She spoke the words as though they ought to hold some significance to Anne. Anne racked her brain frantically, but could recall no mention of any family named Mabberly. However, it seemed likely that Lady Mabberly lived somewhere within the vicinity of Honeywell House, so Anne felt justified in a polite falsehood. "I am very pleased to meet you, Lady Mabberly," she said. "I believe I have had your home pointed out to me since arriving in this neighborhood."

"No doubt," said Lady Mabberly with a complacent smile. "Of course I must be partial, yet there can be no question that Mabberly Manor is one of the showplaces of the neighborhood. And since dear Sir Thomas is the local magistrate, it is naturally a place of importance as well as beauty."

Anne smiled and nodded, and Lady Mabberly turned to her two companions. "This is Mrs. Wrexford and Miss Wrexford," she told Anne. "Like me, they take an active role in the society hereabouts, though you would not likely be acquainted with *their* property. The Beeches is not a bad little place in its way, but compared to Mabberly

Manor it is rather small and off the beaten track, as the expression goes.''

Not surprisingly, the Wrexfords looked a little sour at this remark. Yet it seemed to Anne that sourness was an expression natural to their faces. Mrs. Wrexford was a lady of middle years with graying blond hair, cold blue eyes, and a spare figure. Her daughter was the same in all respects: not so gray as to hair, perhaps, and with the skinniness of her figure partly disguised beneath the ruffles and flounces of her elaborate costume, yet she bore an unmistakable resemblance to her mother all the same. And as Anne curtsied politely to both ladies and received stiff curtsies in return, she felt an intuitive certainty that she was not going to care any more for one Wrexford lady than for the other.

Since they had come to call upon her, however, she was obliged to receive them with politeness. She invited all three ladies into the house, hastily divested herself of her hat, butterfly net, and jar, and sent one of the servants off for tea. ''We will be most comfortable in the drawing room, I think,'' she said, leading the way into that apartment. ''Will you please be seated?''

''You have made no alteration in the room, I see,'' said Lady Mabberly, sweeping a glance around the drawing room with its crimson and gold hangings. ''I had rather expected you would do so. Coming from London, and being acquainted with all the latest modes, I should think you would find these furnishings rather antiquated. At Mabberly Manor we recently had the chief drawing room redone in the Egyptian style.''

Since she seemed to expect congratulations for this feat, Anne duly murmured a few words of congratulation. ''It sounds as though you are tolerably familiar with Honeywell House, ma'am,'' she added. ''Have you visited here often before?''

''Not often lately, but when Lord Lindsay was living here with his family, I came to call quite frequently. Let me see, that was five—or was it six—years ago? Something in that neighborhood, I fancy. And I did call on the O'Reillys a few times when they were living here, though I could not think they were altogether the thing. Irish, you know—and when Sir Terrence ended by marrying his aunt's hired companion, I wasn't the least surprised. Blood will always tell.''

''She was a scheming creature,'' said Miss Wrexford suddenly. It was the first thing she had said since arriving at Honeywell House, and both her mother and Lady Mabberly looked at her in surprise.

''She was a scheming creature,'' repeated Miss Wrexford, with a defiant look in her frosty blue eyes. ''Miss Pearce, or whatever her name was—the companion person, I mean. I told everyone at the outset that she was setting her cap at Sir Terrence, and surely enough, she ended by marrying him. But what can one expect? She was thick as thieves with Catherine Summerfield—Lady Meredith, I *should* say—and everyone knows what she is.''

Anne, who did not know, looked politely uncomprehending. But both Lady Mabberly and Mrs. Wrexford nodded with alacrity. ''Oh, yes,'' said Lady Mabberly. ''You are quite right, Isabel. *Everyone* knows what Lady Meredith is. No doubt even Lady Westland will have heard about her scandalous behavior, new to the neighborhood though she is.''

Lady Mabberly looked expectantly at Anne. Anne shook her head. ''I know nothing of any scandal,'' she said. ''Indeed, I don't think I ever heard anything of the people you mention. But let us not talk scandal, if you please, ma'am. I was wanting to ask you instead if you—''

Her well-meaning attempt to divert the conversation was thwarted by Lady Mabberly. "Oh! Then it will be as well for me to drop a word in your ear," she said, cutting firmly across Anne's speech. "Indeed, it would be better if you were warned, Lady Westland, for otherwise you might be drawn into Lady Meredith's set without realizing how fatal that would be. No decent person in the neighborhood will receive her."

"Except the Percys," said Mrs. Wrexford gloomily. "They persist in letting her birth and consequence outweigh her behavior. And the Winslows do the same, and also the Fitzsimmons, and the Woodwards—"

"But no persons of *real* refinement and elegance," said Lady Mabberly firmly. "Persons such as you and I, ma'am. *We* know what Catherine Meredith is, well enough."

Here it seemed to Anne that the conversation had come full circle without making her a single fact the wiser. But Lady Mabberly continued with her speech, addressing Anne now instead of her companions. "The fact is that Catherine Summerfield was a most improper person before her marriage," she told Anne. "She ran away with an Italian dancing master when she was barely in her teens."

"No better than she ought to be," said Mrs. Wrexford, opening her mouth just enough to admit these words, then shutting it with a snap.

"And though her aunt managed to get that business hushed up pretty well, she went on just as scandalously afterwards. Throwing herself at Lord Meredith, and he engaged to Lady Laura! That would be Lady Laura Lindsay, daughter of the Earl of Lindsay, who was leasing Honeywell House at the time," Lady Mabberly explained to Anne. "A most delightful girl."

"Yes, but it was her own fault she lost Lord Meredith to Catherine Summerfield," said Isabel Wrexford vigorously. "I told Lady Laura that Catherine was an improper person to befriend, but she didn't listen to me."

Anne, looking at Isabel's spiteful face, felt a sympathy for the unknown Lady Laura. *I wouldn't have listened to you either,* she told herself silently.

"At any rate, the damage is done now," said Lady Mabberly with a shake of her head. "Lord Meredith married Catherine Summerfield, and now she queens it over all of us here in Langton Abbots—or tries to, at any rate. Fortunately she is away a good deal of the time. She and Lord Meredith are always off visiting some outlandish place or other. But it happens that they are at the Abbey right now."

"Yes, and the O'Reillys are visiting them," put in Isabel. "If Lady Meredith comes to call on you, Lady Westland, likely she will bring Lady O'Reilly with her. You would do better not to receive either one of them."

Such was the patronage in her voice that Anne felt a surge of rebellion. "It doesn't sound as though either lady has done anything particularly wrong," she said. "The only thing you can find against Lady O'Reilly is that she was once a hired companion."

"But the same cannot be said of Lady Meredith," said Isabel sharply. "I assure you, I should not be surprised to find she has committed every sin in the calendar. And since Lady O'Reilly sees fit to associate with her, she must be regarded as an improper person likewise."

"I don't see it," said Anne, with a bravery that surprised herself. "It sounds as though most people in the neighbor-

hood do not share your scruples about receiving Lady
Meredith. Whatever her past sins may have been, she is
a neighbor now, and I should dislike to omit any obser-
vance that might be due her."

"Then there is nothing more to be said," said Isabel,
and rose to her feet. "Come, Mama, Lady Mabberly: we
had better be going. It's obvious Lady Westland does not
appreciate our attempts to help her."

Mrs. Wrexford immediately rose in support of her
daughter, but Lady Mabberly observed that they were all
being a trifle hasty and remained solidly planted in her
chair. Since the Wrexfords had come in Lady Mabberly's
carriage, they were prevented from making the exit they
would have liked and were forced to remain standing
by the drawing room door instead of flouncing off in a
dudgeon.

"Indeed, I hope you will do nothing rash, Lady Westland," said Lady Mabberly, addressing Anne with a solemn shake of her head. "You are very young and
doubtless inexperienced, and as such, you cannot realize
the depths of depravity to which women like Lady Meredith may descend." She talked on this theme for a good
ten minutes longer while the Wrexford ladies hovered
impatiently at the door. But at last she rose with a final
admonition to Anne to be on her guard and a condescending "Good afternoon." Anne wished her good afternoon
in return, curtsied silently to the Wrexfords (who acknowledged the greeting in equal silence), and accompanied
them all to the door.

As they went out to Lady Mabberly's carriage, Anne
heard Isabel say audibly to her mother, "Well, that was
a wasted trip! We might have known as soon as we
laid eyes on her that there was no use talking to such a
hoyden."

Anne, who had never been called a hoyden before in all her life, was insensibly pleased. It might not be a compliment, but to her ears ''hoyden'' sounded infinitely better than being called a mouse, or a zero, or a little dab of a girl with nothing to say. There was a smile on Anne's lips as she shut the door behind her callers. There was also a resolution in her heart to cultivate the acquaintance of Lady O'Reilly and the scandalous Catherine Meredith if ever the opportunity should offer.

CHAPTER XII

The opportunity Anne was seeking arrived the very next afternoon.

She had just finished putting on a new lavender voile afternoon dress when the callers were announced. The dress had been made for her by a local dressmaker, and the woman had made a good job of it. As Anne stood before the mirror, examining the fit of the dress both front and back, it struck her that she no longer much resembled the girl who had slipped like a pale ghost along the corridors of Queen Charlotte's Palace. Her hair was as silvery blond as ever, but there was a hint of color in her cheeks, and her face looked rounder and less pinched than it had before. Looking closely, she thought her figure had filled out a little, too. She would never be a voluptuous woman, but there was a hint of a curve at her hip and bosom now, and her arms and shoulders had a more rounded look. "Why, I actually look pretty!" said Anne aloud.

Susan, who had been helping her dress, gave her a look of surprise. "Why, to be sure you do, my lady," she said. "But so you have right along. Very pretty and ladylike and elegant."

At that moment a knock sounded on the door. Susan went to answer it and returned a moment later, looking portentous. "You've got callers, my lady," she said. "Ladies, both of 'em—real ladyships, I mean. It's Lady Meredith and Lady O'Reilly. Haywood wants to know if you'll see them, or if he should make your excuses."

"I will see them," said Anne eagerly. "Assuredly I will see them! I have heard a great deal about them both, and I have been hoping they would call."

As she followed the butler downstairs, Anne reflected with amusement that these callers had chosen a more auspicious moment to arrive than had the Wrexfords and Lady Mabberly. Instead of finding her grasshopper hunting in a shabby gown and coarse straw hat, she was in an elegant new dress with her hair freshly coiffed and with a measure of confidence in her heart. But in truth her thoughts were taken up very little with her own appearance. She was much more interested to see what the two ladies Lady Mabberly had called scandalous might look like.

I'll wager they look no more scandalous than I do, she told herself with an inward smile. *Indeed, if Lady Mabberly and the Wrexfords only knew it, I am a trifle scandalous myself. By rights I ought to get along very well with the two local demi-reps!*

When she entered the drawing room, however, she suffered a check. The ladies standing there were both so very beautiful in their different ways that she felt at once she could have nothing in common with them.

"Lady Westland?" said the first lady, coming forward

to greet Anne. "It is a pleasure to meet you. I am Catherine Meredith." She was a tall woman, very slender yet beautifully proportioned. Her face was pale and heart-shaped and possessed to an unusual degree the quality of inscrutability. Yet when Anne looked in her golden-brown eyes, she received a strong impression of force and personality. And after Lady Meredith had regarded Anne for a moment in silence, she suddenly smiled a slow, spreading smile of great charm.

"You are younger than I expected," she said. "And very much less formidable. Thank God for it! I have been quaking in my boots ever since I got here, afraid you might be a haughty, high-browed creature to whom I could not find two words to say."

Again she smiled, and Anne found herself smiling back quite naturally. "I find it hard to believe you could ever quake in your boots, Lady Meredith," she said.

"But I do quite frequently, I assure you. People think me haughty and high-browed myself sometimes, but the truth is that I am only shy."

Anne gave her an amazed look. It was impossible to believe this self-possessed woman could share her own malady. Yet Lady Meredith seemed to be speaking the truth. She went on, turning to the woman beside her. "Allow me to introduce you to my friend Lady O'Reilly. She is only visiting me at present, though I have been trying to coax her into buying a house and settling here in the neighborhood permanently. She well knows its attractions, for she lived at Honeywell House a year or two ago, back when old Lord Westland was still alive."

"Indeed I did live here, Lady Westland," said Lady O'Reilly, curtsying and smiling. "And let me tell you, I envy you the fortune of dwelling here now." She was even taller than Lady Meredith, and much the more striking of the two. Her hair of auburn gold foamed beneath her hat brim in distracting ringlets, her eyes were a warm brown, and her smile singularly lovely.

"It's a pleasant place," Anne managed to say. She felt small and gauche beside these two tall paragons of beauty.

"A magical place," said Lady O'Reilly emphatically. "Especially if one happens to be around the well pavilion at Midsummer."

For no good reason she blushed. It struck Anne that Lady Meredith, too, looked a little self-conscious. "You are acquainted with the well, are you not, Lady Westland?" went on Lady O'Reilly, with the appearance of wishing to change the subject. "But of course you must be. You could hardly fail to be acquainted with the famous Honeywell House well if you have lived here any time at all."

"Indeed, I *am* acquainted with it," said Anne, and felt herself blushing in her turn.

A brief silence followed. It was Lady Meredith who broke it. "I for one should like to see the well again," she told Anne. "I was away at Midsummer, or I should have come down and watched the girls going through their ritual face-washing. It's always such an interesting thing to see. Could we perhaps stroll down there a little later, Lady Westland, after we have had a cup of tea? Your drawing room is very lovely, but formal calls are so—formal."

"Of course," said Anne. She was surprised by this request, but nothing loath, for she, too, found the formal ritual of receiving callers an ordeal. As soon as the ladies had each drunk a cup of tea, she put on her own hat and shawl and accompanied Lady Meredith and Lady O'Reilly out on the terrace and down into the gardens.

She felt at first even shyer walking through the gardens

with her two guests than when seated with them in the drawing room. But the two other ladies soon put her at ease, asking her questions about herself and her experiences since coming to Honeywell House. "You will have met a few people already, I suppose," said Lady Meredith. "Tell me, have you made the acquaintance of the Wrexfords yet?"

"Oh, yes," said Anne, in such a wry voice that the others laughed.

"I can tell from your tone that they made themselves as amiable as usual," said Lady Meredith. "You will find the Wrexfords, mother and daughter, your biggest crosses to bear while you live in this neighborhood. Lady Mabberly is another cross, but not on quite the same scale. I don't consider she reaches anywhere near the same heights of hatefulness as the Wrexfords."

Anne laughed. "I have met Lady Mabberly, too, as it happens. She and the Wrexfords all came together to call on me yesterday. And I am afraid none of them took away a very good opinion of me." She described how she had nearly run into the three ladies while attired for grasshopper catching.

Lady Meredith and Lady O'Reilly were much diverted by her story, but Lady Meredith declared it had not likely made much difference as far as the three ladies' opinions of her was concerned. "They would have found something to criticize no matter what you were doing and how you were dressed, Lady Westland. Indeed, as one woman to another, I would caution you most earnestly to avoid both the Wrexfords and Lady Mabberly as far as you can."

Anne could not resist a gurgle of laughter at this advice. "They gave me the same advice about you!" she said. "Indeed, they warned me long and earnestly against cultivating your acquaintance—and Lady O'Reilly's, too. So long and earnestly did they warn me, in fact, that I developed a positive longing to meet you both!''

All three ladies laughed at this. ''Well, you have gotten your wish,'' said Lady O'Reilly. ''But the Wrexfords will probably wash their hands of you if they find you have been associating with the two scarlet women of the neighborhood.''

''They already have washed their hands of me,'' said Anne. ''Because I told them flat out I would not take their advice.''

Lady Meredith and Lady O'Reilly looked at her with surprise mixed with admiration. ''That showed a deal of spirit,'' said Lady O'Reilly. ''I doubt I would have dared to speak so frankly myself!''

''But are you sure you wish to declare allegiance so soon with the scaff and raff of the neighborhood?'' said Lady Meredith. ''For so I am credibly informed the Wrexfords have called me.''

They had reached the well pavilion by this time. By unspoken assent, all three of them went to the well curb and stood looking down at the clear waters below. Anne, too, looked a moment, then lifted her face to smile at Lady Meredith.

''If the choice is between allegiance to you and allegiance to the Wrexfords, then my choice is already made,'' she said. ''I don't know how it is, but I felt even before I met the two of you that I had something in common with you. With the Wrexfords and Lady Mabberly, I had nothing in common at all.''

These words made Lady O'Reilly laugh, but Lady Meredith regarded Anne with a curiously intent expression in her golden brown eyes. ''Did you indeed feel so?'' she said. ''Because it happens I felt the same way. I could not explain it to myself, for the gossip circulating throughout the neighborhood is that you were once Lady in Waiting to the Queen and are yourself a most exclusive, refined, and elegant sort of woman—the kind of woman with whom I could have nothing in common, in fact. Yet I was driven to call on you by something—call it instinct—that would not let me be until I had done my duty. In general, I am only too willing to let such duties go by the board! But it seems my instincts in this case were sound."

"Very sound," said Lady O'Reilly, smiling warmly at Anne. "We are all going to be very good friends, I feel certain." Turning to Lady Meredith, she added, "This settles it, Catherine. I shall have to take your advice and convince Terrence to buy a house in this neighborhood. Indeed, he is already half convinced that we should; it is only a matter of finding the proper house."

"I understand Mabberly Manor is one of the show-places of the neighborhood," offered Anne with a straight face.

This remark elicited gales of laughter from her companions, who agreed that Mabberly Manor would be a splendid home for Lady O'Reilly to buy if only the Mabberlys could be persuaded to quit it. "Aren't you a sly creature!" said Lady O'Reilly admiringly. "You look so demure, but I can see that is only window dressing. There's a deal of wit behind that innocent face of yours, and a wicked sense of humor, too. Assuredly we shall be friends."

"Assuredly," said Lady Meredith solemnly. "In fact, I am convinced that friendship is our destiny." Taking the dipper that hung from the well curb, she filled it from the well, then held it dramatically aloft. "Let us all drink to friendship! May we love and support one another as long as we live, sharing one another's joys, mitigating one another's sorrows, and presenting a united front against the criticisms and calumnies of the Wrexfords and Mabberlys.''

Anne and Lady O'Reilly could not help laughing at her words, but they arranged their expressions into a look of suitable reverence as Lady Meredith raised the dipper to her lips. She then handed it to Lady O'Reilly.

"Amen," said Lady O'Reilly and drank in her turn. With a smile, she handed the dipper to Anne.

"Amen," said Anne, and drank likewise. She was filled with a glow of happiness. The ritual was a childish one and no doubt intended as much in jest as in earnest, yet there was a nice sisterly feeling about it that warmed her heart. She had never had a close friend growing up to whom she might open her heart. Neither had there been any woman at Court whom she had been minded to make a bosom friend. Now she had not one but two of them. And though she had only made their acquaintance that afternoon, she, like Lady Meredith, felt theirs was destined to be a real friendship.

The vow being duly solemnized, all three ladies began to walk back to the house. "We have already been with you far longer than is appropriate for a first call," said Lady O'Reilly, smiling impishly. "You see how quickly our scandalous disregard for the conventions becomes apparent!"

"I am sick to death of conventions," said Anne frankly. "I had quite enough of them at Court to last me the rest of my life. Feel free to be as scandalous and unconventional as you please."

Lady Meredith smiled her slow smile. "You are a brave woman to give such wholesale permission, Lady Westland," she said. "But in truth, I have no notion to do anything very shocking. What I should like to do more than anything is give a party to introduce you to the neighborhood. Should you have any objection to that? You know it is really my duty to do so, as your nearest neighbor. And what is more to the point, it is something I should like to do, now I have met you and seen what you are like.''

Anne was silent a moment, considering. The idea of a formal party at which she would be guest of honor and would be forced to make the acquaintance of dozens of strangers filled her with panic. But then she considered the circumstances and realized it might not be so much of an ordeal as her mind would make it. She would not be attending the party alone, after all. Both Lady Meredith and Lady O'Reilly would be there to support her, and James would be there, too. She smiled at the thought of him, and Lady Meredith, who had been watching her face, smiled also.

"You will allow me to do it? Good. I think we can contrive to make it an enjoyable evening, even in spite of the fact that I must invite the Mabberlys and Wrexfords if the party is to be a large one. But never fear. You have taken the vow of friendship with Emily and me, and we will take it on ourselves to draw the enemy fire if there should be any. Indeed, with such targets as us around, you are not likely to come under fire in any case.''

Anne laughed. "I hope not," she said. "But after running into the Wrexfords and Lady Mabberly with my butterfly net, I am afraid I have become a target, too. I distinctly heard Isabel Wrexford call me a hoyden as she was leaving.''

Lady Meredith observed that it might have been much worse, and the three ladies took leave of each other with many avowals of friendship. "Indeed, I am so glad you called," Anne told the other two. "It was a pleasure to meet you, Lady Meredith and Lady O'Reilly."

"Catherine," said Lady Meredith firmly. "You must call me Catherine."

"And you must call me Emily," said Lady O'Reilly, smiling at Anne.

"Then you may call me Anne," said Anne, smiling back at them both. "Good afternoon to you both, Catherine and Emily. I shall be looking forward to your party."

This was not quite true, yet as Anne waved a farewell to her new friends and walked back to the house, she found that she was not wholly dreading the thought of the party even if it made her a trifle nervous. Indeed, mingled with her nervousness was a certain excitement at the idea of appearing publicly with James for the first time. *He is my husband,* Anne told herself. *I will be proud to attend the party with him at my side. And I must take care to look and behave so as to make him proud of me.*

She immediately began to give thought to her appearance for the occasion. Lady Meredith had spoken as though the party would be a large one, which meant full dress and jewelry. It had been long enough now since she had been at Court that the planning of a new toilette was a pleasure rather than a chore. And of course the fact that she could choose what she liked without worrying about cost contributed to the pleasure.

I shall have something in aquamarine blue, she told herself. *James always comments when I wear that color. Besides, it will give me a chance to wear the aquamarine set he gave me. I've not yet had a chance to wear it anywhere except here at home.*

James received with resignation the news that he and Anne were to be guests of honor at a large party. "At the Abbey, eh?" he said. "I suppose it was bound to happen. Now the neighbors have discovered us, we'll likely have no peace from here on out.''

Anne looked at him in alarm, for despite the jocular tone of his words she thought he sounded less than pleased. ''I hope you don't mind, James,'' she said. ''I was a little shy at the thought of a party myself, but Lady Meredith and Lady O'Reilly promised to make it easy for me. Since they were being so kind, I did not like to refuse. But I did not stop to think you might prefer not to be bothered.''

''It's not that, Anne. It's only that I've been very happy with just the two of us here at Honeywell House—so happy that I tend to resent anyone else breaking in on our happiness, I suppose. But of course it was bound to happen sooner or later.'' James smiled at her. ''It's only right you should make friends and take your proper position in society. I will endeavor to accept that fact with true husbandly resignation and not resent it when other people claim a share of your time and attention.''

Anne stored this speech in her heart and repeated it over to herself many times in the days that followed. *He is happy with me,* she told herself. *And he would rather it was just the two of us by ourselves. Does that not mean he loves me at least a little?* Anne thought it did, and her whole being sang with happiness as she made her preparations for Lady Meredith's party.

CHAPTER XIII

When James had told Anne he was very happy living with her at Honeywell House, he had been speaking no more than the truth. He was so happy that there were times when he wondered if it might not be tempting fate to exist in such a state of felicity. There lurked in his mind an unexpressed fear that fate, like death, might prefer a shining mark. If so, it seemed likely that some dreadful retribution must be waiting just over the horizon.

As yet, however, no retribution had appeared. He had been married to Anne a little over two months now, and it did not seem to him that earthly happiness could compass more than what he now possessed. He had a home set amid beautiful surroundings that was both elegant and extremely comfortable. He had work to give meaning to his days, yet not so much work as to make his days a burden. And he had Anne, the very best of wives, whom he now knew beyond doubt that he loved with all his heart.

She was so different from what he had expected. There were reserves of strength and passion within her that her frail appearance and timid manner would never have suggested. And yet in some strange way, James felt he had known in his heart all along that she possessed that strength and that passion. From the first moment he had looked in her eyes, something within him had responded to her in a deep and elemental way. What was more, he could not doubt that the response was reciprocal, in the physical sense at least. When he came to her at night, she received him with open arms, gave herself to him without reserve, and left him shaken afterward with a sense that he had just participated in something deeply spiritual as well as passionately physical.

Looking into her eyes at these moments, he was overcome by what he felt for her. Hundreds of times he had been on the verge of telling her that he loved her. Yet always, he had lost his courage at the last moment. The fact was, he not only wanted to tell her he loved her; he wanted to hear her say she loved him in return. And until he could be sure she did love him in return, he did not dare say those three fateful words.

Even after living with Anne for two months, James could not be sure how far she returned his feelings. He thought she was happy at Honeywell House; certainly she looked and seemed much happier than she had been at Court. Slender she still was, but no longer so dangerously frail that it seemed as though a breath would blow her away. Her color was healthier, and she walked with a lilt in her step that had not been there before. She could still be shy on occasion, but when something interested or excited her, she spoke with an energy and enthusiasm that he found endearing. And there could be no questioning her energy and enthusiasm in fulfilling her conjugal duties. James thought this a hopeful sign, but he did not dare read too much meaning into it.

In common with most men of his age and position, he had had a few more or less serious affairs with other women before marrying Anne. He was therefore aware that it was possible for a relationship to be physically gratifying without in any way stirring the deeper strata of one's feelings. He saw no reason why this should not hold true for women as well as for men. Anne might enjoy him as a lover and yet not have any real love for him. Alternately, she might love him with the wrong kind of love. A friendly or sisterly affection would be almost worse than nothing as far as James was concerned. Only a love as full and profound and passionate as his own would satisfy him.

Recognizing this truth, James shied away from the whole subject of love as from an area of danger. He was existing quite comfortably in the present situation, which allowed him to love Anne while hoping and dreaming she might someday return his love. But if ever the subject were brought out in the open, he had a presentiment that there would be no going back. The whole dynamic of their relationship would be changed for better or worse. And since the change might very well be for the worse instead of better, James elected to go on silently loving and waiting and hoping rather than declaring his feelings to Anne.

Yet in making this decision, he forgot the basic truth that change has a way of creeping into human affairs in spite of all attempts to exclude it. This fact was brought home to James on the night of Lord and Lady Meredith's party, when he first beheld Anne in her new dress.

She came slowly downstairs, smiling shyly at James, who was waiting in the hall below. He gazed at her dumbstruck. It had been a long time since he had seen her in formal dress. Since coming to Honeywell House she had worn mainly light muslins and gauzes that were suited to the season and to the informality of country living. Now he beheld her in a rich gown of aquamarine brocade worn over a petticoat of white satin embroidered in silver. The cut of the gown gave her slender figure a fairylike grace, and its color exactly matched her eyes, making their extraordinary beauty even more striking. It also set off her silvery hair and fair complexion. Indeed, it seemed to James that she glowed with an inner radiance: a radiance that reminded him in some indefinable way of moonlight. Before he had well considered, he opened his lips and spoke. "Anne!" he said. "By the gods, but you are beautiful!"

Anne gave him an amused look, which gradually changed to a different kind of look. "Thank you," she said, after a moment's pause. "You are looking very fine yourself this evening, James."

It was, as Anne thought, an understatement. James was wearing black evening clothes whose tailored elegance set off to perfection his tall, well-made figure. His hair, brushed ruthlessly back from his forehead, gleamed golden in the candlelight. She was sure he must be the best-looking gentleman at the party that night, and the thought brought with it a thrill of pride mingled oddly with a sense of pain.

I don't deserve him, she told herself. *He is so strong and true and handsome. Why, he might have married the greatest lady in the kingdom, and she would have counted herself lucky. But he married me—me, Anne Barrington, with nothing in the world to recommend me. And I love him, God help me.*

Then James smiled and said, "Shall we go out to the carriage?" and the moment passed. Anne smiled and nodded, and a few minutes later they were in the carriage and on their way to the Abbey.

The Abbey was a larger house than Honeywell House, built of the same indigenous gray stone. As soon as Anne passed though its doors, she felt a strange electricity in the atmosphere. It was an electricity that seemed to promise that this would be no ordinary night. Once again Anne felt a premonitory thrill. But a moment later Lady Meredith and Lady O'Reilly came hurrying over to her, and she forgot all else in the pleasure of seeing her friends again.

"I must introduce you to my husband," she told them, and proceeded to make introductions. Both ladies professed themselves delighted to meet James and beckoned their own respective spouses over to meet him, too.

Anne shook hands with Lord Meredith, a gentleman for whom the expression "tall, dark, and handsome," might have been coined, and with Sir Terrence O'Reilly, a less conventionally handsome man whose wit and charm more than made up for any irregularity of feature. Both men declared themselves pleased to meet Anne and engaged her to dance with them later in the evening. She was pleased by this attention, though certain that it was accorded her merely because she was guest of honor. To be sure, she thought she looked well that evening— extremely well for her—but she could not believe her own modest charms would have merited so much as a look from either gentleman when their own wives were so abundantly more worth looking at.

Lady Meredith wore a toilette of apricot silk trimmed

with Brussels lace, while Lady O'Reilly was dazzling in white taffeta shot with gold. Anne regarded them a trifle wistfully, envying them their height and figures and striking looks. Yet she could not really be jealous of them. Beautiful they might be, with handsome and charming husbands, but she, Anne, was married to James, Earl of Westland. And as the wife of James, Earl of Westland, she reckoned she had nothing to envy in any lady alive.

It was James who led Anne out for the first dance. She smiled up at him radiantly as he led her out onto the floor. A gentleman standing nearby took one look at her and remarked audibly to his neighbor, "Pretty little thing, ain't she? Countess of Westland, y'know. I'm demmed if I don't envy the earl."

"Jove, yes," said his neighbor with enthusiasm. "By Jove, yes, he's to be envied all right. A regular pocket Venus, by Jove."

Anne, on the dance floor, choked back an incredulous giggle. "How ridiculous," she said. "Me, a Venus? *Me?*"

James looked down at her. "Why not?" he said softly. "He was right about the other. I *am* to be envied, and I am very well aware of it."

Anne was silenced. The music began, and she and James began to go through the movements of the dance. All the while she looked up at James, and he looked back at her. Once more Anne was conscious of something electrical in the atmosphere. It was an anticlimax when, as they came off the floor, she saw Isabel Wrexford glance toward her and then remark in a stage whisper to a neighbor, "She doesn't look much of a countess, does she? I don't suppose her husband thinks so, either. You observe he spoke hardly a word to her the whole dance."

James's hand on Anne's arm tightened. "A singularly

stupid observation," he murmured in Anne's ear. "Who is that young lady, Anne? Ought I to know her?"

Anne explained who Isabel was. James, who had already heard the story of the Wrexford and Mabberly ladies' disastrous call, smiled grimly.

"So that's it," he said. "I should say myself that Miss Wrexford has no room to criticize any woman's appearance. That dress she is wearing looks like nothing on earth."

Anne, surveying Isabel's overtrimmed dress of virulent green and bilious yellow, could only agree. "And who is she to presume what I think about my wife?" said James, casting another look of disfavor at Isabel. "I have a good mind to go and tell her to keep her observations to herself unless she can do a better job of observing. To conclude I do not care for my wife simply because I do not babble like a brook to her the whole time we are dancing!"

Anne smiled. "It was a stupid remark to make," she agreed.

"Not merely stupid but calumnious. As I say, I have half a mind to go and tell her so."

Anne was not sure from James's manner whether he was joking or not. She shook her head, giving him a reassuring smile. "It doesn't matter," she said. "You had better not speak to her, James. It would probably shock her more than my performance with the butterfly net."

"Do her good to be shocked," said James darkly, but then he smiled at Anne. "However, now I know what conclusions weak minds will draw, I can take steps to amend my behavior. Will you dance with me again, my lady? This time, I promise to chatter enough to satisfy the harshest critics."

Anne agreed, and they took the floor once more.

As promised, James kept up a constant flow of conversation throughout the whole dance. "A good party," he said, looking around him. "Apart from Miss Wrexford, I have encountered nobody this evening whom I am not inclined to like."

"Yes, they all seem pleasant people," agreed Anne.

"Still, at the moment, I could wish them all to perdition," continued James. "Because they prevent me from doing what I would really like to do."

"What is that?" said Anne, looking at him in surprise.

"Kiss you, of course," he returned, looking down at her steadily. "And I tell you, I am tempted to do it, party or no party. At the very least, it would give Miss Wrexford something to talk about that is really to the point."

Anne gave an involuntary giggle. "It would at that," she agreed. "But you mustn't kiss me just to shock Isabel, James. It would cause an awful scandal."

"Who said I would kiss you just to shock Isabel? Shocking her would only be an incidental benefit. My real motivation would be what it always is, the pleasure of kissing you." James looked down at her. "The chief pleasure of my life, as it were."

Anne could feel her color heightening. "It is the pleasure of my life, too, James," she said softly.

"Then what a pity that that pleasure should have to be deferred! But it is as I have said before: a pleasure deferred is twice enjoyed. Enjoyed once in anticipation, you know, and once in actuality."

There was something in his eye that made Anne suspect he was not talking only about kissing. "Indeed," she said demurely.

"Indeed, yes," said James. The dance had just come to an end, and as he and Anne came off the floor he caught her hand in his, raised it to his lips, and kissed it. Then, turning it palm uppermost, he kissed it again, a much slower and more deliberate kiss that sent a tingle down Anne's spine. "Until later," he said, and the words were a promise.

Lord Meredith came up just then, seeking Anne as his partner in the set that was forming. She bade James adieu regretfully and went to take her place on the floor with her new partner.

For the rest of the evening Anne danced first with one gentleman and then with another. Some of her partners were better dancers than others, but not one failed to compliment her on her own dancing. "Light as a feather, by Jove," declared one gentleman enthusiastically—he happened to be the same gentleman Anne had overheard complimenting her earlier. "Like a jolly piece of thistle-down, don't you know."

"Thank you," said Anne politely. In truth, she scarcely heard the gentleman's compliments, for her eyes were on James, who was standing across the room in conversation with Sir Terrence O'Reilly. Anne had seen James dancing earlier with his hostess and with Lady O'Reilly, but in general he had seemed to prefer talking to dancing. Anne was just as glad of this, for it had cost her a pang to see him dance with any woman other than herself. She knew this was an irrational attitude, for both the women in question were her friends, and she herself had danced with nearly a dozen other men during the course of the evening. But on the subject of James she could not be wholly rational.

Thoughts of her husband absorbed Anne so deeply that she had little attention for outward things. When one of her partners tried to flirt with her in a small way, she merely glanced at him and smiled, leading him to declare later that Lady Westland was a maddening coquette who could slay a man with a single glance of her glorious eyes. Indeed, the general opinion among the company was that Anne's manners were very soignée and self-possessed, as befitted one who had been a Lady-in-Waiting to the Queen. As far as her appearance was concerned, it was generally conceded that she was not beautiful, but almost everyone agreed in thinking her very pretty and taking. Those few guests who disagreed, such as Isabel Wrexford, were held to be merely jealous.

"And it's no wonder if Isabel ain't fond of the new Lady Westland," said one gentleman, who had drunk enough champagne punch to loosen his tongue. "It's common knowledge that as soon as the earl came into his property, Isabel and her mother did their level best to get the *entrée* at Honeywell House. One of my grooms has a sister in service there, and she told him that the first time Lord Westland came down to visit his new property there wasn't a day when Isabel and her mother didn't call on some pretext or other. Oh, aye; it's a new thing to have ladies calling on the gentlemen, but they dressed it up as well as they could by saying they'd come to offer the earl preserves, or garden produce, or extra servants to get the house in order. But they ended up looking no-how, because he wouldn't see 'em: just sent his servants to say thank you, or no thank you, and kept himself to himself. And then only a few weeks later he appears with his bride—a girl a devil of a lot prettier than Isabel ever was, and one of the Queen's own women, to boot—and that put her nose out of joint properly. No wonder if she's a trifle vindictive."

Anne was certainly aware of Isabel's spite, though not of the reason behind it. She knew that Isabel had repeated to numerous people the story of their first encounter,

exaggerating it to make Anne seem even more of a hoyden
than she had appeared on that occasion. But Anne was
not unduly troubled by this talk. She knew she was not
a hoyden, and she felt certain that her appearance and
manners that evening must put to flight the greater part
of such allegations. Of course there would be those who
chose to believe them anyway, but such persons would
have been prepared to believe the worst of her in any
case.

The majority of the guests seemed almost ridiculously
reverential of her positions both past and present. As a
countess, she was bowed and curtsied to and given the
precedence in everything. As an ex-Lady-in-Waiting, she
was asked respectful questions about the Queen and Princesses and her years at Court. In the past, she had found
social occasions an ordeal because of her shyness and
inability to make small talk, but now her position was
unexpectedly made easy. People did not expect a countess
to be chatty. She had only to answer their questions as
well as she could, and if her answers were brief and to
the point, it was taken as a sign of dignity quite in keeping
with her position.

By the time the party came to a close at last, some
hours after midnight, Anne had found her feet in Langton
Abbots society. She had taken the floor with a dozen
different partners and been roundly praised for the grace
of her dancing. She had spent time chatting with Lady
Meredith and Lady O'Reilly and was now faster friends
with them than ever. She had survived introductions to
dozens of people and had held her own when obliged to
make conversation with them, and now she had the pleasure of leaving the party in a blaze of triumph and on the
arm of her own husband.

''Good evening! Good evening!'' she said, bowing and

smiling as she and James made their way toward the door. They had already tendered their thanks to Lord and Lady Meredith and said good night to Sir Terrence and Lady O'Reilly. Once outside, James took her arm in a slightly more possessive grip as he assisted her into the waiting carriage.

It was a beautiful night, with a star-spangled sky and a full moon hanging low on the western horizon. The air was neither warm nor cool, but that perfect temperature that feels merely comfortable to the skin. Anne leaned back against the squabs of the carriage with a sigh of mingled relief and gratification. James sat down beside her and sighed likewise. "A good party," he said, turning his face to look at her.

"A good party," agreed Anne.

James ran a finger lightly along her cheek. "But I'm glad it's over," he said. "Although a pleasure deferred may be a pleasure twice enjoyed, there comes a time when deferment is no pleasure at all, but merely an exercise in frustration." He leaned forward and kissed Anne on the lips.

Anne shivered at the touch of his mouth on hers. James moved closer to her on the seat, slipping an arm around her shoulders. Anne turned to face him, and he drew her against him, his hands molding her body against his as he kissed her. Anne sighed again as his mouth took possession of hers. She felt the familiar sensation of melting within her, as the touch of his mouth spread its magic through her whole body. All of her seemed on fire with longing for his kiss, his caress. When presently one of his hands slipped to stroke her breast through the fabric of her dress, she caught her breath sharply and shut her eyes at the intensity of the sensation.

"Anne," whispered James, trailing his lips across her face and making the word itself a caress.

Anne shifted her body so as to insinuate herself yet closer within James's arms. "I don't think—however can I wait until we get home?"

James gave a reckless laugh deep within his throat. "Why need we wait?"

Anne took this as mere teasing. "We will be home in a few minutes," she said with a sigh. "Only a few minutes, but it will seem like an eternity."

"Too long an eternity for me," said James. "I've waited all evening, and I'm damned if I'll wait a minute longer." Letting down the window, he called to the coachman. "John! Lady Westland and I have decided that rather than go directly home, we would prefer to do a little sightseeing on the way. Just drive around for a while—by way of Wybolt, perhaps. That ought to be a nice little expedition for us."

"You wish to go to Wybolt, my lord?" came the coachman's incredulous voice. "At this time of night?"

"Yes, we have a fancy to see Wybolt by moonlight," said James firmly. "Or rather Lady Westland does. And you know a lady's fancies in these matters must be humored. Don't bother to spring the horses," he added as an afterthought.

The coachman muttered something in reply and slowed the horses to a walk. Anne was shaking with silent giggles as James closed the window. "James, how can you?" she whispered. "He will think I have gone mad."

"What if he does? Besides, it was you who said you couldn't wait until we got home. This way you won't have to." James then vanquished all further arguments by pulling Anne into his lap and kissing her with devastating thoroughness.

By the time he was done, Anne was in a state of willing submission. She made no protest when he began to unbutton the pearl buttons that closed the corsage of her dress. The chemise beneath he proceeded to get out of the way by the simple expedient of wrenching it from her shoulder. There was a sound of rending fabric, and Anne gave a little yelp of protest, but again James silenced her with a kiss. "Damn it, what's the use of being a wealthy man if you can't destroy a few of your wife's clothes now and then?"

"No use," said Anne meekly, and shut her eyes as his mouth trailed down the bare skin of her chest. When his lips closed over her nipple she stiffened, then went limp with a deep sigh.

For a long time there was no sound in the carriage except Anne's ragged breathing. When she began to make little half-protesting noises and turn from side to side, James released her breast, knelt on the floor of the carriage in front of her, and began to lift up her skirts.

Anne shut her eyes, feeling his mouth caress the most intimate parts of her. The insinuating warmth and wetness of his tongue drove her to a frenzy wherein she called out his name again and again. Just when she thought she could bear no more of such delicious torment, she felt her body soar aloft on a wave of pleasure that rose swiftly to dizzying heights, then fell just as dizzyingly. Anne was left weak and gasping for breath and only remotely conscious of any reality save the pleasure he had just given her.

Dimly she was aware of James rising from his kneeling posture. She turned her head to look at him, then held out her arms to him. He came to her, crushing her against him. Anne shut her eyes. She could feel his desire for her, not only in the hard pressure of his sex between her legs, but in the urgency of his kiss and the eagerness of his hands as he threw back her skirts and unfastened the buttons of his own garments. Anne opened her eyes. James's eyes were only inches away, burning down into hers. Anne looked at him, and as she did so she felt him entering her. Her own eyes flickered, and she saw the fire leap higher in his.

She felt him drive into her again, and again her eyes half closed. James's eyes were fixed and intent. They held her own as he made love to her, and the intimacy of that gaze heightened the sensations his body aroused in hers. Anne felt as if they were not two bodies but one, joined and inseparable. Their pleasure was likewise inseparable. She could not witness his own urgency without feeling her own intensified, while her every move and moan and sigh seemed to feed his eagerness to a positive frenzy. Anne could feel the pressure building. When at last that pressure reached its intolerable peak and she was lifted aloft on a wave of pure pleasure, she saw the same pleasure in James's eyes.

To her surprise, she found her face was wet with tears. James took her face between his hands and kissed them tenderly away. He then folded her in his arms, and Anne shut her eyes once more, rejoicing in the warmth and security those arms offered. But after a minute, as from far off, she heard his voice speaking.

"Anne?"

"Yes," said Anne, tilting her face up to look at him.

He looked down at her a long moment. Then he sighed and drew her more tightly against him with a convulsive movement. "Nothing," he said. "It's nothing."

Anne continued to look at him. "I don't think it's nothing, James," she said softly. "What is it?"

Again James regarded her. His mouth opened, then

closed again. For the final time that evening, Anne felt a premonitory thrill. *He is trying to say he loves me,* she told herself. "Yes," she said aloud, her voice eager. "I know—I know!"

James regarded her for a moment in silence. His expression was frankly bewildered. But then it kindled into a glowing smile. "I'll be damned," he said, and embraced Anne with a fervor that made her squeak. "Witch," he whispered in her ear. Anne lay with her head against his chest, listening to the beat of his heart and experiencing the most sublime and perfect happiness. After a moment, however, James put a hand under her chin and tilted up her face to look at him.

"And you, Anne?" he said. "Do you feel the same?"

"Yes, of course," said Anne simply.

"Yes, of course," repeated James in bemusement. "Of course."

Anne reached up and kissed him. "Tell the coachman to drive a little faster, James," she said. "He may as well take us directly home. I no longer have a fancy to see Wybolt by moonlight after all."

CHAPTER XIV

The rest of that night passed like a dream for Anne. She knew at some point that she and James must have straightened their disarrayed garments in order to exit the carriage, and she could just recall that once they were at Honeywell House, they had gone upstairs to their own rooms, taken their clothes all off again, and made love until the sun was peeping over the eastern horizon. But it was the recollection of the lovemaking and not the intermediary steps that stayed in her memory.

This was not surprising. The discovery that their love was mutual had given to their lovemaking a drive and passion that it had hardly seemed to lack before. But to Anne, looking into James's eyes and feeling the warmth and strength and pure masculine vitality of his body as he took possession of her own, there was a new and mystical element to their union. She had the sense that time had been stayed in its course—that the joining of their bodies, pleasurable as it was, was yet only symbolic of some joining on a deeper level. It was almost as though, in that moment, they had achieved something remarkably like immortality.

Such were Anne's impressions afterward, when she awoke to find James still lying atop her and still, she realized with bemusement, in situ. She had no complaint to find with this, but the weight of his sleeping body atop hers was not strictly comfortable. In point of fact, she could hardly breathe. Yet she did not like to disturb him and did her best to make do with shallow breaths as she lay with him in her arms. Presently he stirred and rolled over of his own accord. Anne drew a deep breath of relief, but her relief was mingled with regret. She felt as though James's withdrawal, unconscious as it had been, had somehow signaled the end of the night—the most magical night of her life. She was just reflecting on this fact, while reflecting also that she ought to get up and dress, when she abruptly fell asleep again.

When she awoke a second time, the morning was far advanced. Anne had a strong suspicion that it was no longer morning at all, but rather early afternoon. She sat up, rubbing her eyes and looking about her. James was no longer there, and for a moment she felt defrauded. Then she espied a note lying on the pillow beside her. Anne picked it up and read:

Dearest Wife,
You can't think what a wrench it is to leave you, but I am obliged to honor the appointment I made yesterday to meet with my bailiff today at noon. I'll look forward to seeing you at dinner.

All my love,

James

Anne looked a long time at the note, and especially at the final salutation. Then she got out of bed and put it away in the papier mâché box on her dressing table where she kept her most precious things.

Anne kept herself reasonably busy that day, though not so busy that she did not have plenty of time to think of all that had happened the night before. She did the flowers in the downstairs rooms, went for a walk, hunted a few grasshoppers, and paid a visit to the spider in the conservatory. After doing this, she found it was late enough to justify changing for dinner. She had just reached the foot of the main staircase when she heard James call her name.

"Yes?" she said, spinning around eagerly. "I did not know you had gotten back."

"Yes, I returned almost an hour ago," he said gravely. "Would you mind coming to my study for a minute, Anne? I want to—*need* to talk to you."

Anne was surprised by his manner and also a little hurt. Anything more different from the ardent and impassioned lover he had been last night could not have been imagined. Indeed, there was a chill in his manner that filled her with apprehension. What could have happened in such a short time to change his manner toward her so completely?

But perhaps it hasn't anything to do with me, Anne tried to reassure herself. *He might have gotten bad news about some investment, or about one of his other properties. Or perhaps he is merely feeling unwell or tired. He certainly has every justification for feeling tired, for he can't have gotten more than an hour or two of sleep last night.*

But though Anne did her best to dismiss her fears in this manner, she could not rid herself of a feeling that there was something more personal in James's coldness

than illness, disappointment, or fatigue. With a growing
sense of unease, she followed James into the study where
he transacted his estate business. Her sense of unease
grew deeper as James pulled the door shut behind her
and turned the key in the lock. Yet when he spoke, his
words were the very last she expected to hear.

"Anne," he said, "I owe you an apology."

Anne looked at him blankly. "An apology?" she said.
"For what?"

"For many things, it seems. But this will do to begin
with." He handed her a letter that was lying atop his
desk.

Anne looked at it in bewilderment. It was a single sheet
that had been folded over in the usual manner and sealed
with a wafer. The wafer had been broken, however, and
the sheet was crumpled, as though it had been crushed
at one time and then an attempt been made to smooth it.
Anne noted all these details, then looked at James. "I
don't understand," she said. "Why are you giving me
this?"

"Because it is yours," said James. "It was addressed
to you, but somehow it got put with my letters instead.
And before I realized the mistake, I opened it and—and
read it."

Anne saw, or thought she saw, the trouble. She gave
a relieved laugh. "That's nothing to apologize for," she
said. "Truly, I don't mind if you read all my letters,
James." She gave him a warm smile.

James did not return it. "I think you would rather I
had not read this one," he said. "Indeed, I beg you will
believe it was an error, Anne. If I had known—" He
broke off and turned away as though unable to continue.

More puzzled than ever, Anne looked again at the letter.
It was indeed addressed to her, its superscription written

in a masculine hand that seemed strangely familiar. She unfolded the letter and began to read.

"Sweetest and most obliging Anne," was the opening salutation. An icy chill swept suddenly through Ann's veins. In that instant she knew fully what was meant by the expression "to have one's blood run cold."

Of course the handwriting had looked familiar. It ought to have looked familiar, for she had received at least a hundred notes in that hand in the days before she had left the Court. It was Timothy who had written the letter. And as Anne's eye swept each damning paragraph, she found herself shaking as though the chill in her blood had permeated her very bones.

Timothy, it appeared, was not going to marry Miss Duval after all. They had been engaged briefly, but then the engagement had unaccountably been broken off. "Unaccountably" was Timothy's term, though Anne, reading between the lines, thought it had probably come about through a desire on the part of Miss Duval's friends and relatives to save her from a mésalliance. Timothy did not touch on that, however, but merely said that the breaking of his engagement had left him in an awkward spot. The creditors who had been silent when he was engaged to an heiress were now all clamoring to be paid. Since Miss Duval had broken with him and taken her thirty thousand pounds with her, there was no possibility of his being able to meet his obligations.

Here Timothy became eloquent. If some kind and generous friend did not come to his assistance immediately, he must either flee England or face the horror of debtors' prison. And in the past, what friend had ever been kinder and more generous to him than Anne? And now that she was newly endowed with wealth and position, she was even more peculiarly fitted to assist him. It would mean nothing to her to lend him a few thousand pounds for old times' sake.

There was more in this vein, plenty more of it. Timothy did not go so far as to hint at blackmail, but he did say that he thought his and Anne's past relations entitled him to consideration at her hands. She would naturally be loath to have her husband know exactly how intimate she had been with him, Timothy, but that was irrespective of the question. The question was whether or not she would lend him three thousand pounds. Timothy was confident she would feel no hesitation about parting with so trifling a sum. He had been assured that Lord Westland was a wealthy man with many holdings both in England and abroad—

Nauseated, Anne put down the letter. She could feel James looking at her, but it was quite beyond her power to meet his eyes. From being cold, she had suddenly gone fiery hot. Shame enveloped her like a garment. Her cheeks were on fire; her hands were moist and trembling, and she wanted nothing so much as to die that instant rather than face the consequences of her own actions.

But death is rarely so obliging as to rescue one in such situations. Anne's heart might be twisted with shame and misery, but it continued to beat steadily. The minutes dragged on, and the silence between her and James grew and grew, becoming increasingly more formidable in its proportions. At last it came to the point when Anne felt it necessary to say something, anything, to break that dreadful silence. "Oh, James," she said with a catch of her breath. "What must you think of me?"

There was a pause before James answered. "What ought I to think?" he said.

There was bitterness in his voice. Anne threw him a quick glance and then wished she had not. With a faltering voice, she spoke again. "Indeed I have done very wrong. You have every right to despise me."

There was another noticeable pause, and then James spoke again. "I don't despise you, Anne," he said.

"But you must," said Anne. Tears sprang up in her eyes as she repeated, "You must despise me. I ought to have told you the truth before now. You had a right to know it before you married me."

James looked at her, then looked away. "There's no point in discussing it now," he said. "What's done is done."

"I am so sorry." Anne could hardly speak through her tears. "What a mess I have made of things! But I will try to make it right now, if I can. If you wish to divorce me—"

She broke off, for James was staring at her. "Divorce you?" he said. "*Divorce you?* Are you saying—are you saying you want a divorce, Anne?"

"No!" said Anne. "I don't want a divorce. But I can see that *you* are quite justified in wanting one, after the way I have behaved."

"But you don't want one?" repeated James. "Forgive me for being persistent, Anne, but I must know your feelings in this matter. It appears from that letter"—he glanced at the letter in Anne's hands, then away again— "it appears that there is a long-standing attachment between you and the gentleman who wrote it. I do not know what circumstances originally conspired to separate you, but it appears there is no impediment to your marrying him now—at least, no impediment that a divorce would not remedy. If your wish is to be married to him instead of me—"

Here Anne broke in aghast. "I, marry Timothy?" she said. "Good God, no, James! How can you think it?"

"I don't know what to think," said James. There was another long silence. At last Anne plucked up courage enough to speak again.

"Indeed, I do not want a divorce, James," she said. "It is only that I cannot imagine your wishing to remain married to me, now you know the truth."

James made an impatient gesture. "Let us set my wishes aside for the moment," he said. "What do *you* wish, Anne? You say you do not want a divorce, but you will have to deal with this situation in some way. At the very least"—he glanced at the letter again, and there was scorn in his voice as he went on—"at the very least, you will have to decide whether you mean to honor the gentleman's pleas for financial assistance."

"Certainly not!" said Anne indignantly. "I would not give him a penny of your money, James. How could you think it?"

"I tell you I don't know what to think," said James. "It's obvious from the letter that you were once deeply attached to the gentleman who wrote it. How could I know what you would or would not do for him?"

Anne was silent a moment. "It's true I was once attached to him," she admitted at last. "But all that is over now, James." She threw a fleeting glance at James's face.

"Indeed," said James, and there was irony in his voice. "The gentleman seems to think otherwise, to judge from his letter."

"His letter! He was wrong ever to write such a letter. Such a *contemptible* letter," said Anne passionately. "How could he have thought I would give him money? And especially after the way he—" She broke off with a flush staining her cheeks, but then took up speech again immediately, speaking slower but with no less passion than before. "I tell you, James, I wouldn't give Timothy a penny, not if he were starving in the street. But I cannot help wondering what he will do when I refuse. You know he could cause a great deal of trouble if he wanted to. For myself I do not care, but such trouble would affect you as well as me. I could not bear to cause you any more pain, James."

James glanced at her. His face was unmoved, but when he spoke his voice was a degree less cool than before. "If that's your only concern, then leave it to me," he said. "I'll write the gentleman myself. I'll let him know I am fully apprised of the situation, and that if he ever so much as mentions your name in public again, let alone tries to extort money from you, it will be at his own peril."

He held out his hand for the letter. Anne gave it to him doubtfully. "This is asking a great deal of you, James," she said. "I cannot like to involve you in this matter."

"I already am involved, it seems," said James grimly. But his face softened as he looked down at Anne. "Never mind, Anne," he said. "We all make mistakes."

Anne shook her head. "Not like this," she said, her voice choked with tears once more. "Never like this, James."

"I don't know. It seems to me that in this affair, your mistake has been less grievous than mine." And with these words he left the room, carrying the letter in his hand.

CHAPTER XV

In after days, James's words haunted Anne until she would have welcomed oblivion as a gift. *It seems to me that in this affair, your mistake has been less grievous than mine.*

Of course she could not doubt what those words meant. They meant that James felt he had made a mistake in marrying her. The idea that he regretted their marriage was easily the most bitter knowledge that Anne had ever possessed.

There were times when the bitterness choked her until she wondered if she could bear to go on living. Her infatuation with Timothy had ruined her life at Court; now it had ruined the new and beautiful life that had miraculously risen like a phoenix out of the ashes of the old. If Timothy had been where Anne could reach him, she felt she could have slain him where he stood. But though such an act might have been a relief to her feelings, she recognized clearly that it would have done no good. James knew the truth about her now. He knew that she had once loved another man—and not merely loved him, but indulged in intimate relations with him. The fact that she had not enjoyed those relations at all made not a particle of difference.

Neither did it make any difference that she loved James with a love against which her infatuation with Timothy was like a raindrop against the waters of the Pacific. James would never believe she loved him now, even if she summoned up the courage to tell him so. Why should he believe her? She had deceived him in other matters. He knew she had deceived him, and he would never trust her again. Nor could he love her any longer, if indeed he had ever loved her at all. All that must have been destroyed in the shock of disillusionment he had felt on reading Timothy's letter.

So Anne told herself, and that knowledge was the bitterest of the bitter things she had to bear in those difficult days. The love she had wanted more than anything in life had been within her grasp, and she had lost it forever. James would never tell her he loved her now. He would never come closer to it than the written word "love" that he had put in his note. Anne felt that if he could, he probably would have taken back that word and that note after learning the truth about her. But this he could not do, for Anne had the note and was not about to let it go. It was her most treasured possession, and she clung to it fiercely, even though it was a possession that now brought her more pain than comfort.

Painful as it was, it was something—a spar saved from a shipwreck of her hopes and dreams. It truly seemed to Anne in these days that her hopes and dreams were thoroughly shipwrecked. In the wake of Timothy's letter, her former happy relations with James had been wiped out almost as though they had never been.

Everything was changed. Nothing was as it had been when she and James had first arrived at Honeywell House. There was none of the joking, none of the camaraderie, no sweet moments of intimacy such as they had once enjoyed. It was not that James had become suddenly harsh and discourteous; on the contrary, he was if anything more polite to her than he had been before. But it was the politeness of a stranger, a chill courtesy that set Anne at a distance and would not let her come near.

Anne felt how impossible it was ever to overcome such a barrier. As much as she had always hated emotional scenes, she found herself wishing now that James had been the kind of man to shout and storm and exhaust his feelings in a fit of rage. If he had been, there might have been some chance that he would have worked through his anger and come around to regard Anne with something like affection once again. But what hope could there be when his only speech to her was to offer her wine at meals or to formally inquire whenever he went out if there were any commissions he could perform for her?

Anne felt there was no hope. Their marriage was now not even a marriage of convenience, but only an empty charade. Night after night, as she lay alone in the bed where she and James had made love so many times, she wondered why he did not simply divorce her and be done with it. Dreadful as such an ordeal would have been, she felt it would have been less painful than to go on living a life from which all hope of happiness had fled.

Yet James did not seem to want a divorce. He had asked her if she wanted one, but when Anne had assured him she did not, he had dismissed the subject with a finality that kept Anne from ever referring to it again. It was remotely possible that if she had insisted long enough and loudly enough, she might have brought James around to her point of view, but she felt she was in no position to insist on anything at the moment. Besides, divorce proceedings would be almost as unpleasant for him as for her, given all the scandal and publicity that would be their result. If James was willing that she should remain his wife, Anne felt she ought to be grateful for his forbearance, even if this actually meant more suffering for her rather than less.

At any rate, there was no further need to worry about Timothy. Anne never knew exactly what James had said and done about Timothy, but she knew the situation had been conclusively resolved. A few weeks after her painful scene with James, Anne received another letter, this one from one of the Royal Princesses with whom she had been corresponding since her marriage. Among other titbits of Court gossip, Her Highness had written that Timothy had abruptly thrown over his position at Court and gone abroad—it was presumed to escape his debts. So Anne felt she had nothing further to worry about in that quarter, but since she had so much to worry about in every other, the relief Her Highness's news afforded her was scant.

Indeed, at this period Anne felt as though everything in life were conspiring to make her miserable. The weather had turned rainy, preventing her from taking her daily airings and making the atmosphere inside Honeywell House as cold and gloomy as it was outside. Then the cook gave notice without warning, leaving Anne and Mrs. Rhodes to frantically scour the neighborhood for a replacement. They eventually located an elderly woman who came with good references and seemed very competent, but her cooking did not agree with Anne as well as her predecessor's had done. Several times Anne was taken ill after eating, and only narrowly made it to her own bedchamber in time to avert public embarrassment.

As if all this were not bad enough, Anne's spider also chose this time to fall ill. At least Anne assumed it was ill, though she had no way of knowing what trouble really afflicted it. She was at first inclined merely to blame the weather. Not only did the constant rain make the conservatory colder and gloomier than usual, but it prevented her for several days from making her usual expedition in search of grasshoppers and crickets. She tried to make do with some black beetles collected from the cellar, but the spider seemed uninterested in these, so she resolved to wait until she could collect the food it preferred before trying to feed it again. But when, on the first sunny day that offered, she returned, bearing a jarful of grasshoppers, she found the spider still would not eat. It crouched motionless in a corner of its glasshouse, ignoring the grasshoppers leaping exuberantly around it and looking as dejected as a spider could possibly look.

"Oh dear!" said Anne. She felt the beginnings of tears prickling in her eyes as she picked up the tongs and began to remove the grasshoppers one by one. She was behaving like a fool, she told herself severely. It was ridiculous to cry because a spider would not eat a grasshopper. James would certainly laugh at her if he knew—assuming he still liked her well enough to laugh at her, and assuming he was here with her now, which he was not. These reflections made Anne's tears fall faster. She was sniffling and trying to wipe her eyes with her sleeve as she sought to corner a grasshopper that had escaped the glasshouse and was leaping wildly through the aisles of plants and trees when Joe Gardiner appeared on the scene.

"Got you, you rascal," he said, neatly capturing the fugitive. "There you go, my lady," he said, presenting it to Anne with a bow and broad grin. But his grin faded when he saw her tearstained face. " 'Ere, what's this?" he ejaculated. "What's the trouble, my lady?"

"Nothing," said Anne, sniffing harder than ever and trying to smile.

Mr. Gardiner was having none of such polite evasion. "*Something* must be the matter," he said, stationing himself in front of Anne and regarding her with a keen-eyed scrutiny. "Else you wouldn't be spouting tears. That gawd-awful spider of yours didn't bite you, did it?"

"No," said Anne indignantly. "Arachne never tries to bite me. She only bites grasshoppers and—and crickets and such things." Then, overcome by misery, she blurted out, "Oh, but Mr. Gardiner, she didn't even try to bite the grasshoppers today. I'm afraid something is wrong with her."

"Is that so?" said Mr. Gardiner. He walked over to the glasshouse to inspect the spider. "Looks a bit under the weather," he admitted after a moment's scrutiny. "You say you tried to feed 'er, and she wouldn't eat?"

"Not a single grasshopper," said Anne desolately. "And she ought to be very hungry, for it's been over a week since I was able to collect any food for her."

Mr. Gardiner looked again at the spider. "P'raps she's just not feeling peckish at the moment," he suggested, with the air of one offering a last-ditch excuse. "Might be all the rain we've had has thrown her off her feed. I tell you what: why don't you leave a hopper or two in with 'er and see if she takes 'em later? You can always take 'em out again if she doesn't eat 'em."

For want of any better plan, Anne agreed to try this. A single grasshopper was left in the spider's glasshouse, and Anne resolved to give her pet a full twenty-four hours to dispose of it. The next afternoon she came tiptoeing

in full of hope, only to see the spider still crouched dejectedly in the corner, and the grasshopper, very much alive,
cheerfully nibbling a leaf of one of its plants.

"Oh, no!" said Anne, dissolving into tears once more.
"Oh, no!" Groping for the tongs, she removed the grasshopper from the glasshouse, dropped it into the jam jar,
then sat down on the floor and began to cry.

She started out weeping for the spider, but once she had
begun, her tears encompassed every unjust, unpleasant,
unfortunate thing that had ever happened in the world.
She wept for the spider that would not or could not eat,
and for the grasshopper that was doomed to be eaten, if
not by the spider, then by some other predatory creature.
She wept for her parents, dead before their time and lying
all but forgotten in a lonely country churchyard. She wept
for the Princesses at Court, doomed to make marriages
of state with men they did not love; she wept for the mad
King in his strait waistcoat; for the unhappy Queen trying
to hold Court in a land where she was a foreigner; and for
the ladies and gentlemen forced to sacrifice their personal
lives for the privilege of waiting on both King and Queen.
Finally she wept for James, who had married her,
believing her to be a woman of honor and virtue, only
to have his life blighted by her betrayal.

So long and hard did Anne weep over this last tragedy
that she had no tears left for herself. Pitiful as her own
plight might be, she simply could not weep for it. She
sat silent and dejected for several minutes, her shoulders
still heaving and her face still wet from all the tears she
had shed. Then she stood up, shook out her skirts, put
away the tongs and grasshopper jar, and went slowly up
to her room.

The dressing bell rang while she was en route, so once
in her room she rang for Susan and set about changing

her dress and tidying her hair for dinner. She carefully avoided any glance at her own tear-swollen face in the glass. Susan noticed it, for she kept glancing at her mistress with a worried air, but Anne kept her remarks brief and to the point while the business of her toilette was going on, and the maid did not dare ask the questions that were obviously trembling on the tip of her tongue.

James was waiting downstairs in the drawing room to take Anne in to dinner. As usual he extended his arm to her, and as usual Anne accepted it with a word of thanks. She avoided looking at him as they went into the dining room, but she thought he looked at her several times. When they were seated at the table, she risked a glance at him and found he was regarding her with a look of concern.

"Anne," he said, "is something amiss?"

Anne looked at him, thinking what a ridiculous question it was. Of course there was something amiss. Everything was amiss, her relations with him most of all. But it was clearly impossible to tell him that, or indeed to make any honest answer. The butler was pouring the wine; the footmen were uncovering dishes on the table; and it was essential to behave with decorum. Decorum! Anne knew a sudden hatred for the word and all the repression and falsehood it symbolized. "No," she said in a thin voice. "Nothing is amiss, James."

He nodded, but she thought his eyes continued to rest on her at intervals through the meal. They began with mulligatawny soup, progressed to buttered crabs, went on to a loin of veal and grouse pie served with side dishes of French beans and potatoes, and finished with raspberry pudding and plum tart. Anne partook only sparingly of the food. She was still subject to queasy spells now and then, though in the last week or two she had noted with relief that her stomach seemed to be adapting to the new cook's regimen. Having finished a small serving of pudding, she began to rise from the table.

"Don't go yet, Anne," said James out of the blue.

Anne looked at him in surprise. He colored and glanced at the servants, who were just vanishing through the doorway with the dishes from the second course. When the door had closed behind them, James spoke again. "I need to talk to you, Anne," he said. "Talk to you privately, I mean. But perhaps it would be more comfortable if we both went into the drawing room. Should you have any objection?"

"No," said Anne. Her mind was buzzing with speculation about what James wished to talk about. Given her obsession with the subject of divorce, that was the first idea that sprang to mind, and she glanced anxiously at James's face as she accompanied him to the drawing room. There was no clue to be found there. His face was solemn and reserved, though also, Anne thought, slightly embarrassed-looking. That was consonant with a man about to discuss such a serious subject as divorce, but it might be equally consonant with other subjects as well.

In a state of suspense, Anne allowed James to assist her into one of the drawing room chairs. He then took a chair himself and sat regarding her with a look of indecision.

"What is it, James?" asked Anne, speaking in a small voice. Now that they had come to the point, she felt more apprehensive than eager to have the subject brought into the open.

James leaned forward, his face more solemn than ever. "Anne," he said, "I have just received a letter."

"A—a letter?" faltered Anne.

Immediately her thoughts flew to Timothy. Was it possible he was going to cause more problems? Something of her thoughts must have shown on her face, for James flushed and began to disclaim in a confused fashion. "Yes, a letter, but not—that's to say, it's a letter from my brother. My half brother, that is."

"Oh," said Anne with relief. "A letter from your half brother." She was too glad to know the letter was not from Timothy to feel anything but relief for a moment, but soon curiosity began to assert itself. "So your brother has written you?" she asked. "I remember your speaking about him before, a little. What has he to say?"

"First, he writes to congratulate me on my marriage." James's lip curled as he spoke these words. Anne, who had begun to feel a little better, was stricken by his evident contempt. Of course James could hardly feel happy at being congratulated on such a disastrous union as theirs had proved to be. But when James spoke again, it was evident that this was not the cause of his contempt at all. "Thomas makes a good pretense of wishing us both happy, but that's mere whitewash, of course. It doesn't suit his book at all that I should marry."

"Oh, yes, he is heir to the title after you, isn't he?" said Anne, with belated understanding.

"Yes, and to the estate as well. But he shan't get either one. At least not—" James glanced at Anne, then looked away quickly. "At least not until I die. And I don't intend to die early to oblige him, I can tell you that!"

"I should think not indeed," said Anne. She spoke with attempted cheer, but her heart sank. It was obvious from James's looks that he was thinking of the heir he had married her to obtain: the heir who would have defended his inheritance from his brother's encroachment. Given the current state of estrangement between him and Anne, no heir was ever now likely to appear. Anne went on, trying to keep her voice level. "What else does your brother say besides congratulating you on your marriage?"

"Why, that is what I wished to talk to you about. He proposes coming to visit us here at Honeywell House for a few weeks—not just him, but also his wife." Again James glanced at Anne, then looked away.

"Oh!" said Anne in bewilderment. "He proposes to come here with his wife? Well, that is very unexpected, to be sure, but I suppose there is no objection to it. Is there?"

"No—o—o," said James. He spoke the word rather doubtfully, however. "There is no objection unless *you* have one, Anne."

"I have one?" said Anne, genuinely amazed. "Why should I have any objection?"

Again James glanced at her, then looked away. "I don't know. If nothing else, it will mean a certain amount of extra work for you and the staff."

Anne was certain there was more James could have said on this subject if he had chosen. Apparently he did not choose to, however. The minutes ticked by in silence until Anne felt compelled to speak again.

"I don't mind the extra work," she said. "And it cannot be much extra work, only to feed and house a couple of extra people. Your brother has no children?"

"No children yet, so far as I know," said James. "But I haven't been in very close correspondence with him in recent years. Not since he and Kate were married."

Anne looked at him sharply. There was something in his manner of pronouncing his sister-in-law's name that made her prick up her ears. "Kate," she said. "Your brother's wife is named Kate?"

"Yes," said James briefly. Anne, looking at him closely, thought his color had risen.

"Were you acquainted with her before she and your brother were married?" she asked, drawing a bow at random.

"Yes," said James. "I was."

He got up very deliberately and went to the window. For a moment he stood there silently with his back to Anne, then spoke again without turning around. "I will give you Thomas's letter, Anne, and let you read it for yourself. It gives all the details as to when he and Kate mean to come and how long they intend to stay."

"Very well," said Anne. There was nothing else she *could* say. But she felt in her bones that the presence of Mr. and Mrs. Thomas Westland at Honeywell House was not going to make her already difficult existence any easier.

CHAPTER XVI

In the event, Anne's forebodings were well-founded. The first moment she set eyes on Kate Westland, she recognized her as yet another cross sent to try her.

In the first place, Kate and her husband made things difficult by arriving at Honeywell House a full day before they were expected. Anne, who was supervising the preparation of the guest rooms, heard the carriage in the drive and went to the window to see who it was. She expected it to be merely some neighbor paying a call, but when she observed the amount of baggage fastened on behind the carriage, some inkling of the truth began to dawn on her.

"Why, this looks like the Westlands now!" she exclaimed. "But how can that be? I am sure they wrote they were not coming until tomorrow. Otherwise I would have taken care that their rooms were cleaned and put in order before now."

The maids who had been cleaning the rooms merely looked at her blankly. Recollecting herself, Anne instructed them to finish their work as quickly as they could, then hurried out into the hall. She stopped briefly in her own room to smooth her hair and clothing. There was no time to redress her hair properly, or to change her dress as she would have liked if indeed this was James's brother and sister-in-law just arrived. But Anne was still by no means certain of her visitors' identity. She paused to take another look through the window to see if she could decide the matter one way or another.

A man and woman had just stepped down from the carriage and stood talking together as their baggage was unloaded. The man was large and bluff-looking, with light hair and a ruddy face. He was not so handsome as James; but Anne, looking at him, thought she could pick out a resemblance between him and her husband. This, then, was James's half brother Thomas. Having surveyed him curiously, Anne looked next at the lady beside him and felt all at once a "prickling in her thumbs."

Mrs. Thomas Westland was a tall woman with dark hair and a buxom figure. Anne was too far away to tell if she was handsome or not, but her experienced eye at once noted the extreme fashionableness of her sister-in-law's attire. Kate's French bonnet boasted a dozen curled ostrich plumes; her ruby red cloth pelisse was trimmed with large buttons, knots of ribbon, and strips of chinchilla fur; and despite the fact that it was a warm September day she had a cape of matching furs flung over her shoulders. She watched as the last of her baggage was placed on the ground, then turned to survey the façade of Honeywell House. Even from that distance, it was possible to discern something critical in her gaze. Anne was just reflecting on this with mild irritation when Kate suddenly raised her bonneted head and looked directly into Anne's eyes. For a startled moment Anne looked back at her. She then quickly stepped backward and let the curtain fall over the window, hiding her from view.

The retreat was pure instinct on Anne's part. But as soon as she had given in to it, she was sorry. She felt almost as though Kate had bested her in some contest, though that was absurd, of course. But absurd or not, Anne could not help wishing she had brazened it out at the window, rather than drawn away as though she had been caught out in a crime. After all, she had a perfect right to look through her own window if she chose.

In spite of these self-assurances, Anne could not rid herself of a feeling of gaucherie as she went down the stairs. Part of it, no doubt, was due to the fact that she was obliged to receive the visitors alone. James had driven over to Wybolt for the day, and Anne did not expect him back until nearly dinnertime. It would be for her to make his brother and sister-in-law welcome and to knit together as best she could those loose ends that still remained in the household, owing to the guests' early arrival.

"Haywood," she said, hailing the butler as she hurried toward the front door, "I believe Mr. and Mrs. Westland have arrived a day early. Will you please inform Cook and Mrs. Rhodes?"

The butler bowed. "Certainly, my lady," he said. "But would you not prefer I open the door to the visitors first, before going to the kitchens?"

"No, I'll open the door to Mr. and Mrs. Westland myself," said Anne grimly. "Just carry my message to Cook and Mrs. Rhodes, if you please. They need to know as soon as possible, so we can try to put together a dinner tonight that will not disgrace us all."

The butler bowed again in a manner that conveyed

clearly his feelings about guests who arrived twenty-four
hours in advance of their time. Anne, who heartily shared
these feelings, waited till he had gone, then went to the
door. She swung it open just as the lady and gentleman
were approaching the front steps.

"Welcome," she said, sweeping a curtsy. When they
had reached the top of the stairs, she ventured to smile
at them. "Have I the honor of addressing Mr. and Mrs.
Westland?"

" 'Deed and you have," said the man, returning her
smile. His resemblance to James was more pronounced
than ever at this close range, though his features were
coarser than James's and his manner of speaking less
polished. But there was a friendliness in his manner that
did much to atone for his lack of polish. Anne found
herself warming to him, though she was uneasily conscious that in doing so she was being disloyal to James.
In an effort to set aside this uncomfortable thought, she
switched her gaze to Kate Westland. Here, at least, she
need fear no partiality. Just looking at Kate's face with
its strong, handsome features and rich brunette coloring,
she felt such a wave of antagonism flood through her that
it took all her self-control to keep the smile on her face

Kate was smiling, too, yet it was a smile that struck
Anne as highly disagreeable. Instead of returning Anne's
curtsy, she thrust out her hand, obliging Anne to take and
shake it. Kate's hand clasp was strong as a man's, and
Anne winced as the rings were crushed into her fingers.
"And so you are Lady Westland?" said Kate. "I did not
look for you to open the door to us yourself. Even at
Four Oaks we keep servants enough to perform *that* task."

Anne opened her mouth to speak, but Thomas inter-
vened. "Why, I thought it very friendly of Lady Westland

to open the door to us herself," he said, smiling again at Anne. "A nice, homely touch, begad."

"At any rate, it was high time *somebody* opened the door to us," said Kate. "I was beginning to wonder if the house was deserted when no one came out to greet us."

"That is because we were not expecting you until tomorrow," said Anne. Try as she might, she could not keep a slight sharpness out of her voice. "If you had arrived tomorrow as you wrote you would, you would have found us better prepared for you."

Kate opened her bold dark eyes. "Did we take you unprepared? The fact is that after we had set out, Thomas and I found we could easily manage the journey in two days rather than three. We had no thought of putting you out, Lady Westland. As I told Thomas, with a household this size you ought to have no difficulty coping with any number of unexpected visitors. Why, even at Four Oaks, which is much smaller than *this* place, I make it a point to always have extra places laid at the table and a guest chamber prepared for just such an eventuality."

Anne could think of no answer to this, so she merely bowed. But in her heart, she reflected that she was already beginning to be tired of hearing about the way things were done at Four Oaks. "Do come in," she said. "I will order tea for us while the servants carry your bags to your rooms."

"So you *do* have servants," said Kate, as though this issue had really been in question. "Very well, let us have tea. I am quite parched with thirst."

Fuming silently, Anne led the way to the drawing room. Kate glanced around it and pronounced it a handsome room in its proportions, though its furnishings were sadly out of fashion compared to Four Oaks. "Yes, I have been told it is a trifle outmoded,'' said Anne shortly. "One of our neighbors recommended I have it redone in the Egyptian style.''

Kate laughed. "Not the Egyptian style, I beg of you! All that is quite exploded now. But there, I daresay you would not know it, living in an out-of-the-way place like Devon.''

"I lived in London until a few months ago,'' said Anne, and once again, she was unable to keep the sharpness out of her voice. "I don't suppose styles have changed as much as that since I left.''

This statement seemed to confound Kate briefly. But then she laughed again. "Oh, yes! To be sure, I had heard you were—what was it?—the Queen's dressing woman, or some such thing as that.''

"I was Keeper of the Queen's Robes,'' said Anne through her teeth. She could not doubt that Kate's words were a deliberate insult. The Queen's dressing woman might have the privilege of dressing the Queen, but her position was merely that of a servant, while the Keeper of the Robes was a position of high honor—in theory, at least. Nettled, Anne determined to get back some of her own. "But there, you could not be expected to know the difference,'' she told Kate in a commiserating voice. "I daresay you have little acquaintance with Royalty.''

This did succeed in silencing Kate, but not for long. "Where is James?'' she asked, looking around. "I would have expected to find him here with his bride. Don't tell me he is neglecting you so soon, Lady Westland? And you but married a few months!''

This was a blow below the belt for Anne, but she bore it without flinching. "Lord Westland has driven over to the nearby township to see about some business,'' she said. "He promised to return in time for dinner, however, so you will certainly see him then."

"I am looking forward to it. Dear James, how fond I am of him." Kate threw Anne a sly look out of the corner of her eye. "Though I was never so fond of him as he was of me. You knew, did you not, Lady Westland, that he used to be one of my beaux?"

Anne was saved answering by Thomas, who broke into the conversation with a broad grin on his ruddy face. "Ah, but then we was all your beaux, Kate," he said, surveying his wife fondly. "There wasn't a fellow in the county who wasn't mad about you."

"Yes, but James was more mad than most," said Kate, her eyes fixed meaningly on Anne. "When I told him I meant to marry you instead of him, Thomas, I assure you he grew quite frantic. I really thought for a moment he was going to do one of us an injury."

"James understood how it was," said Thomas, looking uncomfortable. "Only one of us could marry you, after all. It just happened to be me who was the lucky fellow and not him."

Kate gave a brittle laugh. She looked as though there was more she wanted to say, but in the end she merely asked Anne for a second cup of tea and drank it in silence, glancing around the drawing room with brooding dark eyes.

Her silence was a welcome respite for Anne. She had been surprised by Kate's words and greatly shocked, but it never occurred to her to doubt them. Too well she remembered James's reticence in speaking of Kate, and the resentment he seemed to bear toward his brother. Such a resentment was entirely natural under the circumstances Kate had outlined.

I can see how James might admire her, Anne admitted

to herself, surveying Kate's dark and vivacious face. *She is certainly very handsome. But what a disagreeable woman! She has done nothing but needle me ever since she arrived.*

As soon as the visitors had finished their tea, Anne rang for the housekeeper and bade her show them to their rooms. Ordinarily she would have performed this office herself, but as things stood now she felt she would rather delegate it to Mrs. Rhodes. *Kate will get no change out of her, at any rate,* Anne reflected with grim satisfaction. *Mrs. Rhodes will soon let her know that however things may be done at Four Oaks, they are done differently here at Honeywell House.*

Besides avoiding Kate's tongue, Anne had another reason for letting the housekeeper take charge of Kate and her husband. She divined that Kate would take great pains with her toilette for dinner that night in order to make an impression on James. Being a handsome woman, she would probably succeed, but Anne did not intend to let Kate have it all her own way. She herself might not be tall or handsome or buxom of figure, but she could dress well and make the most of her own attractions. *And I will wear the Westland family diamonds,* Anne told herself with satisfaction. *They're a bit much for a family dinner, but even so I need all the support I can get. I doubt Kate has such jewels, whatever else she may have at Four Oaks!*

But when Anne came down to the drawing room, resplendent in diamonds and pale green brocade, she saw Kate had taken a different tack altogether. Kate's white muslin dress was simple enough for a child to wear, and her only ornament was a red rose tucked among the dark coils of her hair. The austerity of this costume was a perfect foil for her rich coloring and lush figure.

Anne, looking at Kate, felt she had been bested once again. But she stiffened her spine and came forward into the room as though she were quite satisfied with herself and her own appearance. As she advanced, she was not entirely surprised to see James standing at Kate's elbow. She had purposely delayed her entrance into the drawing room so that she need not witness the first meeting between James and his former inamorata. Yet glad as she was to have missed it, Anne found herself wishing all the same that she knew how that meeting had gone.

"Ah, here is Anne," said James, as Anne came forward. "Now we can go in to dinner." Anne glanced at him quickly, thinking there was something like relief in his voice. But he had turned to Kate, offering her his arm, so Anne was obliged to take the arm of Thomas, who declared himself very happy to have such a charming partner.

"By Jove, don't you look pretty, Lady Westland," he said, smiling down at her. "And what sparklers! Did James give you those for a wedding gift?"

"No, these are family jewels," said Anne. "But he did give me jewels of my own for a wedding gift—a set of aquamarines."

She was aware that Kate was listening to every word. The other woman did not speak until they were all seated at the table, but once they were she lost no time in taking up the gauntlet. Smiling at Anne, she said, "My goodness, but you are very fine tonight, Lady Westland! I wish I had known you meant to dress so elaborately. If I had, I would have worn something finer than this old thing." She touched her dress as she spoke, in a way that managed to draw attention to the more obtrusive parts of her figure.

"Your costume is both lovely and suitable, Mrs. Westland," said Anne coldly. "There is no need to apologize."

"Aye, you look deuced fine, Kate," put in Thomas. "Fine as silk."

Kate looked at James as though expecting him to say something. But he only said politely, "Do you care for soup, Mrs. Westland?"

"Yes, certainly," said Kate. "But please don't call me Mrs. Westland, for heaven's sake! I am not a stranger, you know." She gave him a languishing smile. "You used to call me Kate, and I see no reason why you may not continue to do so." Her eyes slid from him to Anne, and her smile became less languishing. "And you must call me Kate, too, Lady Westland," she told Anne. "We are sisters now, and I am sure it is ridiculous for us to call each other by our titles."

Given her feelings for Kate, Anne would rather have preserved all the formalities possible. But she knew that to refuse Kate's request would make her seem ungracious, and she was determined not to let Kate best her again. "Very well, Kate," she said with as much of a smile as she could muster. "You may certainly call me Anne if you like."

"That's the ticket," said Thomas, beaming. "All one family now, don't you know. May as well act like it." Turning to Anne, he bestowed a beseeching smile on her. "And so long as we're Christian-naming each other, I wish you'd call me Thomas," he said. "Every time you call me Mr. Westland, I find myself looking around to see if my governor's standing behind me."

Anne laughed. "Very well, Thomas," she said. "And you must call me Anne." She did not mind Thomas's request nearly so much as Kate's, but when she glanced at James she was taken aback. He had paused in the midst of filling Anne's soup plate and was regarding his brother with a scowl. When Anne caught his eye, he gave a start that sent a wave of chicken consommé flooding over the tablecloth.

"Oh, James, you stupid!" said Kate, whose sharp eyes had caught this as well as every other action taking place at the table. "I do believe sitting down to table with me again after all these years has quite discomposed you." She smiled at him archly, then let her eyes drift slyly to Anne once again. "Tell me, Anne, he is not always so *maladroit,* is he?"

"No, he is not," said Anne briefly. She signed for one of the footmen to help James deal with the spill. When it had been more or less cleaned up, James finished filling Anne's soup plate and passed it to her silently. Anne received it in equal silence, and as soon as everyone had been served, the party picked up their spoons and began to eat.

Kate praised the soup, though she thought it would have been improved by the addition of sherry. When the fish came she praised that, too, while at the same time deploring that it was not so fresh as it might be. "But of course it is so easy to be imposed on where fish is concerned," she said, with a smile of spurious sympathy at Anne. "I find that I must personally inspect what the fishmonger sends us, or we are fobbed off with what is second-rate. I suppose you don't bother to do that, Anne?"

Anne was obliged to admit she did not. As the meal progressed, Kate paid many more seeming compliments which were in reality insults. She wondered that Anne let her cook get away with dressing her poultry in such a haphazard fashion and marveled that she did not serve more than two courses to her company dinners. When Anne reminded Kate tartly that company had not been expected that evening, Kate responded by saying that at Four Oaks she made a point of having her cook keep half-a-dozen dishes on hand for just such emergencies. "A well-made jelly will keep for days, and of course a good fruit cake for months," she told Anne. "And if they are not needed for company dinners, then they can be used up at family ones and new dishes made to replace them."

"Kate's a famous housekeeper," said Thomas, smiling fatuously at his wife. "She can make the ready go a long way—and a good thing, too, by Jove! We've none too much of it, what with one thing and another."

Anne thought Kate did not look pleased by this remark. She advised her husband sharply to hush and hurried to divert the conversation to other channels. "Do you remember, James, that night we danced together at the Owens' ball?"

There was a brief hesitation, and then James shook his head. "No," he said. "I am afraid the occasion has slipped my mind."

Anne was nearly sure he was lying. Kate looked as though she thought so, too, for she tossed her head and said, "What a short memory you have, James! It was only a few years ago, after all. And though I may be wrong, I had thought it had made more of an impression on you than that."

These words brought a tinge of color to James's cheeks. Anne gave him a brief glance, then looked down at her plate. She did not know exactly what had happened at the Owens' ball, but it was easy enough to guess from Kate's manner that it had contained some sort of romantic interlude. It was painful to think of James addressing words of love to Kate and perhaps even kissing her, and more painful still was the idea that he had wanted to marry her. He had by all accounts loved Kate to the point of madness, while he had only married her, Anne, out of convenience.

And then Anne suddenly realized that the truth was even worse than that. When James had asked her to marry him, he had spoken of the necessity of obtaining a direct heir to inherit his title and estate. When pressed, he had admitted that this was because he did not want his half-brother to inherit either one. And why did he not wish Thomas to inherit them? Anne knew the answer now. It was because Thomas had robbed him of the woman he had loved. So in fact James had married her not only in lieu of Kate, but because of Kate. And chances were that in his heart, it was Kate he really wanted to be married to all along. This could only be the more so since Anne had destroyed his respect and affection for her by deceiving him about Timothy.

The knowledge smote Anne like a blow over the heart. In desperation, she turned to Thomas and asked him how he kept himself occupied at Four Oaks. He at once launched into descriptions of the hunting, shooting, and fishing to be obtained in the neighborhood. Anne knew little of hunting, shooting, or fishing, but she was glad to listen to Thomas; glad for any distraction that kept her from her own private thoughts. Even when Kate took advantage of her husband's conversation to embark on a flirtatious tête-à-tête with James, Anne was largely able to shut the words from her ears, if not the knowledge from her heart.

As soon as dinner was over, she gave the signal, and she and Kate retired to the drawing room. This was the part of the evening Anne had dreaded most. In front of the gentlemen, Kate was forced to disguise her barbs beneath the guise of compliments, but now she would be free to bare her claws. It was almost with relief that Anne recognized the familiar sensation of nausea rising in her throat. "Excuse me, please, Kate. I am unwell—I must go to my room," she gasped and fled, leaving Kate looking after her with a startled face.

She made it to her room in time, but only barely. When the wave of sickness had passed, she went into her dressing room and lay down on the sofa. There was no reason she could not have gone back downstairs, for she knew from experience that she would be perfectly well now she had emptied her stomach, but though she might have been physically equal to such an experience, she simply had not the mental fortitude to endure it. Let Kate have the field if she wanted it. She, Anne, could never hope to triumph against such an opponent—an opponent who held all the advantages. She was just reflecting bitterly on this circumstance when there was a scratching on her bedroom door.

"Come in," called Anne. She supposed it was Susan, although the thought occurred to her that it might equally well be Kate. She thought it would be just like Kate to pursue her even to her bedchamber rather than be balked of a chance to vent her spite. *If it is she, I'll soon send her away again,* Anne told herself grimly. *There are things I must endure, but I don't see that having her in my room is one of them.*

But to her surprise, the visitor proved to be James rather than Kate or Susan. He came into her room, looking a little embarrassed, yet worried, too. "Anne?" he said, then saw her lying on the sofa. "Anne," he said again and came into the dressing room. "Kate said you were feeling unwell. I hope you are not seriously ill?"

Anne was surprised by the concern in his voice. Under the circumstances, such a concern was more than she expected. "Yes, I was feeling unwell, but I am sure it's nothing serious," she said. "It's merely that something at dinner disagreed with me."

James was looking more concerned than ever. "Do you think one of the dishes was bad?" he asked.

"No, I think it is merely that Mrs. Laughton will use lard rather than butter in her frying. I ought not to have touched those fritters." Anne summoned up a smile. "Indeed, there is nothing to worry about, James. I will be quite all right if I only rest for a while. Please make my apologies to Thomas and—and Kate, and tell them how it is."

"I will," said James. Yet he did not immediately leave, but stood looking down at Anne as though there was something more he wanted to say. "Anne," he said after a minute. "About Kate—"

Anne was sure that what he was about to say would not add materially to her comfort. She hurried to cut him off. "It's all right, James," she said. "I have already gathered that you were one of Kate's admirers in the past." She reflected briefly that it would have been a comfort to believe his admiration wholly confined to the past, but such comfort she could not look for. "I am sure it is entirely natural. She is a very handsome woman."

"Yes," agreed James. He looked down at Anne a moment longer, then drew a sigh. "Well, if there is nothing I can do for you—"

"Nothing," said Anne swiftly. "You are very kind, but there is nothing, James."

"Then I may as well return to the drawing room. Good evening, Anne."

Anne watched as he went out of the room. Then she sighed in her turn, laid her head against the arm of the sofa, and gave way to a few bitter tears.

CHAPTER XVII

In the days that followed, Anne found herself almost nostalgic for life in Queen Charlotte's Court. She had suffered plenty of snubs, snide remarks, and insults there, but they had been largely impersonal in nature. No one at Court had really resented her as a person. Man and woman alike, they had merely been seeking to elevate their own pretensions at the cost of depressing Anne's.

But it was a different story with Kate. Kate very clearly did resent Anne as a person, and Anne could only guess why this should be. Possibly Kate resented her for having married one of her old admirers, or perhaps she merely resented the fact that by marrying James, Anne's position was now superior to her own. Or perhaps her hostility was purely instinctive, one of those inexplicable antagonisms that sometimes rise between two people.

Whatever the reason, her hostility was an undeniable fact. She needled Anne day and night, alone and in company, until Anne was driven again and again to take refuge in her private rooms to get away from her. She hated herself for taking this craven course, for running away merely left Kate free to do as she chose in the household. Kate was not one to neglect the opportunities this presented; she pried into all the domestic affairs, lectured the servants on the performance of their duties, and even went so far as to contradict Anne's orders.

"I have arranged we should drink our tea in the garden today," she told Anne sweetly one day, when Anne wondered aloud why the servants had not made their appearance with the tea tray. "We often have *al fresco* teas at Four Oaks. The gentlemen thought it a pleasant idea, so I took the liberty of giving the order to your servants. I also told them to make sure the cakes were fresh this time. Those they served yesterday tasted as though they had been sitting about for a week. You know servants will always take advantage if they think there is no one keeping an eye on them, Anne. If I may say so, you are just a *leetle* lax in that direction. When you have more experience in running a household, you will know better how to go on."

Anne was forced to bite her tongue very hard indeed to keep from making a sharp reply to speeches such as this. Sometimes she did reply sharply, but then Kate would only laugh and advise her not to take offense just because she ventured to give Anne a word of advice for her own good. The damnable thing was that often Kate's advice *was* good. The *al fresco* tea, for instance, was a great success. Both James and Thomas remarked several times how enjoyable it was to sit in the garden while drinking their tea, and James even ventured to congratulate Anne on having conceived so pleasant a notion.

Of course Kate could not remain silent at this. She told

James the *al fresco* tea had been *her* idea and proceeded to vaunt her own achievements as a housekeeper while ridiculing Anne's. Anne sat crumbling a fresh-made tea cake and fuming silently to herself. It was humiliating to see another woman in her home, giving orders to her servants and flirting with her husband. It was true that James did not flirt back with Kate, but neither did he make any move to discourage her as far as Anne could see. Nor could she be certain that she saw all there was to see in that regard. Possibly James was a good deal more forthcoming toward Kate when she herself was not around. For all Anne knew to the contrary, he and Kate might even be lovers. Certain it was that she herself spent enough evenings in her room nowadays to give the two of them ample opportunity for amorous goings-on. And as Anne reflected grimly, it was also certain that whoever else James might be making love to these days, it was not to her.

If Kate was a genuine thorn in Anne's side, Thomas was a much more minor irritation. He did have a way of stating the obvious that could be exasperating at times, and his habit of blurting aloud things that were better left unsaid was exasperating, too. But Anne was fairly sure he did not say such things to wound, as Kate did. Indeed, in his bluff and simpleminded way, he seemed to be making every effort to be agreeable. Anne overheard him telling James several times how glad he was to see him again and how he hoped they could do a better job of staying on close terms now they were both living in England again. He really did seem intent on reconciling the differences that had existed between him and James in the past.

Toward Anne, Thomas was invariably friendly in a clumsy but well-intentioned manner. On occasion, he would even defend her when Kate became so aggressive in her attacks that even he could not mistake their intention. "Now, now, Kate, you know you don't mean that the way it sounded," he would say with an apologetic glance at Anne. "You'll have Anne thinking you're trying to criticize her and her household, by Jove. And I'm sure there's nothing to criticize. A dashed fine house, and a dashed fine lady who runs it." And he would smile and bow to Anne, who would smile gratefully back at him, and Kate would subside into silence with a "biding-my-time look" on her face.

Anne was grateful enough for Thomas's defense, but she could not help thinking it should have been James who was defending her. As she reflected bitterly, it would have been more natural to have had her husband speak up for her rather than her brother-in-law. But James was notably silent during these encounters. In fact, he was notably silent most of the time these days.

Anne wondered what he thought about his brother and sister-in-law's visit. She knew he had once suspected Thomas of coveting his title and estate. That was why he had been so anxious to get an heir, and why he had decided to make a marriage of convenience. But Anne saw no sign that Thomas really coveted the earldom. Although he freely admired Honeywell House and was warmly congratulatory toward James on having achieved his present high position, he seemed for himself quite content with his own more modest one.

"Better you than me, m'boy," he often told James, when James mentioned some duty as a landowner that demanded his attention. "Don't know how you manage it. What I mean is, it seems to take a devil of a lot of time and attention to run this show. I'm sure if it was me, I'd throw the whole thing over rather than be saddled with such an all-fired obligation. But then you was always the clever one of the family.''

Kate, who was in earshot during one of these conversations, gave a brittle laugh. "Don't be foolish, Thomas," she said. "I am sure there are many earls who are not clever at all, and yet who function admirably in their positions." It was evident enough that if her husband did not covet his brother's position, then she coveted it for him—assuming she did not actually covet the brother himself. But Thomas only laughed and shook his head at these words.

"Ah, Kate, it'd suit you to be a countess, no doubt! And I'm bound to say you'd make a very fine one. But if you was set on being a grand lady, you ought to have married James here instead of me. You knew all along he was next in line for the title."

This was the kind of remark Anne felt would have been better left unsaid, yet she experienced a certain relief to see it dragged out into the open. She also experienced a malicious pleasure in seeing Kate flush and bridle at her husband's plain speaking.

"Thomas, you old stupid, I never supposed either of you would inherit the title," she said sharply. "The Westlands are famously long-lived, you must know. Why, old Lord Westland looked likely to live forever—and besides, he was just the kind of man to marry and have a quiverful of children on the sly. I wouldn't be surprised even now if some half-bred Scotsman didn't pop up claiming to be the true heir."

"Sour grapes," Thomas laughed with his usual devastating candor. "But you know even if such a thing did happen, Kate, it'd be all the same to you and me. James is married now and has a very pretty wife of his own, and I don't doubt there'll be a little stranger along soon to put our noses out of joint, even if there ain't any half-bred Scots fellow!''

This was another remark that would have been better left unsaid as far as Anne was concerned. Yet it was almost worth her embarrassment to see the venomous chagrin on Kate's face. ''At any rate, Anne doesn't look to be increasing yet,'' she said savagely. ''Only see how skinny she is! I can't imagine how she will ever bear children. Why, she is no bigger than a child herself.''

''Ah, but that don't always follow,'' said Thomas wisely. ''My own grandmother was a little slip of a thing, too, but she had twelve brats besides my mother, and it never slowed her down a mite. Twelve of 'em, and all healthy as horses—and eight of 'em were sons,'' he added, sounding as proud as though he had achieved this feat himself.

His remark effectually put an end to the discussion, much to Anne's relief. She could not imagine what James had made of it all. Was he reflecting, like her, on the irony of Thomas's prediction? No little stranger would ever come along now, given their current state of estrangement. Or was he reflecting that if only he had come into his title sooner, Kate might have married him instead of his brother? Did he still care for Kate? Anne was pretty certain that he did. It was not that he spoke to her much or made a practice of seeking out her company, but when they were all together she had often seen him regarding Kate with a strange, concentrated expression on his face. At her, Anne, he rarely seemed to look at all.

Things had been going along in this manner for several weeks when Anne first got the idea of giving a dinner party for Kate and Thomas. Perhaps it would have been more accurate to say that Kate got the idea first and pointed out to Anne, in the sweetest manner possible, that she had a duty in this direction. "I did imagine, when we came here to Honeywell House, that we might meet some of the local society," she remarked plaintively at the dinner table one night. "When we have company staying at Four Oaks, I always make sure to give a dinner in their honor and usually a dancing party as well. But I suppose you are too inexperienced, Anne, to know what is what in these matters."

"As a matter of fact, I had thought of holding a small party sometime in the next week or two," responded Anne stiffly. "But you have frequently remarked how dull and provincial you find our neighborhood, Kate. I did not suppose you would be interested in meeting any of our neighbors."

Kate gave a shrill laugh. "Anne, what a stupid you are! The whole reason I find the neighborhood dull is because I do not know anyone here except you and James. Once I have met a few people, I have no doubt of making a very good time for myself. You must know that I am a social creature and tend to make friends very quickly— not at all like you, Anne. Why, I haven't seen that you have any friends at all here in Devon, even in spite of having lived here several months."

"I have friends," said Anne, more stiffly than ever. "There are two local ladies with whom I am very good friends indeed. At least, one is a local lady, and the other is hoping to become one. She and her husband are searching for a house in the neighborhood."

Kate laughed again. "They cannot be such good friends as that, Anne, or I would already have met them. At Four Oaks my friends are always popping in and out—"

"You have not met them because neither is in Devon at present," said Anne, ruthlessly cutting short Kate's reminiscences of Four Oaks. "And that is why I have

not yet given a party for you and Thomas. I wanted to
wait until Lady Meredith could be here—and if possible
Lady O'Reilly, too. Her presence will be more uncertain,
I am afraid, but I hope she, too, will be able to attend."

"Lady Meredith and Lady O'Reilly?" said Kate sharply.
Anne thought she looked taken aback, but she quickly
summoned up her most disagreeable manner and gave a
short laugh. "I suppose now that you have a title yourself,
you feel obliged to choose your friends among the aristocracy! For myself, I confess to being more concerned with
whether people are agreeable than with any question of
their pedigrees."

"And I, too," said Anne, congratulating herself that
she had not laid undue stress on these words. "I think
Lady Meredith and Lady O'Reilly the most agreeable of
women. And their husbands are very agreeable, too."

Kate immediately wanted to know more about this subject. Anne described Lord Meredith and Sir Terrence
O'Reilly as well as she could, and Kate listened with
close attention. "And they will be at the party you propose
to give?" she said. "It sounds not so dull as I feared.
Really, I find myself quite looking forward to it."

Anne observed that while Kate objected to titled
females, she seemed to have no objection to titled males.
*She looks forward to flaunting herself before a company
of admiring gentlemen,* Anne told herself. *But I'll wager
Lady Meredith and Lady O'Reilly will be more competi-
tion than she bargains for.*

Anne smiled to think what a surprise Kate would have
if she expected to monopolize the attention of the male
guests at the party. Unfortunately for her, her smile did
not go unnoticed by Kate. "What are you smirking to
yourself about Anne?" she demanded, then went on without waiting for Anne to reply. "Indeed, I have thought

several times that there is something a little—well—*sly* about you, Anne. Not that you mean it intentionally, I'm sure, but you know when someone is as quiet and soft-spoken as you are, it cannot but leave a disagreeable impression on people.''

"Then it would follow that you must leave a very agreeable impression,'' said Anne boldly. "No one could accuse *you* of being quiet and soft-spoken.''

Kate looked at her suspiciously, but finally decided to take her words as a compliment. "Indeed, yes!" she said with a proud toss of her head. "There is nothing sly or underhanded about *me*. I pride myself on always speaking my mind, no matter what the consequences.''

"And so you do, Kate,'' said Thomas, beaming at her. "And so you do.''

Anne glanced at James. He was looking fixedly at Kate, but seemed to feel Anne's gaze upon him, for he promptly dropped his eyes. "I will send out invitations to the dinner for a week from Thursday,'' said Anne. "I received a note from Lady Meredith yesterday saying she and Lord Meredith are back at the Abbey. That should allow them to attend, assuming they have no prior engagement.''

"Don't you think Friday would be the better day?'' said Kate, promptly and predictably. "If I mistake not, James was planning to drive over to Merriweather's Farm on Thursday. He would probably be too fatigued to enjoy a party that same night. You must take these things into consideration, Anne, when you—''

"It's no matter,'' said James, unexpectedly breaking in on Kate's speech. "The drive to Merriweather's Farm and back is not likely to fatigue me. I see no reason why Thursday will not do very well for your party, Anne.''

"But Friday would be better still,'' said Kate obstinately. "The full moon is on Friday, and—''

"There won't be much difference between Thursday and Friday so far as the moon is concerned," said James. "Send out the cards for Thursday, Anne, and let us be done with it."

Everyone looked at him in surprise, for this autocratic way of speaking was not typical of him. But he remained with his eyes fixed on his plate. Kate regarded him a moment, but when he said nothing more, she undertook to salvage her authority. "Of course, James, if you prefer it so, we will send out the cards for Thursday," she told him graciously. "Now I think of it, I believe you are right. Thursday will be much the best day."

No one said anything to this, so Kate went on, planning aloud the details of the party as though it were she giving it rather than Anne. "We must have *assiettes volantes* with the second course," she told Anne. "It's all the crack to serve *assiettes volantes* with the second course nowadays—little light dishes that the footmen carry about in addition to the ones on the table, you know. And I will tell the cook to pay attention to the seasoning of her white sauce. I have noticed before that she totally neglects to salt her white sauce before she sends it to the table."

"Thank you, Kate, but I prefer to speak to the cook myself," said Anne. James's unexpected support had emboldened her, and she addressed Kate with great firmness. "It is I who am giving the party, you know. You need do nothing but plan your dress for the occasion."

For a moment Kate looked as though she were going to object to this, but then she laughed. "Hoity-toity! I merely thought you would appreciate my help, seeing you have never given a formal party before. You haven't, have you, Anne? This will be your first party since your marriage?"

"Yes," admitted Anne reluctantly.

Kate smiled and threw an eloquent glance at James and Thomas. "Let us hope, then, that it will be a success," she said, her voice conveying clearly that she entertained strong doubts on this score. "I will look forward to the occasion, Anne. It will be interesting to see how you manage the business all on your own."

This, of course, was a challenge if there ever was one. Anne saw that Kate not only expected her to fail but hoped that her failure would be a most public and humiliating one. Anne's spirits, so long depressed by despair and unhappiness, had been roused to life by James's support. Now they rallied to her aid, filling her with a grim determination. She would *not* fail. She would plan every detail of the party and show Kate that she was able to make it a success on her own. And she would show James that though he might regret marrying her, he had at least gained a competent hostess when he had chosen her as his wife.

CHAPTER XVIII

The next week was spent in a flurry of planning and preparation. Anne, conscious that Kate would be quick to pounce on any shortcoming, worked hard to make sure that every detail of her dinner party was perfect. A suitable menu was concocted with the aid of Mrs. Rhodes and the cook; floral decorations were discussed with Mr. Gardiner; and the maids and footmen were all thoroughly drilled on their duties for the night. No elaborate ball or fete could have been more meticulously planned than that relatively small and simple dinner party. Anne was aware that she was putting a disproportionate amount of time and effort into the proceedings, but in her mind it had assumed the character of a test. It was a test that she was grimly determined not to fail.

During all the hustle and bustle of preparation, Kate remained conspicuously aloof. When anyone made a comment about the party, she would say, "I wouldn't know about that. This is *Anne's* party, you know, and I have nothing to do with it.'' But still she had an annoying way of following Anne about, watching her preparations with an air of contemptuous amusement that was very difficult to endure.

Anne endured it because she had to, but she was starting to find Kate's presence at Honeywell House an intolerable misery. What was worse, it was a misery that showed no signs of coming to an end. The original period of the Westlands' stay at Honeywell House had been set for six weeks, but now Kate was talking blithely about remaining for the fall shooting season and perhaps even through the Christmas holidays.

''After all, there is no reason why we must go rushing back to Four Oaks,'' she told Anne with a patronizing smile. ''Thomas and I find ourselves growing quite at home here at Honeywell House. And I can tell how happy James is to have us here. Poor man, it's obvious he has been starved for company. And no wonder—living in this out-of-the-way place with no one but rustics and nobodies to associate with! As I see it, Thomas and I have a positive duty to stay here and do what we can to enliven things. If that means remaining on for another two or three months, then I for one am quite resigned to it.''

The thought of Kate picking at her vitals for the next two or three months filled Anne with despair. She decided if Kate did not leave within a few weeks, then she herself would have to. She knew James had several other properties, and she felt that given their current state of estrangement, he would probably offer no objection if she proposed removing to one of them.

The first thing you know, I'll be living like a hermit in Scotland like old Lord Westland, she told herself with wry amusement. *I wonder if his reasons for going there were anything like mine? But no, he wasn't a married man, so presumably he hadn't a sister-in-law to harass him. If he had had one like Kate, I am sure it would be no wonder if he chose to shut himself away from the world and see nobody!*

When the night of the party arrived at last, Anne had very nearly reached the end of her tether. The house was in a state of shining perfection; the food was all prepared or in the last stages of being prepared; and the servants were all letter perfect in their roles. As Anne slipped upstairs to dress, however, she was conscious of a sudden, overwhelming distaste for the whole business. She had worked for days, endured numerous sleepless nights, and worried herself into a mass of nerves, all for what? To impress Kate with her skill as a hostess? But Kate would never own herself impressed, no matter how impressive Anne's efforts might be. She disliked Anne so intensely that she could twist the most positive thing Anne could do or say into a negative. To attempt to convert such implacable hostility would be like trying to reason with a stone wall.

Nor was there much point in trying to impress James. Ever since the arrival of Timothy's letter, he had shown a complete disinterest in Anne and everything connected with her. Nothing she could do tonight was likely to change his feelings.

All that remained was to impress the neighbors, and that was the most futile thing of all. Very likely they would not be her neighbors much longer. If Kate remained at Honeywell House she, Anne, would inevitably be driven away. Anne could read the writing on the wall in large and unmistakable characters. She knew she could not bear much longer the constant conflicts, the incessant veiled insults, the petty torments which Kate delighted to inflict. And it occurred to her now that possibly Kate's actions had all along had this purpose in mind. Perhaps it had been her intention from the beginning to force Anne from Honeywell House and take her place as mistress there.

Turning this idea over in her mind, Anne wondered if it could be true. Of course Kate could hardly marry James, seeing that she was already married to Thomas and James was married to Anne. But she could certainly set up as mistress of Honeywell House in Anne's absence. It was, Anne thought, unlikely that Kate had come to Honeywell House with that express purpose in mind, but after seeing the situation firsthand she might well have seized on the opportunities it offered. Such a course seemed typical of her kind of quick, grasping intelligence. She must have seen that Anne was too weak to resist her alone, and that James did not care enough to come to her assistance. Over Thomas Kate obviously exercised a full control, so that she could do as she pleased where he was concerned.

There was no doubt that living as mistress of Honeywell House would offer Kate many advantages. Neither could Anne doubt that she was a woman with an eye for all possible advantages. From things Thomas had let drop, Anne had gathered that life at Four Oaks, however much Kate chose to boast about it, required a good deal of scrimping and saving and the forgoing of such luxuries as a second carriage and a personal maid. By contrast, life at Honeywell House would allow Kate to enjoy all those amenities without spending a penny of her and Thomas's own money. And she could also enjoy the reflected prestige of James's title—and, possibly, James's presence in her bed as well.

Anne winced at the idea of James in bed with Kate,

but she told herself that it was no affair of hers what he did now. James was hers no longer. In fact, he had never been hers—never but for that one evening, when he had spoken as though he were beginning to love her. And then the letter from Timothy had come and put an end to that budding love as if it had never been.

Let Kate have him if she wants him, Anne told herself bitterly. *Let her have everything she wants. All I want is some quiet corner where I can hide and be tortured no longer.*

She had ordered a new toilette for the occasion of the party, a flowered dress of pink brocade with floss trimmings. But its gay frivolity was out of key with her feelings tonight. On an impulse she put it aside and took instead from her wardrobe the white dress with flowing draperies she had worn the night of the King's Birthday Ball. Her mood tonight was much the same as it had been then. She felt sad and desperate and powerless to escape the afflictions of her existence.

Once arrayed in the white dress, she stood looking at herself a long time in the glass. "You look lovely, my lady," Susan told her. "I don't deny I liked the pink dress better, but I like this one, too, in a different way. You look kind of unreal in it, if you take my meaning— like a fairy princess or something. Seems as if you only wanted wings to fly away."

Anne thought she knew what Susan meant. In her own eyes she looked as insubstantial as a wraith and about as appealing. *Of course Kate will shine me down. But she will shine me down no matter what I am wearing,* Anne told herself. *It will be more dignified to look as though I am not trying to compete with her. She played the same trick on me the first evening I was here; now I'll turn the tables and do the same by her.*

Joy Reed

To this end, Anne elected to wear no jewelry except her wedding ring, much to Susan's disappointment. "Not even your aquamarines, my lady? They're such pretty things, and they'd set you off something lovely."

"No jewelry at all," said Anne. "Just give me my shawl—the blue one with the flowered border—and I will go downstairs."

She found the gentlemen already in the drawing room, engaged in a desultory conversation about hunting. They both rose to their feet as she came in. " 'Evening, Anne," hailed Thomas. "My, but don't you look pretty!" He took her hand in his and kissed it gallantly.

"Thank you, Thomas," said Anne. Out of the corner of her eye she was watching James. She thought he had made as though to approach her, but when Thomas had called out his greeting and come to her first, he had halted in midstep, spun around, and returned to his place beside the fireplace.

Thomas, who labored under the impression that Anne, like all right-minded people, was interested in hunting, proceeded to give her a full account of his and James's conversation on the subject. Anne knew next to nothing about hunting, so her responses were largely limited to "Yes" and "No" and "How interesting." This suited her very well, for she felt in no mood to make conversation. Thomas spared her that trouble, being so intent on his own subject that his listener's reaction was secondary. He had just finished telling Anne about a spectacular run he had made the season before when Kate came into the room.

"I do hope I am not late," she said, glancing at the clock with pretended concern. "The girl who was waiting on me was very clumsy, and it took me longer than I expected to get dressed.''

Anne received this speech in cynical silence. She was perfectly sure that Kate, far from being hindered by a maid's clumsiness, had purposely delayed her arrival in order to make a more impressive entrance. Yet even without such a strategem, she might have been sure of attention. Her orange satin dress was as bright as a dress could possibly be, and color was not its only remarkable feature. It was cut with a scanty skirt that clung to Kate's legs and revealed her ankles, while its low *décolletage* left bare a considerable amount of her bosom. As though to further emphasize this last feature, Kate wore an emerald pendant that nestled between her breasts, and a matching emerald aigrette sparkled in her dark hair.

There could be no doubt that she made a striking figure. Yet as Anne surveyed her narrowly, she realized with a dawning sense of gratification that she was also a vulgar one. The whole costume was too much: too skimpy, too brightly colored, and offering too much contrast between the fiery hue of Kate's dress and her emerald jewelry.

Still, it was obvious that Thomas had no fault to find with it. ''By Jove, Kate, don't you look fine,'' he said enthusiastically. ''I never saw you looking finer than you do tonight. That's a bang-up dress, 'pon my word. You'll take the shine out of every other lady at the party.'' Realizing too late this would necessarily include Anne, he added quickly, ''Except for Anne, of course. She looks very pretty, too, only in a—er—different style, don't you know.''

Kate gave Anne a smile in which malice and triumph were nicely mixed. ''Indeed she does. That is quite a pretty dress, Anne. Although I wonder you chose to wear white, when you are so pale yourself.''

"I think any lady looks well in white," said James quietly. "It is a color that must always appear to advantage, whatever the occasion."

As no one was expecting him to speak, this speech caused everyone to look at him in surprise. Kate was the first to recover. "Yes, to be sure, James," she said. "I was only remarking that white is probably not Anne's *best* color. She has so little color herself that it tends to wash her out."

James looked at Anne. "I think she looks very well in white," he said. "I always did. That dress, in particular, I always thought very becoming to her." Then he turned away, leaving both Anne and Kate to gaze at him with greater surprise than ever.

Once again, Kate was the first to recover. "You haven't said anything about *my* dress, James," she said. "I hope I shan't disgrace you tonight. You don't think I will, do you?" Boldly she placed herself in front of him, turning to and fro so he could not miss any detail of her appearance. As a vulgar performance, Anne thought it could hardly have been surpassed.

James looked her impassively up and down, then shook his head. "I really know very little about ladies' fashions," he said. "It would be presumption to comment."

"But you knew enough to—" Kate bit back the rest of what she was about to say, but its substance was easy to guess from the venomous look she shot Anne. The next moment, however, she summoned up a laugh. Moving closer to James, she reached out and laid a hand on his arm. "Indeed, James, I must not fish for compliments," she said, smiling up at him. "You have paid me so many in my life that I can hardly ask for more. That night at the Owens' ball—I remember your saying that my eyes outshone the stars in the sky, and that Mrs. Owens's lovely roses were nothing to my beauty.''

James said nothing. Anne, who had been watching this byplay with covert interest, turned away to avoid seeing any more. For a moment she had been almost encouraged by James's behavior. He had appeared to be no more impressed than she was by Kate's appearance, but now she realized he was only being discreet. Doubtless he would pay Kate all the compliments she desired as soon as they were in a place of privacy. He merely thought it bad form to pay her compliments in front of his wife. Anne supposed she ought to be grateful for this forbearance, but her heart was heavy as she stood trying not to hear the words Kate was now murmuring to James in a low voice.

Soon the guests began to arrive and Anne was given something else to think about. There were a dozen guests in all, and the Merediths and O'Reillys were among the first to arrive. Anne felt an insensible rising in her spirits as soon as she saw Lady Meredith's slender form pass through the doors of the drawing room. Here was an ally, and one who could certainly hold her own even in conflict against such an unprincipled opponent as Kate.

If only I could do the same, reflected Anne with a sigh. *But even if I can't, at least I can forget Kate for a while in the pleasure of talking to Catherine.* In her haste to speak to her friend, she came close to snubbing her friend's husband, but Lord Meredith accepted her apologies amiably and declared he had no wish to delay the exchange of confidences that both ladies were evidently dying to make.

''I'll just take myself off and—'' he began, when a honey-sweet voice interrupted him.

''Indeed you shall not, sir! We have not yet been introduced, and you cannot be excused until we are. I insist on knowing everyone with whom I am to dine tonight.''

It was Kate, of course. She stood there fluttering her lashes and regarding Lord Meredith with a provocative smile. Turning to Anne, she added with just the faintest reproach in her voice, ''Anne, dear, you are terribly remiss to not introduce me to your guests. One would almost think you wished to keep them to yourself.''

''Don't be ridiculous, Kate,'' said Anne coldly. ''Of course I meant to introduce you. The Merediths have only just arrived.'' She performed the introductions quickly, first between Kate and the Merediths and then between Kate and the O'Reillys, who had just come through the door.

Irritated as she was, she found amusement in the jealous sizing-up Kate gave Lady O'Reilly and Lady Meredith. Indeed, it was hard to judge which lady looked more beguiling: Lady Meredith in a dashing dress of antique gold velvet that just matched her eyes, or Lady O'Reilly in a bronze green taffeta that was a perfect foil for her red-gold hair. Against their stately beauty, the vulgarity of Kate's appearance was more glaring than ever. Even her face with its strong, handsome features and high color seemed vulgar by comparison.

But Kate was not a woman to be impressed by such circumstances as these. Indeed, she was not a woman to be impressed by anything to do with other women, no matter how lovely or exalted in station they might be. Having exchanged greetings with Lady Meredith and Lady O'Reilly, she quickly turned her attention to their husbands. Toward Lord Meredith especially did she pour out a determined stream of allurements. She pouted, she preened, she laughed at everything he said and declared him too naughty for words. She pronounced the Abbey, his home, to be the most delightful residence in the neighborhood, in spite of the fact that she had never laid eyes on it.

Lady Meredith watched this process for a little while with a faint smile on her lips. Then she turned to Anne. "Anne, it is a pleasure to see you again," she said. "Have you other guests to attend to, or can you spare me a few minutes? It has been an age since I have seen you, and I have been dying for a chance to talk to you. Of course I would prefer to talk to you in private if possible, but if not, I will make do with what I can get."

"I have been wanting to talk to you, too," said Anne. "And I don't see why we can't talk privately for a few minutes, at least." She looked around the gathering with a measuring eye. "Everyone is here, and it looks as though everyone is reasonably well occupied." As she spoke, her eye fell on Kate and Lord Meredith. She looked quickly away, only to catch Lady Meredith's eye.

An unexpected grin appeared on Lady Meredith's face. "Yes, Jonathan seems very fully occupied at the moment," she said. "He has not had a chance to even say good evening to anyone except you, as far as I have seen. So that is your sister-in-law?"

"Yes," said Anne, with a barely repressed sigh. "That is my sister-in-law."

"You have my sympathies," said Lady Meredith gravely.

Anne flushed. "I do apologize, Catherine," she said. "I am afraid Kate is—I am afraid you must be offended by her behavior."

Lady Meredith laughed. "Why, because she admires my husband? But you must know I expect every lady to do that. I should rather be offended if she did *not* admire him." She smiled at Anne. "Indeed, Anne, I am neither offended nor concerned—that is to say, I am not at all concerned for my sake. I must say, however, that I am a trifle concerned for yours. I thought when I first saw you that you looked—well, less well and happy than when I saw you last. Will your brother and sister-in-law be staying at Honeywell House much longer?''

"They will be staying forever, I think,'' said Anne bleakly. Then, realizing how this sounded, she forced a smile to her lips. "At any rate, Kate is talking now of staying through the Christmas holidays.''

Lady Meredith was looking at her closely. "That could hardly be congenial for you,'' she said. "Perhaps your sister-in-law is more amiable than she appears—but then again, perhaps she is less amiable. However amiable she might be, you can scarcely welcome her presence when you and Lord Westland are so newly married.''

Anne opened her lips, then shut them again. She could not bring herself to divulge the full tale of her woes, even to such a sympathetic listener as Lady Meredith. That lady regarded her for a moment, then spoke again in a lower voice.

"Tell me,'' she said, "do you really wish your sister-in-law to stay with you forever—or even through the Christmas holidays?''

Anne made a helpless gesture. "No, I do not. But what can I do to prevent it?''

"Fire her off,'' said Lady Meredith with brevity. "That's what I would do if I were in your shoes.''

"But how?'' said Anne despairingly.

Lady Meredith gave her a long, faintly surprised look. "Well, it's your house, isn't it?''

"Yes,'' said Anne doubtfully. "Yes, I suppose it is.''

"You suppose it is? But you know it must be so. The house is yours; the servants are yours; all the advantages are yours, in fact. If you put your mind to it, you ought to be able to make things so uncomfortable for your sister-in-law that she will be glad to go.''

"I suppose I could try," said Anne, more doubtfully still. "But you know it is not only *my* house, Catherine. It is also Lord Westland's house.''

Lady Meredith looked at her a long moment. "You don't mean to say Lord Westland . . . ?'' Her voice tapered off, but the next moment she spoke with renewed assurance. "No, I don't believe it, Anne. I don't believe it for a moment. Lord Westland has always struck me as a man of taste and discernment. He would not be taken in by something so obvious as that.'' She threw Kate a look of contempt.

"You think not?'' said Anne. "But I know for a fact he did admire Kate at one time. In fact, not to wrap the matter in clean linen, he once wanted to marry her.''

"Well, then, why didn't he?'' said Lady Meredith calmly.

Anne stared at her. "Why, because—because she preferred his brother. His half brother, I should say. That is he over there, talking to Mr. Winslow.'' She indicated Thomas, who stood in the corner conversing happily with Mr. Winslow and several other gentlemen.

Lady Meredith followed her eyes. "That stout gentleman with the red face?'' she said. "Why ever would your sister-in-law prefer him to Lord Westland?''

Anne boggled at the question. "Why, I suppose—I suppose—'' She wracked her brain, trying to think of some reason why a woman might prefer to marry Thomas rather than James. "I suppose it could have been money,'' she said doubtfully. "Thomas had a small independence he inherited from his mother, while James had only what he received from his father's estate. I understand that was barely a competence. He had not enough of either capital or property to live on the proceeds like Thomas, and so he was obliged to seek a profession.''

''But your husband was heir to the earldom,'' said Lady Meredith. ''And he was quite capable of making a fair living in his profession, was he not? I think most women would agree that he would be the better marital bargain, speaking from a purely material viewpoint.''

''Kate said the Westlands were all very long-lived, and that old Lord Westland was likely to live forever,'' offered Anne. ''And she said that even if he didn't, he might have a wife and children in Scotland for all anyone knew.''

''That sounds like the utmost sophistry to me,'' said Lady Meredith. ''I should say there was more to the story than that. Have you ever asked Lord Westland why he did not marry Kate?''

''No,'' said Anne. ''No, I didn't like to do that.''

Lady Meredith looked at her, then averted her eyes with an air of tact. ''Yes, I can understand that, I suppose.'' She pondered a moment in silence. ''I don't know what I would do in your case,'' she said at last. ''But I think—I almost think that in the circumstances, I would feel justified in calling your sister-in-law's bluff.''

''Call her bluff?'' repeated Anne doubtfully. ''What do you mean, Catherine?''

''Why, obviously she wants you to believe that your husband still has a partiality for her. I can think of several reasons why she might wish to do that, but the fact remains that however partial he might have been once upon a time, he did not marry her. He married *you,* Anne. And if you will excuse me for saying so, I think he is very much in love with you.''

Anne could hardly disguise her astonishment at this. ''You think so, do you?'' she said, as lightly as she could.

''Oh, yes,'' said Lady Meredith calmly. ''Only look at

the way he has behaved this evening! I have caught him looking our way at least a dozen times during the time we have been talking together, and I have no doubt he is wondering what we are talking about. Not once has he glanced at your sister-in-law, in spite of all her efforts to make herself conspicuous.''

At though on cue, Kate's laughter rang out loudly. ''Oh, Lord Meredith, you are a horrid man!'' she said. ''Fie upon you, sir! If you continue in that vein, there is no saying what will be the result!''

At the same moment, Lady O'Reilly came gliding over to Anne and Lady Meredith. Her face was working with suppressed laughter. ''Catherine, you must call off your husband,'' she said in a low voice. ''He is making the most dreadful game of that poor woman. And she is revealing herself more with every—oh, Anne, dear, I am sorry!'' She looked suddenly aghast. ''I forgot that she is your sister-in-law. Do forgive me for being catty.''

''There's nothing to forgive,'' said Anne. All at once she found she was smiling. ''As it happens, there is no love lost between my sister-in-law and me. Catherine and I have just been discussing it.''

''Well, thank goodness for that,'' said Lady O'Reilly with heartfelt relief. ''Then I can be a perfect cat and say it is the funniest thing I have ever heard. But truly, Catherine, you ought to put a stop to it. It's evident Jonathan means to egg her on as far as she will go—and there appears no limit to how far she will go. As long she thinks she is being admired, she will say and do anything.''

Once again, as though on cue, Kate's laughter rang out loudly. ''Indeed, no, my lord!'' she cried. ''I am convinced that is the veriest flattery. Very well, if you insist— I will admit I was once told years ago, by a gentleman who was accounted to be an authority on such things, that I had a Voice. But it has been many years since I sang for any reason but my own amusement.''

''I am certain you will do it charmingly,'' said Lord Meredith. He caught his wife's eye and threw her a wicked grin. ''Like the gentleman you speak of, I fancy myself a judge on these matters. Merely the tone of your speaking voice tells me you are a natural singer.''

As Kate's speaking voice was more strident than melodious, this speech made Anne, Lady Meredith, and Lady O'Reilly turn away quickly with shaking shoulders. ''Oh, dear,'' said Anne. ''But of course she *may* have a better singing than a speaking voice. I never heard that the two were necessarily linked.''

''At any rate, we shall soon find out,'' said Lady O'Reilly. ''Jonathan has talked her into singing after dinner for the entertainment of the company.''

''Then no doubt she will do it very well,'' said Anne fatalistically. ''She cannot be fool enough to sing in company unless she has *some* musical ability.''

''Ah, but I'd stake my topaz set that she hasn't as much as Miss Winslow,'' said Lady Meredith, nodding toward a young lady in pale blue gauze who was standing nearby, talking to several other people. ''You must be sure to ask her to sing as soon as your sister-in-law is done, Anne. A nightingale's voice would sound like a creaking gate compared to Miss Winslow's.''

Anne smiled, but in truth she felt dubious about following Lady Meredith's advice. It seemed somehow not fair to Kate to expose her publicly in such a way. Lady Meredith must have divined her thought, for she drew near to Anne and addressed her in an impassioned whisper. ''Look here, Anne, this is no time to be softhearted. Has your sister-in-law been making your life a perfect hell these last few weeks, or has she not?"

"Yes," admitted Anne. "She certainly has."

"And has she been tormenting you with the fact that your husband was in love with her before he married you?"

"Yes," admitted Anne again. "She has."

"And did she not this very evening try to put you in the wrong by implying you were derelict in your duties as a hostess? Don't try to tell me that she didn't, because I was standing right here, and I heard her."

"Yes," admitted Anne. "She does that sort of thing all the time."

"Very well, then," said Lady Meredith triumphantly. "You are perfectly justified in giving her a dose of humiliation. And if I were you, I should not be content with a single dose. Regard this as the opening campaign in your battle to drive her from your home. You have the advantage, for it's your ground, and you can order things as you like. If I were you, I should take care that life at Honeywell House wasn't to your sister-in-law's liking after this."

Anne nodded doubtfully. "But Kate is perfectly capable of giving orders herself if she doesn't like the way things are done," she said. "She has countermanded my orders many times in the past."

"Tell the servants to disregard any orders she may give. I'll wager they would be glad of an excuse to do so anyway. Servants always detest that sort of interference."

The butler appeared just then, and informed Anne in a low voice that the dinner was served. "Very well," she said, and turned back to Lady Meredith. "I must go and collect my brother-in-law now. But I will think about what you said, Catherine."

"Do," advised Lady Meredith. "And if you decide to act on my advice, you can count on Emily and me to support you as much as we can. And Jonathan, too." She laughed.

"Yes," said Anne, and joined in her laughter. "Very well. I will let you know if I decide to take your advice."

CHAPTER XIX

Before the first course of the dinner was over, Anne's scruples were at an end, and she had decided to embrace Lady Meredith's advice.

In part, her decision was prompted by Kate's behavior. Flown with intoxication over having made a conquest of a handsome peer in a matter of a few minutes' conversation, Kate was even more than usually officious. She scolded Anne publicly for not having told her butler to air the wine longer and then added insult to injury by assuring her in a patronizing voice that such an oversight was natural in such an inexperienced housekeeper. But this maneuver did not answer very well, for Lady Meredith looked her coolly in the eye and said, "What grounds have *you* to criticize her, Mrs. Westland?"

"I am not *criticizing* her, Lady Meredith," protested Kate with wide, innocent eyes. "I am merely stating she cannot be blamed if things do not run so smoothly as they might."

"That sounds remarkably like criticism to me," said Lady Meredith, her voice cooler than ever. "And as such, I think it is entirely misplaced. Lady Westland is an admirable housekeeper. I am sure we have all been impressed by the hospitality she has shown us tonight. And not only tonight—I myself have visited Honeywell House many times and never seen but that it was managed to perfection."

"Indeed?" said Kate, with a note of polite disbelief in her voice.

"Indeed, yes," said Lady Meredith, her own voice uncompromising. "I should be glad if my own home were as well managed."

Kate gave a titter of laughter. "How generous of you, my lady," she said. "Dare I say you are *too* generous?"

"I am not generous at all," said Lady Meredith briskly. "I am merely being truthful. But I suppose I must make allowances if you are a trifle slow to grasp the measure of your sister-in-law's achievements, Mrs. Westland. I doubt you have any experience in managing a large household like this one."

This remark obviously infuriated Kate. "I have been managing a good-sized household for several years now, my lady," she said sharply. "I assure you, I have as much housekeeping experience as anyone."

"Indeed?" said Lady Meredith with lifted eyebrows. "You surprise me, Mrs. Westland. What sort of household do you manage?"

Unfortunately for Kate, Thomas saw fit to answer this question before she could. "You mustn't be thinking Four Oaks is a mansion like Honeywell House, my lady," he said with a jovial laugh. "I'm sure you could fit half a dozen of Four Oaks inside this place and have room to spare. Still, it's a snug property, and it suits Kate and me better than a big place like this. Doesn't it, Kate?''

There was nothing Kate could do but agree. Her agreement was a very brusque one, however, and she did not speak again until dinner was over. But it was obvious she had not learned her lesson, for as the ladies were leaving the table at a signal from Anne, she turned to address Lord Meredith in a flirtatious voice. ''Remember our bargain, my lord,'' she said. ''I have agreed to sing for you, but if you dawdle too long over your port I may change my mind and think better of it.''

''Yes, by all means hurry, Jonathan,'' said Lady Meredith, before her husband could speak. ''We are all anxious to hear Mrs. Westland sing.''

Lord Meredith glanced at his wife, then at Kate. There was a flicker of amusement in his dark eyes as he said, ''I will be there in ten minutes at the outside.'' It was not altogether clear which lady he was addressing.

The ladies trooped into the drawing room, where they at once polarized into two separate groups. Anne, Lady Meredith, and Lady O'Reilly formed the center of the larger one, but Kate had managed to commandeer Mrs. Winslow and her daughter, who were either too polite or too timid to resist her tactics. ''But you must take your daughter to London by all means, ma'am,'' Kate told Mrs. Winslow in a loud voice. ''She would be the better of it all her life. There is nothing like a Season in London to give a girl town bronze. I had three Seasons there myself before I was married.''

''Which explains why she is not merely *bronzed,* but *brazen,*'' whispered Lady Meredith in Anne's ear.

Anne choked back a giggle, then turned to address Lady O'Reilly beside her. ''Have you found a house to your liking in the neighborhood yet, Emily?'' she asked. ''I do hope you succeed in finding one. It would be delightful to have you and Sir Terrence settled here.''

Lady O'Reilly at once embarked on a lively account of her house-hunting travails. Amid general laughter, she described the last home the agent had shown them, which had been described by him as a desirable residence with a fine situation but had proved to be instead a tumbledown ruin located in a swamp and abounding in both rats and roof leaks.

All the while Lady O'Reilly was talking, Kate could be heard going on and on, telling the Winslows about London and the cultural advantages to be obtained there. Her voice was as loud and self-assured as ever, but Anne noticed she was beginning to repeat herself by the time twenty minutes had gone by. As soon as the first gentlemen came into the drawing room, she abandoned the Winslows in midsentence and flew to greet them.

''There you are,'' she told James, who was among the group. ''Come sit by me on the sofa, James. We have not had a chance to talk all night, and I have a great deal to say to you.''

James greeted her with a polite smile, but seemed not to hear her command to sit beside him. He drifted over to the fireplace and stood leaning against the mantel, looking around the room in a preoccupied manner. Balked of her first prey, Kate turned next to Lord Meredith, who had just entered the room along with Sir Terrence O'Reilly.

''Ah, here you are, my lord! I see you have fulfilled your promise to be prompt. I do appreciate it, for you must know I have been quite impatient to resume our conversation.'' She took him boldly by the arm, flashing a triumphant look toward the other ladies (and particularly toward Lady Meredith, as Anne remarked). However, Lady Meredith had her back to Kate and appeared quite oblivious to her words.

The tea tray made its appearance at this point, and Anne had to attend to serving her guests, so that she missed the exact process by which Kate came to take her place at the pianoforte. It was not until Anne heard the keys of the instrument being sounded that she looked up and saw her sister-in-law seated there.

"Remember, you shall have to make allowances, my lord," Kate told Lord Meredith, who was standing at her elbow. "It has been many years since I performed in public."

With these words, she launched into a song from a recent popular opera. Anne, after a few measures, had to turn away to hide a smile. Kate had not a bad singing voice, but she had not a good one, either, and the song she sang might have been chosen on purpose to expose its limitations.

Nor was her accompaniment much better than her voice. There was no modulation in her playing, and no expression. Every note received a precisely equal emphasis, and this mechanical fingering was not accompanied by a mechanical accuracy. She hit several very audible wrong notes that badly detracted from the overall effect. When she was finished, there was a scattering of polite applause, but no real encouragement to go on. Even Lord Meredith, whom Kate clearly expected to beg for an encore, stood silent and did not assent when she asked, "Well, shall I play something else?"

It was Lady Meredith who answered her. "Yes, do," she said warmly. "That was delightful, Mrs. Westland. Give us another song, if you please."

Kate looked as though she would have liked to disoblige

this request, but her desire to win praise was greater than her desire to snub Lady Meredith. She embarked on a second song, which she performed no better than the first and which won her merely another scattering of polite applause. It was noticeable, however, that Lady Meredith applauded louder and longer than anyone else.

Kate arose from the pianoforte with something like a flounce and sailed over to the sofa. Lady Meredith, having finished applauding her, looked around the room. "Is there no one else who will play for us?" she asked. "Miss Winslow, you have a voice like an angel's. Please won't you honor us with a song or two?"

Miss Winslow blushed deeply and disclaimed having any kind of a voice at all. In the end, however, she was persuaded to take her place at the pianoforte. She did indeed have a very sweet voice, and the fact that she sang nothing save simple ballads was nothing to its disadvantage. The applause that greeted her efforts was considerably more prolonged and enthusiastic than that which had greeted Kate's.

Kate, her cheeks unbecomingly reddened, confronted Lady Meredith as soon as Miss Winslow had stepped down from the pianoforte. "Why don't *you* sing for us, my lady?" she said belligerently. "I'm sure it's the least you can do, considering!"

"Considering what?" asked Lady Meredith, eyeing her coolly.

"Considering that you are encouraging others to perform!" snapped Kate. "Since you claim to be musical, let us see what you yourself are capable of!"

Lady Meredith smiled and shook her head. "I never claimed to be musical," she said. "Indeed, I have never made any *pretension* of being so."

The word pretension was only slightly stressed, but it

contained a sting that Kate seemed to feel. She flushed up to the roots of her hair, stood glaring at Lady Meredith a moment, then turned away without a word and made for Lord Meredith. But he was deep in conversation with James and Sir Terrence O'Reilly, and when Kate sought to draw him away, he smilingly shook his head and continued talking with the other gentlemen.

Frustrated in these efforts, Kate turned again to her old allies, Mrs. Winslow and her daughter. In a condescending way she began to praise Miss Winslow's voice and advised her mother to take her to London so that it might be properly trained. But Mrs. Winslow cut this advice short with the air of one who had heard enough. "Thank you, but I think Sophia is doing well enough right here in Langton Abbots," she said in a voice of decision. "It's my opinion that singers are born, not made, Mrs. Westland. A good singer doesn't need to go to London to learn how to sing—and for a singer who isn't good to start with, I don't see myself that any amount of London training makes much difference."

Possibly she did not mean these words as a direct criticism of Kate's performance, but it was obvious that Kate took them that way. She walked off in a state of dudgeon and did not try again to engage the Winslows in conversation. Instead she attached herself to Anne and the tea table and proceeded to usurp the greater part of the work of pouring and serving the tea.

Anne let her have her way in this, for she was actually feeling sorry for Kate by this time. Even when the guests began to take leave of the party, and Kate accepted their compliments with an air that implied she rather than Anne was the hostess, Anne said nothing to contradict her. "You are too softhearted by half," whispered Lady Meredith, as she prepared to leave the party with her husband.

"If it were me, I would have let her run to the end of her rope and never lifted a finger to help her."

"I don't intend to help her much longer," Anne whispered back. "But I dislike to see her humiliated any more than she already has been this evening. It can do no harm to indulge her a little now, I think."

"Perhaps not," conceded Lady Meredith. "But mind you do not become so sorry for her that you encourage her to stay on indefinitely! The next time I spend an evening with you, I want to sit and talk to you comfortably rather than crossing swords with your sister-in-law."

Lady O'Reilly, who with her husband was next to leave, proceeded to give Anne much the same sort of advice, though not so strongly worded. "I wanted so much to sit quietly and talk with you," she whispered. "I have a piece of news I am dying to share, and I have had no opportunity to tell it to you."

"Have you?" said Anne wistfully. "I don't suppose you could tell it to me now?"

"Well . . . perhaps," said Lady O'Reilly. She glanced around, then bent and whispered in Anne's ear. Anne made a soft exclamation.

"Oh, Emily! I am very happy for you—both for you and for Sir Terrence," she said. "When is it to be?"

"Early next year sometime, the doctor says," said Lady O'Reilly, her face aglow with pride and happiness. "Although there is no pinning these matters down too closely, of course. The doctor will not commit himself to any date more specific than early next year."

"I *am* happy for you," said Anne sincerely. "I thought you were looking very pleased about something tonight— and then, too, you looked unusually well—quite radiant, in fact. But I never guessed the cause."

Lady O'Reilly inspected Anne closely. "Do you know, I have been thinking the same thing about you, Anne. Not that you look precisely happy, I mean—obviously you could not be really happy as long as your sister-in-law is here! But it did strike me that there was something—something *different* about you. Is it possible that you and Lord Westland are also expecting a blessed event?"

Anne assured her that it was not possible, thinking gloomily that such a state of affairs would be almost without precedent given the estrangement between her and James. "But let me know if I can do anything, Emily," she told her friend. "And I hope you succeed in finding a house before the newest O'Reilly makes his or her appearance!"

"I hope so, too," Lady O'Reilly laughed and took a smiling leave of her.

Finally all the guests were gone, and only Anne, James, Kate, and Thomas remained. "A dashed fine party," said Thomas enthusiastically. "It all went off like clockwork, Anne. Everybody looked like they was having a good time." Turning to James, he added, "That Sir Terrence is a dashed funny feller, James. Had me laughing so hard at dinner that I nearly spilled wine on myself. Lord Meredith's a fine feller, too."

"*I* thought him very disagreeable," said Kate loudly. "Both he and his wife. They are both thoroughly disagreeable people, and they quite disgusted me with their behavior."

Anne and James looked at her, caught each other's eye, and quickly looked away.

Kate set down her teacup with a rattle and announced she was going to bed. "But first I shall have a word with your butler, Anne. As I mentioned before, the wine at dinner was scandalously underaired. When he is serving claret, he ought to open the bottles at least an hour before-hand. And there were several points about the service that might also have been improved. When the footmen brought in the dessert, for instance—''

''*No*,'' said Anne strongly. Kate gave her a look of surprise which quickly became one of contemptuous amusement.

''Indeed, I assure you there were a number of points where the service was not quite up to snuff, Anne. Likely you did not notice, being such an inexperienced house-keeper—''

''No,'' said Anne again, more strongly than ever. ''I noticed nothing amiss.'' She drew a deep breath. ''There is nothing you need to speak to the servants about, Kate. In fact, I would appreciate it if you would refrain from giving them any advice or criticism after this. You know if they do need advice or criticism, then I should be the one to give it to them.''

Kate stared at her, then laughed. ''Anne, you needn't be so much on your dignity,'' she said. ''You know we are sisters now, and all I am trying to do is to help you. The plain fact is that you are not firm enough in dealing with your staff. You let them ride over you roughshod—''

''Nevertheless, I would rather undertake the task of talking to them myself,'' said Anne quietly. ''You will oblige me by respecting my wishes in this matter, Kate.''

Kate looked at her, and apparently decided a different tack was necessary. ''I must say, I did not look for this attitude from you, Anne,'' she said in an injured voice. ''I am only trying to help.''

''And I am only trying to be firm,'' said Anne with a

slight smile. "Just as you are always advising me to be. So kindly leave the task of talking to the servants to me, and go along to bed. I am sure you must be fatigued after your exertions at the pianoforte."

Kate stared at her a moment, then turned without a word and flounced out of the room.

Thomas gave no sign that this passage had affected him. He announced that he was ready for bed, too, and wished Anne and James a cheerful good night.

After he had gone, James looked at Anne. "I suppose I must be going to my bed, too," he said. "But it was a fine party, Anne. You managed everything excellently well."

"Thank you," said Anne. The words were welcome enough in themselves, but there was something in James's manner that gave them a weight and value even beyond their surface one. After a second, Anne realized what it was. James was looking at her—really looking at her for almost the first time in weeks.

This surprised her, but she was still more surprised by what happened next. Coming to her, James bent down and kissed her on the brow. "Good night, Anne," he said, then took himself quickly off.

Since the day Timothy's letter had arrived, he had never once kissed her, not even to the extent of a formal salute on the hand. Anne looked after him blankly. "Well!" she said.

Although she had been feeling weary before, she suddenly discovered fresh reserves of energy within her. Instead of going immediately to bed, she decided to go to the conservatory and take one more look at the spider.

She had already looked at it once that evening, shortly before the party had begun. The spider's condition was now a cause of serious concern to her. It had eaten nothing for over a month and spent all its time huddled in a corner of the glasshouse, not moving even when Anne performed such tasks as refilling its water dish and watering its plants. Afraid that it was dead, she had ventured to nudge it once gently with the tongs, whereupon it had taken a few slow steps, then sunk into lassitude once more. Anne could not help fearing that if not actually dead, it was dying.

She entered the conservatory cautiously, holding aloft the branch of candles she had brought from the hall. Making her way to the spider's corner, she peered inside. What she saw nearly made her drop the candles. Over the patch of earth where the spider was wont to sit, it had spun a dense blanket of web and was now lying on it—lying on its back with all eight legs in the air.

"Oh, no!" cried Anne. "Oh, no!"

Her eyes filled with tears. It might be absurd to weep for a spider, but she had devoted many hours to this one's care and had come to feel an interest in it that was more than academic. Like her, it had been driven from its natural home by a remorseless fate; like her, it had been forced to adapt to conditions that were not of its own choosing. Anne had rejoiced to see it adapting so well, as she had thought, but now here it was lying dead. A sob rose in her throat. She started to turn away, but at that moment a movement in the glasshouse caught her eye.

Anne turned back and stared at the spider. Was it her imagination, or had its legs moved ever so slightly? Yes, even as she watched she saw it move again—a feeble movement, but unmistakable. Anne looked around and saw a few feet away the set of steps used by the gardeners when attending to hanging baskets and trees. Setting down the branch of candles, she dragged the steps over to the spider's corner and sat down upon them, tucking her feet beneath her and folding her arms over her knees.

For a long time she watched and saw nothing more than the same feeble movement of legs that had initially caught her attention. Anne supposed she must be witnessing the spider's death throes. She wondered at herself for staying and watching a sight so painful. Yet she felt driven to stay by something—a sense of duty, perhaps, that would not allow her to let even a spider die alone.

"I wish there was something I could do for you," she told it softly. "Poor Arachne, it's a pity you could not have stayed in Brazil. I suppose England was simply not a congenial environment for you."

The spider waved its legs feebly as though in reply. Anne sat watching it, absorbed in thoughts of pity and regret. She wondered if dying was painful to it, or if it would welcome death as a release. There had been times in her own life, as recently as that very day, when she would have been tempted to do the same.

Then her eyes widened, and she leaned forward in her seat. Something was happening to the spider—something apart from a mere movement of legs.

Anne stared at it, unable at first to grasp what was going on. The legs seemed to pulse and elongate, and then, with a rending movement, began to lift away from the body. "No," said Anne aloud in horror. Then she saw the legs were still intact—only they were not the same legs. Neither was the body the same body. Impossible as it seemed, the spider appeared to be wriggling out of its skin. Beneath was a new skin—a skin glossy, plush with hair, and almost black instead of the shabby faded brown it had been before.

Spellbound, Anne watched as bit by bit the spider

worked the old skin off the ends of its feet, like a woman wriggling her fingers out of a pair of too-tight gloves. At last the old skin fell away, and the spider lay on its back, legs folded against the front of its body. It was clearly not dead, for the legs continued to pulse as before, opening and closing slightly as though in rhythm with an unseen pulsing heart.

"Well!" said Anne, drawing a deep breath. "Who would have thought it?" What she had witnessed was not a death at all, but rather a rebirth. She recalled now having heard that snakes and other reptiles periodically shed their skins; she even fancied she had once seen and handled a snakeskin that had been among a collection of curiosities in someone's home. Yet the snakeskin had been a mere ghost of the animal it had once contained, while this was a literal copy. At the moment it looked as though the glasshouse was occupied by not one but two large spiders.

Taking up the tongs, Anne went to the glasshouse, unfastened the catch, and swung open its lid. With the utmost gentleness she removed the shed skin, being careful not to disturb the spider, who still lay on its back as though exhausted by its recent labors. Using the tongs, she laid the skin on a stack of empty planting flats that were lying nearby and bent down to examine it. It crouched there, looking as much like the spider it had come from as possible, save that it was hollow inside.

For several minutes Anne knelt beside it, examining it closely and marveling at the intricacy of its structure. Even the great fangs had been shed with the skin and reproduced anew on the living spider. "Remarkable," she said aloud. "I never would have believed it if I had not witnessed it for myself."

Somewhere in the house, a clock struck two. Anne

realized suddenly she was very weary. She took a last look at the spider, still gently pulsing with life atop its mat of web, then picked up the candles and left the conservatory.

CHAPTER XX

When Anne awoke the next morning, she awoke with a sense of purpose that had her up and out of bed almost before she was fully awake.

It was a beautiful day, fair and cloudless. The sky overhead was a deep, clear blue, and a light breeze drifted through the window, bringing with it the elusive scent of autumn. Anne shut her eyes, the better to appreciate it. The breeze stirred the bed curtains and lifted the hair from the nape of her neck, and she was conscious of life and determination throbbing within her.

Memories of the night before came flooding back to her. When she went to examine them in her mind, she found that those disconnected events had taken on a cohesive and significant pattern. Lady Meredith's advice, Lady O'Reilly's revelation, James's kiss, and even the miraculous rebirth of the spider all seemed to Anne part of a clear message—a message that had been sent to her for some definite purpose. It would be for her to decide how best to profit from that message and achieve the purpose it had been meant for.

The first thing I must do—the very first thing—is get rid of Kate, she told herself. *If I can only accomplish that, I suspect everything else will fall quickly into place.*

As soon as she was washed and dressed, she left her room and went cautiously down the hall. Pausing at Kate's door, she listened a moment. She could hear snoring inside it, and for a moment she thought Thomas must be sharing his wife's bedchamber, but then she realized that the snoring, though loud, was unmistakably feminine. This was satisfying, indicating that Kate was not yet awake, but it was also satisfying to Anne on a more petty and personal level.

"I never imagined Kate snoring somehow," Anne whispered to herself as she tiptoed away. "I may be thin and small and pale, but at least I don't snore."

Making her way to the housekeeper's room, she found Mrs. Rhodes in consultation with the cook. "Good morning, my lady," said Mrs. Rhodes, rising from her chair and curtsying. "You're up early this morning. I hope I find you well?"

"Yes, very well," said Anne. "I am glad to find you here, Mrs. Rhodes. I was wanting to talk to you about a rather private and confidential matter." Here she hesitated. The matter she wished to broach was indeed a very delicate one, and with Mrs. Rhodes's and the cook's eyes both fixed on her, she hardly knew where to start.

Before the silence could become embarrassing, Mrs. Rhodes spoke again. "That happens very convenient-like, my lady," she said. "I was wishful to ask you something in confidence myself." She exchanged glances with the cook, then turned to Anne with the air of one who burns her bridges behind her. "It's about that Kate Westland—about Mrs. Thomas Westland, I *should* say."

"About Kate?" said Anne in astonishment. "You were wanting to talk to me about Kate? But that's what I was wanting to talk to *you* about!"

Mrs. Rhodes looked embarrassed but defiant. "Yes, well, I don't like to be disobliging, my lady," she said, "but you know it says right in the Bible that no man can serve two masters. I'm thinking the same applies to mistresses." She drew a deep breath. "I've done the best I could and kept my tongue between my teeth till I thought I was like to bite it off, but after last night, I made up my mind that enough was enough. It's her or me, as you might say, and if it's her, why, well, then, I'll say no more. I'll just pack my bags and start looking for another position."

"Start looking for another position?" said Anne with dismay. "You don't mean you are giving notice, Mrs. Rhodes?"

"I'm sure I don't *want* to give notice, my lady," said Mrs. Rhodes. "I've been at Honeywell House fifteen years now and looked forward to being here as many more. But it's as I said before: no man can serve two masters. I've enjoyed working for you, my lady, and I always thought we got on as well as any two people could, but ever since that Mrs. Westland came—well! Nothing I do is any good, to hear *her* tell it. It's not that I mind being corrected when I'm wrong, for I'm as like to make mistakes as the next person, and I'm sure I'm always grateful to be set straight when I make one. But it's not mistakes that Mrs. Westland seems concerned about, so much as changing every blessed detail of the housekeeping routine. And for no good reason that I can see, except that she wants to do things different from the way we do things now.''

''I know,'' said Anne, nodding vigorously. ''Believe me, I know exactly what you are talking about, Mrs. Rhodes. It is that which I wanted to talk to you about.''

''It is?'' said Mrs. Rhodes, regarding Anne with doubt. ''As I say, I don't like to be disobliging, my lady, but change for change's sake is something I cannot abide. It's not merely that it's disrupting to me though I'm an old dog to be learning new tricks, I'm thinking. The thing is, though, that I've got my staff to manage, my lady. And when I give one set of orders, only to have to go back and change them an hour later, it not only makes me look a fool but makes it mortal hard to keep my authority with the folk beneath me. I don't know if you take my meaning—''

''I take it perfectly,'' said Anne. ''There will be no more contradictory orders from now on, Mrs. Rhodes. If there are, you have my authority to disregard them.''

Mrs. Rhodes looked at her a moment and it was plain to see hope struggling with skepticism in her expression. ''Well,'' she said, ''you can't think how glad I am to hear it, my lady. Only—only Mrs. Westland spoke as though she had taken the running of the house to herself. And I didn't know but what your ladyship might not have given her leave to do so.''

Anne gave her a wry smile. ''No, I did not give her leave,'' she said. ''Mrs. Westland merely took charge of things without it—though with my own tacit consent, I will admit. She is a guest, you know, as well as being Lord Westland's sister-in-law, and I did not like to seem rude or disobliging. But she has been here at Honeywell House six weeks now, and I think it is time to—how shall I put it? Time to take back that authority which she has borrowed.''

Both Mrs. Rhodes and the cook looked deeply relieved. ''You can't think how glad I am to hear it, my lady!'' said the cook. ''So if Mrs. Westland comes around telling me I need to empty the salt cellar into my white sauce before sending it to the table, I've your permission to tell her to go to the devil? Not that I'd use such a rude expression to a lady, of course,'' she added hastily. ''But in a manner of speaking?''

''You may use any expression you like that carries a sufficient force,'' said Anne, speaking very clearly and deliberately. ''Not to put too fine a point on it, I would not be sorry if Mrs. Westland decided to leave Honeywell House in the very near future. And I think she is more likely to do so if she finds the atmosphere has become somewhat—shall we say, uncongenial?''

The two women looked at Anne, and an expression of something like glee spread across their faces. ''My lady!'' said the cook, drawing a deep breath. ''Them's the most welcome words I've heard in years. You can't think how all of us have chafed to have that hussy picking and prodding at us night and day.''

''That we have,'' said Mrs. Rhodes. With dignity she added, ''Hussy is a word I would hesitate to use, Mrs. Laughton, seeing as we are speaking about her ladyship's sister-in-law. However, a hussy she undoubtedly is, and we won't any of us be sorry to see the last of her.''

''Very well,'' said Anne. ''Let us see if together we cannot persuade her to return to Four Oaks.''

The cook made an exasperated noise. ''Four Oaks! I'm sure I'm sick to death of hearing about Four Oaks,'' she said. ''It's Four Oaks this, and Four Oaks that, until I can hardly stand to hear the name.''

"We've all had a bellyful of Four Oaks, I'm thinking," said Mrs. Rhodes. "And to my mind, the sooner Mrs. Westland's back there, the better." Addressing Anne, she added, "You needn't worry, my lady. There's not a servant in the house that won't join with you in speeding her on her way, now you've given us leave to do so. She's made herself a nuisance from cellar to attic."

Anne expressed herself appropriately grateful. "I am sorry you should have been plagued with her for so long," she said. "I should have done something before now, I suppose, but the situation is a very delicate one. As I said before, Kate is a guest here and my husband's sister-in-law. It's such a pity. If only she were to mend her ways and refrain from interfering in the household routine, I should have no objection to her staying on. If only she could be content to be a guest rather than trying to run things—"

"Her sort never can," said Mrs. Rhodes, with the air of speaking from large experience. "And to speak truth, my lady, I'm surprised you've stood it as long and as well as you have. But there, we always figured you'd stand up to her one of these days. You're a real lady, as all of us servants agree, and a real lady's more than a match for a hussy like Mrs. Westland any day."

Anne had her doubts about this, but when the cook added, "Especially with us to back you up," she felt her heart warm with sudden confidence.

"I am glad to have your support," she told both women. "But you know we must be careful not to step over the bounds of courtesy unless and until Kate does it first."

"That'll be next time she opens her mouth," said the cook cheerfully. "None of us have heard a word of courtesy out of her since she got here, my lady, and that's the truth.'' Looking at Anne, she added, ''I'd be much surprised to hear that you had, either, my lady.''

''Not very many words of courtesy, at any rate,'' allowed Anne. She turned to go, but was stopped by Mrs. Rhodes.

''May I tell the other staff what you have told us, my lady?'' she asked.

Anne nodded. ''Yes, you may, but be discreet. You may tell them that as of today, Kate will no longer be allowed to interfere with household matters. Further than that I would rather you did not go, for you know some of the staff might take it as encouragement to be openly rude to Kate, and that is not what I want at all. I merely wish to show her a cool indifference.''

''As you like, my lady,'' said Mrs. Rhodes, her tone indicating that this was an unnecessary distinction in her book. ''I'll pass the word on as soon as may be.'' Anne thanked her, then took leave of her and the cook, feeling she had left the matter in capable hands.

She went next to the conservatory to see how the spider was faring. She had been thinking of it a great deal since the previous night and hoped it had recovered from the ordeal of shedding its skin. But as she neared the double doors of the conservatory, she heard a startled bellow from within. Anne knew at once what had happened. She plunged through the doors and threaded her way amid trees and flats of plants until she reached the corner where the spider resided.

She found Joe Gardiner cowering back against a rack of seedlings, holding his secateurs in front of him as though to ward off an attack. ''Get back, my lady.'' He gasped on seeing Anne. ''That gawd-awful spider of yours has got loose somehow!'' He pointed toward the stack of flats on the floor beside the spider's glasshouse.

"No, it hasn't," said Anne. "I'm so sorry, Mr. Gardiner." Going over to the flats, she picked up the tongs and removed the shed skin from the topmost flat. She then held it out for Mr. Gardiner to see. "It's not the spider, but only the spider's skin, Mr. Gardiner. It shed it last night."

"No!" said Mr. Gardiner, staring at the object in the tongs. "You're certain sure that's not the beast itself, my lady? It looks deuced like." On being assured it was not, he put down the secateurs and came a few steps closer, still regarding the skin as nervously as though he expected it to take a sudden lunge at him. Once near enough to see, however, his nervousness abruptly gave way to a keen interest.

"Well, now, if that hain't something to see!" he exclaimed, regarding the skin with fascination. "Just like a spider, only 'ollow-like. And 'ow's the old lady herself doing?" He stepped closer to the glasshouse to regard the spider. "Looks fresh as paint, don't she? And bigger, too, if I'm not mistook. I'm dashed if she ain't growed a size in the process of changing her skin."

"Has she indeed?" exclaimed Anne. She put down the skin and approached the glasshouse to take a closer look. After studying the spider a moment, she said, "I believe you're right, Mr. Gardiner. She *is* bigger than she was before."

"A deal bigger," said Mr. Gardiner. "And she wasn't what you could call small before. Unnatural, I calls it." He regarded the spider with gloomy satisfaction. "I don't know what the Almighty was about, creating such a h'animal. Why, it don't even grow like a Christian beast."

"But it is very interesting, all the same," said Anne. "You must admit it is at least interesting, Mr. Gardiner!"

Mr. Gardiner admitted that the spider was interesting,

though he continued to maintain that it was also unnatural. "What do you mean to do with that skin there, my lady?" he added. "You'd best not leave it here, or one of my young lads'll catch sight of it and go off into a fainting fit like a gur-rul."

There was a scorn in his voice that made Anne laugh. "I am sure they couldn't be blamed if they did," she said. "You know yourself it is a rather startling sight, Mr. Gardiner. Perhaps I could put it in the library, in one of those glass-topped cases that are used to hold coins and medals and such things. I think it would make a much more interesting display than coins and medals!"

Mr. Gardiner said he would be glad to fetch an appropriate box for her, if she would stay and see none of his lads got hysterics as a result of stumbling across the spider skin unawares. He returned a short time later, bearing a small walnut box a foot square which was lined with velvet and had a square of glass inset in the lid. " 'Ere you go, my lady. This one looked closest to the right size, and the yellow stuff inside ought to show it off finely." He helped Anne arrange the skin on the velvet and stood admiring it for a moment or two. "Unnatural I still call it," he said at last, "but I will admit it's interesting, as you say."

"I think it is *very* interesting," said Anne. "I wish you could have seen Arachne actually shedding it, Mr. Gardiner. But at least you can see the skin itself, and that is much better than nothing."

It occurred to her as she spoke that James might find the spider skin interesting, too. After all, he had taken an interest in the spider's welfare earlier, even if he had shown no curiosity concerning it—or her—for the last couple of months.

As Anne stood with the box in her hands, debating

whether she dared take it up to show James and risk being rejected for her pains, the conservatory door opened and Kate came storming in.

"Anne, I'd like to know what you mean by—" she began. Then she caught sight of the object in Anne's hands. A piercing scream broke from her lips. It startled Anne so that she nearly dropped the box, causing Kate to scream again. She began to back away, pointing toward the box and gibbering incoherently.

"Kate, do stop that awful noise," begged Anne, trying to retain hold of the box and cover her hands with her ears at the same time. "What on earth is wrong?"

"It's my opinion," said Mr. Gardiner, inspecting Kate with a knowledgeable eye, "it's my opinion that she don't like spiders."

"No more I do." Kate gasped, keeping her eyes on the box in Anne's hand. "I am deathly afraid of them."

"But this isn't a real spider," said Anne, holding the box out to her. Kate screamed again while retreating a dozen paces with amazing speed.

"I don't care if it's real or not," she said through her teeth. "I detest spiders."

"But it's only—" began Anne, then stopped. She could see it was no use to try to reason with such unreasoning fear. "I'm sorry, Kate," she said. "Here, I'll put the box down and come outside." Suiting action to word, she accompanied her sister-in-law out into the hall.

Once in the hall, Kate drew a deep breath. She was trembling all over, and her usually rosy face had faded to a ghastly pale. "You really must be afraid of spiders," said Anne, surveying her with astonishment.

"I am," said Kate through chattering teeth. "I can't bear to look even at tiny ones. Let alone that—that *thing* you were holding. What on earth was it, Anne? It looked like a spider, only''—she swallowed—''only it was *huge.*''

"It's a shed skin from a South American bird-eating spider,'' said Anne. ''James brought one back with him from Brazil.''

Kate shuddered. "Horrible,'' she said. ''Do they really have spiders as big as that in Brazil? Thank God I am never likely to go to Brazil, then.''

"They are really quite interesting,'' said Anne, loyal as always in the spider's cause. ''I was watching last night when ours shed the skin you saw just now, and it was fascinating, Kate. Watching it eat is fascinating, too. Whenever it catches an insect, it does what almost looks like a little dance . . .''

She stopped, for Kate was regarding her with fresh horror. "I thought you said it was only a skin!'' she said. ''You don't mean to say there is a live spider that size in this house?''

"Yes, of course there is,'' said Anne. ''James brought it back from Brazil with him, and I have been taking care of it.''

"Good God,'' said Kate faintly. In a stronger tone, she added, ''It must be gotten rid of immediately. Have the servants kill it, then bring me word as soon as they have. I won't be easy a minute until that thing is dead.''

"I will do no such thing!'' said Anne indignantly. ''I have not been taking care of it for months, only to see it killed!''

"Well, it cannot stay here,'' said Kate. ''I could never sleep a wink, knowing that creature was in the house with me.''

"You have slept many winks with it in the house with

you, and it has never disturbed you in the least," said Anne warmly. "You are being unreasonable, Kate."

"Unreasonable or not, I am determined to be rid of that creature before another hour goes by," retorted Kate. "If you do not give the order to have it killed, I shall." Recollection seemed to come to her with these words, for a sudden fire sprang up in her eyes. "And that reminds me! What the devil do you mean by telling your servants not to obey my orders?"

"What were you doing giving my servants orders in the first place?" countered Anne. "I told you last night that if orders were necessary, I preferred to give them myself."

Kate disregarded this. "I won't have it," she told Anne, placing her hands on her hips and regarding Anne belligerently. "I was down in the kitchen just now to give your cook a hint about the soup, and she was downright rude to me! And when I told her I would see she was dismissed for her behavior, she said she'd like to see me try, for she was only following your orders."

Despite the awkwardness of the situation, Anne could not help smiling. "I am sorry if the cook was rude to you, Kate," she said. "But it is as I told you before: you have no business to be giving my servants advice or orders. They have found it very confusing these past few weeks, having to answer to two different people who have given them what have often been very contradictory orders. I thought it best for all concerned if the authority were limited to me alone."

Kate's eyes were blazing now. "That sounds good," she sneered. "But you know this has nothing to do with the servants, Anne. You are only doing this to punish me, because you are jealous of me. You have been jealous of me all along."

Anne looked Kate squarely in the eye. "Why on earth should I be jealous of you?" she said.

"Because James cared for me first. And because he still cares for me," said Kate, looking at Anne triumphantly. "You know it's true, Anne. James was madly in love with me years ago—madly, insanely in love with me. And he still is. If we were both free, he'd marry me in a minute. He loves me much more than he ever cared for you."

There was absolute conviction in her voice, and for a sickening moment, Anne felt Kate must be speaking the truth. Then she took courage, remembering Lady Meredith's words. Lady Meredith had said she was sure that there was more than met the eye regarding James's supposed attachment to Kate, and that if she were in Anne's position she would call Kate's bluff. Anne could not see that she had anything to lose by following this advice.

"Fiddlesticks," she said in a clear voice. The word pleased her, and she said it again, more loudly. "Fiddlesticks! I don't believe it. I don't believe James cares a straw for you, Kate."

"He does," said Kate fiercely. "He does!"

"I don't believe it," repeated Anne. She looked at Kate for a moment in silence. Kate glared back at her. "However, you are welcome to make a trial of it, if you like," she said deliberately. "Go on and appeal to James, and see what he says."

"I will!" said Kate furiously. "I will tell him what you have said and how you have treated me. We will see what he says to that! And I will tell him also that he must get rid of that damnable spider. And he will do it, because he loves me!"

Anne did not answer but merely smiled in a disbelieving manner. Kate glared at her, then turned on her heel and ran up the stairs. Anne hesitated a moment, then went back into the conservatory. She almost stumbled over Joe Gardiner, who was crouched in front of the door in the classic eavesdropper's posture. He scrambled to his feet, looking deeply abashed.

"Beg pardon, m'lady," he said. "I couldn't 'elp over-hearing—"

"No, I suppose you couldn't," said Anne, smiling in spite of herself. "It was a fine, dramatic scene, wasn't it? I suppose you heard everything that passed just now between me and Mrs. Westland?"

"Most of it," admitted Mr. Gardiner, looking more sheepish than ever.

"Then you know she has taken my Arachne in dislike. May I ask you to stay here in the conservatory and keep an eye on her until I know what Kate intends to do? I am afraid in her current state, she may do the poor creature a mischief."

"I'll be glad to stay," said Mr. Gardiner promptly. "But I wouldn't worry about that 'arpy trying any tricks with your pet, my lady. 'Tis plain to see she's mortal afraid of spiders." He looked at Anne with a glint of mischief in his eye. "After the way she talked just now, 'twould serve 'er right if you tucked your eight-legged friend there into 'er bed tonight, as a gesture of loving kindness."

Anne laughed. "It would serve her right," she agreed. "But I cannot like to take the risk, Mr. Gardiner."

"You mean she might do herself an injury trying to get away from it?" said Mr. Gardiner, tilting his head as though considering the probability of such an event. "If it were me, I'd say the risk was worth it."

"I was thinking more of the risk to the spider,"

explained Anne, and they both laughed. Having extracted Mr. Gardiner's promise not to leave the spider unattended until they knew what Kate meant to do, Anne hurried from the conservatory and went to see what was happening elsewhere in the house.

CHAPTER XXI

Anne fully expected to find Kate with James and already embarked on a scene to end all scenes. But the house seemed quiet—almost ominously quiet. And when she cautiously tapped on the door of James's study and received permission to enter, she found him quite alone.

At her entrance, he rose to his feet with a startled look. "Anne!"

"Forgive me for interrupting you," said Anne formally. One glance was enough to show her Kate was not there, and she was pretty sure from James's manner that she never had been there. He did not look like a man who had just endured a trying scene with a hysterical woman.

On the other hand, he did look like a man mystified by the entry of his estranged wife into his sanctum sanctorum. Anne had been prepared for this and had brought along the shed skin of the spider by way of an excuse. "Forgive me for interrupting you, James," she said again, placing the box on the table in front of him. "But I thought you might like to see this."

James glanced at the box, and his face, already startled, grew even more so. "What the deuce?" he exclaimed. "Is that the spider you've got there?"

"It's the spider's skin," explained Anne. "It shed it last night after the party."

She looked at him as she spoke, but he was busy examining the skin. "Indeed!" he said. "Well, what do you know about that! I had no idea spiders shed their skins. Do you suppose it's a natural process?"

"I think it must be," said Anne. "The spider looks splendid now, like it was made over new. I think it has grown a little larger in the process, too."

"Indeed," said James again. He glanced up at Anne and smiled. "Most people thought it sufficiently large before. It ought to be more impressive than ever if it has grown even larger."

"Yes, it is very impressive," said Anne. In a casual voice, she added, "I take it Kate has not been in to see you this morning?"

"Kate?" said James. He looked surprised and a little wary. "Why should Kate come to see me?"

"I thought she might have come to see you about the spider," said Anne. "She came upon this unawares"— she touched the box—"and it startled her. Apparently she dislikes spiders."

"Does she?" said James. "I didn't know that."

"Yes, she dislikes them intensely," said Anne. "In fact, she took strong exception to the idea of having a spider this size living in the same house with her."

James nodded, but his expression was more amused than concerned. "I suppose many people might have reservations on that score," he said. "To speak truth, I would have expected you to have a few yourself, Anne. It's a wonder to me that you should be such an avid naturalist.''

"I don't know that I'm a naturalist," said Anne. "But I find Arachne very interesting and have grown very attached to her. And I told Kate I should not dream of getting rid of her only because she has an irrational aversion to spiders.''

Anne looked closely at James as she spoke, but he did not appear much impressed by her words one way or another. "Indeed?" he said again, in an absent voice. "Knowing Kate, I don't suppose she took that news particularly well.''

"She didn't," said Anne. "She threatened to come to you and complain.''

James looked up briefly, then down at the spider skin again. "Did she?" he said. After a minute, he looked at Anne again. "Anne, about Kate—" he said.

"Yes?" said Anne.

James met her a gaze a moment, then looked away again. "Nothing," he said. "That is—er—she didn't mention how much longer she and Thomas were planning to stay here at Honeywell House, did she? I thought they had planned to stay only six weeks, but if I mistake not it has been close to that already.''

Anne was sure this was not what James had originally intended to say. But she found comfort in his words nonetheless. They seemed to show he was as eager as she to have the Westlands leave Honeywell House.

Then it occurred to her that it might be only Thomas's presence James objected to. Lady Meredith had scoffed at the idea, but if Kate could be retained while Thomas was sent away, James might well be glad to see her extend her stay. The idea made Anne's spine stiffen. "The last I heard, Kate was talking about her and Thomas staying through the Christmas holidays,'' she said coldly. ''And there are times I think that they—or at least she—would be glad to settle here permanently.''

James sighed, but made no other answer. Anne picked up the box again. ''Forgive me for interrupting you,'' she said again. ''No, don't trouble to get up, James. I will let myself out.''

After she had gone, James remained where he stood, looking after her. He was in a deeply troubled state of mind.

The past months had been the most unhappy of his life. They had seemed even unhappier because of the happy months that had preceded them. In James's mind, those months had come to represent a kind of Elysium. He had rejoiced to find himself married to Anne; rejoiced in the comfort of her presence; rejoiced that she seemed to be coming to share the feelings he cherished for her. Then the letter from Timothy Linville had arrived, and his rejoicings had been vanquished as though they had never been.

That Anne had married him, loving another man, was an idea so painful that there were times James felt it would drive him mad. To know that she had been possessed by another man—and was still, perhaps, possessed by him in spirit—seemed to make a mockery of all he had felt and hoped and dreamed about her. Clearly he had been mistaken in supposing she was coming to love him. Her heart was given to someone else.

And not merely her heart, for the letter had made it clear that she and Mr. Linville had shared physical intimacies. That put the seal on the matter as far as James was concerned. He had not known Anne well before their marriage, but if there was one thing he was certain of, it was that she was not a wanton. If she had given herself to another man, it was only because she had loved him with her whole heart and soul.

And if she had loved another man with her whole heart and soul, then that left nothing for him, James Westland. James had faced this bitter fact squarely and forced himself to accept it. He did not want the remains of Anne's affections—remains that had been left over and warmed up and made to serve in a pinch. If he could not have her whole heart and all her love to himself, then he wanted no part of it at all.

He had made this resolution in the early hours of the terrible night that had followed on the arrival of Timothy's letter. Since then, he had stuck to his resolution faithfully, but he was surprised sometimes to find what a struggle it was. He had supposed he had too much pride to inflict his attentions on a woman whose affections were engaged elsewhere. Yet there were times when he could hardly restrain himself from taking Anne in his arms and begging her to give him whatever of her affections she had left. It was only by a stern exercise of will that James refrained from doing this, and the exercise did not grow any easier with practice. On the contrary, it grew steadily more difficult.

As the weeks went by, he began to hunger more and more for Anne; to feel an intolerable longing for the taste of her kisses on his lips, the feel of her body against his, the sound of her voice speaking his name. Clearly his pride was not so uncompromising as he had supposed. In fact, he began to feel it was precious little safeguard between him and the humiliation of loving a woman who did not love him in return.

The matter had been made worse by Kate and Thomas's

arrival at Honeywell House. Instead of distracting him from his brooding about Anne, having them around had somehow only made him brood the more. To see Thomas's clumsy gallantries toward Anne made him jealous even when he knew there was no cause for jealousy, and as for Kate, her presence seemed to throw into high relief all the things he had come to know and love about Anne.

He marveled to think that years ago he had once fancied himself in love with Kate. He had even considered marrying her at one time, but then they had quarreled over some point of Kate's behavior—as nearly as he could remember, she had been flirting rather too openly with some other man at a party. His pride had been so much offended by her behavior that he had left her severely alone thereafter. Yet even though it had been his own decision to end their relationship, he had been hurt when she had married Thomas. It had seemed just another instance of Thomas getting the thing that he himself desired, and he had felt bitterly that it was his lot to give way to his half brother all his life, as much in adulthood as in childhood.

Since Thomas had come to Honeywell House, however, James had begun to feel that he had been unduly harsh in judging his half brother. There was no denying that Thomas could be irritating, but it was equally impossible to deny that he was also kind and well-intentioned. Concealment either good or bad was impossible for him. He was what he was, an honest, generous, not-very-intelligent but good-hearted man. If his own mother had favored him over James, who was merely her stepson, was that Thomas's fault? James was forced to admit that it was not. Nor could he help admitting that however deplorable he had found his stepmother's behavior, it had been natural enough under the circumstances.

It was a relief to let go of the enmity he had long felt toward Thomas and accept him as a brother and a friend. It was a still greater relief to look at Thomas's wife and rejoice that he had not married her himself. Kate remained almost as handsome now as she had been years ago, but the essential coarseness of her character and looks was coming more and more to the surface. Particularly apparent was it when she was together with Anne. There was something so *fine* about Anne—something so fine and delicate that it made Kate appear gaudy, gross, and overcolored by comparison. The contrast would have been almost an amusing one if James had been sure of the possession of Anne's love and esteem. As it was, it merely made him the more sick at heart to reflect that the wife he loved so devotedly was herself in love with someone else.

"It's such a tangle," said James aloud. "Such an impossible tangle." For the thousandth time, he wondered if he ought to leave Anne at Honeywell House and go somewhere else to live. A physical separation, painful as it would undoubtedly be, might in the long run be less painful than a merely mental and emotional one. As things now stood, he still had to publicly act the part of Anne's husband, and acting it publicly only made him long to do it privately as well.

"But I can't do that," he told himself desperately. "I can't make love to her, knowing she loves someone else. Not even if she were willing to let me. It would be obscene—abominable." The situation was, in fact, hopeless. He was doomed to suffer no matter what he did, and though he was still determined to conduct himself so that he might keep his pride, more and more he felt what cold comfort was this victory of mind over inclination.

Seeing Anne just now had made him even more conscious of how little pride could do to solace a broken heart. Looking into her clear, beautiful eyes, he had felt an urge to throw reserve to the winds and speak to her frankly. Among other things, he longed to tell her that Kate was nothing to him except his half brother's wife. Although absorbed in his own private miseries, he had not been deaf and blind to all that was going on in the household, and he was pretty certain that Kate had said or implied to Anne that he still cherished an affection for her. It irked him that she would misrepresent his feelings, but he admitted to himself that such a misrepresentation could make very little difference in the long run. If Anne did not love him, why should she care if he were in love with Kate?

James was sure Anne did not love him. She had looked and sounded quite cool just now when he had mentioned Kate's name. The chilliness of her response had tied his tongue, making it impossible for him to tell her the truth about his feelings for his sister-in-law. In retrospect, James decided it was just as well. If once he had embarked on a course of self-revelation, he might have gone ahead and revealed his whole heart, including his love and longing for Anne and his bitter regret that she did not return his feelings. And then the fat would have been in the fire. They were only just managing to maintain the pretense of civility now, and if ever such explosive matters as these were brought out in the open, all pretense would be at an end. There would be no option but for them to part.

With a sigh, James looked down at his desk, which was covered with documents having to do with the recent rental of some property. He felt in no mood now to plow through such dry stuff. He decided it could very well be left until tomorrow without causing inconvenience to anyone. Leaving the documents where they were, he went to the study door, opened it, and almost collided with Thomas, who was standing on the other side.

Thomas flashed his teeth in a broad smile. "Beg your pardon, old man," he said. "I was just coming to see you."

"Were you?" said James, forcing an answering smile to his own lips. "What can I do for you, Thomas?"

"Not a thing, old man. I've just come to tell you we're leaving. Kate's decided she wants to be back at Four Oaks for the parish festival, and you know how it is once Kate's made up her mind. She's bound to get her way, though the devil himself should oppose her!"

Thomas laughed as he spoke, with obvious pride in his wife's determination. James smiled, too, but inwardly he was wondering at his brother's words. He had a shrewd idea that more lay behind Kate's decision than a sudden whim to be back at her own home for a parish festival. His mind flew back to the conversation he had just had with Anne. Anne had mentioned Kate's dislike of spiders and her desire that the house be rid of the one kept in the conservatory. But this seemed to James a wholly inadequate reason for Kate to suddenly pack up and leave.

However, he was not one to look a gift horse in the mouth. Kate's meddling ways and assumptions of an authority that was not her own had irritated him many times in the past six weeks. It had seemed to him amazing that Anne should bear it as quietly as she had. But then she bore everything quietly. The thought sent a pang of something like shame through him. For a moment he felt almost guilty, and not merely about having stood silently by when Kate was behaving presumptuously. He had the sense that he had failed Anne in some deeper and more important sense. But he quickly pushed the idea aside. If he had failed Anne, then she had failed him, too. She had married him, loving someone else, and that was a failing that no man of spirit could forgive or overlook.

Since James would not admit he was anything but a man of spirit, it followed that he could not forgive or overlook Anne's deception. Yet he continued to brood about it all the rest of the morning. Even as he took a formal farewell of his brother and sister-in-law shortly after luncheon-time, he kept shooting looks at Anne as she made the polite remarks of a hostess bidding farewell to her house guests. "I am so glad you could both come," she told Kate and Thomas. "You will have to visit us at Honeywell House again sometime soon."

Kate merely sniffed at this, but Thomas said warmly that he was dashed if they didn't take Anne up on her invitation. "And you and James'll have to come visit us at Four Oaks," he added. "For Christmas maybe— though the weather can make traveling that time a year a bit chancy, especially up north where we live. Next spring or summer might suit you better. But whenever you decide to come, you can be sure that Kate and I'll be dashed glad to have you. Won't we, Kate?"

"Certainly," said Kate, showing her teeth in what was more a snarl than a smile. "You must come visit us soon, by all means. I look forward to repaying Anne for the *hospitality* she has shown us."

Soon the last farewells had been exchanged, and the carriage set off down the drive, bound once more for Four Oaks. Anne dutifully waved her pocket handkerchief as long as it remained in sight. James stood beside her, watching the carriage recede into the distance. When at last it had disappeared through the gates, Anne let her arm drop to her side, and both she and James heaved simultaneous sighs.

"Well, *that's* over," said James.

"Yes," said Anne.

James glanced sideways at her. Not for the first time, he wished he knew what was going on in her head. It appeared to him there had been relief in both her voice and sigh. But when he caught her eye, she merely colored a little and turned away. As James watched her walk back into the house, he was overcome once more with a sense of having failed her in some strange, indefinite way.

If he *had* been able to read her thoughts, he would have found he was right in thinking her relieved. Anne felt she had never welcomed anything in her life as much as the departure of Kate from Honeywell House. It was as though a fog that had been obscuring the sun for weeks on end had finally vanished, leaving a day of unclouded beauty behind. Yet it was not as though all her problems had vanished with Kate's departure. Anne reminded herself of this, but still the sense of relief and encouragement remained.

Once inside the house, she went to the conservatory to visit the spider once more. Joe Gardiner was still evidently keeping watch over it, for his face, drawn into a suspicious scowl, reared up over a shelf of potted plants as soon as she opened the door.

Anne smiled at him. "You may be excused from guard duty now, Mr. Gardiner," she told him. "I thank you very much for your fidelity in Arachne's cause, but it appears my worrying was needless. Mr. and Mrs. Westland are gone. They decided of a sudden to return to their own home, and Lord Westland and I have just been seeing them off."

"Aye, one of the lads told me just now," said Mr. Gardiner, his suspicious look giving way to a grin. "So they're gone, are they? We won't none of us go into mourning over *that,* I'm thinking."

Anne could not help laughing, though she thought it more proper to make no acknowledgement of this statement. Mr. Gardiner, having wished her a good day, went off with his secateurs, and she walked over to the glasshouse and stood looking down at it.

If she had not personally witnessed the miracle of the night before, she might have thought she had dreamed it. The spider sat in its usual corner, looking very much as usual. Yet when Anne looked closer, she could see that it was larger, darker, and altogether more resplendent than it had been before. Again she found herself musing on the concept of rebirth and renewal. It might be a painful process, but in this case, at least, the end result was clearly worth it.

"I got rid of Kate," she whispered aloud. "And that's something I never would have thought I could accomplish. But I did it, just by speaking up and making my feelings plain."

A nebulous plan was forming in Anne's mind. It frightened her with its daring, yet when she considered it, she realized that she had nothing to lose by trying. Kate was now out of the picture, but her life could never be whole and happy as long as she was estranged from James. It was worth any risk to be united with him once more.

Of course, as Anne reminded herself, she could not compel him to accept her as his wife again. He might well reject her, even in spite of her best efforts to explain what she had done and why she had done it. But there had been a quality in James's behavior in the last day or two that encouraged her. He might not love her, but it did not seem as though he hated her, either. If she could restore their relations to something resembling their former footing, Anne felt she would be more than satisfied.

She shivered a little at the thought of what she was about to do. There would be no saving face if her efforts went awry. *But it doesn't matter,* she told herself. *If he will not forgive me, then I will have to leave Honeywell House anyway. I can't endure to live any longer as I have lived these last few months.*

As Anne left the conservatory, she caught a glimpse of herself in a pier glass set beside the conservatory doors. She stopped to survey her reflection. Her face wore a look of unusual determination, with set lips and squared jaw. But what chiefly struck Anne was an indefinable something in her looks—a sort of luster or radiance that seemed out of place, considering the nervous strain she had been under. Her mind flashed to Lady O'Reilly's words the night before: *Is it possible that you and Lord Westland are also expecting a blessed event?*

"But it isn't possible," Anne said aloud. "It's absurd, out of the question." Then she caught her breath. Was it so absurd, after all? She had certainly had no recent opportunities to become pregnant, but she and James had made love regularly up till a little more than two months ago. Again Anne stared wide-eyed at her reflection as she made some rapid mental calculations. Her monthly flow had been absent for a month or two, but it was often absent for months at a time. She had thought nothing of it when it had failed to appear the last couple of months. Likewise, the mysterious nausea that had come and gone during the last few weeks might merely have been caused by the new cook's predilection for frying in lard. Or it might have been caused by pregnancy, in which case—

"Good heavens," said Anne aloud. "Good heavens." Wide-eyed, she stared at her reflection in the glass. Her reflection stared back at her. "This bears thinking about," she told it. "Perhaps I had better wait before I speak to James." And she hurried upstairs to her room.

CHAPTER XXII

Now that Anne's mind was awakened to the possibility that she might be pregnant, she found abundant signs to confirm it. Her face, her figure, her recent bouts of nausea: all were unmistakable proof that a child was on the way.

"I can see it now as clearly as if it were written on me," Anne muttered to herself, having gone to her bedchamber, removed her clothing, and looked long and hard at herself in the glass. "Still, there must be no mistake about it. I had better have the doctor, I suppose. I'll just say I'm feeling out of sorts and need a tonic, so neither James nor the servants will have any idea of what's in the wind."

Accordingly, she put on her clothes again, requested that the doctor be sent for, and sat awaiting his arrival with a mixture of hope and fear. She had never had occasion to see the local doctor before now, and she wondered whether she could bring herself to discuss such a delicate matter as a coming baby with a gentleman she did not know. But when Dr. Edwards finally arrived, she found herself reassured. He was a kindly looking middle-aged man whose professional manner was a happy combination of sympathy and authority.

"Now, now, what's all this, my lady?" he asked, looking at her shrewdly over his spectacles. "Not feeling quite the thing, are you?"

Anne gave him a guilty smile. "In truth, I am feeling perfectly well," she said. "But there is a possibility that I am going to have a child, and I wish to be assured of it one way or another before I mention it to anyone else."

The doctor's manner at once became very professional. He asked Anne a few questions, made a brief physical examination, and gave it as his opinion that Anne's suspicions were perfectly correct. "Based on what you tell me, my lady, you can look to be brought to bed sometime in May or June," he said.

Anne sat silent, trying to adjust herself to this incredible idea. The doctor smiled in sympathy. "It's a big thing to take in all at once, but I don't anticipate you'll have much trouble, my lady," he told her. "You're very small, of course, but you look to be in good health, and I've seen women as small and smaller than you manage the business without a mite of trouble. Indeed, to speak frankly, complications seem to arise more frequently with women who are on the heavy side than with those who are very slender."

Anne nodded absently, still absorbed in her own thoughts. The doctor patted her hand and rose to his feet. "Well, I don't suppose I'll be needed anymore here just at present," he said with a hint of playfulness in his manner. "Just keep on as you are going for the next month or two, and send for me if any problems arise. Not that I anticipate it. I expect you will do very well if you just follow your own natural inclinations. Ordinary exercise is quite in order, barring riding and things of that sort, and I don't recommend any restriction in your diet. You don't look as though you were in the habit of eating any too much as it is.'' With a few final injunctions about milk-drinking and meat-eating and avoiding strong spirits, he took himself off.

After he had gone, Anne sank down in her chair again and gave herself furiously to think. The news that she was pregnant made an already complicated situation even more complicated. What would James think when he learned of her condition? Would he be pleased or not? He had spoken of wanting an heir, but that had been prior to his learning about her and Timothy. Anne felt getting an heir could no longer be a high priority with him, or he would not have stopped making love to her.

But now he stood an even chance of getting an heir whether he wanted one or not. On the whole, Anne was inclined to regret this turn of events. Having made a thorough survey of the strengths and weaknesses of her position, she felt that James's desire for an heir might well be the card that would have turned the trick in overcoming his reluctance to take her back as his wife again: back into his bed, if not into his heart. But if she was pregnant, then there was no valid reason for him to make love to her. Besides, he might find it distasteful to make love to a pregnant woman. The doctor had assured her that conjugal relations might safely continue until the last months of pregnancy, but the fact that it might be done was no assurance that James would care to do it.

''And I haven't any reason to believe he would want to make love to me, even if I wasn't pregnant,'' said Anne aloud with a sigh. ''Oh, me, what a tangle it is.''

Once again she reflected on how inconvenient it was

that she should have become pregnant at this particular time. Yet even amid these reflections, she felt a sense of awe at the thought of the new life growing within her. "I am bearing a child," she told herself, laying a reverent hand on her abdomen. "James's child and my child. *Our* child."

But though the child was James's as well as her own, Anne could not think that now was the proper time to tell him about it. There were already enough complicating factors in their relationship as it was. She decided to keep her condition a secret until she had spoken with James and found out how he felt about her and their marriage. Of course he would have to know eventually that she was carrying his child, but Anne did not want that thought to influence him in any way. "I must know how he feels about *me,*" she told herself. "I will not stay with him if he does not want me—no, not if I were having twenty children."

The question that faced her now was how best to ask James about his feelings. It would be necessary to speak to him very frankly indeed, and Anne shrank with all her usual timidity at the thought of that interview. Still, shy or not, she was determined to go through with it. There could be no way of approaching him that would not be awkward, but after some thought, she decided it would be least awkward to do so after dinner. The candlelit evening hours seemed more appropriate to discussing delicate matters than the glaring light of midday. And if there were any conflict, or any decision to be made, she and James might have the whole night to resolve it before they had to face the rest of the world again.

Accordingly, she rang for Mrs. Rhodes and gave orders that dinner that night should be an especially good one. The butler was instructed to see that a bottle of the best wine was brought up from the cellar and a fire made up in the drawing room, but Anne asked that no candles be lit. This subdued lighting would make the elegant, rather commonplace room a place of secrets and shadows, suitable for the exchange of confidences.

Having arranged the setting, Anne gave attention to her costume for the occasion. For a time she considered wearing again her white dress with the floating draperies. James had seemed to admire it, but she did not like to wear the same dress two nights in a row, and she also felt it was too simple and unsophisticated a costume to give her the authority she needed on such a critical occasion. So she put on instead the dress she had worn to Lady Meredith's party, the aquamarine brocade with the silver embroidered petticoat.

After a little hesitation, she decided to wear her aquamarine jewelry as well. James himself had given those aquamarines to her as a wedding gift, and they were a symbol of the vows that bound them together. More than anything, Anne wanted to fulfill those solemn vows, and to resurrect the feelings of those earlier, happier days when the promise of lifelong love and happiness had not seemed an impossible dream.

In his room, James was making his own preparations for dinner.

As he knotted his neckcloth before the glass, he was thinking again of Anne. With the departure of Kate and Thomas, the two of them would once more be dining alone. He wondered why this thought should make him feel so peculiar—half excited and half apprehensive. There was no reason why Kate and Thomas's departure should make any difference at all in the relations between him and Anne. The issues that had separated them before still stood between them, a vast and unbridgeable chasm, and he could see no way to close that fatal gap.

Yet for all the impossibility of the situation, James was nonetheless conscious of a stirring of hope within his heart. He could not put his finger on any material change in circumstances that should give him such a hope. It was simply there in the atmosphere, like distant thunder.

"Which is probably all it is," James muttered to himself. "There's a storm brewing if I'm not mistaken. It's been unnaturally warm for this time of year, and the fine weather's bound to break sometime."

He left his room and came out into the hall at the exact moment Anne came out of her own room. They both halted, and James thought Anne looked as embarrassed as he himself felt. "Good evening," he said.

"Good evening," said Anne, after an instant's pause. James was struck by how lovely she appeared. It was almost as though he were seeing her for the very first time. Her silver blond hair was dressed atop her head in an intricate arrangement of plaits and curls, and there was the faintest tint of rose color in her cheeks. The color of her dress and jewels intensified the crystalline beauty of her eyes, and every ribbon and pin of her toilette was in place. The overall effect was one of neatness, grace, and delicacy. To James, groping for similes, she seemed like a china figure of exquisite make, something rare, fine, and valuable that was meant to be carefully kept and cherished.

Anne's thoughts were much simpler. Looking at James, she was aware only that he was the man she loved and would always love, no matter what his feelings for her might be. So strong was this feeling that it almost choked her. She had to clear her throat to return James's civil good evening. *This won't do,* thought Anne in a panic, and racked her brain for something else to say. "What a beautiful day it has been," she ventured. "And it looks as though it will be a lovely evening, too."

"Yes," agreed James. "Although I think myself there's a storm brewing. You can't see or hear any sign of it yet, but you can feel it in the air."

Anne glanced at him quickly. "Can you? Yes, there *is* a feeling in the air, now you mention it." She said no more, and James, too, was silent, merely offering her his arm. Anne took it, and they went downstairs to the drawing room.

As they stood in the drawing room, waiting for dinner to be announced, Anne was more than ever conscious of a tension in the atmosphere. Possibly James had been right in saying there was a storm brewing, but Anne was not sure whether he had been speaking of a metaphorical storm or a real one. Perhaps he had sensed her purpose and was taking this way of warning her away from an attempt to discuss their private affairs.

For a moment Anne's purpose wavered. She knew an urge to abandon her plan and let the silence between her and James remain unbroken. But then she had a vision of the future: of thousands of evenings just like this one, spent standing around in silence and exchanging an occasional stiff commonplace as though the two of them were strangers. Anything must be better than that, even an open quarrel. So she took up her purpose once more, resolving to speak to James with the utmost frankness as soon as they were alone.

First, however, there was dinner to get through. Given the suspense of her position, Anne had not supposed she would be able to eat much, and she found she was right. Her bowl of soup *à la royale* left the table practically untouched, as did the nicely grilled fillet of sole that succeeded it. She could choke down no more than a few bites of roast pullet, and as for the jugged hare, loin of mutton, and squabs *à la soleil*, or the multitude of side dishes that accompanied them, she did not even make the attempt.

"Is something the matter, Anne?"

The question, addressed to her by James, caught Anne off guard. She looked up with a start. James was regarding her with a quizzical expression, but there was also concern in his eyes as he spoke again. "You have eaten practically nothing, Anne. Is anything amiss?"

"Oh, no," said Anne quickly. "Nothing at all. I am not very hungry this evening, that is all."

"But you must eat something." James's glance swept the table. "Do you think you could eat one of these squabs if I boned it for you? You used to be very fond of squab, as I recall."

Anne could only nod. It was, no doubt, a small thing that he should remember her fondness for squab and offer to prepare one for her, but in her present mood it was enough to move her almost to tears. By making a heroic effort, she was able to eat the squab and, later, most of the pear which James also insisted on preparing for her. "Now I can rest assured that you are adequately nourished," he told her with a smile. "Do you care for a glass of wine with your dessert?"

Anne shook her head. "No wine tonight, thank you," she said. She watched as James drank off his own glass of wine, then refilled it from the decanter. The moment was approaching when she would be expected to leave the table. Anne knew this would also be the moment when she would have to speak up and tell James she wished to talk to him. Otherwise he might go off to the library or the stables or some other masculine haunt, and she would never have a chance to talk to him at all.

"If you please, James," she said, in a diffident voice. "I wonder if you would mind coming to the drawing room when you are through drinking your port. There is something I would like to discuss with you."

James, in the act of reaching for the decanter, looked up sharply. When he spoke again, however, his voice was tranquil. "To be sure I do not mind, Anne. In fact, I will come with you this minute, if you are ready to leave the table. Now I think of it, I believe I have already had as much wine as is good for me."

As he followed her into the drawing room, Anne was reminded of their first evening at Honeywell House. Then, too, James had accompanied her to the drawing room and sat talking with her instead of drinking his port in a solitary state. And after that—Anne tried to close her mind to what had happened after that, but it was too late. The memory had permeated her thoughts and added to the sense of oppression she was laboring under. Any interruption, any postponement would have been welcome to her now that the moment for action was upon her.

She had spent most of that afternoon rehearsing all the things she wanted to say to James in this interview. In her imagination, she had been very eloquent indeed, explaining to James exactly how the situation with Timothy had come about and proving beyond doubt that she had never meant to deceive him by marrying him as she had done. But now she found all eloquence had deserted her. She could not even find words to begin. She sank down in a chair and looked helplessly at James, who had seated himself in a chair across from her. For several minutes they sat looking at each other in silence.

"Well?" said James, breaking the silence at last. "What was it you wanted to talk to me about?"

To Anne's ears, his voice sounded slightly impatient. She opened her mouth, then closed it again. What was the point? Once again, she was filled by a sense of futility. It was futile to suppose she could make any difference in a situation that had been going on for months. It would be better to make up her mind to leave Honeywell House and live out the remainder of her life somewhere else.

James was looking at her oddly, almost as if he were reading the thoughts passing in her head. "Well?" he said again, in a gentler voice than before. "You are very quiet, Anne."

"Never mind," said Anne softly. "I have changed my mind, James. There is nothing I need to discuss with you after all."

As she spoke, she rose to her feet. James gave her a startled look, then got to his own feet. The look on his face was now one of determination. "No!" he said. "Don't go, Anne. There is"—he drew a deep breath—"there is something I need to say to you, even if there is nothing you need to say to me."

Anne looked at him and was suddenly fired with courage. "But there is," she said. "I—I wanted to apologize, James. And I wanted to explain. I have been so unhappy, and I know you have been unhappy, too—"

"Yes, but it's not your fault, Anne," he said quickly. "I realize that now. I know I may have seemed angry before, when I—when you—"

"When the letter came," finished Anne softly. For a moment they were both silent, looking at each other. "I know you were angry, and I don't blame you, James," said Anne, in a softer voice still. "Believe me, I don't blame you in the least."

Once again they were silent. At last James spoke, with an effort. "I don't know that I was so very angry, Anne," he said. "I was surprised, of course, and hurt—"

"Of course you were angry," said Anne. "How could you not be angry? I should have told you about Timothy and me in the beginning. It was not right that you should have married me without knowing the truth."

Another silence ensued. Finally James spoke again in a heavy voice. "I must say, I wish you *had* told me, Anne. Not that I mean to reproach you in any way, but I cannot believe you will ever be happy married to one man when you—when you care for another."

Anne looked at him in amazement. "Are you talking about *Timothy?*" she said. "You think I care for Timothy Linville?"

"Yes, of course," said James, a trifle stiffly. "I had supposed from the things he wrote in his letter that you were—that you were very fond of each other."

Anne made a noise that might have been disdain or amusement. "Hardly," she said. "I was once fool enough to think Timothy was fond of me, but I soon learned my mistake. Between you and me, I don't believe he's even capable of true attachment. All he cares about is getting his own way."

"But—" James hesitated, then went on in a rush. "But even if he was not attached to you, you were attached to him, were you not? You obviously cared for him very deeply—"

"I fancied I did. But I don't care tuppence for him now," said Anne. "All that is over and done with. Indeed, I detest him now. After what he did—"

She broke off in obvious distress. "You are referring to the letter he wrote you?" questioned James, conscious of a rising in his spirits. "That was a rather detestable action, to be sure."

"Yes, but it's of a piece with his other actions," said Anne. "James, how could you think I cared for him? I never did, except in the beginning. And even then I knew he was using me—but I can see now in retrospect that I was using him, too, in a way. I was so lonely and miserable at Court, and he was the only one who seemed to take an interest in me."

At these words, James's spirits took another upward leap. Here was an explanation for Anne's behavior that had never occurred to him. So natural and understandable did it seem that he wondered now how he could have ever overlooked it.

Of course he still disliked to think of Anne making love to another man. But when he considered the matter rationally, he was obliged to admit he had no real grounds for resentment. In the course of his own life he, too, had fallen into the way of one or two love affairs, and he had not been living alone and miserable amid a nest of intriguing courtiers. In such a situation as Anne's, what could be so natural but that she should fall prey to the seductions of a plausible scoundrel?

"I understand," he said compassionately. "Of course I see how it was, Anne. I did not quite understand the matter before."

Anne gave him a peculiar look. "I don't think you do understand, James," she said.

"But I do," James assured her. "You were young, and alone, and Mr. Linville was willing to pay you an attention no one else was. I can see quite easily how you came to fancy yourself in love with him. It's an unfortunate fact, but there are many men willing to take advantage of young women's vulnerabilities to satisfy their own selfish desires.''

''I sincerely trust there are not many men like Timothy Linville in the world,'' said Anne, still regarding James with a searching look. ''You imagine that I let myself be seduced by Timothy, do you not, James? You are very wrong, as it happens. I foolishly put myself in a situation where he was able to take advantage of me, but as for the rest—it was not by my choice, James. Do you understand me? I did not wish to make love to Timothy. *He forced himself on me.*''

James was struck dumb by this speech. He could only stand looking at Anne while his mind struggled to absorb what she had just told him. Several times he opened his mouth to speak, but each time words failed him. Anne was regarding him gravely, and he was struck by a sensation that had occurred to him before, but never so strongly as at the present moment. This was a kind of test. James had no idea whether he was being tested by fate, or God, or circumstance, but he knew with complete certainty that Anne would judge him forever after by the response he made now. And he had only one chance to respond correctly.

Fortunately, Anne made it easy for him. Even as he stood frantically wondering what to say or do, he saw her eyes filling with tears. After that, he had no need to ponder what to say or do, for his response was immediate and instinctual. Going to her, he put his arms around her and drew her tight against him.

''My poor Anne,'' he whispered. ''Oh, Anne, can you ever forgive me? If I had known—''

Anne gulped, and raised tear-flooded eyes to look at him. ''But you couldn't know,'' she said. ''I wanted to tell you before, but I was too much ashamed.''

"You were ashamed?" said James in a rising voice. *"You* were ashamed? What on earth had you to be ashamed of?"

"That I behaved so foolishly. Timothy never would have been in a position to take advantage of me if I had not—if I had not deliberately put myself in his power." Anne gulped again, but went on with determination. "And you know, James, that as far as most people are concerned, it doesn't much matter whether a girl is ruined by her own will or not. Either she is ruined or not ruined, and that is all that matters. Well, I *was* ruined, and I knew I ought to tell you about it, but I was too ashamed. I was afraid you wouldn't want to marry me if you knew the truth."

James was silent a moment. "I don't pretend to know how the rest of the world looks at such matters," he said. "All I know are my own feelings, Anne. And I assure you that if I had known all this earlier, the only difference it would have made is that I would have sought out Mr. Timothy Linville long before now and made him pay for his actions. As it is, I shall attend to the matter as soon as it can be humanly arranged."

Anne, in his arms, was very still. When at last she raised her face to look at him again, it was like a mask of tragedy. "Oh, James! What good would that do? What's past is past, and there is no way of changing it."

"No," agreed James. Something in Anne's expression made him feel the test might not be quite over and he would do well to tread cautiously. "Of course there is no undoing the past, either good or bad," he went on, groping his way from word to word. "But I would like to do *something* for you, Anne—something to make things right. You have suffered so much, and it is intolerable to think that this fellow should get off scot-free."

Anne continued to look up at him. "But punishing Timothy would not change the situation, James," she said. "Are you sure it's not the idea of having a wife who has been intimate with another man that you find intolerable?"

Her eyes searched his keenly, but on this subject James was on solid ground. "No, I do not," he said firmly. "I care nothing about that, Anne. I wouldn't have held it against you even if you had made love to Mr. Linville of your own volition. And since it was not of your own volition, do you not think I shall disregard it all the more readily?"

"You haven't seemed willing to disregard it these past few weeks," said Anne, still regarding him searchingly. "As soon as that letter arrived, your manner toward me changed completely. I could tell you were disgusted with me. You haven't come near me of your own will for weeks."

She expected James to be confounded by this speech, but it was she who ended up confounded. James gave her one look of amazement, then threw back his head and laughed. "My dear girl, do you not know the difference between disgust and jealousy?" he said between bursts of merriment. "That is why I have not come near you all these weeks. I have been eaten alive with jealousy, thinking that you cared for another man and would rather have been married to him than to me."

"Oh, James!" said Anne, her eyes filling with tears once again. "There is no man I would rather be married to than you."

James looked at her closely. "Do you mean that, Anne? Even now, when I have made a jealous fool of myself? And after I have hurt you for no better reason than that I felt hurt myself?"

"Now more than ever," said Anne, tightening her arms around him. "Besides, it wasn't your fault that you thought what you did, James. It is as I said before: if I had been honest with you from the beginning, none of this business would have ever happened."

James shook his head. "I cannot allow that it was your fault at all," he said. "But let it pass. The important thing is that we understand each other now." He looked down at Anne. "And in the interests of better understanding, I think—I believe—that there's something you should know, Anne."

Anne raised to him a face set and determined. "And there's something you need to know, too, James," she said. "Something besides what I have already told you."

For a moment they regarded each other in apprehensive silence. Then, at the same instant, both of them drew a deep breath and spoke in unison: "I love you."

CHAPTER XXIII

For a moment they stood regarding each other open-mouthed. Then James began to laugh. After a moment Anne joined in his laughter.

James nearly suffocated her in an exuberant hug. "I can't believe it. You can't really mean that you—that you—?"

"That I love you," said Anne. "Yes, of course I love you, James. But I can't believe that you love me back." She looked at him shyly.

James's face had sobered. "How could I not love you?" he said. "I believe I have loved you from the first moment I saw you. That day at Court, when I saw you there with the Queen—I couldn't get your face out of my mind afterward."

"And I couldn't get yours out of *my* mind," said Anne. "When I met you again at the ball, it was like a dream come true."

"Yes," said James. "That's how I'd describe it, too."
He shook his head in wonderment. "It's all very mysterious and improbable, isn't it? I still can't believe you care
for me. You know I told you when I married you that
our marriage was one of convenience, just because I was
sure you couldn't have any feelings for me so early in
our acquaintance. I was afraid I'd frighten you away if
I told you how I really felt."

"It wouldn't have frightened me, James," said Anne.
"It wouldn't have frightened me at all."

James sighed. "What a fool I've been," he said. "A
coward and a fool. If only I'd summoned up courage
enough to tell you sooner, this whole muddle could have
been avoided. I almost did tell you that night of Lady
Meredith's party. But then the next day—"

"But then the next day Timothy's letter arrived," finished Anne soberly. "I don't wonder that made you
change your mind, James."

"But it shouldn't have made me change my mind,"
said James, drawing her close against him again. "If I
had spoken to you frankly before, even that letter could
have caused no misunderstanding, or at least only a
momentary one."

"And if I had spoken to *you* frankly before, the question
never would have arisen in the first place," said Anne.
"Because you would have already known about Timothy
and me. So you see it really is more my fault than yours,
James."

"I cannot allow it," said James. He took her hand and
held it tightly in his. "Of course you could not like to
talk about such a terrible experience. But I am glad you
have told me about it now, Anne. I feel we have come
to a real understanding of each other and can, perhaps,
make a better thing of our marriage as a result."

"I hope so," said Anne, looking up at him. "Though I would be content to make it as good as it was before. I have missed you a great deal these last couple of months, James."

"And I have missed you, too," said James. "And when I think that I've wasted those months simply because I was too much a coward to speak out and say how I felt—"

"If you have been a coward, then so have I," said Anne. "Are you willing to forgive me, James?"

"Of course," said James, squeezing her hand more tightly than ever. "Of course I am! As far as I am concerned, there is nothing to forgive."

"And I feel the same way. It was all a misunderstanding, and we have wasted enough time with misunderstandings. Let us try to put the past behind us and go on from here."

"There is nothing I would like better," said James. Looking down at Anne, he felt an overwhelming desire to kiss her. Yet at the same time, he was conscious of a curious reluctance. This reluctance had something to do with shyness, for it had been a long time since he had kissed her, and he felt almost as though they were beginning their relationship over again. But his reluctance had also, as he recognized, something to do with Anne's confession. Now that he knew her history, he could not help wondering if, in her mind, lovemaking must always be associated with pain and fear.

Anne, looking up at him, caught some inkling of his thoughts. Her heart sank. She had thought the ghost of Timothy had been exorcised once and all by her confession, but now here it was hovering over her and James once again. She drew her hand away. "Well," she said in a flat voice. "I'm glad that's settled."

"Yes, so am I," said James, but his ears had caught the discontent in Anne's voice. He studied her speculatively. There were many things that might account for her discontented tone, and he feared it might be presumptuous to assume it was what he hoped it was. Was there a way he might make sure without offending her? Yes, there was a way. "Anne," he said, "I know it's late, but I have a fancy to see the well by moonlight again tonight. Do you care to accompany me?"

Anne looked at him quickly. "Now? Tonight?" she said. There was surprise in her voice, but James was pleased to hear she sounded receptive.

"Yes, tonight," he said. "We needn't stay for more than a minute, but it's been a long time since I've seen the well. Too long," he added, with a sidelong look at Anne.

Her color was a little heightened, but she met his eyes squarely. "I would not mind seeing the well again, James," she said. "But I am afraid you were right when you spoke earlier of a storm brewing. I can hear the thunder quite clearly now."

They both paused to listen to a distant rumble of thunder. "Yes, but you can tell it's still a long way off," said James. "For my part, I'm willing to gamble that we can get to the well and back again before the storm breaks. Still, if you would rather not take the risk, I understand."

Anne looked at him, and an impish smile appeared suddenly on her lips. "What is life without risk?" she said. "I am willing to take a chance if you are, James. But let us bring an umbrella just in case, so if the worst happens we need not get wet walking in the rain all the way home."

James was amenable to this condition, and he also insisted on fetching Anne's cloak in case the worst should happen. Anne was inclined to protest the necessity of a woolen cloak on such a warm night; but certain private reflections caused her to think better of her protestations. She and James left the house by the terrace doors and set off toward the little wood where the well lay.

As they threaded their way amid flowerbeds and formal gardens, Anne was reminded irresistibly of the first time she had visited the well with James. It was almost as warm on this night as on that other one, though the trees and gardens were no longer in the full glory of midsummer. Indeed, here and there the touch of autumn was showing itself in russet leaves and barren branches. But under the silvery glow of moonlight, the landscape looked no less magical than before.

It was a more wavering and uncertain moonlight than on their previous visit. High in the heavens, drifting banks of clouds were wafted continually across the moon's bright face, though there was no trace of wind in the garden. Now and then, but still from a long way off, a distant rumble of thunder was heard, and once the western sky was faintly illumined by a sheet of lightning.

"Still a long way off," said James, and squeezed Anne's hand. "We will make it with time to spare, I feel sure. Are you afraid of storms?"

"Not in the least," said Anne. "I rather like them."

James looked down at her with wonderment. "Now who would have expected that? You know you are a constant source of surprises to me, Anne. Your appearance is so mild and quiet, yet you boldly embrace things that frighten most people into fits. Thunderstorms, for instance, and giant spiders! How to explain such a contradiction?"

Anne smiled. "But you know there are plenty of things I *am* shy about, James," she said. "Crowds, and meeting people I don't know, and things of that sort." She glanced up at him. "Indeed, I have often felt I must be a disappointment to you in that way. If you were wanting a wife who likes entertaining people and playing hostess to large parties, you would have been better off with a woman like—well, a woman like Kate, for instance."

"God forbid!" said James, stopping dead in his tracks. He looked down at Anne with a quizzical expression that brought color to her cheeks. "Now there's a picture to make me shudder," he said. "What the deuce makes you think I *want* a wife who likes entertaining people and playing hostess to large parties?"

"Don't you?" said Anne meekly. "I thought you might. Because in your position, people expect you to do a great deal of entertaining. Kate said—"

"Ah, so it's a question of what *Kate* said," said James. He was smiling broadly now. "But surely, Anne, you must have learned in the last few weeks that what Kate says has everything to do with what is convenient or advantageous for Kate and nothing to do with the truth?"

A gurgle of laughter escaped Anne. "I did just wonder," she confessed. "Lady Meredith was sure she was bluffing, and there were times I was sure of it, too. But some of the things she said about you, James—"

"I can imagine. I can imagine what she said about me." James gave Anne an embarrassed look. "The less said about that the better, perhaps. Only I do assure you, Anne, that if I was once foolish enough to admire Kate, I have long since come to see the error of my ways."

"Have you?" said Anne. She was glad that a cloud had just drifted over the moon, hiding her satisfied smile in darkness.

"Yes, I have. She is an insufferable woman—absolutely insufferable. I can't imagine what I ever saw in her. I was never as glad of anything as when she left Honeywell House today."

"Neither was I," said Anne, and once more smiled to herself in the darkness.

A few minutes later, they reached the well pavilion. Anne looked around the little building with interest. It looked the same as before: the same carved stonework, the same flagged floor, and the same dilapidated wicker furniture. She avoided looking directly at the settee where she and James had made love on their previous visit, but she was very aware of it nonetheless. Together she and James approached the brink of the well and stood looking down into the water that lay dark and smooth within the circle of carved stonework.

"I wonder how many people have looked into this old well through the years?" mused James. "Thousands, no doubt. According to legend, it's been more or less in use ever since pagan times. It's a strange thought, isn't it? No doubt some queer ceremonies took place here in the old days."

"Yes, and still do today," said Anne. She took up the metal dipper that lay on the well curb and regarded it with a reminiscent smile. "Catherine Meredith, Emily O'Neill, and I swore a vow of eternal friendship here, the first day they came to visit me."

"Did you?" said James. "That sounds rather like one of those purely feminine and private rites that men are forbidden to know about. I hope it won't be necessary to put me to death now I'm in on the secret?"

Anne laughed. "No, I don't think so. It was only a kind of jest—although the friendship seems to be real enough, thank heaven."

"Yes, thank heaven," said James. "I am glad you have succeeded in finding congenial friends in the neighborhood, Anne. I always hoped you would be happy here, and after these last two hellish months I want happiness for you more than ever. Do you think it's possible, after everything that has happened? Or does Honeywell House now hold too many unpleasant memories for you to ever live here happily again?''

Anne looked at him in surprise. "Why, James, don't be ridiculous," she said. "Of course the last two months have been difficult, but before that I was very happy here at Honeywell House. Very happy indeed," she repeated, with emphasis.

"Were you?" said James. "So was I, on the whole. But I am much happier now, Anne. This moment, right now, is the true consummation of our marriage. Now we love and understand each other, and nothing will ever be able to come between us again."

"No, it will not," said Anne.

James bent down and kissed Anne on the lips. She stood very still, looking up at him. "Do you remember?" he said. "Do you remember the last time we were here?"

"Yes," said Anne softly. "I remember it very well, James."

"So do I. I will never forget it. You were so beautiful that night, Anne. And you are just as beautiful now. Moonlight is your element." He reached down to touch her face. "I have always thought so, ever since I first saw you. I thought you were like a being of the spirit, a little too fine to live on this earth like the rest of us day-to-day mortals. Not that you're not very lovely in the day, but by moonlight you take my breath away."

Anne could not doubt he meant what he said. The look in his eyes was proof enough of his sincerity, if proof were needed. Anne felt a stirring in her heart, and in that moment she came into her own. She forgot all about

Timothy, all about Kate, all about everything but the reality that was her and James together. She felt that she really was beautiful, that moonlight really was her element, and that at that moment he and the whole world was hers to command. "James," she said. Reaching up, she put her arms around his neck and drew his face down to hers.

James kissed her, a slow reverent kiss that was like a sacrament. Then he kissed her again, wrapping his arms around her and drawing her close against him. "I love you, Anne," he said. "More than anything in the world."

"And I love you, too," said Anne. She felt on fire at that moment with love and desire and a pleasure so exalted that it verged upon pain. In the months past, she had relived countless times in her memory what it had been like to make love to James. She would have been willing to swear she recalled perfectly the warmth and scent of his body; the strength of his arms; the taste of his mouth on hers. But the reality surpassed the memory a thousand times. It was as though their lovemaking had undergone a rebirth, becoming a new and better version of itself: much like the spider had done in the last twenty-four hours, and perhaps even like Anne herself. Anne smiled at the thought of it.

"What are you smiling about?" James whispered in her ear. "You look very mysterious and inscrutable."

"I am smiling because I am happy," Anne whispered back. "And because I love you so much. Never let me go, James."

"I won't," said James. And if he did, eventually, find it necessary to let her go in a purely physical sense, he did at least take the precaution of ensuring she had neither the cause nor the inclination to complain about it afterward.

* * *

It was nearly dawn when at last James and Anne left the well pavilion. James kept one arm around Anne's shoulders as they made their way through the woods. She leaned her head against him, a glow of contentment burning as warm within her as the fires of passion that had burned there before. "James," she said aloud, not because she had anything to say to him but merely for the pleasure of hearing his name on her lips. "James— James—James."

"Anne," he said, and was apparently so much moved by the pleasure of hearing her name on *his* lips that he found it necessary to stop and kiss her. "Did I mention before that I love you?"

"Yes, at least a hundred times. But don't let that stop you from telling me again," said Anne. Whereupon James did tell her, several times, adducing additional kisses as proof. Having received Anne's assurances that his feelings were returned, they started through the woods once more.

"It's hard to believe," said James musingly, "that only twenty-four hours ago I felt as though my life were the most perfect muddle. Kate and Thomas were here, and plaguing my life out, and you seemed as distant as—as that." With a smile he pointed to the moon, which had just peeped out from behind a veil of cloud.

"I was never distant from you, James," said Anne. "But I know what you mean. Things did seem in a muddle not so very long ago, and I would have sworn they could never be right again."

"I will always blame myself for that. But I can't say that having Kate and Thomas around helped the situation. Ah, relations!" James threw Anne a rueful look. "We are rid of them for now, but you know we can never really be done with them as long as we live. Blood being thicker than water, I am sure we will be obliged to see them now and then whether we will or no.''

''I don't know that that's such a bad thing,'' said Anne. Such was her mood of exaltation that she could feel tolerant and loving even toward Kate. ''I will admit your sister-in-law is a thorn in my side much of the time, and I'm afraid I shan't ever look forward to her visiting us again, though I daresay I'll be able to stomach the idea if I'm given a year or two to recover from her last visit. But on the whole, I think visiting her in *her* home might be a better idea. She might not be so offensive on her own ground—and besides, after hearing so much about Four Oaks and the wonderful way things are managed there, I have conceived a genuine passion to see the place!''

Anne laughed as she spoke, and James joined in her laughter. After a minute, she went on, glancing at him rather shyly. ''But, James, I have to confess that though I didn't care for Kate, I did rather like your brother. I know he isn't always the most tactful person, and his mental attainments are not, perhaps, very exalted. But I couldn't help liking him all the same.''

James smiled more ruefully than ever. ''That's the devil of it, Anne! Neither could I. All these years I've felt as though I owed him a grudge, but now I can't even remember why.''

''At any rate, he seems to genuinely like and admire you, James,'' said Anne. ''No doubt that is why I found myself in sympathy with him!''

James smiled down at her. ''You are too good, Anne. But I have to say that it's a relief to let go of my enmity for Thomas once and for all. Keeping it up all these years was more of a burden than I realized. I was always feeling as though I had to be on guard against him. Why, I was so eaten up with envy and resentment that I felt I had to keep myself and my possessions away from him, even after my death! But now I don't feel that way at all.'' His face grew sober as he looked down at Anne. ''I once told you that I needed an heir and that was why I wanted us to be married as soon as possible. Neither of those statements was true, Anne, not even at the time I made them. But if they were untrue then, they're doubly untrue now. If ever we are blessed with children, I shall of course be very glad and grateful—that goes without saying. But not because I have any concern about the succession. As far as getting an heir, I no longer care two cents one way or the other. Why are you looking at me like that?''

''Because it has just occurred to me that there is something else I need to tell you,'' said Anne. ''Dr. Edwards came to see me this afternoon.''

James gazed at her uncomprehendingly. ''You are not unwell, I hope?'' he asked.

''It depends what you mean by unwell! Let me rather put it this way.'' Anne reached up to touch James's cheek. ''I am glad you are not unduly concerned with getting an heir, James. That is always a possibility, of course, but as far as I can tell there is at least as good a chance that you will be getting a daughter instead.''

Watching his face, she saw reflected there a whole succession of emotions: bewilderment, comprehension, shock, and finally a struggling, incredulous delight. ''Are you certain?''

''As certain as one can be about these things. The doctor says my *accouchement* will likely be sometime in May or June.''

''I can't make it seem real. It doesn't seem possible.''

"I feel exactly the same way. Fortunately, we both have six months or so to become used to the idea."

Reaching out, James gathered her into his arms. But almost at once he released her again and looked down at her with an expression of mounting horror. "Good God! What am I thinking of? You ought to be home and in bed this minute. I have had no business keeping you out so late—and probably no business doing other things as well!"

"The doctor says," said Anne primly, "that conjugal relations may continue until a month or two prior to the date of *accouchement*. And there is no need to behave as though I were suddenly made of spun glass, James. It will do me no harm to be out late this once."

"You think not?" said James dubiously.

"I know not," said Anne. She threw James a roguish look. "The doctor says that women in my condition generally have the least difficulties when they follow their own natural inclinations. Well, nothing we have done this evening has in any way gone against my natural inclinations. Quite the contrary, in fact."

There was a sparkle in James's eye now as he looked down at Anne. "You relieve me exceedingly, my love," he said. "But since we are on our way home anyway, I hope you have no objection if we postpone further discussion of this subject until we get there?"

"Not at all," said Anne. She spoke with mock gravity, but there was a hint of real concern on her brow as she looked up at James. "You will not worry about me too much, will you, James? What I mean to say is, I should not like to feel you were afraid to kiss me or touch me because of the baby. Because I *want* you to kiss me and touch me. I want it very much."

James enveloped her in his arms. "Don't worry, dear

wife,'' he whispered. ''I think my natural inclinations and yours are at one on that issue.''

''Thank heaven for that,'' said Anne, and returned his embrace with fervor.

EPILOGUE

Ten Years Later

"Mama, may I show Kathleen the well? I have been telling her about it, and she wants to see it awfully badly."

Anne exchanged amused glances with Emily O'Reilly, who was engaged in bouncing a large and lusty infant on her knee while simultaneously preventing the active three-year-old twins at her feet from pulling the tablecloth from the table along with all the teacups, saucers, and plates.

"Why, I believe that would be all right, darling, if it's all right with Lady O'Reilly," Anne said. "Emily, do you mind? Charlotte will take good care of Kathleen, I know."

"I will," Charlotte assured Emily earnestly. "I promise I will. I'll hold Kathleen's hand all the way and make sure she doesn't get lost, or fall in the well.'' She seized the hand of the smaller girl beside her in a firm grasp, as though anxious to prove this point.

Emily laughed. ''I am sure you will be careful, Charlotte,'' she said. ''And so I will entrust Kathleen to your care. Kathleen, mind you obey everything Charlotte tells you. Your father and I would dislike it extremely if we had to go and fish you out of the well.''

Kathleen grinned and ducked her head at these words. She was a sturdy child of six years with a mop of red curls and a sprinkling of freckles across her nose. Nine-year-old Charlotte, beside her, was taller, but more slender, with a sheet of pale blond hair hanging to her waist. As the two children set off down the terrace steps together, Emily looked after them fondly.

''I do swear that Charlotte is the very image of you, Anne. Even the way she moves—like a feather floating on the breeze.''

''And Kathleen is the image of *you,* Emily,'' put in Catherine Meredith, who was reclining lazily on a chaise longue beside the tea table. ''But then you seem to have stamped your likeness on all your brood.'' She looked with amusement at the red-haired twins at Emily's feet, and at the baby on her knee whose single wisp of hair was already showing a coppery hue.

''You mean that they have the misfortune of being redheads like me! True, but if you can look past that, I believe you will also see a resemblance to Terrence. Especially in the boys. This fellow, in particular, has a great look of him.'' Emily cuddled the baby in her arms, who opened his blue eyes wide and bared his single tooth in a broad grin.

The three women were seated on the terrace of Honeywell House, looking out on the lawn below. Anne, in a dress of sea green muslin, was seated at the table on which still stood the remains of a lavish tea. At her feet, shaded from the rays of the afternoon sun, lay a basket in which reposed her own infant son. He emitted a soft noise halfway between a yawn and a burp, and she glanced down at him with quick anxiety. Her anxiety changed to a smile of relief when she saw all was well, and Catherine, on the chaise beside her, laughed.

"You don't half dote on that child, do you, Anne? Between you and Emily, the display of maternal devotion I have seen this afternoon is quite overwhelming."

"You, of course, care nothing for *your* son," said Anne slyly.

A conscious smile appeared on Catherine's lips, but she shrugged her shoulders with an appearance of insouciance. "Oh, naturally I am fond of him. For a nine-year-old boy, he comes tolerably close to having civilized manners. And he shows signs of turning out to be quite intelligent and conversable someday when he is older."

"Only hear how coolly she speaks of him!" remarked Anne to Emily. "If one had never seen the way she looks at young Jon when she thinks no one else is watching, one might be deceived into thinking her as detached and disinterested a mother as she sounds."

Catherine's lips quirked in another betraying smile, but she shook her head solemnly. "However detached and disinterested a mother I may be, I cannot deceive myself that my son has not inherited some of his father's youthful tendency to misbehavior," she said. "And that being the case, I cannot but view his long absence from the terrace with growing trepidation. Where do you suppose he has gotten to, Anne? Last I heard, Charlotte was going to show him the spider in the conservatory, but he wasn't with her and Kathleen when they came by a minute ago.

You don't think he remained behind in the conservatory, do you? Because when I consider the possibilities of a nine-year-old boy in combination with a nine-inch spider—"

"Oh, you needn't worry about that," Anne assured her. "Knowing there would be children about this afternoon, I ordered one of the gardeners to hover inconspicuously near at hand in case one of them was tempted to do more than look at the spider. Charlotte would warn them against it, of course, but I thought it as well to have an adult nearby to reinforce her authority."

"I doubt she needed it," put in Emily, smiling. "She strikes me as a remarkably mature and self-possessed child."

"Yes, I can't think how she came by such qualities. When I was her age, I was the shyest, most backward creature that ever breathed." Anne looked affectionately toward her daughter's small form, just disappearing around a bend in the path with Kathleen's hand still firmly clasped in hers. "It is a relief to see that even if Charlotte resembles me in looks to some extent, she has at least escaped my youthful awkwardness."

"And speaking of intelligent and self-possessed children," said Emily. "I think I have found your son for you, Catherine." She pointed toward the fishpond, a glinting pool of silver that lay beyond the house's formal gardens amid a fringe of trees and rushes. "At the moment, he seems to be engaged in dragging the pond along with my eldest."

Catherine raised herself on one elbow to survey the fishpond. "So he is! Well, it is a relief to find him so innocently employed." She leaned back on the chaise, smoothing her pomegranate colored gown over her knees. "In that case, Anne, I believe I'll have another cup of

tea after all. And a few more of those little tarts if there
are any left.''

Relieved of fears concerning their offspring, the three
women fell to discussing the improvement in Court fashions that had taken place since the Regent had become
King. Meanwhile, the intelligent and self-possessed
Lady Charlotte Westland was conducting Miss Kathleen O'Reilly along the path to the well pavilion, explaining to her wide-eyed charge the well's history and
the curious rites practiced there on Midsummer morning.

''They come very early, before the sun is up, and wash
their faces in the well,'' she told Kathleen. ''And if they
are very lucky, they see their futures in the well's water.''

''Who?'' demanded Kathleen. ''Who sees their
futures?''

''The ladies who wash their faces in the well. It's only
ladies that see their futures there, you know. Men never
see anything.''

''That's because no man would be fool enough to
believe in such rot,'' said a voice behind them.

''Only a silly girl,'' agreed another voice.

Turning with indignation, Charlotte beheld the two boys
who had a moment before been playing at the pond's
edge. The taller and elder of the two, Terry O'Reilly,
grinned at her provokingly. The other, Jon Meredith, wore
a more sober expression, though his dark eyes sparkled
as they met her own. ''Only a silly girl could believe
she'd see anything in a well except water,'' he said.

Charlotte knew Jon well. He was a neighbor and just
her own age, and she had always thought him quite nice,
for a boy. So she relaxed the stern expression on her face
a trifle as she said, ''That just shows what *you* know,
Jon Meredith. My mama says the well does have magic

powers, and she would know a deal more about it than you would!''

Jon shook his head skeptically, although there was interest in his eyes. ''How would she know?'' he demanded. ''Did she ever see *her* future in the well?''

Charlotte longed to give an affirmative to this question, but her conscience would not allow her to lie. ''I'm not sure,'' she confessed. ''Mama never really said whether she saw anything in the well or not. But I *am* sure she believes in the well's powers. It is a regular joke between her and Papa, that the well decided her future for her.''

The four of them had by this time reached the clearing where the well pavilion stood. Kathleen ran forward eagerly to look at the well, and Charlotte, mindful of her responsibilities, hastened after her. The two boys sauntered after at a more leisurely pace and joined the girls where they stood beside the well's stone curb. *''I* say it's nonsense,'' said Terry O'Reilly, reaching out to dabble his fingers in the water. ''There's no such thing as wells that tell your future. They're like faeries and ghosts and that sort of thing. Everybody knows they don't really exist. Even Katie knows that. Don't you, Katie?''

''There *might* be faeries,'' said Kathleen stoutly. ''And there might be magic wells, too. You can't be sure, Terry; there *might* be.''

''Well, if this well's magic, then I'm going to turn you into a toad,'' said Terry. He flicked water at his sister, then recoiled in pretended horror. ''Good Lord, I was wrong! The well *does* work. Poor Katie, I do beg your pardon. Whatever will we tell Mama and Papa?''

Katie's face reddened alarmingly at this badinage. Jon and Charlotte, having some experience of her temper, stuffed their fingers in their ears and prepared for the roar that would follow. But instead of letting out the roar, she merely dipped her own hand in the well and splashed a generous handful of water in her brother's face. This precipitated an exchange of hostilities that caused Charlotte and Jon to step back hastily from the well's curb to avoid being drenched.

"I still say it's silly to think a well could show you your future," said Jon to Charlotte, picking up their conversation where they had left off. "What I mean is, how could it? It simply isn't sensible."

"Lots of things aren't sensible, but that doesn't mean they don't happen," pointed out Charlotte with nine-year-old acuteness. "*I* believe in the well."

"That's because you're a girl," explained Jon kindly. "Girls will believe anything. But boys don't believe in things until they see the proof, and where's your proof, Charlotte? I can't see proof of anything except that the well contains a deal of water." He glanced at the O'Reillys, who were still furiously throwing water at each other.

"I should think the fact that the well's been famous for hundreds of years would be proof of something," said Charlotte in a withering tone. "Besides, I know lots of people have seen things in it. Mrs. Rhodes, our housekeeper, tells me stories about it sometimes."

"Stories!" said Jon with a pitying smile. "Stories aren't proof. I'd have to see something in the well myself before *I'd* believe in it."

"Well, you can't, for you're a boy," said Charlotte with triumph. "Only girls see things in the well."

"Well, did *you* ever see anything in it?" challenged Jon.

If he expected this question to confound Charlotte, he

was disappointed. She merely gave him a superior smile. "No, of course not," she said. "I'm far too young. Mama says she doesn't think it's a bit of use my looking into the well until I'm at least twenty-one."

"Well, I'll wager you don't see a thing even when you're twenty-one," said Jon.

"I'll wager I do," said Charlotte.

"I'll wager you don't," said Jon.

"I'll wager I do," said Charlotte. This bickering went on for some time, until at last Jon proposed putting their wager in formal terms.

"I'll tell you how we can settle this thing," he said. "We'll both come here on Midsummer morning, the year you are twenty-one. You can go through the whole riga-marole of washing your face and looking in the well, and we'll see if anything comes of it. Done?"

"Done!" said Charlotte. They shook hands solemnly, and Jon warned Charlotte that she must not forget the terms of their wager, for her failure to appear on the appointed date would be taken by him as an admission that he was right and she was wrong.

"I won't forget," she said. "I'll be here at five o'clock, in the year—" she paused a moment, calculating. "The year 1839! My, that seems a tremendous long way away, doesn't it?"

"It does," said Jon. "But I won't forget."

"I won't either," said Charlotte, and they shook hands again.

Notice appearing in the *Morning Post*, June 1839:

Engaged: Jonathan Summerfield Meredith, only son and heir of the Right Honourable Jonathan Arthur Meredith, 8th Baron Meredith, to Lady Charlotte Westland, only daughter of the Right Honourable James Edward Westland, 14th Earl of Westland and Viscount Bemis. The wedding is to take place at Honeywell House, Devon, on the 24th of August.

ABOUT THE AUTHOR

Joy Reed lives with her family in Michigan. Joy loves hearing from readers and you may write to her c/o Zebra Books. Please include a self-addressed stamped envelope if you wish a reply.

COMING IN JUNE 2001 FROM
ZEBRA BALLAD ROMANCES

or money order (no cash or CODS) to: **Kensington Publishing Corp., Dept. C.O., 850 Third Avenue, New York, NY 10022**
Prices and numbers subject to change without notice. Valid only in the U.S. All orders subject to availabilty. **NO ADVANCE ORDERS.**
Visit our website at **www.kensingtonbooks.com.**

Put a Little Romance in Your Life With
Shannon Drake

__Come The Morning   0-8217-6471-3 $6.99US/$8.50CAN

__Conquer The Night   0-8217-6639-2 $6.99US/$8.50CAN

__The King's Pleasure   0-8217-5857-8 $6.50US/$8.00CAN

__Lie Down In Roses   0-8217-4749-0 $5.99US/$6.99CAN

__Tomorrow Glory   0-7860-0021-X $5.99US/$6.99CAN

Put a Little Romance in Your Life With
Janelle Taylor

__Anything for Love	0-8217-4992-7	$5.99US/$6.99CAN
__Lakota Dawn	0-8217-6421-7	$6.99US/$8.99CAN
__Forever Ecstasy	0-8217-5241-3	$5.99US/$6.99CAN
__Fortune's Flames	0-8217-5450-5	$5.99US/$6.99CAN
__Destiny's Temptress	0-8217-5448-3	$5.99US/$6.99CAN
__Love Me With Fury	0-8217-5452-1	$5.99US/$6.99CAN
__First Love, Wild Love	0-8217-5277-4	$5.99US/$6.99CAN
__Kiss of the Night Wind	0-8217-5279-0	$5.99US/$6.99CAN
__Love With a Stranger	0-8217-5416-5	$6.99US/$8.50CAN
__Forbidden Ecstasy	0-8217-5278-2	$5.99US/$6.99CAN
__Defiant Ecstasy	0-8217-5447-5	$5.99US/$6.99CAN
__Follow the Wind	0-8217-5449-1	$5.99US/$6.99CAN
__Wild Winds	0-8217-6026-2	$6.99US/$8.50CAN
__Defiant Hearts	0-8217-5563-3	$6.50US/$8.00CAN
__Golden Torment	0-8217-5451-3	$5.99US/$6.99CAN
__Bittersweet Ecstasy	0-8217-5445-9	$5.99US/$6.99CAN
__Taking Chances	0-8217-4259-0	$4.50US/$5.50CAN
__By Candlelight	0-8217-5703-2	$6.99US/$8.50CAN
__Chase the Wind	0-8217-4740-1	$5.99US/$6.99CAN
__Destiny Mine	0-8217-5185-9	$5.99US/$6.99CAN
__Midnight Secrets	0-8217-5280-4	$5.99US/$6.99CAN
__Sweet Savage Heart	0-8217-5276-6	$5.99US/$6.99CAN
__Moonbeams and Magic	0-7860-0184-4	$5.99US/$6.99CAN
__Brazen Ecstasy	0-8217-5446-7	$5.99US/$6.99CAN

Call toll free **1-888-345-BOOK** to order by phone, use this coupon to order by mail, or order online at www.kensingtonbooks.com.

Name _____

Address _____

City _____ State _____ Zip _____

Please send me the books I have checked above.

I am enclosing	$_____
Plus postage and handling	$_____
Sales tax (in New York and Tennessee only)	$_____
Total amount enclosed	$_____

*Add $2.50 for the first book and $.50 for each additional book.

Send check or money order (no cash or CODs) to:

Kensington Publishing Corp., Dept. C.O., 850 Third Avenue, New York, NY 10022

Prices and numbers subject to change without notice.

All orders subject to availability.

Visit our website at **www.kensingtonbooks.com**